ONE

December 1831

Some mornings were so cold that the only thing that could tempt Charlotte from her warm covers was the scent of apples baking. The wood inhaled the apples, breathing them into its pores, making the room so sweet that Charlotte felt as though she were nestled in a barrel of cinnamon. A barrel packed in ice, she thought, tugging the blankets to her chin. No matter how she snuggled, the cold always found its way in, tickling her skin like a warning of what she would face if she stood up. Even the fire at her bedside did nothing to heat the drafty attic. Bears knew well enough to hibernate in winter, she thought. Why didn't Vermonters?

Her mother's calling began, the start of a daily ritual. Charlotte sometimes loved the sound of her mother's textured voice, but not first thing in the morning, and not when it was calling, "Charlotte! Get out of bed! Where are you?!"

"Just a moment!"

Charlotte pushed herself from bed, shuddering when her bare feet touched the icy birch planks. She tried to stretch, but was on the short end of a lopsided ceiling and nearly scraped herself on the rough-hewn wood. She hated to be up, but as long as it was so, she knew exactly how she wished to start her day. She scurried to the window. How could she resist? It was nearly Christmas, and the world was alight with the magic people believed in only once a year. She wiped frost from the icy panes, startled by the cold of the glass. The country morning was white and crisp, with just a streak of soft peach smoking on the horizon. A horse-drawn sleigh glided by, its bells jingling in the wind, its driver breathing clouds. It looked like a painting, thought Charlotte. It looked like the sort of morning on which miracles were born. Miracles. Oh God, how she could use one of those.

"Charlotte! Come down here and help!"

"I'm coming!"

Frantically, she ran to her closet and swung open the creaking door, causing a chip of white paint to fall at her toes. She chose a drab dress. It was the brown one, the beige, or the tan, she wasn't sure; they were all as colorless as her days. She didn't even look at the garment until she'd tossed it on the flattened feather bed. It appeared she'd picked the tan, as good a color as any, she supposed. Anxiously, she fought with her bodice, a morning routine that always had the unpleasant effect of making her remember her girlhood. Even then, she'd been too buxom to fit in any of the undergarments her mother made for her. She'd always had to squeeze and prod and poke, as she was doing now. That's why the boys had taunted her. That's why they'd called her "Peaches," a name so humiliating, no girl could bear it. It still hurt to remember. How pleased they must be, she thought stonily, to know that their favorite scapegoat would soon be a spinster, as unloved at seventeen as they'd made her feel at twelve.

Not that she wanted a husband, she reminded herself . . .

"Charlotte! Where are you?!" That was the sound of the final bell.

ANTICLIMAX?

He kissed the top of her head scarf and whispered, "Are you warm enough?"

"It's very cold," she replied. And for that, she got an extra-tight squeeze. Her life would never be the same.

When at last they reached the three-story white house, they hurried to the hearth to warm their hands. Charlotte raced to her mother's bedroom to whisper that she was home, and then announced to Shaun, "She was fast asleep."

"She must trust me," he grinned.

"She must not know you," Charlotte retorted.

Shaun took no offense. Instead, he held out his hand.

Shyly, with a bit of a tremble, Charlotte accepted it and let him lead her all the way to the attic. But at the door, she turned and said a cautious "Good night."

Shaun did not move. His eyes were fixed upon her. "Are you . . ." she swallowed, "are you going to . . . kiss me again?"

With a powerfully intent look, Shaun reached out his hand and cupped her jaw, stroking her with his thumb. Charlotte could barely stand to look at him. He was so beautiful. She worked up the courage to ask again. "Are you going to kiss me?"

He stopped touching her and reached around her, turning the doorknob that she'd tried nervously to block. He flung open her bedroom door just to prove he could do it. "Actually," he said, "I had something a little more intimate in mind."

Charlotte's eyes turned heavenward as he brushed his lips against her ear, holding her and stroking her neck.

"I . . . I . . ." She was going to tell him that she couldn't. That he mustn't ask. That he mustn't even think such a thing. But she couldn't bring herself to say the words. Not when he was making her melt so, not when he was nearly bringing tears to her eyes with his affections. And besides, he interrupted her.

He said, "I want you to show me your drawings."

<u>BOOK YOUR PLACE ON OUR WEBSITE</u> <u>AND MAKE THE</u> <u>READING CONNECTION!</u>

We've created a customized website just for our very special readers, where you can get the inside scoop on everything that's going on with Zebra, Pinnacle and Kensington books.

When you come online, you'll have the exciting opportunity to:

- View covers of upcoming books

- Read sample chapters

- Learn about our future publishing schedule (listed by publication month *and author*)

- Find out when your favorite authors will be visiting a city near you

- Search for and order backlist books from our online catalog

- Check out author bios and background information

- Send e-mail to your favorite authors

- Meet the Kensington staff online

- Join us in weekly chats with authors, readers and other guests

- Get writing guidelines

- AND MUCH MORE!

Visit our website at
http://www.kensingtonbooks.com

A COUNTRY CHRISTMAS

ELIZABETH DOYLE

ZEBRA BOOKS
Kensington Publishing Corp.
http://www.kensingtonbooks.com.

ZEBRA BOOKS are published by

Kensington Publishing Corp.
850 Third Avenue
New York, NY 10022

All Kensington titles, imprints and distributed lines are available at special quantity discounts for bulk purchases for sales promotion, premiums, fund-raising, educational or institutional use.

Special book excerpts or customized printings can also be created to fit specific needs. For details, write or phone the office of the Kensington Special Sales Manager: Kensington Publishing Corp., 850 Third Avenue, New York, NY 10022. Attn. Special Sales Department. Phone: 1-800-221-2647.

Zebra and the Z logo Reg. U.S. Pat. & TM Off.

First Printing: October 2002
10 9 8 7 6 5 4 3 2 1

Printed in the United States of America

Charlotte straightened her woolen petticoats and stockings, and laced her narrow boots, crying, "I'm coming, I promise!"

She was still braiding her silky brown hair when she swung open the splintered door and raced down the steep, winding stairs. She had to duck to avoid spots where the ceiling hung low and switch stairwells on the second floor. None of this boded well for her braiding, but she kept at it, following the warm, savory smoke until at last it stung her eyes. She had landed in the kitchen. "Sorry I'm late."

Her gray-haired mother did not enjoy apologies. Her skin was pale and aged from a lifetime of bending over a hearth, breathing smoke and moving in darkness. Margaret's hands were beating a ball of dough into submission. "Grab the beans," was all she said, "I've already got the pudding in the bricks."

Charlotte cast about, frantically scanning the flaming brick hearth, the blackened stove, the narrow window which let in barely a ray of winter light.

"Oh, for heaven's sake," said her mother, "the beans are in the pot by the washing board."

"Thanks." Charlotte scurried to the counter as though racing could make up for a half-hour of absence.

"Push them to the back," said her mother. "I need room for the bread."

Charlotte sniffed deeply the strong scents of pork and onions. Cautiously, she removed three bricks from the hearth, revealing a secret passage. She saw a bowl of apple pudding snuggled deep into the wall and sent the beans in after it. "Shall I light it?" she asked, testing a wooden panel for warmth.

"I already did," scowled her mother, "nearly an hour ago."

"Oh." Her lashes fluttered in her embarrassment.

"Now, I need you to stay home from the academy

today," said her mother, taking a moment's break from kneading, wiping her thinning hair only to smear a streak of dough into it.

"Stay home?" asked Charlotte. "But I have a knitting assignment." It was her most challenging subject, one in a long series of domestic arts classes which Charlotte abhorred. Peacham's was one of the very best academies in Vermont, but its girls' curriculum was not at all as interesting as the boys'.

"Never mind the assignment," said her mother. "You've learned as much as the academy can teach you. You're seventeen now, and I need you at home."

"You mean . . ." Charlotte didn't know whether to be frightened or relieved. No more trouncing through the snow each morning to be scolded for her domestic incompetence? She could be saved the trip, and receive all such scoldings right here at home? That seemed a worthwhile proposal. Perhaps she could even sneak in some drawing . . .

"Besides," said Margaret, "your brother is coming home for Christmas and it'll take a lot of work to make the holiday suitable for a guest."

"A guest?"

"Yes. Peter is bringing home a friend from Harvard."

"Peter has a friend?"

Margaret Bass scowled at her daughter in warning. "Yes, of course Peter has a friend. He's a year ahead in school—about nineteen, I think—but that's all we know about him. He comes from Boston, and I don't want him thinking we can't be hospitable just because we're country folk. I'll need you to help me get this house ready for the holiday."

"Peter has a friend?"

This time, her mother thrust fists against her sides. "Your brother happens to be a very nice young man."

"My brother?"

Mrs. Bass had very little sense of humor when it came to her only son, whose Harvard education would soon make her so proud. She knew he and Charlotte had their difficulties, but she hoped that in time, Charlotte, too, would grow proud of him. In the meantime, she would not coddle her unseemly jests. "The young man's name is Shaun Matheson," she said, turning her back on both Charlotte and the topic. "I trust you to be a good hostess. Oh, that reminds me—here." She reached a sticky hand into her apron pocket. "The post rider went by this morning. Go to the postmaster's and see whether Peter has sent another letter, telling us the date of their arrival. Here's some money in case he has."

Charlotte cocked her head inquisitively. "Did you ever find it strange," she asked, "that we must pay for our own mail? I've sometimes wondered whether it wouldn't make more sense to have the sender pay the bill. After all, we can hardly help it if someone decides to send us a letter, can we?"

"Charlotte." Her mother's impatience made her eyes close as though she were holding tight to an outburst. "If there were a better way to run the post, someone would have thought of it before you. Now go check for that letter."

"Yes, Mama," she said resentfully, knowing that if Peter had said it, it would have been declared brilliant. But she knew young women weren't supposed to waste their time on thoughts. They were supposed to be too busy for them. So with great annoyance, she wrapped herself in a bundle of scarves and faced the bitter cold. There were dull chores to do.

She opened the back door, relieving the kitchen of half its smoke. The icy wind chilled her through the cloak and slapped her painfully in the face, even though she was wrapped in scarves to the eyes. Hardened snow glistening with bits of silver crunched under her boots.

She could barely look up into the wind, it was so power-ful, but when she did, it was a red-domed barn that told her where the road lay. It was her father's barn, trimmed primly in white, and home to a wealth of friendly ani-mals, some of whom had been companion to her since childhood—when she'd had no one else to talk to. Be-yond it, through the blinding white, were rolling hills, decorated with pine trees laced in snow. Beyond those were more hills, trussed in blue. It was a beautiful, freez-ing white world, but to Charlotte, those hills marked the edge of the earth, and sometimes looked like the walls of her personal prison.

A sleigh passed her by, its bells jingling. She grinned even though she was forced to taste scarves. That was the one thing she always looked forward to every year—the sleigh bells, the festivity, colors that weren't drab. How she loved the sound of Christmas! Something about bells jingling in the wind always lifted her spirits. They reminded her of something. Something she may have known long ago, but had forgotten somewhere along the way. That miracles were not so unnatural. That life was not a circle but a spiral, always moving a little for-ward even in the course of its routines. That maybe someday . . . something wondrous might finally come her way.

TWO

"Would you quiet those sleigh bells?!" Peter rapped on the tavern's window, shouting at a passing driver, "I hate that sound," he told his companion. "Our own sleigh was jingling all the way from Barnet. I think I have a permanent ring in my ears."

Shaun Matheson was barely listening. He savored a swallow of rum, which warmed his throat the way the crackling fire warmed his face. His posture was casual, but there was always such an elegance about him—even Peter admired it. He was dressed in a slender waistcoat and creamy silken cravat, a style he seemed born to wear. His pale brown hair was short but waved enticingly, while his modest sideburns handsomely framed his face. There was a sharpness in his sly smile, a confidence in the way he dared to slouch, as though he didn't need to draw attention to his handsomeness. His silver eyes were more than dashing; they peered at the tavern with a quiet humor that made strangers wish to know him. It was this natural charm that made him the polar opposite of Peter, whose charms were much more difficult to discern.

Peter Bass was a new student at Harvard, a chunky fellow with dark hair that protruded randomly in clumps beneath the brim of his top hat. He seemed clumsy, and laughed loudly, but Shaun had defended him against any who would call a rural boy inelegant beyond his hearing. He couldn't tolerate chastisement, and went out of his way to compensate for the rudeness of his classmates. When a night of drinking had ended with an invitation to Peter's hometown for Christmas, Shaun had been delighted. He thought it might be just the thing to spare him the agony of his own house at holiday time. But after a week of listening to Peter complain about everything from sleigh drivers to scarves that made his nose itch, Shaun came to the conclusion that no holiday, no matter how quaint, could be worth this amount of suffering.

"I think it's rather charming," he said of the sleigh bells, pleased by the sights and sounds of his first visit to the rural north. Truly, he found himself captivated by Vermont, the state of green, covered in a foot of white. He was entranced by the rolling hills and by the scent of pine made more pungent by chill and ice. Despite Peter's trying company, Shaun would never wish to forget their sleigh ride through the white flurries. He could still recall the sunsets of cornflower blue when the snow seemed to brighten under the early stars. He had often heard the term "home for the holidays." Only now did he understand its romanticism. "Are you sure your parents don't mind my visit?"

"Of course not," said Peter, fidgeting with his cup of apple cider. "Why should they mind? All they need do is cook a few pies, slaughter a pig. It isn't much trouble."

"But you did ask them," he demanded suspiciously, "and you did give them the dates."

"Uhhhh . . . yes, I think so. I'm fairly sure I did."

Shaun only tipped back his chair and glared. If Peter had misled him about his welcome, or failed to deliver dates to his host, he might just have to throttle him.

"I don't see why we're even staying at the tavern," said Peter between careful sips of burning-hot cider, "My house is only a short way out of town."

"Because it's the middle of the night," said Shaun, "and it's bad enough I may be unexpected. I don't wish to rouse my hosts from sleep by way of a grand entrance."

"You certainly do worry a lot," chuckled Peter. "I don't see why. When you meet my family, you'll see there's no cause for concern. You know my father's only a drummer—he's not wealthy like yours. He fills up shops' supplies around New England. Very boring work. He's hardly ever home, probably won't be there now. And my sister is—"

"You have a sister?"

"Why, yes."

That was a surprise. Why it was so startling, Shaun wasn't sure. But somehow, he found it difficult to imagine. Peter—with a sister. It changed the whole image of him somehow. "What does she . . . I mean, is she . . . pretty?" He knew it was clumsy and in some ways an awful question. But he was so curious. What would a sister of Peter's be like?

"No, she's not pretty at all."

Shaun dryly lifted a corner of his mouth. "That's a fine way to speak of your own sister."

"Well, you asked, didn't you?"

His head shook slowly side to side in distaste, but still, he couldn't resist asking, "How old is she?"

"Sixteen or seventeen. I don't remember."

"Getting ready to marry, then?"

"Oh, no!" Peter laughed, "No, no. My sister shan't marry. No, she's going to be a spinster. Nobody would ever marry Charlotte."

He'd said it between slurps of cider, as though Shaun really should have known better. But Shaun was visibly put out by his declaration. "Why would you say such a thing?"

"It's simply true."

"But why?"

"I don't know. Partly her temperament, I suppose."

"Temperament? Is she a horse now?"

"No, I just meant . . ."

"Personality?"

"Yes, exactly. That. She has a terrible personality. Rather discontented all the time, lazy about doing her chores. She's also plain. And . . . well, you know how these things are. Everyone knows that nobody wants her, and who wants someone no one else wants? I wouldn't."

Shaun couldn't tell whether his companion was joking or not. But he didn't smile, so he had to believe he was in earnest. To speak of one's own sister that way—it was unthinkable. He wished he had met her so he might have some evidence by which to come to her defense. But as it was, all he could do was speculate. If Peter called her personality "terrible," the poor thing was probably an angel.

Peter started laughing, spitting bubbles into his cup. "Do you want to hear the most embarrassing story about Charlotte?"

"Not especially."

"When she was twelve, she wore an awful dress whose hem was always dragging through the mud. One day we were at church . . ."

Shaun thought it would be gallant of him to stop listening, and so that's precisely what he did. As Peter rambled on, he gazed about at the tavern, its dim lanterns and ruggedly attired clientele. He was impressed that a town as small as Peacham had a tavern, and that it was so lively at night. He hadn't realized there would be so many travelers to a small town, moving to and from the dormitories at Peacham Academy doing business at the mills, or resting on their way to St. Johnsbury. It was close to the midnight hour, and there were still men awake and playing checkers at the long, rustic tables. The lanterns were burning low.

When it seemed Peter was finished with his story, Shaun said, "I see," and downed the last gulp of his hot brandy. He was about to struggle with a turn in topic when something more appealing caught his eye.

What a beautiful woman. It seemed the servants had changed shifts and the new serving woman was fair of hair and skin. He had never seen such dark eyes on a blonde. And Shaun was always the first to notice . . . she had magnificent breasts. Furthermore, her bodice was peeking out from the top of her generously cut gown. And he knew well what that meant. The young lady was more than a house servant. "Do you want another drink?" he asked Peter.

"No, thank you. I've never cared much for spirits. I know I should drink more of them to fight off the cold and keep from getting thin, but I just don't care for them."

"Then why don't you get some rest."

Peter was puzzled by his chum's fixed stare. It was almost as though he were being given an order to leave. How strange.

"I believe the straw piles are upstairs," said Shaun, eager to help him make a hasty disappearance.

"But this is our last night before we're burdened by my family. Shouldn't we stay up late? We could play a game of chess."

As much fun as that sounded, Shaun found that his heart was already set on a more appealing evening's activity. "Perhaps another time?" he suggested.

"Well, all right." Peter pouted but rose from his seat. "Aren't you coming?"

"I have to pay the servant," he said with a twinkle in his silver eye.

"Very well then. Until morning."

"Until morning."

The servant trotted to his table, offering to refill his steaming cup. He touched her wrist to show he wanted something more.

She met his eyes with shyness before breaking into an endearing nod, answering his unspoken question. "There is a private room," she confessed. "Will you wait for me to finish these tables?"

Shaun shook his head. "No," he said softly. "We'll go now."

She bowed her head, a bashful blush speckling her cheeks. "I'll have to charge you more for interrupting me."

"I understand."

She dared to look up from her hands. "Then I'll go fetch the other girl to tend the dining room. I'll be right back."

"Wait," he said, fondling her pulse with his thumb.

She gazed at her wrist, surprised that after all these years, a handsome young man could still give her a flutter. "What is it?" she asked.

"I'll pay you in full," he said with a strangeness that made him all the more appealing, "but I'm not paying for this." He touched the lace of her revealing bodice, making her blush at his strong touch so near her breast. "This isn't what I want tonight."

"Then what—"

"Just sleep," he said, with a devilish smile that made her wonder whether to believe him. "I just want to hold you, touch your hair." He fingered a flaxen tress, watching it shine in the firelight, making her sigh with anticipation.

"You mean to say—"

"Yes."

His silvery gaze was so intense it thrilled her. She wondered at the handsome young man, his chiseled face adorned with such stylish, light-brown sideburns, his silver eyes so alluring. Surely he had young ladies fawning all over him day and night. She knew she would join them in the chasing if she could. Why, then, would he pay her only to hold her in his arms? But the more she studied him, the more she understood. Indeed, most men came to her because they longed to escape. But there were those who had nothing to escape. There were men who had known so little of warmth that they longed only to imagine, just once, that they had a place to call home.

"I am running away."

Charlotte chided her sandy-haired friend with a goading look of disbelief. "You are not."

"I am," said Sarah Brown, tossing a frizzy braid over her shoulder where it belonged. "Whatever I do, I am not going to die here in Peacham. Charlotte, don't you remember all of our plans?"

"The ones we made when we were six?" She chuckled, nearly stabbing herself with a sewing needle in her momentary lapse of concentration.

"You say that as though we gave up on them," said Sarah, disappointment wrinkling the creases around her round, brown eyes. "We never gave up on them. We've just been waiting for the right time, haven't we?"

Charlotte's hands dropped to her lap, bringing the quilt down with them. "You aren't serious, are you?"

"Of course I am. Do you mean to tell me that you've changed your mind? That you're going to stay put and become just like our mothers?"

"No, not that, but . . ."

"Yes, you are," said Sarah with an accusing glint in her eye, carefully designed to shame her friend into a change of heart. "You've given up on all of our plans and you're going to stay here and get married, just as they want us to do."

"I am not."

"Are, too."

"Oh, please. Even if I wanted to, who would I marry?" She made it sound as though the question were rhetorical, though in truth, an intriguing answer might have been welcome.

"Giles Williams."

"Giles Williams?!" An intriguing answer might have pleased her, but an offensive one did not. "Giles Williams? The boy who first called me Peaches?"

Sarah made every effort to appear suddenly engrossed in her needlework, as though she had said nothing out of the ordinary. "He only called you Peaches because he fancied you."

"Fancied me?! He had the entire school calling me that for two years! I thought I would never see the end of it. And to this day, he still sometimes tosses that horrible name at me. He should be horsewhipped!"

Sarah tossed her tiny nose haughtily in the air, feeling quite proud to have created such a stir. "Yet, he is unmarried and his father runs the printing press, which would make him a good provider, you know. And I insist he is taken by you." She turned woodsy eyes on her fuming friend, prepared to strike the final blow. "And if we stay here, he will most likely be your husband. There aren't many to choose from, you know."

Charlotte wanted to expel her friend from the parlor. "I am not going to marry anyone!" she cried. "I will not become a wife, and I will not spend the rest of my life doing mindless chores." Realizing she was in the midst of performing one, she tossed aside her quilt.

"Then run away with me," Sarah urged, her goading look immediately replaced by an enticing one. "We'll leave this place late one night and not send a letter home until we've become wildly successful in our own right."

"Sarah," she drawled, her voice rich with a maturity Sarah's still lacked, "when you are seventeen, it is no longer called 'running away.' It is called 'going mad.'"

"Oh, come. It will be exciting! I will be an actress and you will sell your drawings to all the art vendors across Europe."

"Europe? Now we're going to Europe?"

"Why not? Or we could go to Philadelphia. It will be just the two of us, alone on a grand adventure, and . . ."

"And starving?"

Sarah was gravely disappointed by her friend's mature stagnation. Her disappointment showed all over her tiny, round face and doll-like brown eyes. She couldn't allow herself to be the only one in Peacham who longed for escape. She couldn't let her partner bow out. "Charlotte, we live only once. If we run, we may find peril, but it will be no loss. We'll miss out only on a lifetime of *this*." She waved her tiny hands left and right. To someone else, it may have seemed a beautiful room, this wooden parlor. It was host to a comforting fire, attractive albeit uncomfortable straight backed chairs, and tall windows chopped into tiny squares, framed by white cotton curtains roped gracefully to the side like ponytails. But to the girls, there was something stifling about it. The smoke mingled with the strong scent of wood, making the room smell like a locked barrel.

"If only we had somewhere to go," Charlotte mused quietly. "If only we were boys." She crumpled the quilt in her fist, not harming it, but wrinkling it quite thoroughly. "Do you know why I'm mending this quilt?" she asked angrily. "Because Peter's coming home and everything has to be just right for my royal brother." Her face was flushing, she was so mad. "He gets to travel, he gets to leave the house, leave Vermont, and on top of that, he gets treated like an honored guest every time he returns home. And why? Because he's a boy. No other reason." She gazed helplessly at the torn quilt she had struggled all morning to mend. "I can't believe I'm being asked to play servant to my own brother, just because he sees fit to pay us one visit from Harvard."

"It's humiliating," Sarah agreed with a dramatic pout.

"My whole life is humiliating. It's as though I was born into servitude just because I wear a dress. Oh, Sarah, wouldn't it be a dream to return from college and have the whole family cook for us and ask us to share our brilliant thoughts?" Her blue eyes alight with wonder, she moved to the window, watching the glittering snow fall as though the freezing outdoors were calling her. She crossed her arms tightly, for the cold had a way of seeping through the glass, forming a field of chill all around the panes. "Imagine being somebody," she said wistfully, "being known for something we had achieved. Oh, Sarah," she said excitedly, "my parents would be so frightened if we ran off. But if I insisted, how could they stop me? And we could always come back if things got bad." Her pulse quickened, giving her little chills that ignited her blood. "Sarah, you're right!" she cried, spinning around. "We should try it! We should leave here and strike out on our own. Let's do it!"

"Well, I didn't mean right away." Sarah buried her nose in her needlework, pretending to have reached a very crucial moment in it that required immense concentration.

"What?!"

"Well, I . . . I meant sometime, perhaps after we've finished school. But I . . ."

"Sarah, you . . ." Charlotte stomped her foot, struggling between the affection and the frustration she felt toward her childhood playmate. "You are nothing but talk. You always do this to me. You get me excited about some harebrained scheme, and then you . . . you just pretend it never came up."

"I do not."

"You do, too."

"I do not. I plan to leave just as soon as . . . well, as soon as everything is finished here and we have time to adjust our parents to the notion, and we have a good plan, and—"

"And hell freezes over."

Sarah pointed brightly at the window, a mischievous look dimpling her cheeks. "I think it already has."

Charlotte's glare slowly melted, becoming a radiant smile. She couldn't help laughing. "Oh, Sarah, it *is* hard to stay angry with you."

Sarah beamed brightly. "I'm sorry if I led you to believe I wanted to run away so soon. That's not what I'd intended to say. I just . . ."

"Oh, never mind it," said Charlotte, waving her hand dismissively, "let's just get back to our chores." With a heavy sigh, she plunked herself back on the floor and looked mournfully at the unfinished task before her.

"So when is Peter coming back?" asked Sarah.

"I don't know." Charlotte took a stab at her quilt. "Mama expected a letter from him at the postmaster's but there wasn't one. I imagine it won't be until Christmas Eve, for I'm sure he would have written by now if he were coming any sooner."

It was so rare, she felt, for anything exciting to happen in Peacham that Sarah couldn't help shaking her head wistfully at the thought. "It seems so strange to think of Peter at Harvard. I wonder whether he has changed."

Charlotte snorted undaintily. "Doubtful."

"Well, he'll have to change a little bit if he wants to make any friends."

This brought forth a good-hearted chuckle, straight from Charlotte's breast. "Oh, my. You're not going to believe this. But speaking of friends, Mama said he has already made one. In fact, that's really whom this quilt is for. It's our guest quilt."

"You don't mean . . . here? Someone from Cambridge is coming here?"

"I hear he's from Boston, not far from the school. The only other thing we know of him is that he has poor taste in friends."

Sarah looked positively starry-eyed. "A Harvard man? Eligible? In our town? One who isn't Peter? How thrilling!"

Charlotte's eyes rolled. "Please, Sarah. He's bound to be perfectly awful."

"You don't know that. Maybe he's handsome!"

"Will you listen to yourself?" Charlotte clucked her tongue. "We were just talking about how humiliating it is to get married and to spend one's life in the servitude of a man. One mention of Harvard, and you look as though you're about to put on a white lace dress. I declare, your thoughts and schemes are as fleeting as the summer."

"I wasn't thinking of marriage," said Sarah. "You know I want to see the world before I'm burdened with babies. I was only thinking that I look forward to meeting someone who hasn't been stuck here all his life. Someone who has seen the city!"

"I'll bet you were."

"It's true! So what do you suppose? What do you suppose he will be like?"

Charlotte stopped her sewing long enough to close her eyes and sigh. "I suppose," she said after a long pause, "I suppose that . . ." She tried to envision Peter walking through the door, all covered in snow, whipping off his top hat to receive hugs and kisses from Mama and Papa. She pictured it until it seemed true to life in every way, then imagined a figure standing behind him, waiting to be introduced. What would he be like? "Very boring," she said at last, "boring and full of himself, as city folk always are."

"But what will he look like?"

"Like someone who wishes he'd never come to a dull town like Peacham. Now, enough talk about men. Who needs them anyhow?"

"Of course." Sarah watched her own small hands move over the quilt square to which her mother had assigned her for the afternoon. Vaguely, she was aware of her size, smaller than petite, smaller than delicate. Too small. Knowing well that her mother had never grown past her own height, she didn't expect a growth spurt to rescue her from her childish stature. It worried her, for she truly feared for her attractiveness. The notion of a handsome man in her life had always been a critical element in her fantasy about the future, second only to becoming an actress in a distant land. "You know, if Peter matured a lot in school, he might not be so unappealing."

"We're talking about my brother, Peter? Not some other Peter?"

"That's right."

"Oh. In that case, I would have to say you've lost your mind."

Sarah pouted her lips and stabbed her needle at the same time. "Well, you can be as bitter as you like, but I plan to keep my options open. You say Peter's friend is from Boston? Now, that would be a nice place to live."

"Nothing but a servant," Charlotte reminded her. "Boston or Paris, a wife is nothing but a servant and I won't be one. I won't." But Sarah noticed something odd in the way she said it. Disappointment. She said it as though life had let her down. As though she had once hoped. So Charlotte had once hoped for a more romantic future, had she? How intriguing. Sarah strained to imagine what it was Charlotte might have wished for. Magic? She studied Charlotte's restless hands, moving across her mending without care or pride. Had she hoped for a miracle? She thought about the drawings Charlotte hid in her room. Perhaps she had hoped for more leisure time, more frivolity. Like Christmas or like . . . like love. A mischievous smile lifted Sarah's cheeks. Could it be that despite all of her saucy talk, Charlotte would have liked to meet a dashing man? No. Sarah shook her head. It couldn't be.

THREE

A snowball smacked Charlotte squarely between the blades of her shoulders. And it wasn't a soft snowball; it was the kind so full of ice that it would surely leave a nasty bruise. She spun around, not in the least surprised to see Giles Williams, pointing and laughing at her. "Ignore him," said Sarah, tugging at her friend's mittened hand, "He won't follow us all the way home. Let's just go."

But to see him laughing, to see his stringy black hair and cruel eyes dancing in delight over having embarrassed her once more, was lighting a fire in Charlotte's brow. "Won't you ever grow up!" she screamed, drawing sweat to her heavily scarved face.

Her fury excited him, for he was one who grew stronger when others grew weaker. He loved to make people angry and watch their helplessness in the face of his torment. Particularly when it was Charlotte, though why that was, he still wasn't old enough to comprehend. "Hi, Peaches."

"Let's go," said Sarah, now tugging more desperately at her friend's hand. "He's not worth it."

But he had called her Peaches, so there was no turning back now. "You take that back!" she cried.

"No."

"Someone should wash your filthy mouth with lye!"

"Why don't you come over here and try it?" he grinned, "and your short, ugly friend, too."

Sarah suffered a spontaneous change of heart about leaving. "Sh . . . short? I'm not short!" The ugly part really hadn't bothered her, because she knew it to be untrue. "How dare you! You . . . well, Charlotte, you're not just going to stand there and let him call me 'short,' are you?"

"Of course she is," said Giles. "She doesn't have the gumption to do anything about it."

"Oh, that's it." Without a plan or a thought, Charlotte ran at him, causing him to flee in a fit of laughter. But she wouldn't let him go. She couldn't. She followed him as fiercely as she was able, her boots sinking a foot deep in crisp snow with every step. Some of it spilled over, sliding into her socks, melting when it hit her feet. But she didn't let it stop her. Giles was being slowed by the same snow, and she was determined to catch him and . . . strangle him or . . . punch him or . . . well, she didn't know what. But she had to do something.

Charlotte ran so hard that even Giles was surprised. He'd expected her to give up half a mile sooner, but every time he checked behind him, there she was, her fists swinging by her sides and her boots kicking up snow. If he kept running, he knew, he would reach Charlotte's house and then, surely, she would give up and go inside. So that's the direction he headed, for he feared he was running short of breath and would soon need to pause to rest his stinging ribs. Charlotte absently construed a new plan. Her thoughts seemed to appear before her in the form of white breath, and the harder she gazed at her very own steam, the more certain she was of what she had to do. She had to learn to aim a snowball very well, and very quickly.

She stopped, causing Giles to stop as well, grinning with hands on knees, laughing at her as best he could on every desperate exhale. But when he saw she was patting snow into a ball, he curtailed his rest and fled once more. She aimed mightily, but missed. He was too far ahead. So again, she broke into a run. Sarah's breathy "Stop, wait for me," barely reached her. She noticed her family's red barn to the right, and knew there was danger if her mother saw her throwing snowballs. But she was too determined to stop now. It was time—long past time—to teach Giles a lesson. If it meant a scolding, it would still be well worth it.

There was a sleigh parked ahead. Charlotte feared Giles would hide behind it, making it nearly impossible to hit him. Her fear was well founded, for he was already ducking beyond her sight. "Coward!" she cried, packing up a nice, hard snowball. "Come out right now! I swear I'll get you." She saw him take a peek, and aimed where his head appeared, but he did not stay put long enough to take the impact.

Giles ducked behind the carriage, and her snowball landed squarely in the chest of a gentleman emerging from the sleigh. It hit him hard enough to land with a pound, and it splattered a snowy stain all over his expensive-looking woolen coat. Charlotte's jaw dropped so wide, she had to slap a hand on her face to hide her tonsils. She didn't even take notice of Giles scurrying off with a taunt. All she could see was a handsome, tall gentleman in a fashionable top hat with light-brown waves peeking beneath it, flashing an adoring smile her way, dripping with watery droplets of melting snow. Then she saw something else—her brother, chunky and scowling, fumbling awkwardly from the sleigh. Squinting curiously, wondering whether this might all be a dream, she also took note of her mother, peering through the parlor curtain, mouth as wide as Charlotte's. It took some thought to put it all together, but soon she realized what she had done. She had accosted their guest.

"I am—" Charlotte couldn't decide whether to laugh or get on her knees and plead forgiveness. It was one of the more surreal moments in her dull life. "I am so sorry," she managed to blurt out, her head swaying back and forth in disbelief. "I am . . . so . . ."

"You must be Charlotte," he grinned, offering his hand in a gesture so forgiving, she couldn't bring herself to accept it.

"I . . . no . . . I . . ."

"Charlotte!!!" Her mother flew through the front door wearing nothing but a shawl for warmth, screaming her daughter's name as though it were a curse. "Charlotte!"

"Mother, I . . ."

Margaret Bass wanted so desperately to throttle her daughter that only her absolute humiliation forced her to forgo the pleasure. "I don't want to hear it right now." She turned to her guest with a look so apologetic, it lacked only tears. "You must be Shaun Matheson," she supposed, no less mortified by his early arrival than by the scene her daughter had caused. "I am . . . I am so sorry about Charlotte." This was said in a tone that made Charlotte wonder whether she was apologizing for the snowball or for giving birth.

"Oh, it's really no trouble."

"You moron!" cried Peter, grabbing his sister round the neck, trying to shove snow into her dress. She squirmed and fought him, but he held her still. "You stupid little . . ."

"Oh, leave it be, Peter," his mother said gently.

But it was Shaun who reached out an arm to stop it. "Peter," he said. And it was all he said. It made Peter turn around and catch the eye of someone he secretly thought better than he. Somehow, he sensed Shaun would think of him less if he didn't let Charlotte go. Why, was absolutely beyond his comprehension. But many things were. So he let her go, but not before sending her for a tumble into the snow. "Peter," snapped Shaun with bitter distaste. He moved to Charlotte, offering her a hand, but she was too embarrassed to be grateful. Where once she had felt remorse for her deed, she now felt only anger at her punishment.

"Don't touch me," she snapped, slapping away his gloved hand.

"Charlotte!" gasped her mother.

But Shaun understood. He understood far too well. "You're sure you're all right?" was all he said, and in a voice so quiet only Charlotte could hear.

She was too embarrassed to reply. Being scolded in front of a stranger was bad enough; humiliating herself with that snowball was even worse; but to take a forced tumble in the snow, right in front of a guest, was more than she could bear. She hid her awkwardness behind anger and refused to look him in the eye. Without a word, she helped herself from the snow, stomping angrily past her mother and into the house.

"I'm so sorry," said Mrs. Bass, thinking only of the letter her poor guest would surely send home to the city, relating the brashness of simple country folk. He was such a well-dressed young man, and so very handsome. She hated to think Peter's first real friend might be frightened away. "Please come in. We'll find you some dry clothes."

"Oh no, really. It didn't soak through. I'll be just fine."

"Are you sure?"

"Absolutely." His eyes followed the trail of Charlotte's departure, for in truth, he worried more over the embarrassment of a young girl than over the state of his coat.

He followed his hosts to their rickety front porch and inside the grand, white, three-story home, steeped in the scent of burning wood. He noticed that there were no holiday decorations about. Just as he'd feared, his visit had come earlier than expected. Peter had never sent the dates of their arrival. With exasperation, he closed his eyes and let the cursing take place only within the echoes of his mind. He loved the cozy house; he loved the snowy scenery; he found the mother kind and the daughter appealing, but his dislike of Peter was growing stronger by the breath. Immediately, he went to work complimenting the house. "It's lovely," he said, and this was the truth, for though his father's home was more lavish, this one echoed under his footsteps as if it knew he was there, and held snugly the scent of apple pudding, as though the house itself were enjoying the smell. In addition, there were bonnets hanging from pegs, announcing the presence of women to all who entered—something sorely lacking at home. It was a house where people not only dwelled, but lived. "It is beautiful."

"Why, thank you," said Mrs. Bass. "I know you don't mean that, but you're awfully kind. Come sit down, and I'll bring you boys some pie."

"We eat it all day long," Peter informed him with a nudge. "Pie for breakfast, pie for dinner, and pie for supper, too. No avoiding pie."

"Why, Peter, I thought you liked my pie. I've been storing the blackberries since summer."

"I like it, I like it," he said. "I just thought I'd warn someone who comes from civilization."

He didn't know he'd hurt his mother, but Shaun did. "My mother used to do the same," he said, casting his hostess a small but comforting smile. "We had pie at every meal. She always said no self-respecting Yankee would go without."

His words had the desired effect of putting a smile on Margaret's face. Warmed by her guest's practiced grace, she led the two young men from the tiny entry where their coats and hats were hung to the dining room, full of winter light and warmed by a most welcoming fireplace. Shaun could tell a great deal just by looking about the room. The family did not have enough money to order wallpaper, he observed, but they had enough taste to have carefully painted the walls' borders with rows of tiny pink roses. The straight backed chair he was offered was not of the finest quality, but it was more comfortable than most. And Mrs. Bass, he noted, brought out the family china for his pie and cider. He knew this to be a compliment, though his father would have scoffed at the thick, clumsy quality of the snow-white dishes.

"You're not drinking your cider," Mrs. Bass observed when he was several bites into his pie. He was carefully chewing, thinking of a kind way to respond, when Peter broke in.

"He doesn't like soft cider. He's not a child, you know."

Shaun's eyes cast Peter a long, disapproving glare. He wanted to throttle him. But before he could, Margaret chimed in. "Oh, dear. Then let me put a splash of brandy in that for you. Oh, I'm so sorry. I didn't think to ask."

"Thank you," was all he could think to say as she whisked away his cup. But the moment she'd left, he turned stern eyes on his schoolmate. "Peter."

"Yes?" He had blackberry juices splattered all around his mouth, and was still shoveling.

"Why don't you let me speak for myself henceforth, eh?"

He shrugged. "Just trying to help."

"Well, you're not. You're not helping at all."

Peter snorted, nearly losing some of his own cider in the process. "Don't see why you'd want to impress my family. They're just my family."

"But they're not mine. I . . . thank you." Mrs. Bass had returned with the spiked cider, and replied to Shaun's courteous nod with her own.

"Well, boys," she said, "you must be tired from your journey. When you're finished, why don't you run upstairs for a nap." In truth, she wanted them out of her way so that she might make some minimal preparations for her guest. "Shaun, I apologize that Mr. Bass isn't here to welcome you. He's away on business and won't be home until the holiday."

He'd rather be treated by a hostess than a host, at any hour of any day. But this, he did not say. Instead, he replied, "Oh, I'm . . . I'm sure I have more than enough pleasurable company," bringing a flush to her cheeks.

"Well, I'm not in the mood to nap," said Peter. "Can't we play a Christmas game?"

"Well, I . . ." She had five hours worth of chores to do in the next one hour. "I . . ."

"Actually, Peter, I fear I'm not up to it," said Shaun, dabbing his jaw with a napkin. Margaret let out a sigh of relief. "Our trip has been rather long. I could use some sleep."

Margaret beamed at the handsome young man until he downed his cider in one breath and rose. That hadn't been an elegant thing to do at all. That cider was strong, too strong for one gulp. For a moment, she looked suspiciously at her guest, reevaluating him, wondering whether there was something in him she hadn't seen at first. But her uneasiness was quickly forgotten when he offered her a small and elegant bow and thanked her profusely for her hospitality. "Well, you're most welcome. I—"

"Can we play a Christmas game tomorrow then?"

"Yes, Peter," she said irritably, "anything you want."

"Even the caroling game?"

"Even the caroling game." She gazed upon him with

annoyance, but could not maintain her glare. He was so tall, so broad in the shoulder, and in her eyes, so very handsome. He was her son. And he was home from Harvard. "Oh, Peter," she said, wrapping him in an unwilling embrace, "it is so good to have you home. I am so proud of you."

"Stop it," he grumbled, writhing from her clutch. He looked miserably at Shaun, fearing he'd seen that hug. But Shaun was turned away, pretending to admire an ornate grandmother clock perched on a marble table. Peter was relieved, but Shaun was not. All he could think of was the injustice of Peter's having so much, and appreciating it so very little.

"Shall I show you your room?" asked Margaret.

"No, no. I uh . . . just tell me the way," Shaun said, heading for the trunk he'd left in the entry. "I'll find it."

She directed him, and he climbed the rugged front stairs, noticing the banister's wood was unpolished. Charming, he thought. Natural. His room was a pleasant one on the second floor. It was host to a lovely canopy bed, which he could tell had not been fluffed for his arrival. There were windows divided into tiny squares, creating an odd, artistic frame for the falling snow. The fire was not lit, and so he lit it himself, borrowing flame from the hallway, and admiring the ornately woven fender which protected the room from his fiery creation. The walls were nicely whitewashed, the room bright as snow. And he did enjoy the coziness of that woodsy smell rising from the planks. But he had no intention of staying put. After making good use of a spacious clothes closet and an interesting maple dresser, he turned his boots to the rear stairwell. There was a little girl who needed to be reassured.

He found her in the attic, whose ceiling was so low that he had to duck in order to avoid being knocked unconscious. Her bedroom door was open, which made him sense that the entire attic was her own, and that he might already have intruded just by climbing the stairs. "Hello." He said it as gently as he could, not wishing to startle her.

But she was startled nonetheless, and with frantic hands, shoved something into her rolltop desk. When she spun around, it was with wide-open eyes, for she'd expected her brother. With something between relief and further annoyance, she sighed, "Oh, it's just you."

Her rude welcome was met with a smile, because it had been so terribly honest. "Do you mind if I disturb you?"

"You're doing a fine job of it already." Her words were harsh, but her tone was soft. It was the tone of someone who wasn't comfortable being so curt, but who had learned to defend herself. Shaun recognized it immediately and smiled again.

"What is it you were doing?" he asked, nodding at the rolltop desk.

"Nothing."

She had wonderful breasts. He hadn't gotten a glimpse of them when she'd been all huddled in scarves. But now that she was indoors, he could see. She was not a "little girl" after all. What had Peter said? Sixteen or seventeen? He supposed it was not a sin to look, then . . . "Nothing?" he asked. "Well, I find that interesting."

Charlotte shot him a look to burn. She had big blue eyes, laced with sooty black lashes. Not surprisingly, Peter had not done the girl justice in his description. There was nothing plain about Charlotte Bass. He wondered what her long brown hair would look like unraveled from its braid. "What do you mean?" she asked rather sharply.

"Well," he said, leaning casually on the door frame, "I've always found that 'nothing' can mean one of two things. Either it means nothing, or it means the exact opposite. Something terribly important."

"Well, in this case, it means nothing," she assured him. Was it her imagination or did he have a very handsome face? His nose and jaw were perfectly carved, his eyes squinted and silver, sparkling with intelligence. Peter couldn't have a good-looking friend, though. Not good-looking and rich. That would be ridiculous. What would such a man be doing with Peter? There had to be a glaring flaw somewhere—she just hadn't spotted it yet. Her eyes moved up and down his tall, sleek, but broad-shouldered frame. Glaring flaw, glaring flaw. Where could it be?

"You're looking at me rather oddly."

"I am not." She turned from him as though to attend to her desk, but there was nothing on it.

"You seem to have charcoal on your fingers," he said, momentarily forgetting that he'd come to apologize. She was too interesting to leave be, too pretty to be left with only a simple message of regret.

Charlotte looked about for a badly stained cloth and began to wipe.

"Well, I don't consider myself particularly astute," he said, "but I would suppose that you've been drawing."

Every muscle in Charlotte's back stiffened. He had come to tease her. He was going to poke fun at her for trying to draw. Just like every boy she knew, just like Peter. "My drawings are none of your concern!"

And to her astonishment, he quite agreed. "Of course not," he said, rather in earnest. "An artist needs her privacy. I wouldn't ask you to show me anything unless you were comfortable."

Charlotte was too young to mask her gratitude. Something distinctly tickled in her chest at being called an "artist," and her pleasure made her rosy skin shine. "Well, I'm not an artist, really. I . . . I just like to draw."

"That would hold true for most artists, I should think."

Charlotte bit her lip, sucking on its flesh in a poor attempt to conceal her expression of pride. "I . . . I don't really draw, I . . ." She checked his eye contact and found it to be exemplary. He was hanging on her every word. "I just . . . I just draw in lieu of keeping a journal. You see, I . . . for example . . ." She suddenly wanted to show him every drawing she had ever concealed. "I . . . I draw people I meet, or things that happened to me today. Well, I . . . I can't draw an event, but I draw something that reminds me of it. Like maybe a . . . a . . ."

"Snowball?" he suggested with a wry grin.

Charlotte blushed. "I am truly sorry about that," she confessed. "It was just Giles Williams. He . . . he has tormented me ever since we were . . . well, since we were . . ."

"Ten?" he suggested.

Head cocked, she looked at him rather curiously. "Yes, ten, I would say. But how did you know?"

He shrugged. "Lucky guess." It was the usual age for boys to start wishing to be chased down the road by snowball-wielding girls. Though seventeen was well beyond the usual age of stopping.

"Well, he's been tormenting me all of my life, and I was just so angry, I . . . I . . ."

"Apology accepted. May I see your drawings?"

Charlotte clenched her fists. But it wasn't a gesture of anger, it was nervous anticipation. "No, really. I . . . I couldn't."

His nod held mischief. "Well, if you say so."

"Well, perhaps I could."

"No, no. Not if you aren't comfortable. I know these things are delicate."

"Well, I . . . perhaps sometime."

"Perhaps," he shrugged. "When you're willing."

She was willing at that very moment. But he wouldn't give her the push she needed. That he was tormenting her on purpose, that he was trying to build her longing to share, did not occur to her. All she knew was that she wished he would *demand* to see those drawings. "Well, I'll give it some thought," was all she said. But a terrible notion was dawning on her. "Wait," she said before he could spin around. He raised his eyebrows most attentively. "You're not . . . Peter didn't ask you to come up here, did he? You're not . . . just setting me up to be teased?"

His head shook slowly as she studied his mellow expression, trying to determine his integrity. "I'd be honored to look at your drawings," he said, when he grew tired of being scrutinized. "I'll leave you to them."

The moment he departed, Charlotte felt a loneliness she'd never before felt in the privacy of her bedroom. It lasted only a moment, but it was powerful. She hadn't quite wanted him to leave, and she didn't know why. She heaved a sigh. Somehow, as a disgruntled sister she felt it her sworn obligation to despise her brother's new friend. Yet something told her that hating him was going to take an awful lot of effort. She took out her charcoal and returned to her drawing, but this time, with a vivacity and confidence she'd not had only minutes ago. It had been a long time since anyone had expressed an interest. It had been a long time since she'd thought of herself as a budding artist. Somehow, that afternoon, she found herself drawing the finest picture she had ever created.

FOUR

Charlotte walked into town late in the afternoon without any intention of making mischief. She planned only to purchase some sugar for her poor mother, who was frantically trying to transform their house into a suitable place for a guest to spend the holiday. But unfortunately, she bumped into Sarah, her surest accomplice when it came to avoiding chores. The two of them were soon on the front stoop of Richter's General Store, talking about anything but buying sugar. "So has Peter changed?" asked Sarah, waving kindly to a sleigh driver whose horse trotted inches away from their boots.

"I think it's safe to say not."

"Why? Here, have a peppermint."

"Thank you." She reached into the striped paper bag with fingers that could barely grab hold, they were so well mittened. "Let us just say, within his first five minutes home, he stuffed snow into my dress." Tasting sweet spice, so warm against the chill of the wind, she was tempted to ask for another candy right away, but knew it would be more proper to pause.

"Well, you did, after all, throw a snowball at his friend." Sarah finished her sentence by shoving five peppermints in her mouth at once with an open palm.

"It was an accident! You saw what happened. And thank you so much, incidentally, for fleeing rather than coming to my defense. Another, please."

She held out the bag invitingly, but cried, "I did not flee!" Her cheeks flushed beneath her scarves. "I merely thought it was best we didn't complicate matters by having another person arrive in the midst of an already very confusing greeting."

"You fled."

"Well, you didn't even wait for me to follow you, you were so busy seeking revenge. You didn't give me a chance to catch up. I hardly thought you'd notice my disappearance."

Charlotte was stumped by that one. It was true—her speed had been rather inconsiderate.

While she thought, she gazed at the mix of red-brick and snowy-white shops, and the rolling hills beyond. Her scenic town was as beautiful as it was chilly on this crowded afternoon. Sucking hard on her peppermint, she began to lose herself in her meandering thoughts, wondering whether the church had yet been decorated for the holiday, wondering what she might present as gifts to her family, wondering when her father would return. But her thinking was interrupted by a sudden clasp of her arm and a positively scandalized look in her friend's brown eyes. "Listen," she whispered loudly.

Charlotte strained, and at first could hear nothing. So with agitation, she asked, "What is it, Sarah?"

Sarah's mouth was widening with every breath, as though her sensitive ears were being treated to a delicious pleasure. Charlotte was motivated to listen harder. And then she heard it.

"He made me feel so . . . I don't know. I can't describe it. Not wanton exactly, but . . ."

"Behind the hat shop," said Sarah. "Come." Bouncing to her feet, she tugged her reluctant friend by the gloved hand and led her to the source of the sound. Around the double-walled brick they went, until they were at the rear of the shop, hidden only by a corner. Sarah lifted a finger to her lips, begging her friend to be quiet, but she broke her own rule by whispering, "It's that tart from the tavern."

"Oh, stop that," whispered Charlotte with agitation. "You have no right to call her a tart. That is only a rumor. My mother says she does nothing but wait tables and provide for her family. They're nothing but ugly rumors."

"Oh, grow up, Charlotte. Everyone knows." She prevented a reply by demanding silence with a breath to her finger.

"I never knew a man could make me feel that way." The waitress's voice was light and crisp as the color of her hair. "He held me all through the night with such tenderness and strength."

Charlotte was not as excited about this as her friend seemed to be, and had the distinct urge to flee. "I don't think we should be eavesdropping," she began, but she was harshly shushed.

They missed some of the talking in their brief commotion, but when they returned to full attention, they heard, "And the strangest part of it is I never learned his name. I spent the whole night in his arms, in his bed, and yet I never learned his name. Though I do know he came in with the Bass boy from Cambridge."

Charlotte's jaw stretched wide open. Sarah mouthed, "Oh—my—lord."

When Charlotte arrived home, she plunked a bag of sugar before her hardworking mother, then raced to the stairs before her expression could be detected. "Wait!" called Margaret, forcing her daughter into an awkward freeze. "Where are you going in such a hurry? I need help down here."

"I . . . uh . . ." Charlotte forced the blush out of her

cheeks with every ounce of willpower she had before turning around. "I'm just going to change aprons. I wore my good one into town."

"Aren't you even going to take off your coat?"

Realizing it was a bit awkward to be so encumbered on her way to the bedroom, Charlotte reluctantly unwrapped. As she did so, the blush returned alongside a mischievous smile. "Say, then . . . is Peter's friend here?"

"Hmmm?" Margaret was too busy kneading bread to grant her full attention. "Peter's uh . . . Peter's friend? He's upstairs. Why?"

"No reason." But her tone so gave her away that her mother looked up suspiciously.

If she could have thought of a single possible reason for the mischief, Margaret would have given a warning. But as she could think of nothing her daughter could possibly be up to, she merely watched her prance up the steep stairs, praying she wasn't going to do something awful. Strangely, after a few more turns of the dough, she had forgotten all about her concern. That was a funny thing about chores—they kept life from becoming an abstraction. And so for Margaret, they kept life manageable. She wished she'd been able to teach her daughter to appreciate that. That to work was to touch life, and to think was to drift away from it. But she feared Charlotte would never understand. She seemed to want something intangible from life, something so translucent that even she didn't seem to know what it was. But this much was for certain. Whatever Charlotte's wish, if it didn't involve washing, mending, cooking, and obeying, then she almost certainly could not have it. And this, Margaret hoped, she would not have to explain.

A horrible thought occurred to her. It was so horrendous, in fact, that it caused her to stop her kneading, and it took a great deal to cause something like that. Charlotte. Asking about the Matheson boy. No. She clasped a floured hand to her mouth. She wouldn't be so foolish, would she? Charlotte had never expressed interest in a boy before, never. She wasn't . . . she wasn't . . . *hopeful,* was she? Oh, no. No, this could never be. The families were no match. And Charlotte was not handsome enough to steal the heart of such a young man. A boy like that most likely had young women lined across the Commonwealth of Massachusetts, awaiting his proposal. Oh, no. No, surely Charlotte wouldn't be such a fool. Perhaps she was merely . . . merely instructing him with regard to suppertime. Hmmm. That would be awfully sensible and courteous of her. Suspiciously so.

"Why, hello." Charlotte found him in his bedroom, the door wide open, and his nose buried in a leather bound book.

He closed the book and stood. "Hello, Miss Charlotte."

"No, no. No need to stand." She invited him back to his chair with a dramatic wave of her hand and took a seat at the desk. "I only came to ask how you're enjoying your stay in Peacham so far." She managed to blurt that out without laughing, but only barely.

Shaun cut his eyes to the side, trying to discern what her mischief was, but could not make a guess. So he decided he would sit after all, and made himself at home in a stiff-backed chair with a strong wicker seat. Charlotte didn't know it, but snow was floating behind her in the window. The dark brown of her hair was striking against the soft white beyond. And the warm flush of her cheeks was soothing against the chill which fogged each little glass pane. Shaun never failed to observe women during picturesque moments. Life was too short to miss them. "I'm enjoying Peacham and Vermont very much," he said. "I find great beauty in the rolling hills and the pines."

"And the taverns?" she asked, giving her joke away long before she'd intended, "Do you like our taverns?"

Shaun was quick enough to guess everything from her one clumsy question. It startled him for a moment to be caught so brazenly, but he was careful not to let it show. He leaned forward, using his knees as armrests, and intensified his silvery gaze. "Why don't you just tell me what's on your mind?" he asked, with just a flicker of a kind smile.

Charlotte was far more embarrassed than he. She could scarcely stand to look at him, and her sooty lashes fluttered nervously in laughter and shyness as she struggled to blurt out her discovery. The more he watched it, the more his smile broadened. She was precious. "Yes?" he asked patiently and encouragingly, as one who had not been on the spot, but rather, was interrogating someone else.

"You . . ." She just couldn't think of any delicate way to put it, and before she knew what had happened, she had turned from the aggressor to the defended, speaking out in a voice that begged for a gentle reception. "I heard you . . . enjoyed our little inn."

Shaun just watched, his hands clasped together, his eyes alight with humor. She was struggling so hard not to look at him, he felt rather sorry for her. But not enough to let her go easily. She deserved a small punishment for snooping and for her lack of restraint in revealing her findings. So, in good humor, he asked, "What did you hear?"

"Well, I heard that you . . . well, that you . . . met a woman there." She forced herself to look incensed at the last of these words. She straightened her back to an awkward arch and let him have a look at her big blue eyes, which were supposed to be burning with disgust, though she wasn't sure she was managing it.

"I see. And did you find that shocking?" he asked calmly, inviting her to keep looking by softening his own gaze.

"Well, it's . . . it's not so much that, as . . . as what can only be presumed about your . . . lodgings."

"All right." He thought about that for a moment, his eyes losing focus for just a flash while he pondered Charlotte's perception. "Then I see I'm being accused. Would you like to tell me exactly what I'm being accused of? Exactly?" he emphasized with a grin. She turned her cheek so stubbornly, and was silent for so long, that he added, "Do you even know?" It amused him to think she did not. He had to control his smile, lest it look like he was laughing at her.

"Well, naturally," she said, still offering him nothing but her cheek to view, "naturally, I don't know about such things."

"Then perhaps you came up here to learn."

Charlotte gasped. He looked so calm, as though he had said nothing at all. But she clutched the fabric at her bosom, instinctively fearing she was about to be harmed.

"I think it's true," said Shaun, making not a move with his body or hands. "I think you came up here not to accuse me, but to ask me. To find out what men do to women that creates a scandal."

Charlotte was relieved. She let go of her dress, realizing he hadn't intended to "teach" her in the way she had feared. Shaun watched her relax with a smile. "Isn't that right? Isn't that why you came?"

Charlotte shook her head, her long, dark braid moving across her back like rope. "No."

"I think it is."

"Well, you're wrong!" It suddenly became very important to her that she should make herself clear. After all, what if he told Peter about this?

"I'm not wrong."

"You are!" she cried. "I don't want to hear anything about what you did!"

"Not even one thing?" he asked, lifting an eyebrow. "Not even one little thing? I promise. It's fairly intriguing."

Charlotte, of course, wanted desperately to hear. But she only stuttered, "Well, I . . . well . . . well, what is it?"

He leaned deeply into his knees and said, "You're sure you want to hear?"

She nodded emphatically.

"Very well. Here it is." He met her eyes intently and said, "I didn't do anything to that servant. Nothing."

He looked unmistakably truthful, but his story made no sense. Charlotte knew what she had heard. "I don't believe you," she said.

"Well, there's not a great deal I can do about that."

She furrowed her dark brows. "You're lying."

But he would not allow her to regain the upper hand. "Do you think I'm lying?" he asked, "or are you merely disappointed?"

"I am not! I am . . . that is, I am of course relieved if what you say is so."

She said this so unconvincingly that he had to let her get away with it on the grounds of pure appeal. "Well, good. You should be," he said with such subtle face-tiousness that it was undetectable to Charlotte. "Had I done what you accuse me of, it would have been grounds for shunning me, no doubt."

Charlotte knew there was something odd about the way he spoke, as though he were making fun of her. But he wasn't being clear enough to warrant confrontation. So she said, "No doubt," and rose to her feet.

"Is that all then?" he asked, speaking to her stiff profile.

"Uh, yes." Awkwardly, she made her way to the open door, but before she reached it, he called out in a soft voice, "Charlotte?"

She froze, butterflies rising in her belly.

"Charlotte?"

She felt as though she'd been caressed. It was the way he spoke her name. "Y—y—yes?" she managed to ask.

"Are you available tomorrow?"

Her stomach did a free-fall. "Uhh . . . yes. Why?" Still, she did not turn.

"I wish to ice-skate."

"With . . . with Peter?"

"No," he said, his soft voice brushing across her breasts from across the room. She felt them harden. "No, not with Peter. With you."

She bowed her head pensively, struggling with something wordless. "I . . . I don't know how."

She heard him rise, though he barely made a sound. He came a step closer, and then another, and she thought, *If he touches me, I'll die.* To her unacknowledged disappointment, he did not touch her, but merely stood near, saying, "Then I'll teach you."

"I'll . . . I'll have to think about it," she blurted before he could take another step closer. Then she raced from the room as though fearful, leaving him curious over her behavior. Had he really done something so dreadful? Quietly, so that no one would hear him distance himself, he closed his bedroom door, absently making certain that she would not return and catch him in thought. He had merely asked her to go skating. Was it so odd a request from a guest in Vermont? And could he really be expected to choose Peter as a partner? He hoped he hadn't made her fear his advances, for truly, he felt Charlotte was too young—if not in age, then at least in maturity. And besides, she was the sort who must marry first. He knew that. He had not been raised in a cave.

It took him only another moment to make a more as-tute guess about her sudden disappearance. It had looked like fear, but how close were fear and pleasurable excitement? Of course. She suspected him of having bedded a strange woman at a tavern. Disgusting, surely, but intriguing? Absolutely. He smiled with a sniff as he imagined what a rosy-cheeked young lady like Charlotte would think of a man who touched women for pleasure. In her world, touching was for procreation. Such had been the case in his world, too, until he'd found that his adoration of anything female far outweighed his com-mitment to propriety. What would Charlotte make of a man's peeking under gowns for pleasure? She was prob-ably curious beyond reason, and that is what made her run. Fear that her excitement would show, and that her curiosity might be misinterpreted as affection. Some-thing about this conclusion satisfied and pleased him.

Charlotte breathed in the heavy fumes of the attic, shivering as the fire was never warm enough to fight the icy snakes of draft. Her hands moved over paper as though they were touching it, as though no charcoal stood between her fingers and her creation. Her lips quivered, and there were tears at the back of her eyes. But they were the sort of tears that did not even threaten to fall. They were nothing but liquid emotion, every kind of emotion, neither sorrow nor joy, and nor fear, but all three. The closer her drawing came to resembling its subject, the more those tears wet the back of her eyes. Charlotte was falling, falling, falling for the first time. It was the sound of her name on his breath. As though he were meant to speak it. As though it were a name that mattered. But when she'd finished her drawing, all she had was a picture of something that brought her as much anxiety as it did curiosity. Something that meant the difference between achievement and servitude, something that caused some to tease, and others to be teased, that ordered some to stay home and allowed others to roam free. It was something she was not allowed to see, but never allowed to ignore. It was a drawing of his lap.

FIVE

At the supper table, Charlotte was forced to wait on her own brother as though he were an honored guest. She had to ask him whether he'd like another slice of bread with his beef stew, and fetch him more water when his pewter cup ran dry. All the while, he spoke of his professors, his studies, and the sights and sounds of his journey to Cambridge and back. Charlotte scowled so noticeably that Shaun thought it peculiar he was the only one to observe it. When it was his turn to answer a question, he did so with sensitivity to his perturbed audience. "And Shaun, what has been your favorite thing about Harvard?" It was hard for Mrs. Bass to steer her focus from the son who made her so terribly proud, but manners required it.

Shaun cast a concerned eye at Charlotte and answered, "Actually, I'm finding it rather lonely. With no women about, that is."

"Pshaw, I'm relieved to be away from them," said Peter, snatching the opportunity to return the topic to something more interesting—himself. "At home, I'm surrounded by them, with Father always away."

"Now, now," said his mother with a look of endearment, "you know your mother and sister would be lost without you. What would we do without our boy?"

"Live longer?" suggested Charlotte, though she dutifully refilled a stew bowl as she did so.

Her mother was aghast. "Charlotte! Apologize."

"I'm sorry," she said with more hesitation than sincerity. Before she could be asked to show more heartfelt remorse, she disappeared to the kitchen, leaving Shaun to smile after her. He noticed she was paying him very little mind this evening, for someone who had been so very curious this afternoon. He wondered whether that meant she had decided he was all right, or that he was beneath contempt. Almost immediately, he decided on the former. Charlotte didn't strike him as a "thou art beneath contempt" sort of a young woman. She struck him as one to light sparks, not put them out. He believed he would still have an ice skating partner come morn.

"Hey—hurry, will you, Charlotte? I'm hungry here. Bring me more food, wench."

"Peter, don't call your sister 'wench.'" Mrs. Bass clucked her tongue. "It isn't funny."

Peter, who thought he was very funny indeed, and normally found his mother to be an appreciative audience, replied, "All right then, I'll just call her 'ugly.'"

"No, you're not to call her that either."

"Why not?"

"It isn't polite."

"But it's funny."

"Well . . ." She cocked her head, not quite wanting to wound him by declaring his joke less than amusing. "It's . . . it's not good behavior. And it's very untrue. Your sister is lovely."

"For a sow, maybe."

"Stop it, Peter."

"Well, it's true."

"Please."

"Come, wench, we need some service!"

"Peter . . ."

It was too late. Charlotte had not only arrived, but be-

fore anyone had noticed her, had dumped the entire re-
mains of the hot stew from the hearth directly into
Peter's lap. It was not scalding, but it was hot. He leaped
from his chair, determined to strangle her just as soon as
the agony wore off.

"Charlotte!!!" Her mother's scream could undoubtedly have been heard from the neighbor's house, and
that was a long way off. Charlotte laughed every time she
managed to escape her brother's attempts to grab her
neck. Never had a suffocating person looked so happy
or smiled so brightly. It had all been worth it for the sight
of the stew dripping on his shoes. "Charlotte, you go to
your room now! And you are not to come down until
morning!" Mrs. Bass was on her feet, fury in her blue
eyes. A few gray hairs flew free from her bun, as though
her anger had caused her hair to dishevel. "You heard
me! Go! Peter, please release her neck so that she may
leave us."

Shaun hated to break into a family quarrel, but this
had gotten ridiculous. He sprang from his seat and man-
ually pried Peter's fingers from Charlotte's throat,
wincing when he saw the deep, red indentations left behind. Amazingly, she was still laughing as she choked out
her freedom to breathe. "Charlotte, are you all right?"
he asked, resisting the urge to punch Peter square in his
fat nose.

"If Papa were here, he'd whip you," said Peter, trying
to thrust a finger in her face, a gesture Shaun prevented
with a light shove to the elbow.

"Are you all right, Charlotte?" he repeated, trying to
catch her eyes.

Her big eyes, blue and bright with cheer, met his.
"Yes," she said, "I'm fine."

"Go to your room!" her mother yelled, her voice now
scratching through a raw and tired throat.

"I'm going," she laughed, "I'm going." Then she

hiked up her skirts and ran before any more could be said about it. Shaun wished he could run right after her. It didn't hit him until she was fully out of sight that not only was she the prettiest thing in the house, but also quite possibly the only sane one.

"I'm so sorry," said Mrs. Bass, first to her son, and then to their guest. "Oh, Peter, please put on some fresh clothes. I'll have your dessert ready before you return. And Shaun, you must just think horribly of us. I don't know what's gotten into Charlotte. She's normally not like this. She's . . ."

"Yes, she is," said Peter, his square head still visibly swollen with the blood of rage, "she's always like this."

"She's getting better," his mother pleaded for him to believe, "she really is. She's not the tomboy she once was. She's really trying."

"You should whip her."

"She's too big for that, Peter. She's . . ."

"You should do it anyway."

"You know, I don't see anything wrong with her." Shaun's voice was a shock, for it had been so long since he'd spoken. Mother and son alike cocked their heads at him as his words sank in, almost as though they were having to translate from a foreign language.

At last, Mrs. Bass was sure she'd understood. He was being kind. Yes, of course. "Shaun, thank you. Thank you for understanding. Why don't you boys relax and let me clean these dishes and fetch the pie. Shaun, I'll bring you a bit of brandy," she added, revealing a warm acceptance of the fact that he was a drinker in a household that sanctified it less than most.

"That's all right," he said, an image of chatting by the parlor fire with the likes of Peter flashing in his mind, "I'm . . . I'm rather tired still from . . . from our journey. I think I'll declare it a night."

"Oh. Well, are you certain? I've made the pie with a touch of mint for the holiday."

"Sounds lovely. Still, I must retire. Thank you. Thank you for all of your hospitality."

"Certainly."

He offered a stiff bow, glancing once at Peter in the course of it to make sure it seemed he wasn't rudely ignoring anyone, and then did what could only be described as fleeing. He all but held his breath on the way to the stairs, hoping he wouldn't be stopped by another word of farewell. Once he was safely on the second floor, he leaned against the banister and exhaled, suddenly feeling quite alone in the world. Even better. The snow fell furiously behind a window, illuminated only by the night sky. The woodsy scent of the house flowed deeply into his chest. White and soft outside, brown and warm inside. He was better than alone in the world, he was alone in a place as cozy as Vermont. How he had always longed for a home like this. Minus the insane war between the sexes, of course. Otherwise, it was exactly the place of his dreams. A real home. A place to feel snug and unafraid. Only one thing could make it better, he thought, catching the faint scent of perfume floating down the stairs.

Taking the steps three at a time, he climbed to the attic and to Charlotte. Her door was closed, but before he knocked, she had already opened it. "I heard you on the steps," she said, and seemed to be in a most peculiar state of mind. Her smile was faint, her expression not nearly as defiant as usual. She had been crying. But she was over it—he could see that. And she seemed to welcome him in. "I've just finished my drawings," she said, implying that they were safely put away, in the way another woman might have told him not to worry, for she was fully dressed. "I'm using only a small candle for light," she said, lifting a partially empty candelabra from the wall, "that's how I like it at night. I hope you can see."

Shaun hesitated in the doorway. He didn't think he should come all the way in. In the daytime, he wouldn't have minded. He and Charlotte were both rule-breakers at heart, he could see that. And surely no one would catch them at their impropriety. But there was something about walking in there at night. He had rather hoped to fetch her so they could meet somewhere more neutral. "You must have decided I'm not the scoundrel you thought I was," he mused, "or I wouldn't think I'd be welcome in your bedroom at this time of night."

"People can hear me scream," she said, flashing a spark from her eye that let him know the fire had not been strangled from her. "In fact," she added, dragging a second chair to her favorite window, an invitation for him to join her, "if you're caught in my room, it's you who's most likely to be horsewhipped. Just a peep from me should be enough to send you on your way."

A warm smile crossed his handsome face. "I see, then. It is I who will have to trust you, rather than the other way, eh?" He moved into the room with ease, completely unafraid to take the seat beside hers.

They sat before her window, watching streams of snow fall furiously rather than float to the ground. The flakes themselves lit the room more brightly than her lone candle. "Thank you for trying to make Peter unhand me," she said, though she seemed to be talking to the window. "I think you don't like violence."

"That's true," he said, following her example by keeping his eyes fixed on the cold air that seeped in, and his ears alerted to the crackling of her bedroom's fire. "I'm a pacifist," he added, his voice low but soft as the night.

"What is that?" she asked.

"Someone who never fights."

"You see, I would know these things," she said, "if I, too, got to go to Harvard. Or anywhere at all."

He didn't pretend to understand. He let his silence speak whatever answer she hoped to hear. Strangely satisfied by his response, she asked, "Do you know what I like about Christmas?"

For some reason, he was tempted to guess. After shaking his leg a bit in thought, he ventured, "Your father comes home?"

"No."

"Gifts? Singing?"

"No," she said, leaning deeper into the night, farther away from her room, "I love Christmas because it's the only time anyone admits that there's magic. All the rest of the year, they tell me that only hard work will get the job done, we only get what we earn, chores sustain life and life is a chore. But once every year, we're allowed to forget all of that and believe in magic, in miracles, in wishes that come true even though we haven't earned them."

He leaned forward until his knees were a prop for his elbows and asked, "If you could have a Christmas wish, what would it be?"

Her answer made his heart fall. "I would wish never to be a wife," she said, her eyes alight with wonder. "I wish to be no man's servant, and just once, to be free."

It was a long while before he was able to swallow the tight lump that had suddenly and mysteriously formed in his throat. "N—never?" He didn't know why his voice sounded so odd, so strained. It was just that she sounded so certain, so . . . settled on the matter. It just didn't seem healthy, that was all. He was just concerned . . . about the well-being of a nice young woman.

The strange sound of his voice moved her to glance his way, and there, she caught the flash of his silvery eyes. The bright snow was making shadows on his perfectly sculpted cheekbones and jaw. His hair and slight side-burns waved so nicely. "Never," she said. But this time, she was so unconvincing that Shaun smiled warmly. She was only trying to convince herself.

For a moment, he understood her perfectly. She felt she'd been humiliated. To him, it hadn't looked like humiliation. To be throttled round the neck was many things, but not embarrassing. But to the one whose breath had been smothered, whose face had been made beet-red before a small audience, it was belittling, and her laughter had been a defense. Alone in her room, the shame had set in, and then the desire always to be alone. How many times had he himself suffered the very same feeling. How could he have missed it? And then he knew what she needed. She needed what he always needed in times like this—distraction. "Let's go now," he said, his voice no longer soft but loud and awakening.

Charlotte was shaken. "Go where?"

"To the skating pond. Is it far?"

She was having trouble adjusting to the change of topic, and this delayed her response. "Uh . . . no. It's less than a mile, but . . ."

"Then I'll fetch my skates. I've packed them in the trunk. Do you have skates for your shoes?"

"Yes, they were a Christmas gift from my father, but . . . I . . . I've never used them."

"I said I'll teach you." Somehow, he had risen to his feet without her noticing. Now, his hand was within inches of taking hers.

"But Mama will say no. It's the middle of the night!" This last bit she gasped out with a big grin on her face. It was an exclamation of thrill more than protest.

"I imagine she'll soon be asleep," he said.

"You mean, we should sneak . . ."

"I mean we should go quietly," he interrupted, "so as not to disturb anyone."

Charlotte bit her lip, glancing at the closet where she supposed her skates must be hiding in a dusty box. "Won't it be too dark?"

"The winter sky is light. Come, stop making excuses. Are you coming with me or not?"

There was no way she could look in his determined, handsome face and say no. The "yes" broke out as soon as she allowed it.

One side of his mouth lifted into a magnificently dashing smile. "Good. I'll help you strap them to your boots. Now remember," he added with a finger to his firm lips, "be quiet. I don't want them thinking I've kidnapped you."

Charlotte gazed up at him as though he were her savior. And that's what he was—for one night, anyway. "How will I know when they've gone to sleep?"

"I'll knock six times on your door, like this." He demonstrated a memorable pattern, and repeated it until he had her nod. "Excellent. If you've fallen asleep by then, we'll just wait till morning." After all, he thought, if he found her in slumber, most likely that meant she was feeling all right again.

"I won't sleep," she promised him. "I'll wait for your knock."

His smile burned a heart-fluttering memory into her mind that would stick with her for an hour to come. As she watched the falling snow and gripped her skates, waiting for his knock in the dark, she grew rather sleepy. So she pressed her face nearer to the windowpanes, letting the cold air brush her cheeks and enliven her. It would be frigid out there. She would wear every scarf she had and still probably grow numb. She would miss precious sleep, and be exhausted come morning when her mother wanted her to string berries and wash clothes. She would be murdered if she were caught. But she didn't care. She didn't know much about this very strange stranger who had arrived in her home like a mysterious Christmas package. But she knew one thing. No matter where he had come from or where he was going, tonight, he was exactly what she needed.

SIX

Charlotte had never dreamed escaping could be so easy. She'd always imagined there was more than a door between herself and blatant disregard of her mother's rules. But she could see now that it wasn't so, that the cold night had always awaited her, that all she'd needed to do was dare. "I can't see a thing!" she cried through her scarves, amazed that they were already beyond the range of her mother's hearing.

"Just hold my hand," he told her, squeezing her mitten. "Our eyes will adjust."

Snow was managing to land on the one place she was exposed, her eyes. It was crackling under her boots and floating into her mouth. It tasted like metal, like ice-cold silver landing on her teeth with the texture of tiny sponges that melted before she could study them with her tongue. She was shaking violently despite her wrappings. It was the wind that really caused it. Every time she thought she might adjust to the temperature, a gust of icy breeze nearly toppled her and started her sniffling. Shaun became concerned enough by her shaking to wrap an arm about her waist. "Stay close," he said.

She leaned into him, finding it was much harder for the wind to disorient her when his weight was added to her own. He was warm . . . and so strong. "Sorry for holding on so tight," she said, checking for a reaction.

He looked down at her brilliant blue eyes and answered, "You're just fine," emphasizing this with a squeeze of her heavily clothed waist. Despite the padding, his squeeze reached her heart, and she felt a gentle thrill blow through her.

The air smelled of sweet pine, though breathing in the scent with too much enthusiasm drew snowflakes into the nose. They were magnificent, those pine trees. Even in the thick of winter, they not only survived but prospered. They grew all along the roadside, taller than the tallest building and in the richest, darkest green, accented with laces of snow. "The fastest way is to cut through the woods," said Charlotte, though she hoped he would discourage the suggestion. The pale night sky was illuminating flakes of silver on the road, guiding their way, more and more so as their eyes adjusted to the dim. But in the forest, the majestic pines would block so much of the sky, it would be nearly impossible to see. And then there were the wild animals . . .

"Very well," he said. "You lead the way."

"Well, it is very dark in there," she said, peering into the thick of the forest, which encroached upon the side of the road.

"Well, then, I guess it's one of those decisions," he said mildly, "to risk being lost or to risk being a coward." His smile showed that he was not actually daring her in the most childish sense of the term, but merely inviting her to be wild, if she so chose.

"You really are a troublemaker," she said, observing the handsomeness of his square jaw even while it was flushed ruggedly by the wind. There was a devilish light in his eyes. "Are you always so reckless?"

He shook his head rather defensively. "No, I'm not reckless. Not at all."

She wondered about that. And she wondered about his night at the tavern. Was he capable of hiring a trollop right under the nose of a small, snooping town?

Something told her yes. She was developing the impression that his gentle demeanor was a clever guise to hide a very irreverent and scandalous young man. "All right," she said, "we'll go through the woods. But if we get lost, it's your fault. You're older than I, and you should have stopped me. Come," she said and flashed a smile at him, which he could barely see through the opening in her scarf, and pulled him by the hand into the forest of pine.

"Oh, I'm sure everyone will believe that," he chuckled. "I'm sure anyone who's never met you will believe I could have stopped you."

"Come," she said, tugging his hand. It was strange. His was the first non-familial hand she had ever held, and yet she was already comfortable enough to tug at it.

"Not so quickly," he said, closing tightly around her fingers, demonstrating a surprising strength that made Charlotte's hand feel completely encased. "If we lose each other, we're dead. We'll walk slowly so we're sure not to lose our grip. Come." With a gentle hand upon her back he led her at his own pace, deep into the dark where nothing seemed to stir. That was the frightening thing about it. Nothing seemed to stir, and yet, it was a forest. Surely there were many creatures about, just none of them willing to be heard.

"Why, if I didn't know better," she beamed, "I'd think you were scared of the woods."

"Well, I am a hopeless city boy, you remember." His gaze flitted about cautiously. Some of the pines were so tall overhead, he felt the size of a mouse. And though they were green, they looked black. He had the distinct sensation that forests did not like to see humans at night. That disturbing them during the day was bad enough, but disturbing them at night was a tremendous breach of hospitality.

"You really are scared," she laughed as though she had no fear at all. But that was her fatal error, for Shaun's power of observation was strong, and the moment he heard her false laugh, he knew that he was not alone in his jitters.

"Well, we can't all be fearless. Say, what's that?" he asked, pointing.

"What?" She turned, but just as she did, something touched her back. She screamed just as it started to move and tickle her through her coat.

Shaun caught her and kept her from running. "I'm sorry," he said. "I couldn't resist. I'm sorry."

"That wasn't funny!"

"Oh, I know," he said, laughing, "but I think your scream scared the bears away."

He could tell through her scarves that she wasn't smiling. In fact, her eyes looked rather distraught. "Bears hibernate, silly." There was a twinge of hurt in her voice. "There aren't any bears out at this time of year."

He shrugged one shoulder. "I know. I was only teasing."

"Well, I don't like being teased," she said so emphatically that his eyes narrowed curiously. "Teasing is just a way of insulting someone without giving her the option of objecting for fear of being a poor sport," she said, turning away from him pensively, "and I don't like it."

His smile was slow and barely visible in the dim evening light that sifted through the pines. "Then I won't do it again," he said solemnly touching her shoulder.

And when she turned, she saw that his words were in earnest. A nod was all she gave him, but it said a great deal. It said that she was willing to try, that she was willing to put some small amount of trust in a stranger, even a man. "Come," she said, "I think I know the way, but you must follow more quickly. I don't want my mother to wake and find us gone."

Obediently, he allowed himself to be pulled. It was warmer somehow in the forest, for the trees seemed to block the wind. There were places where his feet hit soft pine needles rather than snow, so dense was the coverage overhead. He might even have found the forest peaceful if it hadn't been so eerily quiet. But with the friendly scent of pine wafting through the air and a girl as lovely as Charlotte at the other end of his hand, it was hard to feel intimidated by the night. The trees had so little in the way of lower branches, their walk was a smooth weave around massive, sappy trunks. Somehow, though these were not maples, the sight of their sticky bark made him long for some johnnycakes and syrup. He tried to think about breakfast and what Mrs. Bass might prepare. He tried to think of it so that he might avoid another thought that was encroaching. That it would not be too difficult to seduce Charlotte.

It seemed true. It was dark, and they were so far from anyone who could disturb them. Oh, it wasn't that he wanted to ruin her—she was the sort of young lady for whom that would be the end of the world. He would never do that to her. At least, he didn't think so. "Never" was a long time, but . . . no, he would never do that to her . . . probably not. Still, the fantasy of it was making him long for a more concealing coat. He wondered what she would do if he stopped her. Would she take his kiss if he demanded it? Would she swallow her pride if he asked to see her breast, if he helped her unstuff it from her gown? He imagined if he were firm enough, she would. He believed she was just uncertain enough to respond to certainty. Stubborn though she was, a lifetime of being the underdog would undoubtedly leave some cracks in her foundation. She could be toppled by just the right suitor.

It angered him to think that a less scrupulous young man, a young man who cared less for her soul, might someday have the same thoughts and act upon them. His mind went back and forth between moralistic outrage and imagining her on her back in the snow, her plump breasts tickled by the wind, and his own finger spreading sticky sap over each of her mounds. It was rather unlike him to consider something so base as licking sap off a woman, when the woman in question was so innocent and endearing. The only explanation he could muster was that he must be furiously attracted to her. There must have been something in the scent of her hair.

"What are you thinking?" asked Charlotte, still leading him by the hand, her ice skates dangling over one shoulder.

"I was uh . . . I was thinking about calculus."

She wrinkled her nose. "Well, you shouldn't think about schoolwork when you're on holiday. You should try to think of something more interesting."

"Thank you. I'll try." He swallowed hard. "Are we almost there?"

"That depends on where we are." Her eyes beamed over her shoulder. "I'm joking. I know where we are. It isn't far now."

They walked until the forest became friendly, until it no longer seemed silent because their ears were tuned to the subtleties of sound. They walked until the scent of pine seemed to be the scent of air. And they walked until their gloved hands seemed always to have been linked. For a moment, Charlotte could barely imagine how it would feel to walk with an empty palm, without the strength and warmth of his large hand, without knowing that he was near, and that somehow, she was safe in his strange company. She didn't know why, but she was quite certain of it. He would not let anything harm her. Every glimpse at his thoughtful silver eyes told her so. Charlotte had never been alone so long with a handsome young man, and had to admit, there was a thrill to it. There was an excitement in knowing that he could . . .

touch her . . . even though she was hoping and trusting with all her heart that he wouldn't.

"We're here," she announced.

They stepped into a clearing away from the forest that had become their eerie friend, and saw an enormous round patch in the snow that could only be hiding a pond. The sky seemed bright without the trees overhead. Squinting, Charlotte looked up, finding that the night sky was almost a very dim white. Mountains, blue and green, rolled in the distance, creating a picturesque platform for her first ice-skating lesson. "Oh dear, the pond is covered in snow."

"We'll brush it off," he said, patting her hand. He went in search of a low branch, and when he found one, tore it off with surprising strength and used it for a broom.

"Shall I put on my skates?!" she called, but he gestured to his ear that he could not hear. So she plunked herself down in the snow and grasped her knees, watching him shine the ice. He didn't clear the whole pond, but just a big enough circle for one couple to enjoy. The moment he was within hearing range, she repeated her question.

"I'll help you," he answered, chucking his broom like a spear. "Let me see your skates." The skates themselves were nothing but blades with leather laces. "It's hard to make them tight enough," he explained, venturing near her foot. "May I?"

She was nearly stumped by the question, but realized he was asking permission to touch her boot. All she could do was nod. Somehow, by the courtesy of his question, it had become an intimate touch. She watched wide-eyed as he went to work, wincing once when he yanked the straps too firmly. For this, he apologized and tried again. And when he had finished, he patted her ankle in a gesture they both knew was sinful, but neither dared to acknowledge. "Now, I've never done this before," she reminded him, worried over the thought of appearing clumsy.

"I know," he said, helping her to her feet, catching her by the arm and waist when she wobbled. "Whoa, are you all right?"

"Yes," she said, giggling at her own clumsiness.

He responded in kind. "Believe it or not, it's easier to balance once we're on the ice." His smile was so infectious, she could hardly remain embarrassed.

"Then let's go," she said, allowing herself to be led like a lame stallion.

The moment she stepped on the slippery pond, she nearly slid all the way to her backside. She would have, if Shaun hadn't predicted the event and caught her. "The ice doesn't have any tracks yet," he said, making it sound as though it were the pond's fault and not hers, "It will get easier as we move along. Come." He held her securely round the waist, letting her feel the weight of his body, letting her know that she could not fall when he was so near. Her ankles wobbled and her blades slid out from her many times. But it was as though he were carrying her, and together, they glided effortlessly. "Such beautiful hills," he said.

"Yes," she replied, but her heart was not in it, because she was too familiar with the hills to appreciate them. She nearly slipped, but caught herself.

"You're all right?" he asked, sliding an arm around her waist, just in case she needed it.

"I'm all right," she replied, disappointed that this meant he would unwrap his arm. Still, she had his gloved hand.

"Want to see how long we can glide?"

She grinned at the challenge. "All right."

They each gave one hard push forward and then stood erect, waiting to see how long before they stopped or were toppled by a curve. They did well, but Charlotte stumbled out of her glide with several frantic steps at the last moment. To her delight, he did not laugh at her as her brother would have, but chuckled gaily in the spirit of friendship, in the spirit of a shared joke. "That was pretty good," he announced.

She laughed at herself—something she rarely did, for fear of others joining in. "I think I need practice."

"Then we'll keep going as long as you like," he said in a voice as warm as sunrise.

Her answer was a sparkle of the eye. So they skated on, and though the snow kept falling, their blades tore through it, revealing streaks of shining ice everywhere they went. The wind was cold, but they'd been in the cold so long, they no longer shivered. Even their breath seemed to take form in thinner clouds, as though it, too, had grown accustomed. Circle after circle they skated, the mountains growing ever more visible in the distance, and the black forest changing into moist, dark green. They rarely spoke, and with each rotation, the silence became more comfortable. Soon, they could say much to each other with only a smile. And Charlotte very much regretted the moment she had to announce, "My ankles are very sore."

With a nod of understanding, he led her to the pond's edge and settled her on the snowy banks. Stepping on dry land felt like a harsh landing from a breezy flight. Charlotte could no longer glide, only take ordinary steps on very wobbly blades. It was a disappointment, but her ankles were not strong enough or practiced enough to keep going. "I'm sorry," she said, thinking she had ruined Shaun's fun.

"Not at all," he said, collapsing casually into the snow. "You stayed out much longer than I did my first time."

Charlotte sat by his side, hoping the snow would not seep through her coat and wet her. "Did you skate in Boston?" she asked.

"Yes." And she noticed he had the grace not to point out the stupidity of her question.

"Was it very different there?"

"More crowded," he said. "It's very different when you've got to dodge other skaters."

Suddenly, an unexpected thought troubled her. "Did you skate with someone? With a . . . with a girl?" Why this mattered, she wasn't exactly sure. But somehow, the notion that she wasn't the first to hold hands with him on the ice would seem to cheapen what they'd just shared.

It wasn't the sort of question Shaun liked answering, so he drew traces in the snow and eyed her thoughtfully. "Don't remember," he lied.

Charlotte liked the way he looked at her, maybe even a bit too well. That silver glint to his iris was like a reflection of his quietly devilish streak. His face was so perfect, even as the night stubbled his jaw with a roughness men of his breeding were inclined to hide. It only added character, it only illuminated the spark of barbarism he concealed behind sly eyes. "What did you really do with that servant?" she blurted out.

Shaun was shocked to hear the question fly so effortlessly from her lips. He nearly asked, "What?" but as he'd clearly heard her, he stopped himself in time and pondered. When he was ready, he lifted an eyebrow and said, "I think I told you."

"Yes." She huddled her knees to her chest, protecting herself from the tender topic. "But did you tell me the truth?"

His frown was charismatic. "Well, yes. But if I hadn't, why would I change my story now?" He finished with a smile, hoping it would distract her. But it did not.

"Because we've skated together. Because we've held hands."

Again, he was taken aback. Hers was a mature reply, not what he'd have expected from one so young. It was possible, he reasoned, that she was grown up enough to hear the details, but he would not give them. He himself had little in the way of these kinds of sensibilities. He had no shame in telling her what he had done, especially as it had not been much. But he suspected that she would blush if he spoke even of having caressed the woman's neck with a breath. "Just tell the truth," she urged him, her blue eyes growing round behind her scarves.

"The truth?" he asked lightly. He thought her bright eyes were awfully pretty, especially when a strand of dark hair fell near them and contrasted so brilliantly. "The truth," he sighed, "is that I suppose there are certain things only your husband should explain to you someday."

"Do you really believe that?"

He thought about it a moment, then shrugged. "Yes, I suppose I do."

"Why?"

He was surprised by the question. "Well, I . . . I don't know, really. I just suppose you'll regret delving deeper into this conversation . . . with anyone besides . . . besides a husband." His eyes landed so intently upon her that she felt a rush in her bosom.

"Maybe you should let me decide what I would regret."

"I think you shouldn't be so bold," he said, and he wasn't talking about her words. He was talking about the look in her eye. The look that said he could kiss her if he wanted.

"Why not? I'm only asking a question." She tried to sound cheerful, but it was hard when he was looking at her as though in warning. "What is it?" she asked nervously.

"Unwrap your scarf," he dared her.

Something in the way he said it made it sound as though he were asking her to disrobe. It was only a scarf;

it covered only her face and hair. But his voice was so low, so eerily soft, and the stare of his beautiful eyes was so piercing. It sounded like a threat. "What for?" she asked.

"Because I asked."

He hadn't asked. He had ordered. But she didn't want to nitpick just now. She wanted to remove her scarf. And so she did, one long coil at a time, noticing that his gaze never wandered and never softened. When her plush lips were revealed, it was as though she were showing him a breast. When her dark-brown waves fell free, it was as though she were standing naked before him. "Why?" she laughed awkwardly.

"Sit closer to me." His arm reached out welcomingly, but his eyes remained fierce. Charlotte didn't even notice the chilly air tickling her neck and ears, she was so consumed by his strangeness. And by the thrilling and frightening notion that she was about to be kissed. Something that had happened to Sarah two times, but never to her.

"Yes?"

He answered her vague question by wrapping a confident arm about her waist, a gesture that made Charlotte swallow in anticipation. She could feel his fingers moving over her coat. Her fright only excited him. He fingered a lock of her hair, making it wave through his hand and finding it to be silkier than he'd expected. He dropped it near her face so he could look at the beautiful contrast between the darkness of the tress and the porcelain-white skin. He couldn't remember the last time he'd been so drawn to a woman. "Have you ever been kissed?" he asked, speaking dangerously near her lips. His voice was tender, but his stubbled jaw looked ruggedly masculine, his hands felt strong and sure.

"Not very often," she said.

He knew it for a lie immediately, and loved her for it. He could tell she'd never been kissed. "May I?" he asked.

Charlotte blushed and lowered her gaze. What he loved about it was the genuineness. She was trying with all her might not to flush, but was failing. She kept trying to look up bravely, but her eyes kept lowering. It was positively endearing. To put her out of her misery, he reasoned, to ease her awkwardness, he should just do it. And so, with such selflessness in mind, he leaned into a kiss, guiding her gently with a touch to her chin whenever she tried to evade. Charlotte didn't know what to do. It was hard to absorb the knowledge that she was being kissed for the first time. His face felt so warm, his lips were so soft, his nearness seemed like a sin. When they parted, his eyes were still closed, but hers were wide-open in awe. When at last he noticed that, he smiled. "Have I scared you?"

Charlotte tried to look haughty, for somehow, she thought she ought to. "No," she replied, stiffening her back, "although I . . ."

He took another kiss from her. This time, he took it with passion, tangling her hair in his fingers, forcing her head back, caressing her lips with his teeth and with his tongue. Charlotte's mouth fell open before him. She felt immobile, unable to squirm from his embrace, and strangely uninterested in doing so. She found herself breathing heavily as he brushed her hair aside and nibbled hotly on her ear. *Show me,* she wanted to say, *Show me what men do.* But she could not. Her nipples hardened against her gown, and she had to fight not to rub them against him, not to let his chest soothe them into ecstasy.

Then suddenly, it happened. One squeeze of her breast was enough to awaken her to reason. It had been a gentle squeeze, an impulsive one, barely more than a passing gesture on his way to her waist. But aroused as she was, it was electrifying to feel his fingers press and squeeze her . . . . there. Charlotte gasped and recoiled. The moment she had him at arm's length, she struck him, palm of her hand against his rough cheek.

Shaun only winced in reply. "Ouch," he said mildly. "That seemed unnecessary." But he unhanded her and cast his eyes elsewhere so she wouldn't see the lust-turned-to-fury in his eyes.

Charlotte was still gasping. She had gotten carried away, she knew it. She couldn't decide what was most shocking—that he had blatantly fondled her breast, that she had yearned for it, or that she had actually struck him across the face. She had behaved first as a tart, and then with violence. But she couldn't exist within such self-hatred, and so she defended herself. "How dare you," she blurted out.

Shaun knew he had misbehaved. In fact, the more he thought about it, the worse it became. To touch a woman's breast on the way to lovemaking was natural. But Charlotte had not been on her way to lovemaking. She had been engaged only in her first kiss. And to touch her there, no matter that her breasts were ripe and juicy and unavoidable, had been an unforgivable crime in the eyes of her society. And the society that was supposed to be his. "I'm sorry," he said, making sure his coat was yanked well below the hips, "I behaved inappropriately. I . . ."

"Take me home!" she cried, standing up with an air of great purpose. "Take me home now!"

Shaun closed his eyes. It was his own stupid fault. How could he let himself become so aroused, so taken by a girl who was too young and too proper to bed? Quite a houseguest, he was.

"Take me home now!" she cried again, wrapping her face up in scarves as though tidying up the morning after a scandalous affair.

"Take you home?" he asked, pushing himself to his feet. "I don't even know the way. Remember?"

"Well, then, follow me home!" she cried, "and stay ten paces behind me! I can't trust you any closer than that."

"Then how can you trust me to stay ten paces behind?" Tearing off his skates, he tried to gather himself so that his next remark wouldn't be so flippant. But it was hard.

"Good point!" she cried. "I'll let you find your own way home." And with that, she unfastened her skates with urgency.

He was about to let her go. He was sure he could find his own way eventually, and if she wanted to be alone, he hardly wanted to force his company. But as he chewed on his cheek and watched her turn away through narrow slits in his eyes, he knew he couldn't let her walk away. "Wait," he called, surprised that Charlotte turned immediately, and at full attention. He strolled up to her and tried to approach her as the graceful gentleman he sometimes was. "Charlotte," he said, making her knees tremble at the soft sound of her name on his lips, "Charlotte, I'm sorry." His face was sincere, and his eyes were strong, narrow, and full of heart. "Please don't be frightened. I just . . . I made a mistake. It won't happen again."

For a moment, she met his eyes with fluttering blinks and remained silent. It almost seemed as though she were going to accept his apology. But then she spat, "It was no mistake. I think you have control of your hands and I think you should be horsewhipped."

"If that would excite you," he called to her turned back. "I'm only joking. Charlotte. Don't just wander off by yourself. Charlotte!"

He raced after her, but stopped short of catching up. She stomped into the forest, the forest that had once been theirs. And he let her go, but never let her out of his sight. He couldn't. Every time she looked back, he said, "Don't worry about me. Just keep walking." And she turned away in a huff to continue her journey. And Shaun watched her prance ahead, with increasing affection stirring in his chest. She was forcing herself to remain angry. He could see it, and it was adorable. Her marching was exaggerated and she was not moving particularly quickly. She was not actually trying to get away from him. It was . . . well, it was cute. The more he thought about it, and the longer he followed behind, the more he was certain. Charlotte was exactly the stubborn, but warmhearted and vulnerable, young woman he could come to love. But contrary to his earlier musings . . . there was one problem foreseeable on the horizon. She would not be easy to seduce.

SEVEN

The morning after a long night is never welcome. Charlotte awoke to the most startling sound. "Good morning!" The voice of her dearest friend was carried from the parlor, up the smoky steps, and into her private little attic.

"It's so nice to meet you," she heard Sarah say. "You must be Shaun Matheson. I've heard so much about you." Charlotte pulled a pillow over her face.

"Oh? Good things, I hope?" asked Shaun in his most mannerly tone of voice. Mannerly. What a joke that was. If only everyone could have seen him last night, dragging her into the wilderness and groping at her breasts. He was horrid. So horrid that the sound of his voice made her belly flutter with enthusiasm.

"Oh, nothing special," answered Sarah. "Nothing . . . bad or . . . scandalous or . . . "

Charlotte could only imagine the expression on Shaun's face. She knew exactly how he must look—that mildly amused, *Yes, I just guessed your meaning, and I don't care, nor will I give you the benefit of acknowledgment,* kind of expression. She hated that look. "Well, I'm certainly glad to hear that," she heard him reply. Curse this house, thought Charlotte, curse it for not letting her shut out the conversation. It carried every word to her as though it thought she might like to hear.

"And where is Charlotte?" asked Sarah.

It was Mrs. Bass's voice that growled, "She has not yet risen. Please go awaken her and tell her we've had breakfast without her, and that her chores will be doubled for the day."

Charlotte groaned. There was nothing quite like starting off a new day, deeply in trouble. But then she heard Shaun's deep, elegant voice. "Actually, I'm afraid her sleepiness is my own fault." Charlotte's heart did a pleasant free-fall. "You see, I awoke rather hungry last night, and Charlotte heard me move about the kitchen. She offered to make me something to eat, and I'm afraid I may have kept her up a long while." What a smooth liar he was! Had he come up with that off the top of his head? What a natural talent for evil.

"Oh." Mrs. Bass sounded quite taken aback by his story. Her voice lost its grit. "I see. Well, then—well, go fetch her anyhow, Sarah. I'll need help slaughtering the pig." Oh no. Not slaughtering the pig. Her mother knew she couldn't do things like that, she knew it. Why did she torture her so?

She heard Sarah's footsteps clicking up the stairs. She rolled over and pretended to be asleep, fantasizing that it was still the middle of the night, that she was not late rising, that she hadn't been talked about . . . and that she would not be asked to help slaughter anything. "Be gone," she groaned when she heard the knock at her door. She was not in the mood for company.

"Charlotte, it's Sarah," she said, not realizing that Charlotte had heard everything.

"I'm asleep," called Charlotte.

"Well, you'd better rise," she whispered through the door. "Your mother is very annoyed."

Charlotte did not answer.

"Oh, I'm coming in," Sarah pouted, inching open the door, letting in the scent of the morning's strawberry pie. Charlotte was sad she had missed it. "Get up, Charlotte."

"I don't want to."

"Then I'll just come in." She moved across the room, her brown skirt rustling noisily against her thick stockings, her tiny hands still red from the outdoors. She settled herself in the desk chair, and depressed Charlotte terribly by looking as though she'd been awake for hours. Her pixiesque face looked fresh, all splattered with golden freckles and a rosiness at the tip of her narrow nose. Her liquid brown eyes were bright, as though sleep had gone well for her. And she had spent a good deal of time on her hair. The sandy braids, usually adorned with frizzled pieces falling out this way and that, were plaited tightly today and fastened together in back in a rather adult fashion.

"You look nice," said Charlotte. "Is there an occasion?"

Sarah looked deeply offended. "No," she said, tiny brows furrowed. "Don't I always look fetching?"

"Uhhh . . . yes, of course. Just especially so today."

That pleased her greatly, and she lifted her shoulders and chin proudly. "Well, I'm experimenting with a new image. We're not girls anymore, you know. We're eligible young ladies, and I imagined it was time to start looking the part."

"Who did you meet?"

"Meet?" She turned her cheek away. "No one. Why do you ask that?"

"Hmmmm. I don't know. Just a suspicion."

"Well, speaking of meeting," said Sarah, leaning forward in her excitement, "what about that Shaun Matheson?"

"Ugh. What about him?"

"Handsome!" she squealed in such a high voice that she hardly made a peep.

"Oh, please," groaned Charlotte unconvincingly, "I don't think so."

"Oh, come! I've never seen someone so dashing in all of Peacham. And his clothes are so stylish!"

"All of Peacham? Now, that's saying a great deal, isn't it?"

"Oh, Charlotte," her dear friend scolded her, "just because he is a friend of Peter's doesn't mean he's horrid. The tart at the inn certainly didn't find him objectionable," she giggled.

"He didn't do it."

"What?"

"He didn't do it," said Charlotte. "I asked him."

"Oh, you didn't!" Sarah's mouth fell wide. "You didn't! What did he say?!"

"Keep your voice down," she whispered, waving her hand downward. "Everyone will hear you."

"What did he say?" she repeated in a rasping, loud whisper.

"He said it was untrue."

"Then he's a liar," she said lightly. "There's no other explanation. We know what we heard."

Charlotte was about to object, but then she thought about the lie he had told downstairs in her defense. And then she thought about his kiss. "You're probably right," she concluded with a bite to her lip. "He'd probably ravish a serving girl in a heartbeat. And no doubt demand his privacy."

"Well, I think it's perfectly wretched," said Sarah, "coming to a town like this and behaving in such a way. Lucky serving girl," she pouted, stuffing her fist into her chin.

"Sarah!" Charlotte gasped laughingly. "How can you say such a thing?"

"Well, he is very handsome. I know it was awful, what he did," she added quickly. "I don't condone it, you understand. Not at all!" She sighed into a slouch. "I only wish it had been me."

Charlotte laughed. "Well, I think he's a cad," she said, rearranging her pillows so that she might sit up more attentively. "I feel sorry for the poor woman."

"Oh, please. You heard her—she enjoyed every moment of it. I only wish we were from the city, and we could do things like that."

"What he did isn't any more proper in Boston than it is in Vermont."

"Surely it is! Those city folk do things of that sort all the time. They throw big soirees, undermine their marriage vows. It's all very normal there."

"Oh, honestly, how would you know?"

"I've heard!"

"Well, then, perhaps he should return to the city, because we certainly don't want that sort of thing here."

"Don't we?" Sarah's eyes rounded into a startle. "The first good-looking man to arrive in Peacham, and you want him gone? That's masochism, Charlotte. I personally don't want him to leave here without at least getting a kiss," she giggled embarrassedly.

She wanted to tell her, she wanted to tell her, she wanted to tell her. "Well, just be glad *you* didn't get one," she said haughtily.

"What . . . what do you mean?"

Don't blurt it out, don't blurt it out, don't blurt it out. "Well, just that—well, that, as we've said, he's a very inappropriate young man."

Sarah's eyes narrowed in suspicion. "Do go on."

"Well, there's . . ." She tossed her hair over one shoulder, "There's really nothing to say. I just . . . well, I had something of an . . . encounter with him . . . last night."

Sarah screeched so loudly that Charlotte found herself shushing her as her mother called up the stairs, "Are you girls all right?"

"Yes, Mother!" she cried guiltily, and then huddled into a shared laugh with her friend, red-faced and arms locked together.

"Oh my goodness, oh my goodness," whispered Sarah, bouncing Charlotte's arms up and down. "Tell me everything. What happened?"

"Well," she said, more enthusiastically than she'd intended, "he took me to the pond last night."

"After dark?" she squealed.

"Yes, yes. Mama and Peter were fully asleep."

"Oh my goodness! I can't believe you went!"

"I can't either," she grinned, her blue eyes wide and alight with magic. "I wouldn't have gone, but he was so persistent. And he held my hand the entire way there."

"He held your hand?" Sarah gasped. "Oh my goodness! Charlotte, do you know what this could mean? You could marry him and move to Boston. And then you could be a famous painter, and—"

"Shush, shush. I haven't finished. I haven't gotten to the bad part."

"Bad part?" she gasped. "Oh, no! Did he reject you?"

"Hardly. In fact, at the skating pond, he swept me into a kiss."

"Charlotte!" she cried. "You've been kissed!"

"It's not so important," she said defensively. "In fact, I didn't even want to. He really pulled me into it."

"Did he force you?" she asked excitedly. "I would find that just awful if he had forced you to kiss him. Just awful." She waited expectantly and with great hope for the affirmative answer.

Charlotte recalled the events of her long night with an overwhelmed sigh. There were so many ways to tell a story. Should she choose the exciting take on it? Or the one that made it sound as though very little had happened. She settled on something in between, something that made her sound both desirable and highly moral.

Yet, something that didn't stray too far from the truth. "Well, he . . . he didn't force the first kiss. He—"

"The first kiss!" Sarah broke in. "How many kisses were there?"

"Oh, come now. You make it sound as though kissing were exciting. It was really nothing. He just . . . well, he leaned forward and kissed me, the first time. But the second time, he nearly forced me."

"How awful! Did he use his tongue?"

"Sarah!"

"I only mean, did he . . . well, how bad was it exactly?" She conjured up a very noble attempt at looking sympathetic and concerned.

"Well, it was bad. He . . . well, his hand, he . . ." This part of the story, she really did find difficult to face.

"What is it?" asked Sarah, a flicker of genuine concern glimmering through her feigned one. "Did he . . . did he hurt you?"

"No. No, not at all." She pulled apart a knot in her waist-length hair, pretending to be preoccupied with it. "His hands wandered where they should not. But I properly admonished him!" she added with haste. "I shunned him properly, and so should you." Why this second part was so very important to her right then, she wasn't sure. She just didn't like the idea of Sarah's fancying him.

"Oh, Charlotte! I'm so sorry! Were you able to get away?"

"Oh, there was no 'getting away' about it. I scolded him, and that was the end of it. I demanded he take me home."

"Oh," she peeped, looking a tad puzzled. "Well, at least he was a gentleman about it."

"A gentleman? Are you mad?"

"Well, no, no, I didn't mean for what he did at first, I only meant . . . oh, never mind. I'm just glad you weren't in any danger."

Charlotte tugged thoughtfully at the flesh of her lip. "No, I don't think I was," she said after some thought. "I really don't."

"So where exactly did his hands go?"

"Sarah," she snapped, "it is not important."

"But you can tell me. I'm your dearest friend!"

"Why does it matter? You have the gist of it."

"Who wants a gist? Gists are what we give to our parents. I want the details!"

"Well, honestly, where do you *think* he touched me?" Sarah was unable to look down without catching an unavoidable glimpse of her friend's rather impressive bust. "Oh, yes. I suppose that was obvious."

"Thank you very much," she said, crossing her arms in a huff.

"Oh, I didn't mean it that way, Charlotte. I meant it as a compliment! I've always been envious, truly."

"You have not."

"Well, 'envious' is a strong word. But I have always thought you were . . . well, beautiful."

Charlotte tilted her head. "Really?"

"Yes. Absolutely. All the boys think so. I know they do, even though they have a bad way of showing it. And that Shaun Matheson certainly must," she added, with a mischievous lift of her chin.

"Oh, he does not," Charlotte giggled. "He's just an ill-mannered city boy who seduces all the ladies," she said, longing desperately to be contradicted.

"I'm sure not all of them. Only the special ones," said Sarah with a bright smile. "After all, he hasn't tried to touch my bosom yet."

"You haven't spent a moment alone with him," drawled Charlotte. "If you did, it would doubtless be only a matter of seconds before he tried." But she did not believe her own cynicism. She believed that Shaun thought her special somehow. The tender way he looked at her told her that. But for all the life of her, she couldn't think why—why would he think her special? She shunned the thought. He probably would have done it to any young woman. She shouldn't flatter herself by thinking otherwise. He was a cad.

"Charlotte!" Her mother's cry was fierce.

"Ikes!" Charlotte shrunk into her bed. "Sarah, quickly. Please go downstairs and tell her I'm nearly ready."

"You mean lie?"

"Yes, please, if you would."

"Right away." Sarah gathered her skirts and trotted at full speed. But before she touched the door, a self-conscious hand went to her hair. "Charlotte?"

"Hmm?" Charlotte was already in frantic search of her stockings.

"Do you really like my hair this way?"

Charlotte spared her a glance. "Uhh . . . yes, yes, I think I do."

Sarah broke into a mysteriously enormous smile. "Thank you!" And with that, she raced to the stairs.

Charlotte shook her head in puzzlement, but not for long. She had some fast dressing and braiding to do if she didn't want this Christmas to turn into the first one she was forbidden to attend. The thought made her hands run frantically.

Downstairs, Sarah was stopped at the exit. "Where is she?" asked Mrs. Bass, a fireplace crackling behind her in the entry.

"Uhhh, she'll be right down, Mrs. Bass. She was almost ready."

Margaret eyed her suspiciously. "I see. Well, won't you stay for some cider? I'll even let Charlotte join you."

"I can't. I have to get ready for the . . . uh, well, I . . . I have to go."

"You have to get ready for the *what?*" She scrutinized the tidy appearance of the tiny young woman and concluded, "You look lovely."

"Really?" Sarah touched her hair. "Thank you. I . . . well, the thing is . . . I . . . "

"You *what.*" What should have been a question came out as a dark demand. Mrs. Bass could have such a sternness about her at times. Sometimes, though she felt guilty for thinking it, Sarah hoped she would not be present during her visits. She tried to be nice, but something about her straight posture, her stern voice, and the graying hair tied so practically into a knot was rather naturally intimidating. So much so, that Sarah was forced to utter the truth.

"Well, I . . . well, I really mustn't tell Charlotte where I'm going," she confessed, warming her gaze in search of understanding.

"Why not?" she asked coldly.

"Well, you see . . ." With some nervousness, she noted that both Shaun and Peter were in the parlor playing checkers and, no doubt, listening. "You see, there's a Christmas dance tonight at our old schoolhouse," she answered quietly, though she knew they could still hear.

"I see." Mrs. Bass showed no expression. "And why mustn't Charlotte know?"

"Oh, no! You see, she knows about the dance. She just . . . well, she doesn't know that I'm attending it."

"Why isn't Charlotte going?" she asked as only an ignorant mother possibly could.

"Well, she . . ." Sarah glanced awkwardly at the boys. "I don't think she was asked."

Peter burst into laughter, all but spitting on the checkers board. Mrs. Bass tried to silence him with a warning look, but he did not catch her eye. So she returned her attention to Sarah rather stoically. "I see," she said stiffly. "Well, do enjoy yourself."

"Thank you, ma'am. Thank you." She backed out of the house just as inconspicuously as she was able, given that she was moving under a strange stare.

Margaret bowed her head just as soon as the girl had departed. It was a pensive and troubling moment, but it did not last. She was a practical woman who did not value Christmas dances and frivolous courtship. And just as soon as she was able to remind herself of that, she stopped being troubled and spun about to the kitchen. "And you still hope she'll find a husband?" Peter laughed to his mother.

"Silence, Peter." She moved passed him as though he weren't there and let herself into the dark kitchen. It *was* a dark kitchen, wasn't it? She looked around at the black stove, the burnt maroon hearth, the dark tin cups and hanging pots. The room was filled with smoke and the windows were small. She'd never realized how dark it was before, though Charlotte had said it many times. Pensively, she bit her lip.

"Nobody will ever ask Charlotte to anything," chuckled Peter, making a terrible move with his checker.

Shaun had the opportunity to take a number of his pieces, but was distracted and chose not to. "If you'll excuse me," he said.

"What? Aren't you going to finish our game?"

"Later," he promised, "I'm just going to . . ." His thumb pointed behind him, ". . . to help your mother."

"She doesn't need help. It's easy. She just bakes it and we eat it."

"Yes, uh . . . nevertheless." Shaun strolled casually into the kitchen just in time to keep Mrs. Bass from dropping a heavy platter.

"Oh!" she cried. "Thank you. Thank you very much."

He carried it with ease to the counter, then cast concerned eyes upon her. "Are you all right?"

"Yes, yes," she said, sucking the tips of her fingers. "I

don't know what I was thinking, grabbing something so heavy with just the ends of my fingers."

"They're all right though?" he asked, reaching for her hand and turning it under his gaze.

"Yes, yes," she said. "It's perfectly fine, you see?"

Satisfied, he gave back her hands with a gentleman's smile. "Good."

"Well, whatever are *you* doing here?" she asked after giving her stinging finger one last suck. "Are you hungry? Can I fetch you something?"

"No, you've fed me handsomely," he assured her. "I'll not be able to fit in any of my clothes by the time I return to Cambridge."

She grinned, for there was no greater compliment to her cooking.

"What I actually wanted," he said, leaning against a counter and crossing his arms expectantly, "is to ask you a question."

"Oh? What is that?" She had already returned to her chores, and was on her knees scrubbing the hearth before he could reply.

"It's about Charlotte, actually."

"Mmm-hmmm." She rubbed and rubbed and rubbed.

"Did you know that she draws pictures?"

Mrs. Bass halted her scrubbing. After pausing, she spun around to look at him. "Oh, dear. She didn't show you her drawings, did she?"

"No," he said with a frown and a raised eyebrow. "Has she shown them to you?"

"I'm afraid so." Mrs. Bass put down her scrubbing brush and rose to her feet, slapping her hands against both sides of her apron. Then, with a sigh, she told him the bad news. "The poor thing doesn't know it, but she's terrible."

"Really?" For some reason, he found that hard to believe.

"Yes," she said, pacing to the edge of the room, for it was so hard for her to stop moving. Absently, she grabbed a rolling pin, somehow thinking there must be something she ought to do with it. Ah. There it was. Some dough she had prepared. As she began rolling, she said, "It was a bit touchy for a while, you know. Charlotte was in the habit of showing her charcoals to everyone for some time, always hoping to receive some encouragement. But I'm afraid we couldn't give her any," she said, sparing him a glance of regret. "She's perfectly awful."

"What is awful about her?"

"Well . . ." The dough was stiff and in one place, requiring several poundings with the roller. With a scrunched face, she delivered them and then said, "Her pictures don't look like the things they're meant to represent. Sometimes they don't resemble . . . anything."

Shaun slipped into his most diplomatic tone of voice. "Perhaps she draws impressionistically."

"Perhaps she draws what?" Mrs. Bass wiped a streak of flour from her nose.

"Impressionistically. Maybe she draws things not so much as they are, but as she sees them."

"Well," she gave the dough a merciless punch, "yes, that sounds like her drawings. The 'not so much as they are' part, anyway. I'm sorry to say it, but they're pretty awful."

Shaun reflected on what Charlotte had once told him. Rather than drawing anxiety, she draws a snowball. Her drawings weren't meant to be literal. He was sure of it. And for some inexplicable reason, he was also sure that she could draw well. He didn't know what gave him that impression. But when he looked at Charlotte, he did not see a woman who would live in the illusion of being able to draw when she couldn't. In fact, he couldn't imagine her pursuing anything at which she did not excel. There must have been something that her mother was not seeing, and he intended to find out what.

"Charlotte! There you are!"

At the sound of her name, Shaun found himself warming into a natural smile. He was excited to see her, and was not disappointed when she came rushing in, her hair messily braided into one dark plait, her blue eyes the brightest lights in the room, and her face flushed from panic. "I'm sorry, Mama. I overslept. I . . ."

"Shaun told me what happened. It's no excuse, though. I've taken you out of school so that you can help me, not so you can linger in bed."

"I'm sorry, Mama." She patted down her white apron, wanting at least to look like a hard worker. "What can I do to help?"

"First you can tell me why you're not going to the Christmas dance."

Mrs. Bass had no notion of how cruel it was to ask this in front of a handsome young man, so near to Charlotte's age. Charlotte's eyes flitted immediately to Shaun, and her cheekbones fell. He had the courtesy to look the other way, to seem disinterested, but it barely helped. "It's just a silly dance," said Charlotte. "I didn't want to go."

"Sarah said you weren't asked."

Charlotte felt tears burning in wells behind her eyes. Why did she have to embarrass her? It was as though she were trying! "I didn't want to be asked," she said. "I wanted to stay home."

Her mother knew better. "Maybe if you would carry better posture," she said with a wise glint in her narrow eye, "and plaited your hair more fashionably."

"Mama!" she cried, fighting to keep from screaming it, "I didn't want to go!"

"Well, then, you'll stay and slaughter the pig with me."

Charlotte couldn't make any physical gesture that would soothe her. She tried turning, gritting her teeth, tearing at her hair, but nothing could ease the painful frustration. "I don't want to!" she cried. "He's a cute pig!"

Shaun thought his heart might slide out from inside him.

"I've told you not to play with the animals!" her mother growled. "I've warned you of that ever since the first time you grew attached. The animals are our survival, not your companions!"

"I haven't been playing with him!" cried Charlotte. "I haven't even gone near him. I saw him only a few times. I had no choice—I had to go into the barn. And I just can't slaughter him!"

"You will!"

"Why can't Peter do it?!"

"He's home for the holidays! Would you make him a servant?"

"Why must *I* be a servant?!"

"Because you're a girl!"

Charlotte glared. "Well, perhaps that's why I'm not going to the dance," she cried. "Maybe I don't want to find a husband, maybe I don't wish to be a servant!"

Something about that troubled Margaret more deeply than she herself could understand. Marriage as a work contract—it was an unseemly implication, one that she would not entertain. "Go to your room," she said, her low voice shaking with fury, "while I decide your punishment." And the quiver in her narrow, pale eyes told a great deal about how awful the punishment would be.

Charlotte raced up the spiral kitchen stairs before another word could be spoken, and she had only one thought in her mind. *I'm running away, I'm running away, I'm running away from home.* Knowing that it wouldn't happen didn't bother her. The words themselves, empty as they were, helped her race to the smoky, cold attic. Her mother was left behind with both floury fists on her hips, and her head bent down in anger. It seemed she was unable to speak, but she knew that she must. She just had to gather herself first, control the tremble in her voice and soften the bite in her eyes before she apologized to her guest.

At last, she lifted her chin to speak, but was momentarily frozen by a glare. Shaun was looking at her not as a guest, but as a man. Just a man. His fixed gray eyes spoke plainly of hatred and disgust. "I'm . . . I'm sorry for Charlotte," she began.

"Stop apologizing for her."

Mrs. Bass hardly knew how to reply. She felt strangely humbled by his intensity. For though his posture was casual—he was, in fact, leaning on a counter—his cold expression was absolutely unwavering. She had to play with his words quite a bit to construe a meaning that would lean in her favor. But at last, she did it. "Yes, it would be better if she apologized herself, but the way she's been behaving . . ."

"That's not what I meant." Casually, he leaned away from the counter, making himself upright. But there was nothing casual about the bite in his eyes or the stubbornness with which he locked them to Margaret's. He strolled up to her and said, "Mrs. Bass, with all due respect, there is nothing wrong with your daughter." And then he walked past her, leaving her to guess where the problem might lie.

"What was Charlotte screaming about this time?" laughed Peter, just as Shaun strolled past him.

"Go to hell."

He hiked the front stairs three at a time, clutching the banister for speed. When he reached the door at the top, he knocked softly. He watched the snow fall through a triangular window as he waited for a reply. At last, he knocked again and said, "It's only me."

"*Only* you?" The indigence on the other side of the

door made him smile. "What do you mean, 'only you'? Have you come to attack me again?"

"Charlotte," he said cheerfully, "will you let me in?"

"A known cad? Certainly not. If I had a lock on this door, I would use it. As it is, I may cry for help."

He sighed good-naturedly. "Charlotte, we can talk about that if you wish, but you'll have to let me in first."

"Anything you have to say to me, you can say through this door."

He thought about simply pushing it open, but he decided not. She'd been humiliated enough for one day's time. If being proud helped her recover, he would let her be so. "Very well," he relented, "I've come to ask you to the dance."

There was a long silence.

"Charlotte? Did you hear me?"

"Yes, I heard you. And no, thank you."

"Oh, come now. It'll be fun."

"Fun like last night?"

He flitted his eyes to the ceiling in an expression of adoring annoyance. "Charlotte, I've only come to ask you to a dance. Nothing more."

"Well, I don't want to go."

"Why not?" It really wasn't spoken as a question.

"Because I'm afraid of you, you wolf!"

"You are not. A little insulted, maybe, but not afraid. What's the real reason you won't go?"

"Because I'm insulted!"

"I shouldn't have given you that answer. Sorry. Let's try again. What's the real reason you won't go?"

There was a long pause. When at last she spoke, it was with more soul and less volume. "Because I won't . . . I won't like anyone there."

Shaun could guess what that meant. She felt that they didn't like *her*. "Then we'll ignore them," he said. "It'll give us a chance to talk."

"I don't want to talk to you. And I certainly don't want your charity! You're doing me no favor by asking. I don't want to go to this dance."

"A moment ago I was a cad, and now I'm charitable? Try to keep your defensive exaggerations consistent."

He thought he heard a laugh, but it was a muffled one.

"Come on," he said brightly, "I don't want to be stuck in this house tonight, and I know *you* don't. If we don't have fun, I'll take you to the tavern for a cider."

There was a painfully long pause. Shaun could feel her thinking through the door. "You heard your mother," he said by way of cinching it. "If you come to the dance, you won't have to help with the pig."

The door flung open. He was thankful he hadn't been leaning on it. And before him was a cross-armed, tight-mouthed Charlotte, her round, blue eyes big and laced with lengthy lashes. "You'd better not lay a hand on me," she said.

"I make no promises." But his face was teasing. Within a moment, he broke into a full smile.

"Well, then," she announced, "I shall carry a crowbar."

He laughed so brightly that she had to fight to remain petulant. She didn't last long, though, and had to bend her head to hide her smile. "I don't have anything nice to wear," she told him.

"You don't need it," he said firmly. "You're beautiful."

Charlotte felt as though he had caressed her face. Her lips, her hair, and her cheeks all tingled at the thought of being beautiful. "You're being improper again," she snapped disingenuously.

He only smiled mysteriously in reply. "I'll come get you when it's time. Oh, by the way," he said, just before departure, "what time does it start?"

"Chaperones arrive at five, we're to arrive at six."

Again, he wore a mysterious smile. For someone who

had "forgotten all about" the dance, she certainly had memorized its details. He nodded cordially, then descended the stairs, leaving Charlotte breathless in the privacy of her room. At first, she was so confused, she could hardly decide what she felt or what she ought to think. That she shouldn't agree to be alone with him after what he did? That she shouldn't attend a dance where she had so few friends? That everyone was going to faint when they saw her walk through the door with such a handsome stranger? In the end, this was the thought that prevailed, and she closed the door, spinning around with whispering screeches.

EIGHT

Charlotte had a dress, after all. When Shaun asked Mrs. Bass whether she might have a gown Charlotte could wear to the dance, adding, "She's fine as she is, of course, but I think she'd enjoy something fancier to wear," she stopped what she was doing and went pallid.

"She has one!" she cried, "That is . . . let me fetch it."

So Charlotte was forced to suck in harder than she ever had before while her mother clasped a merciless corset around her waist. Her arms outstretched, her hands whacking the bedpost every time she turned, she was rather miserable about it. She wouldn't be able to sit, much less dance, in the brutally attractive gown her mother had sewn. "This corset doesn't fit," she groaned.

"It's not meant to fit," said her mother, tugging. "It's meant to make *you* fit."

"Ouch, that hurt." She winced in the direction of the gown. Though green for Christmas, its color was a coincidence. Her mother had sewn it three years ago, hoping ever since that she would be invited to a dance. What a disappointment Charlotte imagined she had been. "Did you go to many dances when you were young?"

"Oh my, yes," said her mother.

That's what Charlotte had been afraid of. Her eyes dropped down, for she was truly ashamed that this was her first dance. That her mother was making such a fuss over it only confirmed her anxiety that her social failures had been noticed.

"Why, the first time I met your father, it was at an Easter dance," said her mother in a tone that was uncharacteristically whimsical.

"How old were you?"

"Fifteen." Two years younger than Charlotte. Her eyes fluttered downward again. "Of course, I had gone to it with another boy," Mrs. Bass reflected. "Charles Ashbrooke. I'll never forget him. What a mistake it was for him to take me to that dance! If he hadn't done so, I never would have met your father and forgotten all about him," she chuckled.

Charlotte, though saddened by the comparison, was also strangely curious. "What was it about Papa that you liked so well?"

"Stop breathing so deeply. I can't get these last laces."

Charlotte sucked hard.

"Good. Ummm . . . what was it? What was it that I liked about him . . . well, he was very . . ." She stopped her lacing and reflected for a moment. "Well, very handsome, I suppose."

"Handsome? My father?"

"Why, yes," Margaret laughed. "Is it so shocking?"

Actually, it was. It was very difficult for a seventeen-year-old to see her parents as human, much less attractive to the opposite sex. "But he . . . he's so . . . ordinary looking."

"That's only because you're used to seeing him. And because it's hard for a young woman to see an older person in his proper light. Our eyes are better tuned to the subtleties of faces our own age. Turn around. Let me see the front. Good." She patted her daughter's waist, checking the depth of its curve. It was not as dramatic as she'd hoped, even with the corset on. But Charlotte had a sturdy frame, and there was little that could be done about it. She was a beautiful, grand height, and had wonderful padding in the places she needed it most, but that waist simply would not crunch. "I don't believe you wear your corset to bed," she accused her.

"I do . . . usually."

Mrs. Bass frowned, but said nothing more about it. She would make her daughter as beautiful as possible on this night, no matter what her shortcomings. She held up the velvet dress and squinted. "Mmmm," her lips twisted disapprovingly, "I should have made it blue for your eyes. Or red to contrast with your hair." She sighed a deep sigh. "Oh well, this is what we have. I hope it will be warm enough with your cloak."

"May I wear my hair up?" Charlotte asked excitedly, sensing that her mother was in a yielding mood.

"No." So much for her senses. "You may wear your hair up when you're eighteen."

"But I am nearly eighteen, Mother."

"You're barely seventeen."

"Then may I at least wear it down? I'll look a child if you braid it."

Mrs. Bass flanked her hips with fists and cast an imposing glare upon her daughter. But her eyes fluttered and she relented. "I'll braid the front strands and tie them with a bow. The back may hang free, *if* you brush it properly."

"Thank you!" It was a style Mrs. Bass normally disliked, because she believed that hair was unclean and ought to be put away somehow. Even in early childhood, Charlotte had not been allowed to wear it thus. That she was allowed to be so impractical on this night only proved how important it was to her mother to see Charlotte go to a dance.

As the petticoats were fluffed over her legs and the dress smoothed against her corsets, Charlotte got to thinking again about her father and mother. She wanted to know something, but didn't know how to ask it without receiving an automatic reply. She attempted anyway. "When did you know that Papa wanted to marry you?"

"When he asked, I imagine." She stood back and studied her daughter like an unfinished work of art.

"Not until then?"

"Mmmm, I suppose I had my suspicions. Turn around. If you're going to wear your hair down, I'm going to brush it senseless. Turn."

"What sort of suspicions?" she asked with an obedient about-face.

"Well," she said, whacking at her head with the brush, holding hairpins in her teeth, "he bought little gifts from time to time. My mother did not let me keep any of them. She found it highly improper for a young lady to receive a gentleman's gifts, mind you. But he did try. And I think I suspected he would soon speak to my father."

"But when did you know that he loved you?"

"Oh, I . . . I don't think you can truly love someone until you've known him for years. I don't think we even began to love until we were ten years married."

"But when did you know that he . . . that he had feelings for you, special ones?"

"I don't know what you mean."

"Well, just . . . just how would I know . . . or would anyone know . . . that someone really liked her . . . as more than just a friend?"

"He would propose marriage."

"Before that? Surely there are signs."

Margaret spun her daughter around and took her by the shoulders. "Charlotte, I didn't want to say this, but your questions are worrying me."

Charlotte looked like a puzzled doll, with her sooty lashes batting over her round eyes.

Her mother took a deep breath but did not soften her

stare. "It was very kind of Shaun to ask you to the dance, Charlotte. I hope you will have a wonderful time, and I hope you will wish to attend more dances after this. But . . ." Another deep breath ended in a helplessly worried look. "You know that he cannot be your husband. Not ever."

Charlotte tried to shrink away from her mother's grasp. "Husband? I . . . I don't want a husband. I . . . I wasn't thinking of . . ."

"Good," said her mother, "because I don't want you to get hurt. Believe me, I know, Charlotte," she said with compassion. "I know what it's like to be young and to meet someone so handsome, and be asked to a dance for the first time . . ."

"I wasn't!" she cried, her eyes wrinkling to hide from the pitying look that was so painful to receive. "I don't have any interest. I'm only going with him because" She couldn't say because of the pig. But she wanted to. She wanted to say something that would make her seem like the finicky one, and him seem like . . . like someone she could have if she wanted to.

"Charlotte, you don't have to tell falsehoods."

"I'm not! I'm not. I'm not." The third time was a whisper.

"All right," she relented, "then I suppose I have nothing to worry about."

Charlotte's heart was sinking and the backs of her eyes were filling with water. All her blood seemed to drain to her extremities, pulling her downward into sadness with each stroke of the hairbrush. "Out of sheer curiosity," she asked, "why is it that I could never have him? If I wanted to, which I don't."

Margaret didn't want to hurt her. She didn't want to say that Charlotte was not quite beautiful enough, was not well-behaved enough or didn't possess enough grace to charm a man as refined as young Mr. Matheson. So she stated the reason that seemed the most impersonal and, therefore, the least hurtful. "We're simple country folk. We could barely scrape together your brother's tuition. We're not the sort of family his will want to join." There. That was highly diplomatic. She'd made it the fault of the family, and not of Charlotte.

"I don't believe that," Charlotte said faintly without thinking. "I don't believe Shaun thinks that way. I don't think you know him." But what she meant by that wasn't clear to either of them, so nothing more was said. They finished her dressing in silence.

Shaun had dressed in his finest, which was awfully fine. He would be the most exquisite-looking man at the dance, for he could hardly help it, given his wardrobe. But he'd been careful not to add any flair that might draw undue attention to his father's wealth, or overshadow the simple beauty of his lady's homemade gown. Buttoned waistcoats seemed to have been invented for men like Shaun, for his black one fit over his white shirt with a perfect emphasis on his strong, tight waist. The slender fit of his buckskin breeches was a blessing to his long, strong legs. And his high, white collar and cravat rose nearly to his fashionable sandy sideburns, drawing out the perfection of his face and the bright glitter of his eyes. How he got his short hair to wave so perfectly, Peter could not understand. It was one of the many things about Shaun that set him in awe. Elegant silken ruffles peered out from under his dark, stylish waistcoat, making him look the model of a city gentleman gone courting.

But he'd worried needlessly over keeping his dress simple, for there was no chance he could have outshone the green-clad lady who descended the stairs so expectantly. His eyes sparkled at the sight of her. Her dark, walnut hair was longer that he'd ever imagined. It hung in thick, gentle waves to her waist. Her skin looked ghostly white beside the dark of her pine-green gown. Her lips were so lush, her face such a perfect oval, her brows so dark, her eyes so blue . . . she looked like a painting. And then there was her corset. Yes, Shaun knew that he was gazing upon a woman wearing a much-too-tight corset. The poor thing could hardly breathe, he imagined. Though he was stylish himself, he had never cared for the fashions of women, particularly these new tighter corsets.

A woman, he thought, was magnificence at birth. She was nature's most startling creation—beautiful by definition, by virtue of being able to create breath within her belly and equal to a man in all else but in the art of warfare. Of slaughter. Of all that Shaun despised. Why would anyone try foolishly to improve upon nature's greatest achievement? And yet . . . he had to admit the style worked on her. The corset may have had an unnatural effect upon her waist, but it did wonders for exaggerating the beauty of what lay above. Her breasts, enormously inviting in all their glory, begged him to pinch them through the velvet, even if she herself would slap him for doing so.

He offered a courteous bow, but was unable to take his eyes off her during the course of it. "I am charmed," he said in a way that would have seemed impeccably polite if he hadn't ruined the illusion by fixing his eyes on her breasts before remembering to lift them.

Charlotte was charmed as well. He looked exactly as she'd hoped. Exactly as she needed him to look, if he were going to impress all of her classmates. "Thank you," she said, remembering to sound stiff, as though she would not be there if he hadn't twisted her arm.

"You look ridiculous!" cried Peter, who was watching this potentially romantic greeting from the parlor sofa.

"If you're going to make my friend take you to a dance because no one else will take you, you could at least try to look nice so you won't embarrass him."

"Peter." The name rolled from Shaun's tongue like an utterance of annoyance that forced him to rub the weariness from his eyes. "Your sister looks beautiful. All right?"

Mrs. Bass trotted down the stairs at an anxious pace. "Shaun," she called apologetically, "Shaun, I forgot to tell you, there's no sleigh. Mr. Bass uses it to make his rounds and we haven't afforded a second one. I'm sorry that you'll have to walk."

"It's no inconvenience," he said smoothly. "We'll enjoy it, I'm sure."

"I'm sorry to send you unescorted—I know it's improper. But really, you're more of a brother than a beau, Shaun. Here, won't you take a lantern for the walk home? It will be dark by then." The sun had already turned a stinging bright orange, and no longer illuminated the entire sky, but only a small circle of it.

"It isn't necessary," he said, smiling at Charlotte. His smile was so handsome that she flushed. "The moon should be full tonight. I think we'll find our way."

Somehow, Charlotte knew why he didn't want to carry a lantern. She had known him such a short time, yet she knew. It would be more romantic without. She would cling to him more needily in the darkness. They would be more at one with the night. That is how Shaun thought, she was sure of it. And as he took her hand, resting it firmly on his elbow with a reassuring squeeze, she looked shyly into his sparkling eyes and thought, *My mother is wrong. I know she's wrong. If I wanted him to, he would marry me.* After all, her mother hadn't seen him trying to take advantage of her on the ice pond. She hadn't seen their kiss—the kiss Charlotte had to fight off with a vengeance. If she'd known those things, then she would not have likened him to a brother. She would have seen the truth. That somebody in this world really did want Charlotte. And that her solitude really was her own choice.

"Shall we go?"

NINE

The road to town was lined with fences, glowing white under moonshine. The fences were short, white wood, incapable of holding in even a dog, but they were important. They separated what was hers from what was his from what was no one's. The road was slippery under their feet, but Charlotte held tight to Shaun's arm, somehow believing that while she might slip, he never would. And somehow, as it turned out, she was right. "Have you been to a dance before?" Shaun asked her, feeling in the brightest of moods, for the pine smelled fresh and he was learning to like the chill. And most importantly, he was excited to have Charlotte's full attention for the night.

"Yes, of course," she said, feeling cheered by his contagiously bright mood. There were sparks of excitement and nerves firing in her belly. She didn't know whether this would be the most exciting night of her life, or the most terrifying.

Shaun realized his mistake. He had asked a question that forced a lie, at least from one as tender as Charlotte. "Well, I've rarely been to them," he said, hoping to make her feel he'd suffered some social failures of his own, though in truth, they were few in number. At Saint Paul's Academy, there had been no girls, and that was the reason for the lack of dances. At home, he'd gone to a few, and even been invited to some by ladies at a finishing school, most of which he declined out of sheer lack of interest.

"Really?" asked Charlotte. "Do they even have dances like this one in Boston?"

"Well, I always attended boarding school, so I really don't know."

"Was that lonely?" she asked, her eyes bright and curious, framed in concealing scarves. "Boarding school, I mean?"

He shot her a look of bafflement. "No, of course not. I always enjoyed school. The only thing I dreaded was coming home."

Something told Charlotte to reply only with a smile. Now was not the time. She didn't know how she knew it, but she knew. All he wanted was a tender smile. He nodded appreciatively in return.

Already, they could hear fiddling and laughter. The old schoolhouse seemed to be the only thing alive in the dead of night. Its windows glowed a soft orange, and there was movement in and out of the creaking front door. It was a rugged white house, right in the center of Peacham Corner. Charlotte had gone there as a child, before being sent to the academy. Because she'd rather draw, she had always thought of school as a tedious place that opened its doors every morning and bored itself to sleep by late afternoon. It always seemed to be dead by nightfall. Then, every morning the teacher came in and kicked it until it grudgingly awoke. Ordinarily, Charlotte would steer a wide ring around it, for walking by unprepared for a day's lesson felt dangerous, even years after her departure, and even on the night of the dance. "I wish they'd held it in church," she said, glancing at a tall, white cross in the near distance. "I hate the schoolhouse. I always feel I'm going to get caught at something."

Shaun laughed. "I know exactly what you mean. I think they give schools that intimidating air on purpose.

But come," he grinned, taking her hand. "If anyone suggests a pop spelling bee, we'll make a run for it."

At his grin and wink, Charlotte let him lead her to the source of all the friendly commotion. She could see immediately that there was little to fear. The schoolhouse was not a schoolhouse at all on that night. It had no tables or chairs, the bell was not ringing, and no one was at attention. Instead, there was a giant Christmas tree whose breadth imposed itself upon the room, scratching not two but three of its walls. Alight with yellow lanterns and draped in strings of berries, the pine tree would allow no one to think of schoolwork on such a night that belonged to celebration. Fiddlers played spirited tunes while the adult chaperones danced, their skirts and tailcoats fanning out. The scent of pine mingled with the heavy scent of ice-cold wood. And whenever the band paused, the crackling of the fireplace became the music. Cider, gingerbread cookies, and a colorful Christmas cake adorned with candied fruit were spread out plentifully along a splintered table of birch. And that is where most of Charlotte's neighbors, some too shy to dance even with their own escorts, were gathered.

At first, Charlotte could hardly recognize anyone. She'd never seen her contemporaries dressed so elegantly, not even for church. All around her was velvet and lace and even a few pieces of jewelry. Some of the young women wore their hair pinned up, though they were younger than Charlotte. And the boys . . . they looked like . . . well, like Shaun. She glanced at her escort. Well, maybe not that good, but they did look awfully sophisticated.

The first person to approach them was Mary Whittaker, and this was a surprise, for as far as Charlotte could remember, the young woman had never spoken six words to her before. Presently, she scurried to the entrance, beaming as though she and Charlotte were the best of friends. Her strawberry blond hair had been molded into perfect curls, and her mother had let her wear her hair on top of her head. Charlotte didn't think her cream dress was as pretty as the one her own mother had made her, but she liked the silver lace at the neck and wrists. "Charlotte!" she cried, "I'm so glad you came!"

She was? "Thank you! I'm glad I came, too."

Shaun quietly took her coat, scarves, and mittens, and as he momentarily drifted off to hang them, Mary's eyes followed. "Who is that?" she asked, biting a delicate nail.

Charlotte beamed. "Oh, that? That's just my escort. He's very nice."

Mary couldn't take her eyes from him. This pleased Charlotte to no end, for Mary was known to be one of the most sought-after young ladies in Peacham. So to have her gazing enviously at her own pretend beau was rather flattering. "Where is he from?"

"Harvard," said Charlotte with a shrug, knowing the more accurate answer would be Boston. She just thought it was a good opportunity to misunderstand the question.

"Oh, then he's a friend of Peter's?" she asked, some light of hope burning in her pretty green eyes. Charlotte didn't much care for that light of hope. It implied that if he were a friend of Peter's, then his escorting Charlotte was nothing more than an act of kindness.

"Oh, yes," she said, thinking quickly on her feet, "I suppose, now that you mention it, that *is* how we met."

Mary did a double take. "Then you . . . he's your . . . your beau?"

"Oh, my! Is that Sarah over there? I'm sorry," she said, touching Mary boldly on the elbow, "I must greet my friend. It's so good to see you!"

Mary was left with a puzzled look, interrupted by an occasional lustful gaze at the tall, handsome, fashionably dressed man who seemed to be Charlotte's new beau. And "man" was the word to describe him. He didn't look at all like the country boys Mary had grown up with. Even the handsome ones did not bear his quiet, sophisticated charm. Just watching him move gracefully across the room gave her the flutters. No. It couldn't be that he was interested in Charlotte. He must be using her as an excuse to come to the dance and meet someone better-looking. She decided it was her duty to help him.

Before Charlotte could reach Sarah, she was stopped by another friendly young woman whom she barely knew. "Charlotte!" Mandy Weatherford screeched, "Charlotte, you look wonderful!"

Charlotte clasped her hands proudly behind her back and grinned. "Thank you. So do you."

"No, I mean it," said Mandy, her eyes moving up and down Charlotte's dress in astonishment. "That is a beautiful dress. And your hair . . ." She was tempted to touch it. "It's so long! You really look fabulous."

"Thank you."

"No, I mean it! I've never . . . I've never seen you look . . ."

Before this compliment got any worse, Charlotte decided to interrupt. "I've never seen you look pretty before, either," she beamed innocently.

Shaun came up from behind her with a glass of cider. "I took the liberty," he said, rubbing her back with fondness. Charlotte accepted the drink and beamed lovingly at him. Shaun was bright enough to know that it was for the benefit of her friend, but he didn't mind. He liked her insecurities. He would rather she adored him in truth, but he wasn't offended by the act. He'd surmised that posing as a doting beau might be part of his duty on this night, and he was glad to be of help.

Mandy's jaw dropped at the sight of him. Charlotte

rather liked her expression and decided to encourage it by asking, "Have you met Shaun?"

All she could do was shake her head.

"Well, Mandy Weatherford, may I introduce Shaun Matheson? Mandy and I haven't gotten to know one another as well as we'd like to," she explained mischievously, "but we are working on it."

"I'm pleased to meet you," he said, for she didn't seem able to say a word.

All she did was nod.

"Well, it's been really wonderful to see you," beamed Charlotte, "but I really must see Sarah. Come along, Shaun." She pulled him by the hand, perhaps bragging in some small way that she was at liberty to touch it. She left a wide-eyed Mandy for the warmth of her only true friend at the party, Sarah Brown.

Sarah looked lovely, dressed modestly in a simple gown of red with black lace trim. She was quite possibly the shortest person in the room, but with her braids tied together in back, a compromise between the childhood and grown-up styles, her neck looked long, and that helped her a great deal. In fact, to Charlotte, she looked like one of the prettiest girls at the party; her smile was so cherubic and genuine within her small, round face. "Sarah," Charlotte screeched, catching her by surprise.

Sarah was startled when she turned her head. A tiny hand flew to her mouth. "Oh, my goodness!" She jumped up and down, spilling a little cider from her cup before remembering with a laugh to hand it to her escort. "How are you?!" She wrapped her arms tightly about her friend, casting a pleased glance in Shaun's direction.

"You didn't tell me you were coming here," Charlotte pretended to accuse her, though it really didn't bother her one bit.

Sarah, feeling caught in deceit, blushed humbly in the

direction of her flaxen-haired escort. There was no need for introduction. Everyone knew most everyone. Charlotte recognized him as Kevin Gordon, one of the gentler, more shy local students at the academy. He had never teased her, but always kept to himself even through the worst of the "peaches" epidemic. For that reason, she smiled kindly and said, "It's good to see you."

His nod was nervous. Charlotte thought he must like Sarah an awful lot to have worked up the courage to ask her there. "Well, now that we've surprised each other," said Charlotte with a bounce, "shall we dance?"

Sarah laughed uncomfortably. "Oh, I couldn't," she said. "So few others are dancing."

"All the more room for us," said Charlotte, whose confidence had blossomed since her grand entrance. "Will you hold this, please?" she asked Shaun, thrusting her glass at him.

"By all means," he said so perfectly that she thought she might swoon.

"Do you mind?" Sarah asked of her escort.

Kevin was quick to shake his head and urge her, though he had the sinking feeling that he should have been the first to ask her to dance, rather than Charlotte. He just hadn't worked up the courage yet. So he was forced to watch dejectedly as Charlotte led his date to the dance floor, the two of them looking like a Christmas package, red mingled with green. As they stepped before the fireplace, Shaun sensed the young man's distress and said mildly, "Why don't we cut in after the first song, eh?" The relief on Kevin's face was apparent. Not only would he have the chance to dance with Sarah, but he wouldn't have to walk out to the dance floor alone. He and Shaun would ask together.

The fiddle launched a new song, and the young women spun each other around, holding hands, letting gravity keep them from tumbling backward while their long hair flew out behind them and their laughs mingled with the fiddle. The young men enjoyed the sight, and couldn't help smiling at the beauty of their dates, multiplied by two, and linked to each other's hands in friendship. The rough wood floor squeaked under their soft boots, and their smiles were radiant enough for Christmas. The snow began to fall behind them in the windows, just in time to create a perfect picture of holiday cheer. Shaun thought he might weep at the feeling of home that was all around him. How lucky these people were, he thought, to have a place like this. A warm fire, a fiddle played with marvelously cheerful mediocrity, and a woodsy-smelling room full of friends. There wasn't much he wouldn't give to live in a place like Peacham. And Charlotte, he realized, gazing upon her bright-eyed, laughing form, would always represent this place in his memory. Just as every city woman he met made him think of Boston and the lair of his horrid father, Charlotte would always make him think of this peaceful place for which he longed.

Before he could get thoroughly lost in the moment, his thoughts were interrupted by a false laugh. There were few sounds that grated on Shaun's nerves more painfully than that. Glancing left, he was not surprised to see the laugh had sprung from a false woman. The one to whom Charlotte had introduced him at the front door—Mary Whittaker, a woman who looked to him like a doll designed for admiring and not for touching. She was just too perfect for his taste. "Oh, I dropped my muff!" she cried, pointing at his feet.

Grudgingly, Shaun leaned down and fetched it for her. "Here you are," he said, then immediately turned away.

"Oh, I'm so sorry!" she cried, "I was going to step outside to look for my escort when I dropped it. Where could he be? Oh well, perhaps I'll wait here for him."

Shaun cast her a weak smile, then returned his attention to his two favorite dancers—Charlotte, and the one young lady who seemed to be a true friend. For that, he already liked her.

"You haven't seen him, have you?" Mary asked, settling herself within inches of his side. "You haven't seen my escort?"

"I'm sorry," he said coldly, "afraid I didn't notice him."

"Oh well. Perhaps he'll turn up." She stretched her arms backward, pretending to ease her muscles while thrusting her small breasts into his line of sight. "I'm so tense," she said.

"Oh dear, be careful," he remarked, "you don't want to fall out of your dress there." He hid his smile by taking a sip from Charlotte's glass.

Mary looked down and laughed. "Oh, no. I hadn't realized! That *would* be embarrassing." She giggled, but did not blush. She didn't have enough shame to blush.

"I would think," he answered mildly.

She realized this wasn't going to work. She was a big fish in a small pond, but perhaps she wasn't practiced enough to impress a man from the city. She tried another tactic. "Has Charlotte had a chance to show you our town?"

"Uh . . ." He swished the cider around the cup as though it were cognac. "Yes, uh . . . yes, we took a lovely tour of the skating pond." A devilish light sparked his eye.

"The skating pond?" she laughed. "I think I can do better than that. Why don't you allow me to show you about? I'm sure the Basses are busy with preparations for the holiday. Perhaps I can take you off their hands for an afternoon," she nudged him cheerily.

"Why, thank you, that's very kind. But I don't have much time here," he said, giving her a glimpse of his face in full, handsome enough to take her breath away in the pale firelight. "And I'd like to spend as much time as I can with Charlotte."

Mary's cheekbones fell. "What?" she asked either nervously or angrily, neither of them was sure. "Are you her beau now?"

He smiled mysteriously. "Ah, the song is over. Excuse me. It's been my pleasure, but it's my opportunity to cut in. Kevin?" he asked, nodding at his partner in intrusion.

Mary felt positively like an idiot as the two men strode to the dance floor, taking Charlotte and Sarah on their arms. What could he possibly see in her? She glared at Charlotte's obscenely lush figure, so poorly masked by the painful corset she could barely wear. Mary touched her own small waist and fumed. What had been the purpose of binding herself morning, noon, and night since birth if sloppy, lazy Charlotte could merely sit at home drawing awful pictures and have a man like *that* come along and steal her. She saw the way he looked into her eyes as he took her hands in his and led her. And she saw the way Charlotte looked up at him, smiling so confidently, her face so fresh and alive. It wasn't fair. Mary had done everything she was taught to do, *been* everything she was taught to be. She was given all the secrets of catching a man, and had devoted herself to the art. And all this time, no one had ever told her . . . that love doesn't know about beauty or poise.

"Oh, there you are. I've been looking everywhere." Her cocky escort winked, then boldly scrutinized her from hair to tiny boot. "You really are beautiful."

She yanked her cloak from a hook and said, "I don't think I ever want to hear that again. Let's go." And she stormed out ahead of him.

Charlotte saw her go from the corner of her eye and couldn't help biting her lip to suppress a giggle. It wasn't that she harbored any particular animosity, but to think she had made the most popular girl in Peacham jealous!

Jealous of *her!* She never thought she'd see the day. Shaun distracted her with a tender clasp of her hand, reminding her that she was in the midst of a dance. She looked up at him, her face radiant and happy. And he looked down, his face eerily sincere. He led her in a most practiced fashion, charming the audience with the grace of his steps. Somehow, he even made Charlotte seem a talented dancer, for he guided her with fluid perfection, making it easy to stumble into just the right footing. When he led her in a turn, he did so with a hand on her back, gently steering her so she could make no mistake. Soon, even Charlotte began to believe she was gifted.

Watching them gave some other young couples the courage to step away from the buffet. And the more crowded the dance floor became, the easier it was for even the shyest to step out. None of the boys felt as elegant as Shaun, for they hardly knew how to lead their partners with such grace. And none of the girls felt as beloved as Charlotte, for their escorts did not look at them with the same rapture and attention. But some of that melted as the grand fire flickered on into the night. The boys became less self-conscious, more confident, and thereby turned their attention from themselves to their dates, some of whom began to feel the warmth of being adored. Still, many an eye turned to Charlotte and her dashing stranger. And many a young man wondered, "When did Charlotte become so pretty?"

It was with near exhaustion that Charlotte finally put her hand to her throat and announced she could dance no more. Shaun grinned understandingly, and took her by the hand. "Will you cut me a slice of that Christmas cake?" she asked. "A giant slice like this?" With a grin she held her hands at an exaggerated width apart.

"Shouldn't we save some for everyone else?" he teased, leading her to the buffet.

"No, they can have the gingerbread cookies. I've never cared for those."

He chuckled and said, "I admire your generosity."

Then, just as he turned to slice the cake, Charlotte felt a tug at her skirt. She whipped around to the sight of Giles Williams, grinning with absolute wickedness. His stringy hair had been swept from his eyes with some gooey substance. His wealthy father had dressed him in a suit of gray, much too charming for such a mannerless boy. And Charlotte imagined that somewhere in the room, he must have had a dance partner. Bullies tended to despise their own company, and were not inclined to declare independence at a social event. Somehow, Giles must have found someone to escort. But at the moment, she was nowhere to be seen, and Giles seemed to be giving Charlotte his undivided attention. Why, she had no doubt. He must have come in while she was dancing. He must have seen her frolicking in happiness and soaking in admiration. No doubt, it was time to destroy her.

"Having fun?" he asked, his black eyes twinkling hatefully.

"I was until a moment ago." Charlotte accepted the cake Shaun passed her with a thankful nod.

Giles examined her escort as though searching for a fatal flaw. "Who's this?" he asked Charlotte.

"None of your . . ."

"I'm Shaun Matheson," said Shaun, extending his hand.

"Giles Williams," he said, taking a moment to recover from the politeness. "So did you mean to be here with Charlotte or did your real dance partner die?"

Charlotte turned scarlet. "You worthless . . ."

Shaun stopped her with a calm raise of his hand. "You seem rather obsessed with my dance partner, in a backward sort of a way. I can't say that I appreciate that." He spoke so calmly, he might have been discussing his studies.

"Obsessed? I'm not obsessed," snarled Giles. "Trust me, if you knew her, you wouldn't be at a dance with Charlotte Bass. I'm just trying to warn you."

"Giles, you are a . . ."

Shaun stopped her once again with a wave of his hand. "Then I'm warning you, too," he told Giles with a cool stare. "I don't like people fawning over my dance partners, whether it's with charm or with venom. So leave."

Giles didn't like being confronted so directly. Particularly by someone his own size, even taller. He thought it was much more fun to harass Charlotte when she was unprotected, and so he made up his mind to move on. But his evil instincts couldn't resist one little "accidental" bump into her side as he left. That this caused her cake to smear her dress was a fringe benefit he'd not anticipated. There was nervous laughter all around as Charlotte looked down at herself and saw moist cake plastered to her velvet gown, the last crumbs of it falling to the floor. Thank goodness it had only sugar for frosting, lest the dress would be ruined. She looked up and saw confused faces. Those who had come to admire her only moments ago suddenly remembered the inadequate girl whom Giles had tormented for their audience, years on end.

But then, the entire punch bowl of cider flooded over Giles's head, drenching his greasy hair and making him gasp for breath as though he'd dived into a deep pond. There was a huge uproar of laughter, and even a little applause as Shaun put the empty punch bowl back on the buffet. "Get out," he told Giles in a tone so menacing that the printer's son scurried out in a sudden hurry to wash himself off. As the door slammed behind him, Shaun got down on bended knee before Charlotte with a napkin, taking care as he wiped every last crumb from her handmade gown. Charlotte looked up and saw that the faces had changed once more. Everyone watched Shaun's humble gesture, and the caring way in which he groomed her. And once again, their eyes turned to Charlotte with respect. She was loved. They believed it. She held the secret to something they all wanted so badly. The girls gazed upon her only with admiration, and upon Shaun with longing.

Shaun chucked the napkin on a nearby chair and rose, extending his hand gallantly. "Another dance?" he asked.

Charlotte smiled so brightly, it seemed to him that she was the most vibrant thing in the room. "Yes, please," she said, resting her hand timidly upon his.

Smiling nearly as magnificently as she, he led her to the dance floor under the watchful eye of an appreciative audience. And when the fiddles started up once more, they danced before the snowy windows, the crackling fire, and the grand Christmas tree. And they soaked in the comforting scents of pine, of wood, and of well-wishers all around them. But most excitingly of all, they melted into each other, and allowed themselves to smile openly into each other's eyes. It was nearly Christmas, the time when miracles were said to be real. And for the next five dances, they secretly, momentarily thanked the heavens for what the season had brought to them.

When the chaperones sent them all home, Charlotte raced happily into the freezing night. "That was lovely!" she told Shaun, bouncing for excitement and warmth. "Everyone I like had a marvelous time, and everyone I hate was made to suffer in some small way. An evening can hardly go better than *that!*"

He laughed along with her and said, "That's the Christmas spirit."

She waved to Sarah and Kevin as they passed by, then asked, "What shall we do now? I'm too excited to go home."

"I can't keep you late," he said. "Your mother would never let me see you again." But before she could point her nose eastward, he grabbed her firmly by the arm. "Where do you think you're going?"

"Home," she said. "Didn't you just say . . ."

He shook his head. "No, not yet." And before she could ask any more, he pulled her against him so there could be no mistaking his intention.

Charlotte's whole body could feel him, even through all of their winter clothes. She was shivering, but he was hot. She felt as though she'd crawled inside his coat. When she tried ever so meekly to worm away from him, he held her still, gazing confidently at her, as though she had not struggled at all. "Wh—what are you doing?" she asked.

A smile was his only answer. His breath drifted off to the side in cool white clouds. The schoolhouse behind him still shed light, for the chaperones were now cleaning. And in that light, his face, perfectly chiseled, seemed to taunt Charlotte with what was to come. His lips, laced with a masculine shadow for the evening, curled warmly and warningly. "You didn't think I danced with you all night only to leave without a kiss, did you?" He took the scarf from her hand, a gesture to ensure that she didn't cover her face yet. And he touched a wisp of hair at her temple, sending a thrill down Charlotte's neck.

"Let go of me," she demanded unconvincingly. Her voice was gentle and curious, not at all the way it sounded when she was angry.

He wrapped her in his arms and wove his fingers

through the back of her hair. "That doesn't seem likely, does it?" His smile was haunting. Sometimes Charlotte thought she hadn't really met him yet. Sometimes he looked like a man with a secret.

"If I scream, they'll hear inside," she warned him through a half-smile.

"You won't be able to scream once I have your lips."

"I told you I would come here only if you kept your distance. I warned you not to touch me again."

He touched the flesh of her lips and said, "You're much too trusting." Then, with a smile, he gently pulled her hair, tilting back her head until her lips were spread wide before him. He almost kissed her, but then he stopped. He rather enjoyed gazing for a moment. Her eyes were closed, her sooty lashes spread like black lace upon her cold, alabaster cheeks. Her very life was visible with each breath, and the lips which exhaled gentle streams of smoke were as full a pair as he'd ever seen. He thought about biting one. He wondered how she would look if he gave her just a pinch of pain, and soothed it with a caress. He knew she could feel his body against his, and liked to think it was making her curious. In another moment, she'd be able to feel his arousal, an arousal he'd like to press into every soft spot of her tender body. The thought was killing him. She was so vulnerable to his touch, so sensitive to the slightest tickle, even to the back of her neck. There was so much he could teach her. So much could be done with a pair of full breasts, with hair so long, and with lips so lush.

He thought about dipping a finger into her mouth, just to see how her lips would wrap around it. He realized now why his body responded so strongly to her. She was as innocent as a baby doll. And unlike the other women to whom he'd made love, she would not react like a flirtatious love goddess. She would tremble, then she would enjoy. She was real. Oh God, if only he could take her for a wife. He closed his eyes and wished. Then he dove in for his kiss.

Charlotte thought that if he wanted to eat her alive, she would let him. His lips were so soft, and all around her, she felt his warmth. She was powerless under his determined grasp and forceful lips. He was so tall, she hadn't realized how tall until she was forced to look up at him. Her breasts brushed against him, and she could feel it as though they were bare. His body was so hard and so warm, she wanted him to lift her and carry her off. She had never been so excited in all of her life. For the first time, she had an inkling of why women tolerated men. If he would hold her like this forever, there wasn't much she wouldn't give him. She was disappointed when he pulled away, but had sense enough to pretend she was not. "Have I paid my debt?" she asked cheerily, though she bent her head to hide a blush.

Shaun loved to see her blush. "Mmm, not quite," he said, playing with a strand of her hair. Every time his finger accidentally touched her ear, she felt a spark. "But I'd better take you home anyway." He released the strand of hair and offered a cloaked elbow. "May I escort you home?"

"I don't know," she said playfully, "I'm told I'm too trusting."

"Yes," he grinned, "but without a gentleman, who will fend off the bears? I'm afraid you've no choice. All the trustworthy men have gone home."

She took his elbow with both hands. "I didn't know pacifists fought off bears," she teased.

"Oh, no," he said, leading them in a walk, "we don't fight them, we just reason with them." He sauntered on through her giggle. "And if diplomacy doesn't work . . . we challenge them to a game of wits. The winner gets to eat the loser."

"Ah," she said, giving his arm a tender squeeze, "then

I feel so much safer knowing I'm with you. Whatever would I have done on my own?"

"Undoubtedly, you'd have resorted to violence." He gave her a friendly wink. "It's a pity, really, that there aren't more of us who understand the value of peacemaking."

"What, you mean more peace-loving humans or more peace-loving bears?"

"Both, really. The whole thing is saddening."

"I see," she said, tapping her chin with some drama, "then tell me this. When you poured an entire punch bowl of cider over Giles's head, was that peace-making?"

He cut his eyes in her direction. "That was artistic expression," he said. "Pacifists are always very artistically inclined."

"Is that a fact?"

"Oh, absolutely."

"And why is that?"

He shrugged. "It's simply part of our image. Even if we aren't fascinated by art, we have to pretend to be or the other pacifists will make fun of us." He winked.

Charlotte found herself snuggling deeper into his arm. And he did her the favor of not seeming to take notice as she leaned increasingly into his sturdy side. By the time they were at peace in one another's company and could stop chattering, Shaun had gently slid his arm around her waist. Fresh snow crunched under their feet in the moonlight. The trees were so tall on either side of the road that looking straight up, Charlotte could not see their tops—only millions of freckled stars. As they walked on, she began to believe. She began to believe in the tenderness of his gestures, in the respect he had afforded her all evening, and in the kiss he had gently forced upon her when they'd departed. She began to believe he was for her. It was something she'd thought would never happen to her, something she didn't know she wanted. But it just felt right. He didn't seem the least bit shocked when she rested her head on his broad shoulder for the remainder of the walk. He just kissed the top of her head scarf and whispered, "Are you warm enough?"

"It's very cold," she replied vaguely. And for that, she got an extra tight squeeze. Her life would never be the same.

When at last they reached the three-story white house, they hurried to the hearth to warm their hands. Charlotte raced to her mother's bedroom to whisper that she was home, and then announced to Shaun, "She was fast asleep."

"She must trust me," he grinned.

"She must not know you," Charlotte retorted.

But it was a friendly retort, and Shaun took no offense. Instead, he held out his hand.

"Wouldn't you like something hot to drink before bed?" she asked him.

He shook his head, and still held out his hand.

Shyly, with a bit of a tremble, Charlotte accepted it and let him lead her all the way to the attic. But at the door, she turned and said a cautious "Good night."

Shaun did not move. His eyes were fixed upon her, they were intense, and they made her belly flip in a ticklish manner. "Are you . . ." she swallowed, "are you going to . . . kiss me again?" she asked, as though she had no control over the matter.

With a powerfully intent look, Shaun reached out his hand and cupped her jaw, stroking her with his thumb. Charlotte swallowed hard and could barely stand to look at him. He was so beautiful. She worked up the courage to ask again. "Are you going to kiss me?"

He stopped touching her and reached around her, turning the doorknob that she'd tried nervously to block. He flung open her bedroom door just to prove he could do it. Then he said, "Actually, I had something a little more intimate in mind."

Charlotte's eyes turned heavenward as he brushed his lips against her ear, holding her and stroking her at the neck. "I . . . I . . ." She was going to tell him that she couldn't. That he mustn't ask. That he mustn't even think such a thing. But she couldn't bring herself to say the words. Not when he was making her melt so, not when he was nearly bringing tears to her eyes with his affections. And besides, he interrupted her.

He said, "I want you to show me your drawings."

TEN

Charlotte led him by the hand, closing the door softly behind them, praying that they would not be heard and caught. She lit candles from the fireplace, as though illuminating a temple, but she didn't light many. She didn't want him to see her drawings in full light. "I feel shy," she said, backing herself up against the desk that held her treasures. But there was a big, anticipating grin on her face, and she sought signs of encouragement.

"Don't be shy," he said, making himself comfortable in a chair. "I'll be very gentle."

She glanced at the drawer under her round hand. "My drawings are very small," she warned him. "I've wanted to paint something large, but . . . but I've only done small ones, and they're all in charcoal."

Shaun tried to repress a grin. "Size doesn't matter," he told her. "It's what you do with what you have."

Charlotte's hand trembled over the knob. "I don't know that I have the courage," she said.

But his answer was firm. "I know you want to. I can feel it."

"That's trickery," she teased him. "Your manipulation won't work on me."

"I'll use force if I have to," he warned gently. "If I have to, I'll go over there and tear those drawings from your desk."

"You wouldn't!"

He raised an eyebrow to leave her guessing.

Charlotte gave in with a sigh. Submission would be easier than argument. "Very well," she said, sliding open a wobbly drawer, "but I have to warn you, many people have said I am terrible."

"But you don't believe them."

She shook her head at the wall.

"How do you know?" he asked. "How do you know they're wrong?"

Charlotte bravely scooped out a stack of drawings and faced him. "First, I'll have to make sure you're not one of them," she said. "Then we can talk."

He nodded at the dignity of her answer. And with steady hands, he accepted the first drawing. "It's smudged," she said, "they're all smudged. I shouldn't keep them in the drawer like that, but . . . well, I like to hide them, and there's nowhere else. I tried the closet once, but it has no lock, and Peter went in there and pulled them all out, dragging them about town to embarrass and mock me. After that, I decided I would simply . . ."

He put a finger to his lips for silence. "You don't have to be nervous." He watched her swallow hard. "You're safe with me."

Charlotte dared to let go of the first drawing, and leave it at the mercy of his inspection. Immediately, she turned away so as not to observe his expression. But after a moment of tapping her foot, she could bear no more and took a peek. She couldn't tell what he was thinking. He was staring very intently, rubbing his knuckles along a short sideburn, but she couldn't sense his opinion. She decided that if she chattered, she might be able to help shape his thoughts. "It's hard to tell what it is, I know," she said, her words jumbling together with unnatural speed. "It's actually meant to be a tree. A maple tree. But you see, I only drew a knot on its wood because that was the most distinctive thing about the tree. You see, I didn't want it to be a generic tree, I wanted it to be that particular tree. And the only way I knew how to portray it as an individual was to zone in on the one characteristic which set it apart. Oh, I know I could have drawn the entire tree, and simply included the knot, but then I really wouldn't have been making a statement about the tree. It would have been a literal portrayal, which of course, would be pleasant from the standpoint of alerting viewers to the fact that it was a tree, but . . ."

His handsome voice, like a low breeze streaming steadily into the room, interrupted her. "You were sad when you drew this."

Charlotte gripped a piece of skirt in each tight fist. He was asking a question. Did that mean he liked it? "Umm, well, yes," she said, her voice nearly an octave lower than it had been in her frantic, apologetic explanations. "I was very sad. I . . ."

"Felt that you had a giant knot on your trunk that set you apart from everyone else?"

Charlotte nodded.

"Let me see the next one." He held out his hand expectantly. And as though in a trance, Charlotte handed it over.

"This one is a . . ." she began to explain. But he interrupted her by raising a hand.

"I know what it is," he said.

Charlotte peered over his lap to get another look at the picture. "Really? You know what it is? No one else ever does. In fact," she squinted curiously, "if I hadn't drawn it, I don't think I would know, either."

"It's rage," he announced softly, never taking his eyes from it.

"Why, yes! Yes, that's right. Well, of course, technically it's a . . ."

"A flower."

"Yes! Yes, it's a flower. But . . . but how did you know that? I drew the petals so strangely, and I really scribbled the stem . . ."

"It's a flower that's been trampled."

Charlotte touched her heart. "My God."

His eyes looked hotly up at her. "Show me one about passion," he said. "Show me one about love."

Charlotte could barely bring herself to speak. "I . . . I . . ."

"Don't be shy." He stood up, and she cowered. To get close, he had to back her against a wall. "Show me everything," he said, touching that wisp of hair at her temple that drew him so, "I won't leave until I've seen every last drawing."

"They're on the desk." She pointed, but hid from him in a crumpled posture, fearing his closeness at a time when she felt so very naked.

"I want you to bring them to me," he said, "and I want you to bring them to me like this." He released her from his gaze and caress, and stretched himself across her very comfortable bed. For a moment, he stared at the ceiling, and thought, *So this is what Charlotte sees every morning*. But it wasn't enough. He wanted to know more. He unbuttoned his vest and loosened the collar of his silk shirt. "Lie with me," he said. "Lie with me and show me passion."

Charlotte approached with caution and with a dizzying thrill in her belly.

"Uh-uh," he grinned, "not without the pictures."

"Can't you just ruin me?" she asked half-jokingly.

He laughed. "Bring me those pictures and lie down." His eyes sparkled with sincerity. "I mean it."

He had a funny way of giving orders. He was indeed playing the role of master, but his tone was so caring, it was difficult to take offense. Charlotte grabbed her stack of drawings and laid them across his obscenely displayed chest. She could not see much of it, as the shirt was still mostly buttoned. But she could see more than she ought, and what she saw was terribly handsome. "Lie down with me," he said. And Charlotte did so, though stiffly and awkwardly, as though lying in a tomb.

Shaun lifted the picture she had put on top, and it sent a frisson up his spine. It depicted yearning—a woman with no hands. With trembling fingers, he flipped to the next, and his hair stood on end. It was a drawing of an explosion, a burst of ecstasy. My God, he realized, Charlotte had—he glanced sideways at her awkward recline—well, she had . . . done something ladies are not supposed to do. She had taught herself ecstasy. He loved it! He flipped to the next drawing, a picture of sorrow so real, he felt a trickle of sweat drip across his forehead. He had to brush back his hair before looking at the next, and then the next. The images burned so richly within his heart that he could barely breathe them in. With each flip of the page, he knew her more profoundly in his bones, and yearned to feast his eyes on more and more. "You're brilliant," he whispered, his breath coming out in gasps. He squeezed her round the waist and pulled, despite her stiffness. He didn't care. He had seen the passion—he knew it was there.

"I'm not," she told him. "The ones I draw with my own hand are terrible. The good ones are those which . . ."

"Those which what?" he urged her, finding that his hands could not resist the touch of her ivory cheek.

"Well . . . those which pass *through* me instead of originating *from* me."

"That's why you never gave up drawing, isn't it?" he said. "Because you had faith in the winds that passed through you."

Charlotte nodded. "I only hope I don't ruin the drawings on their way to earth."

Shaun kissed her. He absolutely couldn't help it. He wanted to be inside her, and not in the literal sense of it. He wanted to crawl into her skin and feel the warmth of her blood flowing over his wounds and healing them. His hold on her was gentle, although he rolled her and forced her to face him. He offered no mercy on the kiss this time. He opened his mouth, and when that startled her, he did not let her retreat. He made her feel his breath and then the warmth of his tongue until she had relaxed just enough for him to thrust fully into her mouth. Charlotte didn't know whether he would stop, whether there was a line that he would draw . . . or not. It felt as though he would hold her as long as he liked, and kiss her as passionately as he wished. And if she could stop him . . . she didn't want to know. She rather preferred thinking she couldn't.

At last, he withdrew of his own accord. His face was moist with masculine need. But he had control. "Tell me about this picture," he said, hastily flipping through the stack, which he'd been careful not to crumple in his enthusiasm. "Tell me about this one."

To Charlotte's horror, he held up the drawing of his own lap—the one she had created after confronting him about the tavern. Instinctively, she tried to writhe away. But he wouldn't let her. "No, don't be scared," he said. "Tell me what it is. It's a man, isn't it?"

Charlotte nodded.

He took another glance. "It has an intimidating look about it." He stared harder. "Yes, I think . . . I think it's a drawing about domination, isn't it?"

Charlotte turned her head away.

"It's all right," he said. "That wasn't a criticism. I think it's fascinating." He pecked her comfortingly on the cheek.

Charlotte swallowed frantically, and for some reason, found herself confessing, "It's you."

"What?" He looked at it again. "Me? Hmmm." Then a wonderful look of mischief came over him. "Look at me," he said, touching her chin. Charlotte turned her head, but only grudgingly. "Do you want to see?" he asked her.

Charlotte's heart did a free-fall. "What??"

"Do you want to see?" he grinned, touching the waist of his trousers. "Do you want to see what it really looks like? It's not so intimidating as this drawing makes it seem."

Charlotte pushed his hand away from his trousers, and he accepted her reprimand with a laugh. "You're sure?" he asked brightly. "Because I'd be happy to let you look. I wouldn't lay a hand on you, I promise."

"You're scaring me," she said, though her eyes were delirious with curiosity.

Shaun frowned with a light air of apology. "I didn't mean to. I'll tell you what. If it would make you feel better, you can show me yourself first." His grin was delightfully evil.

Charlotte gasped so hard that it ended in a laugh. "You should be horsewhipped," she whispered loudly. "You are a guest in this house, and an unmarried man. Coming in my room was scandalous enough, then kissing me, and lying on my bed, but . . ." She gazed into his eyes, impressed by the utter lack of shame she found there. "Are you evil spawn?"

"Oh, no," he said, taking her hand in both of his and caressing it. "Just a little anarchistic. It's really not the same thing, though some would argue." He gave her fingers a kiss.

"Who are you?" she whispered, reaching up to feel his face under her hand. It was a gesture he welcomed, and from which he did not flinch. His skin was not as soft as her own, but it was pleasant to the touch. She liked that he allowed her to do it, to feel the slight scrape of beard that was darkening him for the night, and that he did not make her feel wanton or wicked for her curiosity. "Who are you?" she repeated. "You don't seem like a son of wealth nor a gentleman from the city."

"I might ask the same of you," he answered evasively. "What sort of a wholesome country girl allows a young man into her bed late at night?" His smile told her that he, in fact, thought little of it.

"You're not *in* my bed—you're merely on it," she grinned, "and besides, I *am* the spawn of evil. I didn't realize that was even up for debate. Why, just ask anyone in town and they'll tell you. I am as useless a member of society as I shall be a wife. I have little to lose."

He returned her smile and said, "Then let me have a look at you."

Charlotte shook her head adamantly.

But his silver eyes sparkled with reassurance. "We can share a great deal of passion without ruining you," he said quite seriously. "Trust me. Small intimacies can bring us just as close as giant mistakes ever could." He gave her an encouraging nod. "Show me your breast," he whispered, "or just touch it. Touch it and I'll take it as my clue that I'm free to open the gown myself."

But Charlotte did not move. She yearned to do his bidding, but she was paralyzed with fear. It was too much. She did not have his experience. Shaun understood the look in her eyes. She wasn't merely being coy. She was scared. So he nodded his understanding and said, "When you're ready, all right? When you're ready." And he rose from the bed after offering her only a friendly kiss.

"Wait!" she called instinctively. She sat upright and watched him rebutton his vest. "Where are you going?"

He winked to let her know he held no animosity. "I'm going to bed," he said. "Would you like me to tuck you in?" He smiled wickedly.

Charlotte frowned. "Thank you, I think not." But her voice was as cheery as his, despite her attempt to be stern. "Are you . . . are you angry?"

"No," he said, a look of deep concern coming over him. "No, not at all." He moved to her and knelt by the bed. "I enjoyed this evening very much," he said, taking her hand to his lips. "Thank you."

"But what about the . . . well . . ."

"When you're ready," he repeated. "Just think about how it would feel. And if you would like it . . . if you would like to show me . . . you know where I'll be."

There was a sinking in her gut. "I . . ."

"Don't answer," he said, pressing a finger to her lips. "Don't answer." He replaced the finger with his own lips and snuggled hers for a good-night kiss. "Sleep well."

She watched his handsome form casually stride out the door, then heard the gentle click of his departure. He closed the door gently, as though he were leaving something precious behind. And Charlotte collapsed on her bed in a swoon. What an evening she'd had! She felt as though she had grown into a woman in one short night. He had kissed her, he had adored her, he had let her show him off to all her schoolmates. She'd been pretty! She'd been smart! She'd been everything she'd always wanted to be. And best of all . . . *he liked my drawings,* she thought, clutching one at her breast, *he really liked them.* Immediately, she popped back up out of bed and drew another. This time, the subject was obvious. It was a reflection of the erotic thought he had planted in her mind. It was the wish she was not brave enough to fulfill, but more than brave enough to entertain in face. It was a portrait of closeness and of sharing. It was a rendition of sexiness in its simplest and most appealing form. It was a woman bearing her breast to the eyes of her lover.

ELEVEN

"Good morning, Mama! Isn't it a beautiful day?!"

Mrs. Bass glanced out the window to where the pale sun was only beginning to rise through the gray, and then back at her daughter. "Who are you and what have you done with Charlotte?"

"Oh, Mama," she laughed gaily, "did you think I would sleep the day away?"

"Yes."

"Well, I shan't. Now come, what needs doing? Shall I prepare the boys' breakfast, or do some sweeping?"

"Christmas decorations," said her mother flatly. "It is less than a week to Christmas Eve and the house is plain. It won't do. Your father could be home at any hour."

"I would've thought he'd be home by now," said Charlotte, feeling just a hint of neglect.

Her mother turned scolding eyes upon her for that subtle sadness she detected. "Christmas is the busiest time of year for a drummer. All of the general stores across the state are looking to stock up on goods and gifts. And how do you think we could buy gifts of our own if he weren't so hard at work?"

"I know, I know," groaned Charlotte, too young to realize that her mother was covering her own hurt at his perpetual absences. "Just tell me where you want the Christmas trinkets scattered out."

"They're in the attic outside your room—in the first

closet, in a wooden box. Set the dolls on mantels and the nativity scenes on the windowsills. The little Christmas village will go in the parlor, on the coffee table. If you have time, begin stringing the dried berries on ropes. We'll need them for the Christmas tree when your father cuts it down. But don't work long, as I'll need your help serving the boys when they get up."

Charlotte's eyes flashed with enthusiasm. "When do you think they'll be up?"

"Soon, I imagine." Her mother's brows furrowed suspiciously. "Why such concern?"

"No reason," said Charlotte gaily, "I just . . . I just wondered how much time I had. That's all."

Her mother did not let her walk out so easily. She stopped her with a stern question. "I take it you enjoyed yourself at the dance then?"

"Dance? Umm, yes. Yes, it was just fine."

Her mother stared at her so icily, she got the impression she wasn't supposed to have enjoyed herself quite so well. And to think her poor mother didn't know the half of it.

"Ummm." Charlotte looked all about her for a quick change of subject. At last, she found one. "Is that bacon you've sliced over there? Do you . . . do you not need help with the pig after all then?" She would never have brought it up if she hadn't been certain the answer was no.

Margaret kneaded her dough ball with furious strength, thrusting concern into every push. "Shaun helped me with it last night," she said shortly. "Before you went to the dance, he told me he'd like to help with the slaughter. Said he'd never seen it done before and wanted to." She eyed her daughter with suspicion, a gray flap of hair beating against her forehead with every stiff push into the dough. "Frankly, I think he was trying to spare you from it."

Frankly, so did Charlotte. And she didn't know how she could ever thank him. "I'm . . . I'm glad you had help," she said, her voice touched with tenderness. But before she could turn around to fetch the Christmas things from the attic, she was stopped once more by her mother's stern voice.

"Charlotte," she called, as though the girl had done something wrong. Charlotte turned around, still feeling a warmth in her bones over what Shaun had done. "Charlotte," said her mother, "I don't want you growing attached to that young man. Do you understand me?"

No, she didn't. She didn't at all. "Who said I'm attached?" she pouted. "And if I were, I still don't see what is so wrong with it."

"I knew this would happen. I knew you'd get your hopes up if he kept giving you such attention."

"So what if I am!" she cried. "What if my hopes are up? What if?"

"Charlotte, don't be a fool!" she rasped. "He's a young man on holiday. He would pay heed to any young woman who lived in this house. It's the nature of young men."

"Maybe you're the fool!" cried Charlotte. Her mother gasped, but it didn't stop her. "Maybe I'm not so undesirable as you think. Maybe . . ." Her hand moved to her long, brown braid. "Maybe I *am* pretty. Maybe I *can* draw well. Maybe . . . maybe if you opened your eyes and looked at me the way . . . the way Shaun does, you would know that he can care for me. Tell me, Mother. What is so awful about me that I can't have any man worth his salt?"

"Oh, Charlotte," her mother moaned sympathetically, "Charlotte, this is awful. I've waited so long for you to take an interest in the boys, and now that you have, you've set your sights too high. There is nothing wrong with you," she implored. "Oh, if only you had more experience, if you'd had more suitors, you would know. You would know how to read a young man. You would know that no matter how much he seems to like you, he is only entertaining himself for the holiday. When the season is over, he will be gone, and it will be the end of it. Charlotte, don't lay your heart out to be broken."

"You don't know that," said Charlotte, "you don't know any of it. You're only guessing. And you only guess in that way because you think I am unlovable."

"Of course you're not. I love you dearly."

"It's not the same. And you know it's not the same. You think no one could love me the way . . . the way a man loves a woman."

"That isn't true."

"Well, you're wrong!" she cried, disregarding the protest. "You don't know him, and you don't know me, either. You'll see. It isn't what you think it is. He isn't going to leave me. He does care for me—you'll see that he does!"

Margaret bent her head in sorrow when her daughter stormed out. She would punish her for her tongue, but there was no punishment so dreadful as the sorrow she would bear the day Shaun Matheson rode out of her life forever. That would come in about two weeks' time. And Margaret predicted many long, tearful nights. He was such a nice young man, too. If only she had warned him not to bewitch her naive daughter. If only she had known her daughter had reached the age of bewitchment. She would never have let them go to the dance.

Charlotte had never before been so cheerful about serving breakfast. She liked the way Shaun looked first thing in the morning with one ankle crossed over his knee, and wearing his casual morning suit, which was as elegant as everything else he wore. The fire crackled behind him at the dining table, giving the whole room an overwhelming scent of burning wood. It was light beyond the white-curtained windows, but not sunny. The outdoors were just bright white. It looked so cold out there, Charlotte was grateful to be trapped indoors, even if the whole house smelled like a burning log cabin. The scent of bacon smothered in maple syrup enhanced the snug feeling of the otherwise elegant dining room, its walls painted white, trimmed with colorful little flowers. "May I get you more strawberry pie?" she asked Shaun, eager to take his plate.

"No, thank you, Charlotte." She liked the way he responded, as though waiting on him were unnecessary, as though he could have gotten his own if he wanted, but that he appreciated the gesture. His eyes had been smiling at hers all morning, reminding her of the little secret they shared, and letting her know that he didn't regret it one bit. Charlotte was thankful for the reassurance that her mother was horribly wrong, and that Shaun really did want her. Even the morning after their scandalous night on the bed.

"I want more pie," Peter griped, "and I want it now, lazy. How come you didn't ask me?"

"Get it yourself, you slob. Shaun? May I get you more maple syrup for your bacon? Or perhaps a cup of water?"

"Oh, why, no, thank you, Charlotte. I'm just fine."

"Charlotte!" her mother snapped, "did you just call your brother a slob?"

"He called me lazy!"

"How old are you? Get in that kitchen and get your brother some pie. I swear, you're acting half your age."

"Fine. I'm going, I'm going." She would have put her tail between her legs if she'd had one. It was so humiliating to have to serve the likes of Peter.

When she returned with a slice of pie in hand, she found that she'd missed the beginnings of a most interesting conversation. She dumped the plate before Peter's greedy mouth and heard, "Why, yes. I wrote him just as soon as I got Peter's letter, thanking him for letting you spend the holiday here."

Shaun looked as though something was terribly wrong. She'd never seen him look so worried. He always had a calm confidence about him, as though nothing would ever surprise him. But at the moment, he looked lost, his eyes moving worriedly from the wall to his lap and back.

"Is it a problem?" asked Margaret. "Should I not have written him?"

Shaun was too polite to say no, though Charlotte could tell he wanted to. "Of course . . . of course it's not a problem. No problem at all." He forced a smile, but let go of his fork. It seemed he had lost his appetite.

"What did I miss?" asked Charlotte cheerfully.

"I seem to have committed some kind of a foible," admitted Margaret, looking worriedly at her guest.

"Who did you write?"

"Mr. Matheson. Shaun's father. I really meant no harm," she told him. "If I'd known you didn't want him to know of your holiday plans . . ."

"It's . . . it's all right," he said, taking a deep, shaky breath. "It's all right." To accentuate his point, he lifted his fork and began eating again.

Charlotte had the strangest urge to go over there and give him a hug. To squeeze him and tell him that whatever it was, it would be all right. But she did not. Instead, with a flutter of excitement in her belly, she reached into her apron pocket and fingered a note she had written the night before. This, she thought, might bring him some cheer. She waited until everyone at the table had risen, and in the commotion, she "accidentally" brushed against him, leaving the note in his hand. Shaun was smooth enough not to glance at it until he had a moment's privacy. He tucked it discreetly into his vest pocket and waited until he was the last in the room. Even Charlotte had scurried out, perhaps more quickly even than the others. She could not bear to see his reaction to the note. She would die if it made him frown or laugh. But it didn't. As soon as he had the opportunity, he unfolded it and smiled good-heartedly at what he saw. It read: *Meet me at the birch tree behind the red barn. 5:00, just before supper.* Shaun took it to a desk and scribbled a note of his own. He wrote: *Don't wear any undergarments.*

TWELVE

Charlotte found his note propped on her pillow like a visitor to her bed. With numb fingers, she lifted it and grinned wildly at its words. Though no one could see, she blushed. She bit her finger, and she checked over each shoulder to make sure she was alone. Then she forced herself to stop smiling, to shun him privately for his naughtiness, and begin the inevitable debate with herself. Did she dare? Did she dare follow his instructions? She felt a burning between her thighs. But no. She mustn't do as he said, lest he find her unbecomingly easy to tempt. For as shocking as it was for him to suggest it, it would be far worse for her to comply. Because . . . why was that? She cocked her head in thought. Oh, yes. Because she was a woman. Because for a man to seduce was quite natural, while for a woman to tempt was a sin. It was the way of things. And that did it. She tucked the note under her pillow and decided. She would do exactly as she pleased. If Shaun lived by no rules, she would show him that she, too, could be free. And sexy.

It was after a very hard day of housekeeping that Charlotte headed out for the birch tree. She had begun to think nothing could be so sweet as the anticipation, for her chores, though tedious, had gone by quickly, because her mind had never truly been on them. It had been somewhere much more exciting, somewhere where both thrill and anxiety awaited her. It had been under that birch tree, behind the red-crisscrossed barn, from where Shaun now watched her draw near. Charlotte would almost have rather kept this moment in her daydreams than live it. So much could go wrong. But nonetheless, she found herself warmed by the sight of him, leaning so elegantly against the tree with his arms crossed. He smiled welcomingly, and she returned the gesture without even meaning to. She just couldn't look at him without smiling.

"You came," he observed casually, the cold wind catching his sandy hair.

Charlotte noted he had arrived first, and knew in her heart that he had done so to save her the embarrassment of waiting. What a gentleman he was, even when he was being a rogue. "I did," she replied.

Shaun smiled softly as the deep-brown ends of her hair lifted with the wind. She had taken it down for him. For him. He liked that. "I wouldn't have picked the great outdoors myself," he said, reaching out, caressing her cheek with a gentle knuckle, "but you Vermonters are tougher than we pretty boys from the city."

Charlotte joined him in a smile. "It's the only place I knew we wouldn't be caught," she told him.

He took that as an invitation for a kiss. And he accepted, his lips gentle upon hers, but his hands unyielding in their restraint. He had her round the back and behind her head, and would not let go until he'd completely had his way with her lips. When he came up for air, her eyes were closed. Stroking her face with a thumb, he asked, "Why did you come?"

Charlotte had not rehearsed an answer, but one came nonetheless. "Because I have so little to lose," she whispered. Then her eyes fluttered open and she asked with a most curious expression, "Why did *you* come?"

He sniffed a laugh. "Because I have so very much that I would *like* to lose."

He tried to kiss her again, but she held him off in protest. "No, truly," she asked, "truly, why?"

And Shaun knew by the fragile look in her giant eyes what it was she was asking. Not, *why this* but *why me*. "Charlotte," he said, "do you need to hear flattery?" It was an honest question, not an accusation. He brushed her cold, silken cheek and watched her thick, sooty lashes move in thought.

"No," she said, "no, I only want to be sure that . . ."

"That I care?" he asked when she paused.

Charlotte nodded with embarrassment.

"I care," he said, assaulting her with a brush of his lips.

"But we have nothing in common . . ."

"We're outsiders," he said, "we're both strangers here. I, because your family's not had time to know me, and you, because they've never bothered."

Charlotte melted into his embrace, her eyes rolling heavenward in relief. All of her life, she had longed to hear words of compassion, assurance that she was more than anyone seemed to realize. And secretly, she had known from the moment she'd lain eyes upon Shaun that it would take a stranger to redeem her in the eyes of those she knew. She had hoped for this. She had hoped for it even as old habits had forced her to resist it. She allowed herself then to enjoy his firm embrace and the warmth of tucking herself inside his coat. She did not feel the sting of the cold, but only his hot tongue wrestling hers, and his bold hands sliding lower and lower down her back. She rejoiced in her moment of The Quickening, when all past was made good and the sun managed to shine through the winter sky to cast golden shadows upon her dark hair. And she was held high in the eyes of one—the only one whose eyes she cherished.

"I don't take promises lightly," he warned, touching the neck of her gown, sliding his fingers beneath its cloth, stretching them as far as he could toward her breast.

"Nor do I," she assured him, yanking the gown from her shoulders with determination and courage he didn't think she'd have.

"Whoa, easy there, easy there," he whispered. "Not all the way off. You'll freeze. Just to the ribs. Here, I'll show you." He reached in as far as he could, wrapped his hand around a plump breast, and guided it gently to freedom. "See?" he said to a wide-eyed Charlotte, who could not believe her breast was bare to his eyes. Holding the dress firmly in place so it would not fall to the ground, he freed the other, and then gently pinched both, tenderizing what would be his feast.

"What if someone sees us?" she asked anxiously, checking over her shoulder.

"Wouldn't that be exciting?"

"No!"

He cocked his head charmingly. "Oh, well. Then I suppose we'll have to make sure they don't." He tickled her cold, bare breasts, and watched them rapidly harden in the wind. Protecting them with both sides of his coat, he studied them through the tunnel of fabric. They were round and heavy, forced low by their sheer, delicious weight. Yet, their pink tips were placed high, as though they were peering at the sky. He wanted to hold them, to love them and shield them from the wind. He warmed them by rubbing them in his coat. Then he got down on one knee and began to suckle.

"Stop that," laughed Charlotte, who didn't know that such a thing was ever done.

But he looked up mysteriously and told her, "I have to warm them. I wouldn't want you to catch your death."

She accepted this reply with a naughty smile, accepting the wet of his tongue. Her eyes rolled. She couldn't believe how much she loved it. How much she adored seeing him down there, kneeling as though in worship, suckling as though she had something he needed. When he stopped, she wanted to force him right back where he'd been. He gave her breast a little pinch and asked, "Does this hurt?"

"No," she panted.

"Good." She was not too sensitive then, so he could devour her a little more ferociously. This time, he teased her with his teeth, and raked his fingers over the breast that was not being licked. Charlotte held onto his short, wavy hair, and fondled the rims of his ears. She wanted more. She wanted to wrap her legs around him.

She wanted it so badly that she found herself blurting out. "You know, I did as you said."

He took back his mouth and looked up with a raised eyebrow. "Did you?"

She nodded pantingly.

"Good." He winked.

"Are you going to . . . I mean, under my skirt . . ."

His head was shaking before she'd even finished. "No," he said, rising to his feet. He gently hooked her sleeves over her shoulders until she was sloppily concealed. "No, I'm not," he said, putting a finger to her plush lips. "You're not ready for that."

"Then why—"

"I just wanted you to know it," he said, "I just wanted you to know that you didn't have anything on under there." He tickled her leg through her gown. "I thought it would be exciting for us both."

"You're so strange," she said with love in her foggy eyes.

"No, no," he said, always resisting this statement of the obvious. "It's just that . . . well, that passion is purely psychological, you see." He searched her eyes for any sort of understanding. "We don't have to make love, Charlotte. I don't have to ruin you. Some men make love with less excitement than I feel just touching your face." He smiled pointedly as he was doing just that, caressing her silken cheek and fondling the tips of her ears.

"You make me feel like a princess," she said distantly.

He blinked heavily, wondering what that meant to her, wondering what it was about princesses that were so appealing to some young women. "You're too good to be a princess," he said at last. "Princesses are prisoners of perfection. You've got a mind all your own."

Charlotte flung her arms around him and gave him a kiss, forcing him to lift her off her feet with a laugh. "How did I live before I met you?" she asked.

He rubbed his nose against hers, as it was so irresistibly close. "Perhaps you knew I was coming."

"Yes," she grinned, "perhaps I did. Perhaps I've always known."

"We'd better not make your mother worry," he said, glancing anxiously at the dimming sun.

"When will we meet again?" she asked.

"At supper in half an hour?"

She laughed brightly. "No, not that, silly. I mean, when will we meet again like . . . like this?"

"Oh, that." He pretended to think about it. "Well, I do have an awfully full schedule, but . . . probably any hour of any day would be fine."

"I shall leave you a hint then," she said, remembering his words about the subtleties of passion. "I'll hide a note somewhere in your room, and if you don't find it, then you simply won't be able to meet me."

He liked the idea very much. "I'll tear out the floor boards if I have to," he assured her. And with that, he squeezed her hand. "Come, we won't get you in trouble."

Charlotte allowed him to lead her away from the sunset, past the red barn and cows, and toward the old white house. The sun glimmered faintly behind the massive rolling hills, but it could not melt the snow which frosted them. Icy winds froze even the ends of Charlotte's hair, and forced Shaun to huddle her to his side, cradling her in his coat as they walked. Charlotte foresaw a whole new image of her future. The gloomy adulthood she'd once imagined shattered like a nightmare she should have known wouldn't come to pass. Working like a slave for one of the unappealing Peacham marital candidates or living forever in her mother's home, sewing stitches as they both grew old—none of that seemed real anymore. Her new future seemed much more plausible, as though she'd always known it was meant to be. Though it was far away, she began to envision it. Life in a big city. Life with Shaun. A happy chill ran through her at the thought. Someday, she would be Mrs. Shaun Matheson.

THIRTEEN

It was a wonderful morning, even though Charlotte had overslept. She had stayed up much of the night with excitement in her belly, thinking about Shaun and the birch tree. When at last she had drifted off, it was late, and she knew she'd be in terrible trouble for oversleeping. But in the white, early morning light, she knew that nobody would be scolded on this day. It was a day to rejoice, a day to forgive all, even a lazy daughter. For immediately, her eyes had fluttered open to the ring of sleigh bells. Instantly, she ran to her frosty window and knelt by it to watch the sleigh pull into the drive. Christmas season was really here. There would be gifts and laughter, feasts and games. Although she would have to work through all of it, there would still be such joy! Everything was finally falling into place for the holiday. Her father was home!

It was so unthinkable to descend the stairs in her nightgown, that even in her excitement, she put something on. But her hair was loose and messy as she raced to the front parlor. And the only thing that could stop her wild grin was the sight before her—Charlotte stopped running and glimpsed the startled faces of her family. There was an eerie silence. And there was a strange man standing in the parlor. That's when Charlotte knew. All of her excitement had been for naught. It was not her father at all who had come to pay a call. It was an angry-faced, stout man with gray, thinning hair, dressed in finery too elegant to become his gruffness. "Where is my son?!" he demanded, hat clenched in a fist.

Charlotte looked at her stony-faced mother, and could tell this man had afforded her no pleasantries. She was clutching Peter as though he were still a little boy, and she looked as though she were hiding fear. Charlotte supposed it was a little frightening, having a strange man barge into the house with such anger. "Where is he?!" repeated the man, his face reddening in rage.

"I'm here."

Everyone turned around to see Shaun make a graceful but somber entrance. He leaned casually against the fireplace, but came no closer than that.

"What the hell are you doing?" demanded the balding man.

Mrs. Bass tried to cover Charlotte's ears from the word "hell," but, of course, was too late.

"I'm sorry I misled you," said Shaun, whose mere presence in the room was enough to give Charlotte a thrill, even under these awkward circumstances.

"I didn't raise my son to be a liar."

"You gave me no choice!" yelled Shaun, his eyes firmly fixed on his father, his posture casual against the mantel.

Mrs. Bass felt obligated to interrupt, as this was, after all, her house, and she had exactly enough courage to do so. "I beg your pardon," she said, her pale gray face held firm, "but what exactly is the matter here? Shaun is here as my guest."

"Ma'am," he said, nodding formally, "it's best that you stay out of this."

"I disagree. What exactly is the problem?"

He would not answer, but his son thought it was right to do so. "I'm afraid I told my father I was elsewhere for the holiday. I apologize, Mrs. Bass. I didn't anticipate that he would learn of my whereabouts."

"Then it's my own fault," she said to the elder Mr. Matheson. "I shouldn't have written you my thanks. Your son is a grown man and ought to make his own holiday plans."

"Stay out of this," warned the gentleman. Then he turned burning eyes on his son. "You told me you were with Miss Shepherd this season."

"I lied."

"Her family wants to meet you!"

"Her family doesn't *need* to meet me!"

"They do!"

"They don't!"

"What's the matter with you?" he growled, gazing upon Shaun as though he were a monster and not his son at all. "Have you no interest in a pretty young woman?"

"'Pretty' does nothing for me."

"Maybe *women* do nothing for you." It was an unthinkable insult, one Shaun hoped the women did not understand, lest their sensibilities be shaken.

He glared at his callous father and retorted in a low voice, "Maybe the women *you* pick do nothing for me."

"Then you're being childish. She's a lovely woman and she comes from a good family."

"I don't plan to *bed* her family!" He yelled it, but then immediately cast a repentant look in Mrs. Bass's direction. "I'm sorry." But it did no good. She was wide-eyed and appalled. Shaun rubbed his weary face hard.

"Get your things and go," rasped his father.

Shaun worked his way into a gradually increasing nod. "Yes. That's probably best."

Charlotte wanted to say something in protest, but her mother, sensing it, tugged her arm.

"You're a disappointment to me," said his father with a sincerity that gave everyone chills. "Always have been, but never more so than now."

Shaun barely flinched, a sign that he was used to hearing it. His eyes held quiet rage, but his voice was soft and low. "If you loved me, you wouldn't care who I marry."

"Loved you?" His father tried to laugh. "What made you think I love you?" His eyes pierced into his son's, as though he were trying to speak straight to his heart. "You are a pacifist and a weakling. If our country went to war, you would stay home and frolic with the women. You embarrass me."

"I love you, too."

"The one useful thing you could do," he growled, "is make a good marriage, and you won't even do that."

"We have enough money. We don't need to bring in more."

"*We?* What do you mean by *we?* You don't have any money. And if you think you're going to inherit mine, I suggest you stop paying tribute to the local brothels, and start paying visits to Miss Shepherd!"

"You can't blackmail me."

"I don't have to! I'll kill you if that's what I have to do. I've got no feeling for you but that deep disappointment that hits me every time I lay eyes on you."

"That's enough," said his son weakly.

"Oh, I hope you aren't going to cry," said his father. "I have to worry about that, I know. It's not like I'm talking to a man."

"You don't know what it means to be a man."

"You worthless . . ." He punched his son square in the jaw with a clapping sound that made Charlotte and her family jump. They all turned to see whether he was felled. But he was not.

With repressed anger seething in his eyes, Shaun wiped the blood from the corner of his mouth and straightened. His eyes were murderous, but he did not retaliate. All he said was, "Did that prove something?"

His father moved to grab him by the neck, but Char-

lotte stepped between them. "Leave him alone!" she
cried, her face hot with rage. Her mother tried to draw
her back, but Charlotte shook herself free. "You're an
ogre!" she cried. And though he tried to ignore her,
tried to weave around her, the moment of vengeance
was lost for him. Before he could get by, his son announced calmly, "I'll just pack my things. Step out of the
way, Charlotte." And he nudged her gently upon her
shoulder. "Come," he said when she wouldn't budge and
wouldn't stop glaring at Mr. Matheson. "Move out of the
way, Charlotte. It's all right."

Poutily, she stepped to the side, and Shaun glided past
her and his father both to reach the staircase. His father,
still purple in the face, spun around and called, "I'll wait
in the sleigh," much to the relief of all. For a moment,
Mrs. Bass was willing to bask in that relief, comforted in
knowing that the conflict was behind them and whatever
was to come would no longer concern her or her family.
But she was fundamentally braver than that, and it took
her only a few moments of recovery to remember it.

"Oh, dear," she clucked her tongue at her children,
"we can't just let him ride off like this. Wait here. I'll go
talk to Shaun."

"No, wait!" cried Charlotte, tugging her mother's
elbow. "Let me! Let me do it!" And without waiting for a
reply, she fled to the stairs. Margaret nearly ran after her,
but paused at the banister. Charlotte was already at his
bedroom door. She tossed up her hands with a sigh.
Maybe Charlotte was the best person to send anyway. Just
so long as someone tried to stop him. Just so long as
someone made it known that he would not be cast from
their home so callously.

When Charlotte received no answer to her delicate
knock, she let herself in. She found Shaun folding shirts

and stacking them neatly in a trunk. He spared her only the most casual of glances before returning to the task. "Shaun," she implored, touching a hand to her heart, ready to explode in a ramble of sympathy.

Shaun smiled weakly, unfazed and uninterested. "What?" he asked curtly.

"Shaun," she breathed again, shaking her head, wishing her eyes would fill with tears, but unable to force it. "Shaun, I . . . I don't know what to say."

He looked at her quite rudely, as though she were insane and speaking nonsense. Not once did he interrupt his task.

"Oh, please stop packing," she said, swiping a shirt from his hand, imagining that he couldn't leave without it.

Shaun swiped it right back and piled it on top of the others. But he said nothing.

"Shaun," she pleaded once more, "I don't want you to go."

"Well," he shrugged, "I didn't want to go either, but I have to. Now that he's here, he won't leave till I go with him. And believe me, you don't want him to stay."

"But Shaun, I'll . . . I'll miss you."

"Well, I'll miss everyone, too," he said, turning his back in search of more belongings, "but I hope you'll all have a merry Christmas. Sorry I can't join you."

Charlotte pounded her foot, making as startling a noise as she was able. The clapping made him turn around and see her fiery eyes. "That's not what I meant," she announced stonily. "I said I will miss *you.*"

It was hard for Shaun to turn away this time. She was glaring in a way that could scarcely be ignored. But he managed to turn partially, using the excuse of fumbling through a cherry chest of drawers. "Well, thank you," he said lightly.

Without a blink, Charlotte watched him move. Occasionally, he glanced at her with a raised eyebrow as though to say, *Yes? May I help you?* And then went back to packing. Charlotte felt as though all the blood had drained from her body and what was left could fall over at a touch.

She thought up a thousand possibilities of things to say and for a long time couldn't settle on one. She couldn't decide which were the magic words that would bring him back, that would let her in. At last, she tried, "When will I see you again?"

He kept moving, as though he'd expected that question to pop up and wasn't in the least surprised to hear it. As though he'd prepared his sloppy answer. "I don't know," he shrugged, slamming a drawer shut with a bang. "Maybe never."

Charlotte gasped. She made no attempt to hide the impact his words had on her trembling knees. When she spoke, it was in a pathetic screech. "What do you mean, never? Shaun, I . . ." Her mouth was wide open when she paused, "I thought . . . I thought you cared for me. I thought . . . I thought we might . . . that we might . . . get to know one another even more." She couldn't say "marry." It was like a jinx. As long as she didn't mention it, he couldn't tell her no, and it might still happen.

Failing to mention the word didn't save her from anguish. Shaun knew exactly what she meant by "get to know one another even more," and was candid in his reply. "I'm sorry if I misled you," he said as one who was in quite a hurry.

Again, Charlotte gasped. *"Misled* me?" she asked from that uncomfortable hallway between anger and hurt. "But . . . but at the pond, and you . . . and then you . . . and then . . . then the tree and . . . the . . . the dance and . . ."

"Charlotte, I never asked you to marry me," he broke in, sliding his arms through his coat sleeves with a shrug. "I'm sorry if . . ."

Charlotte might have interrupted him to argue semantics. She might have told him that any young woman would have "misconstrued" his behavior. Or that she was certain his feelings had been different only hours ago. But instead, she found the maturity to strike at the heart of the matter by touching her breast and saying with all of her soul, "You're killing me."

Shaun was taken aback, and something changed in his eyes. But only for a moment. As soon as he was able to harden himself against the hurt all over her lovely face, he slammed his trunk closed with finality and lifted it by its fine leather handle. "I'm sorry," he said with a tad more sincerity than before. He gazed at his trunk for a while, soaking in the silence he had summoned. "I'm sorry," he said again, "but you're much better off. You've got to believe that you are." And with that, he reached for his top hat.

"I don't believe it," she said hurriedly, but he was already walking by, and he was too strong to stop with a grab of the elbow. "Shaun, stop! Stop going. Shaun . . ." He had already reached the stairs and had begun his descent. "Is it that woman you're supposed to marry?" she asked. "Are you going to marry her? Is that what this is?"

Shaun hesitated on the steps. But all he said was, "Good-bye, Charlotte," and touched the brim of his hat.

Her mother and brother now closed in on him, eager to wish him well and to express their regrets. He received them with broader smiles and more appreciation than he'd received Charlotte. She spun around and raced back into his room, shutting the door behind her. She couldn't look. She couldn't watch him go. And most importantly, she couldn't cry in front of an audience. Crumpled at the foot of his bed, she breathed heavily, trying to absorb whatever spirit he had left in the room, trying to consume some piece of the air that had spilled from his own lungs. She wept in silent sobs, her face red and wet, but her open mouth not making a sound. She just couldn't let them hear.

Anxiously, she scrambled to the rear of the drawers and retrieved the enticing note she had hidden the night before. He had not yet looked for it. Unable to bear the humiliation of the romance and seduction of her own written words, she tore it into tiny shreds so that no one, not even five hundred years from then, could find it and know what a fool she'd been. But when she heard the crack of reins, she simply had to go to the window. She simply had to watch the sleigh pull away from the house, else she might have hoped that it never would. That something had changed his mind at the very last minute. But away it rode, carrying two passengers, its horses turned away from the blue hills of Vermont, heading back to the mysterious, untrustworthy world from which Shaun had come. Charlotte tossed the pieces of her note into the fire and snuggled up on Shaun's bed, curled like a kitten, her hands tucked under her cheek. She hoped she might miraculously fall asleep and never wake again.

FOURTEEN

Charlotte spent Christmas with her face in half-shadow like one of her more melancholy charcoal portraits. "I'm so happy to see you," she told her father on the day he at last arrived, his arms full of wrapped gifts and his coat full of snow.

But he saw immediately that his presence—and his presents—were not enough to bring cheer to his daughter this holiday season. He twisted the end of a very long chestnut sideburn speckled with gray and said, "I'm sorry I've been gone so long, but I didn't want our tree to be bare. You knew I wouldn't miss Christmas, didn't you?"

"Oh no, Papa, it isn't that. Of course I knew you'd come. Of course I knew. Welcome home." And she wrapped him in an embrace that went on too long, and that let him know something was very wrong.

"She's grown so pretty," he told his wife late that night as he watched her brush her hair by the frosty window. "I didn't know she'd be such a beauty when she bloomed."

Charlotte, who could hear every word through her floor boards, listened with gentle delight. She could always hear their talking at night, but had never told them so. Their bedroom was just beneath hers. In her father's absence, there was never a thing to hear, as her mother did not even snore. But whenever he was home, their room rumbled with soft talking upon each dusk.

"I fear you see her through the eyes of a doting father," said Margaret, causing Charlotte to scowl.

"You don't think she's lovely, Margaret?"

"She's fine," sighed the woman. "She'll be just pleasant enough to get a husband, I imagine."

"Well, I think she looks like a princess," said her father, making Charlotte stick out her tongue at the imaginary vision of her mother.

"Well . . . it's right that you should think so."

Charlotte whispered, "Better than a princess. Because I have a mind of my own." Despite all that had changed, Shaun's words still gave her comfort.

"She seems sad, though," said her father in a much lower mutter, as though on some level, he knew someone might be able to hear.

"Well," said Margaret with a weary sigh, "I'm afraid she had her first heartbreak this season."

"Heartbreak? Is she old enough for that?"

"Of course she is. She's turned seventeen."

"Well, by the dickens, I suppose she has. How did she get so old?"

"Time steals everyone's children."

"I suppose you're right. So who was this young man who broke my daughter's heart?"

"Oh, a very nice gentleman named Shaun Matheson. Quite handsome and quite exciting—all the way from Boston. Peter brought him home, and he was to spend the holidays with us. He had to leave in a rush, but I hope to persuade his father to let him join us next season. He was most welcome around here, as I'm afraid Peter is hardly any help at all when you're gone."

"Well, that's why we sent him to school. He was too

useless to keep here." Charlotte snickered into her blanket.

"Oh, he means well," said Margaret, always quick to defend her only boy, "and I know he mustn't toil while on holiday, but there are times I need some help. For instance, the pig. We had to slaughter him, but you know how Charlotte is about the animals. I couldn't get her to do it, and I'm not strong enough to do it without help. There are times I wish Peter would step forward. I'm just grateful the other young man was here for a time."

"Well, I hardly think Peter needs rest for the holidays. His performance in school doesn't seem to imply he's been breaking his neck."

"I hope he doesn't fail."

"He'd better not fail. We paid good money to get him accepted. I had to work hard for that sum."

"Well . . . he's never been the more clever of our children."

"Yes, but he's the only boy we've got. If putting a top hat on Charlotte would have made her a boy, I might have suggested that as our tactic for raising a Harvard graduate."

They both laughed, and Charlotte smiled. She'd never known her parents felt that way.

"Especially if it would make her stop drawing," teased her mother, turning Charlotte's grin into a fierce frown.

"Is she doing that still?"

"I'm afraid so. We've tried everything to discourage her, but she's just so stubborn. I really believe she doesn't know how awful her drawings are."

Charlotte whispered, "They're not awful. Shaun says they're not awful."

But her father said, "Well, I'm sure when she's married, she'll have more chores to distract her."

That made her mother sigh loudly, after which a long silence ensued.

"What is it?" asked her husband at last.

"Oh, nothing. I just . . ." she clucked her tongue in frustration, "I just wish she hadn't gotten her heart broken so. I tried to tell her, George. I tried to tell her that Mr. Matheson was not within her reach. But you know how young girls are. Once they get their hearts set . . ."

"Ah, she'll get over it. It was just her first romantic flirtation. There will be many more."

"That's what troubles me. She doesn't need romantic suitors, she needs a husband. You should have seen her with her eyes full of stars. She even found the courage to scold me for telling her the truth, for telling her that she wouldn't be a bride for Mr. Matheson."

"She shouldn't scold her mother."

"Oh, I didn't mind her ill manners, not just this once, not when her heart was so fragile. But what really troubled me was that she refused to believe. I just fear it was a hard lesson for her. I hope she really learned it."

"Well, she does seem awfully sad."

"I know, and I hate to see her that way."

"Well, just don't tell her you were right. Don't put her nose in it."

"Oh, no. No, I won't do that. I think she knows," she decided with some satisfaction, "I think she knows now that she can't simply have anyone she wants. Maybe now she'll choose someone sensible."

"But who?"

There was a lengthy pause and then in a voice of cheery illumination, she announced, "I believe Giles Williams will be courting soon."

"Ah yes, the printer's boy."

"Yes, and I've always suspected he had an eye for Charlotte."

"Excellent. So then you see? All hearts do mend, and Charlotte may not have to set her sights too low after all."

"You're so right, George. Just wait until Charlotte recovers from her grief and sees what a fine young man has been waiting for her in the wings."

"I suspect that smile will return."

Charlotte pulled the blankets over her stricken face and pretended once more to be dead.

FIFTEEN

December 25, 1831

Dearest Shaun,

Today is Christmas and I write only to thank you for the gift you left behind. My mother presented it to me before the close of the day. She said you had left it in her care, and for that I cannot thank you enough. How delighted I was to open it and find watercolors! I shall begin painting with them immediately. I shall do it for you, for you are the only one who has ever sought to encourage me. Thank you for the lovely gift. I only wish I had thought to give you my own before your departure. It would not have impressed you, I fear. I had merely drawn the pond where once we met. Perhaps someday, if you wish, I might send it to you.

Christmas was wonderfully gay, particularly now that my father has returned. The goose was tender and my mother must be the only woman alive who knows six different varieties of applesauce. Indeed, that is how many were served. Poor Peter forgot to fetch me a gift, but that's his way! He's always been terribly forgetful. I know he felt just awful about it, though his feelings are difficult to discern. I did receive some lovely gifts including a new apron from my mother, which is far more detailed than any I've had before. Oh my, listen to me. I should be sharing what it is I gave rather than what I received. I fear I gave everyone very sensible gifts this year—scarves I knitted which were far from spectacular. I would have given them drawings, of course, but I'm afraid they would rather have the scarves!

As you see, it was a splendid Christmas Day, although, of course, it would have been more joyous if you had been here to share it. "Everyone" misses you.

My dearest Shaun, if I were wiser I would say less, I know, but I wonder how lonely it is to be wise. I wish that we had not parted as such strangers. I fear we may both have said words we didn't intend, and I hope that in the calm after said storm, we may find a point of reconciliation. May you at least call me a friend?

Anxiously awaiting your reply and all news about your holiday.

Yours sincerely,
Charlotte Lynn Bass

January 25, 1832

Dearest Shaun,

I hope you'll forgive me for writing you again so soon. A great deal has happened over the past month, and I'm bursting at the seams to tell you all the news.

I know that nothing that happens here in Peacham could ever be so interesting as what probably occurs every day in the city! But to me, having nowhere else to turn for excitement, even the smallest incident is worth a letter, I'm afraid.

Do you remember Mary Whittaker? The most amusing thing has happened since I've returned to school. She has invited me to join the other girls in all of their outings and gatherings. This may not sound like such a startling turn of events, but had you lived here over the course of the past seventeen years you would see that it is shocking indeed. I have never been invited to join the other girls in their frolic, not since Giles began taunting me years ago. I suspect they always feared they, too, would fall prey to taunts should they seem to be my associates. I have been delighted by their new friendliness, but have delicately declined their invitations. I shall remain loyal to Sarah, who has always loved me, no matter what the consequence.

Perhaps most amusing of all is a bit of news I suspect even you will find laughable. Giles Williams, of all people, has tried to court me! I tease you not. I fear I burst into laughter at his approach, but it was not my intention to be rude. I merely thought he was in jest. He was not, however, and I had to work heartily to regain my composure and decline his most interesting request. For years people have told me that Giles torments me out of fondness, but that has never seemed likely until now. What a strange notion of flirtation he must have to think I would adore him for his rudeness. I believe "hopeless" is the appropriate word to describe his chances of courting me. But it is this event which prompted me to write you, for I could hardly keep something so enormously funny to myself.

I do so look forward to your correspondence. I have been asked many times about your well-being and have been too ashamed to confess my ignorance of the matter. Perhaps some people think you are my beau. Silly of them, isn't it?

I do hope all is well and that your studies are progressing or, at least, not causing you anxiety. I imagine it must be very difficult to study at the university, though I would surely like to try it. Do take good care of Peter and write me just as soon as you are able. Until I hear from you, I shall fear that I have lost even your most innocent of affections.

Yours sincerely,
Charlotte Lynn Bass

July 6, 1832

Dearest Shaun,

I still await your reply.

I do so wish that you could see Vermont in the summer as I imagine that nowhere else is the season so lovely. On some days it is so hot I can scarcely gather the energy to leave the house. I wonder how those in warmer climates get any work done at all, or how they think. Sometimes my mind is so hazy from heat that creative inspiration seems an impossibility. Of course, these days are the exception, for normally there is a lovely pine-scented breeze. Every now and then, I must even wear my coat if the weather is not in the mood for summer.

You know that you would always be welcome to visit, no matter what the season. I know that my mother would be delighted to have you again. She truly raves about your fine manners, and has declared you a thoughtful guest. How delighted she would be to hear that you were coming again.

Giles is still trying to court me! I tell you this only as a friend, and certainly not to stir jealousy in you. It would be awfully presumptuous of me to suppose I could make you jealous, and thus, I assure you it is not my intention. But my, it is amusing! Although it was not so amusing on the Saturday afternoon that he came calling and my mother invited him to stay. I was forced to entertain him when I had pegged the day for painting. Speaking of which, I must thank you again for the lovely watercolors you gave me! They yield much more intriguing results than the charcoal ever did. I am so delighted with them that I find myself painting with much more frequency than ever before, and I proudly leave them to dry in the attic where any familial visitor is forced to view them.

My mother has allowed me to return to school on

certain days when there is not much work in the house.
It is tedious as always, and increasingly a waste of
valuable time. There is really no cause for a woman my
age to be in school, and the teacher, well aware of this,
is more likely to assign me quiet reading than any ac-
tual work. He, as my mother, is hoping I will soon
marry and be out of his care. But I doubt this will hap-
pen! Do you suppose?

My dearest Shaun, it has occurred to me that your
silence may be a reflection of your intention to marry
another. I hope that this is not so, but please let me as-
sure you that I wish to remain an acquaintance, no
matter what your circumstance. I am lonely, Shaun. I
am lonely and you have been dear to me. Please
write.

Yours sincerely,
Charlotte Lynn Bass

It was on a glorious day that Charlotte dropped her
pennies on the postmaster's counter and raced home
with a letter in hand. To see Shaun's writing on the en-
velope, to see his name, was almost more than her
pounding heart could bear. The joy of receiving it was
so great, in fact, that she could hardly stand to open
it, lest anything written inside should diminish her joy.
She took it to the farthest corner of her bedroom,
where she had closed the door as tightly as it would
shut. Carefully, she took her letter opener to the seal,
but then put it down, danced around in nervous anticipation, and with trembling hands, tried again.
Again, she could not bring herself to do it. The con-
tents were just too important. She couldn't bear the
moment. So she put down the letter opener once more,
jumped off some excess nervous energy, took a deep
breath, and tried again. This time, she successfully
broke the seal in one brave slash. With wildly shaking
hands, she pulled out the letter and took one more

deep breath before unfolding it. At last, she swallowed and read:

> *Dearest Charlotte,*
>   *I'm sorry. Good-bye.*
>
>   *Yours,*
>   *Shaun Jackson Matheson*

SIXTEEN

The wonderful thing about absolute heartbreak is its finality. It doesn't demand to be carried around and studied like its weaker counterpart, sorrow. It sweeps through its victims like a wave, carrying away their insides, leaving behind nothing, not even itself. It has the mercy not to linger and fester. And it's for that reason that Charlotte was actually smiling as she balanced at the edge of the sparkling brook that trickled through the forest of pine and birch. A month had passed since she'd burned the letter, and she no longer lived in its gloom. She frolicked in the freedom it had granted by forcing her to let go. She had let go of her hopes and wishes, her frustrations and yearnings. She lived only for the next meal, the next joke, the next refreshing night's sleep. And sometimes the simplicity of it put her in a very bright mood.

The sun was gentle on the bed of dried pine needles which covered all the forest. It danced through the leaves overhead and made spots on the ground where it could. The brook was noisy, its rocks slippery underfoot. Charlotte balanced on its edge, spreading her arms, occasionally losing her footing on a round rock and getting her boots wet. The air was perfect. A gentle breeze carried the green scent of pine, warm but not hot upon her face. Charlotte looked up at the steep hill she'd had to descend to reach this part of the forest. She had nearly slid all the way down, clutching tree trunks to prevent a serious tumble. She felt quite alone down there, skipping across brown needles, balancing on rocks and listening to the chirps of birds and chipmunks singing over the high-pitched brook. She was supposed to be gathering blackberries. And she had . . . just before eating them all. She would have to return to the fields of tall grasses, she thought, examining her purple-stained hands. Her mother would be angry if she returned with an empty basket. She certainly hoped that the dark red of the strawberries she'd been eating all morning would mask the new purple she'd added to her lips. Come to think of it, she'd been eating a great deal lately. . . .

Charlotte walked and walked, sometimes hearing footsteps that sounded like a moose's. She would stop and wait, anxious to catch a glimpse, but she never managed. Oh, well. There would be beavers ahead, and they were almost as interesting. She stopped to take a drink from the brook, and worried that the sun was dimming. Looking up, she could see the yellow sun in all its detail. It no longer hurt to look at it, so clearly it was getting late. Another breeze wafted over her as she dipped her hands in the racing water. The water felt like ice and looked happy in the flickering sunlight. She brought it to her lips and felt healed by its joy. She could hear a waterfall in the distance and wished she had time to reach it. But just as she was busily wishing, a sound interrupted her thoughts.

It was laughter. At first she wasn't certain, but the longer she paid attention, the more clear it was. And furthermore, she would recognize that bright giggle anywhere. It was Sarah's. Charlotte picked up her empty berry basket and raced toward the sound. There was something fun about running in the forest, she noticed, for she'd been of a mind to notice these subtle joys lately. She couldn't run a straight path because there were so many trees in the way, and that made her slow jog acceptable rather than lazy, which greatly enhanced the joy of it. She liked the way her boots barely made a sound, they were so well padded by needles. And she liked the way the fresh scent of the forest washed through her lungs more thoroughly with each heavy breath, cleansing her and filling her hollow insides with nature.

At last, she saw them and slowed down, both to catch her breath and to spy. She clung to a narrow tree and watched Sarah giggle gaily at Kevin Gordon. They were reclining in the forest, leaning against a maple tree which had been freshly carved with their initials. Their legs stretched out before them, they were holding hands, sharing softly spoken jokes and grinning at one another. Charlotte prepared to creep away, but was caught. "Charlotte!" It was Sarah, and she was pulling free of her suitor's casual embrace, dusting herself clean of pine needles and waving her arm welcomingly. Kevin didn't look quite so delighted by the intrusion.

"Sarah," said Charlotte, returning her friend's warm eye contact and welcoming her small hands into both of her own. "I'm so sorry, I didn't mean to intrude."

"Oh, no!" she cried, "no, not at all. She didn't intrude, did she, Kevin?"

Kevin's smile was weak. "Why, of course not."

Charlotte knew how shy he was, and how hard it must be for one so self-conscious to be caught at an intimate moment. "I really should go," she told Sarah, brimming with forced pleasantness. "I feel it is late."

"No, no. Please stay. It isn't very late, is it, Kevin?"

"Actually," he said, rising to his full height, which had come to be rather impressive, "I'd been thinking the same thing. I really should be going. I . . . Charlotte, it's so good to see you."

She accepted his handshake with a smile she had to

suppress, lest he think she was laughing at him. "You also, Kevin. Again, I'm sorry . . ."

"No, no. I'm . . . it's really good to see you. And Sarah," he added, taking the tiny woman's hand to his lips. It was an awkward gesture for him, because it was one that required confidence to be carried out effectively. But Sarah didn't notice. Her big smile said it all. He could do no wrong in her eyes. The barrier of judgment, of evaluation and analysis, had been broken. She had moved beyond it and was in love.

Charlotte looked from the towheaded boy to her dearest friend, then back again, over and over until he'd wandered out of sight. At last, she said lightly, "I'm afraid I frightened off your beau."

"Oh, no," said Sarah, "he's just a little shy. Besides, we've been out here the better part of the day. He had really better get back if he doesn't want to raise suspicions." She giggled expressively.

But Charlotte's stare was as firm as it was kind. "Sarah," she said in gentle earnest, "why didn't you tell me?"

"Tell you what?"

"Sarah." She took her friend's hand and gave it a loving squeeze. "I haven't seen you with Kevin since the Christmas dance. Why didn't you tell me he was your beau?"

"Oh, that." Sarah bowed her head guiltily. "I uh . . . I'm not sure. It wasn't very important, was it?"

"Why, of course it's important," chuckled Charlotte. "I'm your dearest friend. How could you go so long without telling me? You should have been at my house with gossip after the very first kiss!" Her laugh held absolute forgiveness.

"Well, I . . . I just didn't think . . ."

"You didn't think what?" She paused a good long

while, studying Sarah's face, holding her hands with care. "You didn't think *what?*"

Sarah looked up bashfully, but with soul. "It's just that you didn't have anyone."

"Oh, Sarah," she breathed, "Sarah, you mustn't pity me."

"I don't! Oh, Charlotte, believe that I don't."

"Then swear it," said Charlotte, "swear that you won't hide from me again. You're my dearest friend, Sarah. You should always include me."

"I'm sorry," she said, shaking her head imploringly. "I'm sorry, Charlotte. I should have told you, I just thought . . ."

"Well, you should have thought better of me. You should have known that I could find pleasure in the happiness of my best friend."

The young women shared a smile they'd shared countless times since they were tiny children. They locked hands without saying another word, and swung their joined arms as they walked along toward home. "I'm sorry," Sarah said once again.

But Charlotte scolded her. "Don't be sorry, just make up for it. Tell me everything I've missed."

Sarah's blush said a great deal. "Well, I—"

"He's going to marry you, is he?"

Sarah bit her lip and nodded. "I think so. He hasn't said anything, of course, but I think he might."

"And who is going to be your maid of honor?"

"You are, of course."

Charlotte gave her friend's hand an extra squeeze. "I wouldn't miss it for the world."

The two walked on, their footsteps made brisk by the threat of coming darkness. Forests were dangerously dark at nightfall, and knowing that they must reach the road by then made their race for it rather exciting. They held onto one another, pretending not to hurry, never mentioning the obvious threat of being forever lost if the pale sun moved faster than they did. It was fun, being in minor trouble like that, as they had been so many times before. They felt just like little girls again, fearing the wrath of their families, and basking in the comfort of knowing that whatever trouble they were in, they were in it together. But they weren't little girls anymore. Charlotte knew that. Sarah was thinking of getting married; it was hard to be any more grown up than that. Charlotte knew that years from then, it simply wouldn't do for Sarah still to be pitying her best friend. Nor for Kevin to scurry away each time he saw her, knowing that she was the poor nosy spinster with nothing better to do but spy, gossip, and steal away his bride. Charlotte knew what she had to do. It was time to take others' lives into account: Sarah's, her mother's, her father's, everyone's. It was time to accept the courtship of Giles. . . .

SEVENTEEN

Beacon Hill may have been aesthetically entrancing, but it was an absolute hassle to climb. The narrow, winding streets were lined with red-brick town houses that seemed taller than they were because they were crammed so close to the sidewalk; a pedestrian had to look straight up to see the tops. On a rainy day, the windows were all dotted with thick drops that didn't want to fall. Golden light radiated from French doors, gently interrupting the afternoon's moody gray. Shaun's shoes clapped against brick, just like the horses' hooves that trotted by periodically. The rain was gentle and warm against his face. And the gray was soothing to the eyes, for foggy days were the only days he could look absolutely anywhere, open-eyed, without squinting. There was a peacefulness in the solemn faces of every carriage driver and every stroller in a top hat. But Shaun was never able to feel at peace when he climbed that tedious hill, for what awaited him at the top always made him tense.

He fumbled with his key in the large, elaborate keyhole. His father's town house was as beautiful as any of the others—the second from the right in a row of four. Some of the windows stretched from ceiling to floor on all four stories. But to Shaun, it was the ugliest house on the block, and had been ever since his mother's death. Before that, it had been a place where cookies were baked, where warm smells filled the entry and crackling fires welcomed him home. But it had been many long years since he'd associated the staunch-looking building with anything but his father's short temper and quick fist. Shaun no longer hated his father, though. As the years had passed the hate had cooled into something best described as . . . distaste. He simply had no respect for the man and rarely bothered to be enraged. At least not openly.

"Ah, there you are," said his father the moment Shaun's key opened the door.

Shaun looked at him unreceptively, as though to say, "I hate it when you pretend you're happy to see me." But he said nothing, only listened.

"We've received an invitation," said his stout father, holding a pipe in one hand and waving a feminine-looking piece of stationery with the other. It was the femininity of it that drew Shaun's eye. It had a lacy border—it reminded him of a woman. And anything that did that was always a welcome sight.

"What is it?" he asked, still flustered that his father was home. He had hoped for his absence, and would not have journeyed home for the weekend if he'd known his father planned to laze about.

"It's from Margaret Bass," he said, causing Shaun to forget all about his other trouble. "A rather lovely letter, actually," he added, stuffing the narrow end of his pipe between his lips. "Remarkable woman."

"What does the letter say?"

"She's invited us to stay the next holiday with her family in Vermont."

Shaun was already shaking his head.

"In all candor, I have to say the notion sounds tempting. A couple of bachelors like you and me can hardly put on a festive holiday. Your aunt and uncle live so far away, and . . ."

"You dragged me away from their house only a short while ago."

"Well, yes, but that was only because you lied to me. This is quite different. This is a proper invitation, and it's for us both."

"I can't go." Shaun was already fumbling through some papers on the front coffee table, searching to see whether there was anything of importance before he retreated to his room. As far as he was concerned, there was nothing here to discuss.

"Why not?" asked his father, a hint of temper worming its way into the gentleman's voice he had tried so affirmably to maintain. "You were eager when you knew it was disobedient. Now that I'm giving approval, you've lost interest?"

"It has nothing to do with that," said Shaun quietly, still shuffling through papers, entirely unfazed by his father's tone of voice.

"Then *what?*" cried his father. "You can't bear to spend Christmas with your own father? Is that it? If that's it, then I'll give you some good news. I was planning to send you ahead of me so I can attend to our affairs right up till the holiday. You'll only have to spend a few days with me if that will appease your fears."

"No, not that."

"Then what?!"

Shaun looked up with an expression like the one he'd have if he'd only just noticed his father was in the room. "It isn't any of your concern, Father. I simply can't go."

His father shoved the coffee table hard enough to make it topple, though it did not. A few of Shaun's school documents fell to the floor. Shaun put up both hands in surrender. "If you're going to start this, I'm leaving," he said to his father. "If you want to break our furniture, that's fine, but I'm not going to stand here and watch."

"You afraid to fight your own father?"

Shaun shook his head regretfully, disgust all over his face. "You're an idiot."

"You know, when I fought in the war, we had a name for people like you."

"Civilized?"

"Cowardly."

"Oh, that's right. That was going to be my next guess." He touched the banister and was thoroughly prepared to disappear, but his father would not let him go.

"Don't be smart with me, young man," his father growled. "If I'd a mind to, I'd beat you down and drag you to that farmhouse."

"Oh, that's lovely," drawled Shaun. "That's the Christmas spirit."

"Don't think I wouldn't! If you won't come with me to the Basses', then I'll see to it you spend that time wisely, courting Miss Shepherd as any real man would do."

Shaun rolled his eyes with a sigh. "I'm not marrying her, Father."

"We'll see about that. Fine." He tore Mrs. Bass's letter dramatically into shreds. "If you don't want to go, then we'll stay here. And I'll have the Shepherds pay us a visit for the holiday. Maybe that's what you need—a little more time with the young woman. You don't like beautiful girls? Then I'll try to explain to the family that my sensitive weakling of a son needs to 'get to know' the young lady," he whined in a falsetto.

"Don't invite them here. I don't wish to spend time with her and I don't wish to hurt her feelings."

"Oh, how sensitive."

"I'm immune to your condescension, Father. All I ask is that you don't invite them."

"I'll do as I please in my own home."

"No, wait!"

"Don't disturb me. I'm going to write them immediately. I'll marry you off if it's the last thing I do."

"What do you mean Shaun is coming for Christmas?"

"Now, Charlotte, I know how you feel. But I simply couldn't let the boy spend a holiday alone with that awful father of his. I invited them and received their kind reply today. They were both quite enthusiastic."

"I can't believe this. I can't believe this is happening to me!" Charlotte pressed her hands over her eyes and leaned back, screaming quietly from the rear of her throat.

Her mother barely glanced from the washboard where she was busily scrubbing stockings. "Charlotte, I know you were hurt. But it isn't his fault that you were so easily smitten."

"Easily smitten?! Mother, you . . . you have no idea what he's really like! You have no idea what he did!"

"Charlotte," she snapped, "he is a fine young man and it is unseemly to speak ill of someone because you're wounded by rejection."

"Oh my lord!" screamed Charlotte, spinning in circles in her frustration. "Mother, you are so wrong about him! You have no idea! He is not a fine young man at all—he is a wolf!"

"Charlotte, I am not going to listen to any more of your resentful sentiments. And quite honestly, I'm rather disappointed in you for bearing such a grudge. I would think now that you're being courted by Giles, you would be quite over this matter."

"Over it? Mother, how could you invite him here?!" *And how could he agree?* she wondered quietly. Could it be that he had changed his mind and now wished to make amends? Ohhh! She punched her thigh to make the gullible thoughts cease. Never again. Never again would she open herself to such hurt! How could he? How could he stomp on her heart and then come back for a casual visit? "Please recant the invitation," she begged, folding her hands as if in prayer. "Please tell him something has come up and we can't possibly have him. Please. I will never ask anything of you again."

"Oh, stop being so dramatic," her mother chuckled. "It will be lovely to have more people in the house for the holiday. Can't say I'm delighted to have the father," she confessed, "but I felt it was necessary to invite them as a pair. He says he'll be arriving late so we'll get to have Shaun to ourselves for some time anyway."

Charlotte could see there was no use pleading. Her mother saw Shaun as a polite, innocent gentleman to whom Charlotte had naively attached herself. She didn't know about the waitress at the tavern. She didn't know about the night on Charlotte's bed or the sunset by the birch tree. And Charlotte could tell her none of this, for it would just be too humiliating. She would have to live forever with the lie that Shaun was the good-natured son her parents had always wanted, and that Charlotte herself was a fool for thinking otherwise. He had outwitted her. The most irreverent boy she had ever met had convinced the entire town of Peacham that he was a gentleman. And he had nearly convinced Charlotte as well. But he would pay for it. He would pay for it with every turn of her chin and strike with her tongue. If he thought he could come back and charm her again, he was in for a dreadful surprise. Never again would Charlotte be a fool.

"Now, you listen to me, Giles. For the next few weeks, you are going to be madly in love with me. Not just mildly intrigued, but madly in love. Do you understand?"

"No, not really." Giles had grown slightly more handsome over the year. His dark hair, though still quite straight and stringy, was cut more fashionably, in the style of an urbane young man, short on the back and sides, longer in front. His dark eyes, though still rather cocky, were mellow for longer periods of time now, as age sometimes softens people. He had grown to fill out his suits rather nicely, and his father kept him well dressed. He now towered over Charlotte, though she was reasonably tall.

"Then let me explain again," she said impatiently. "I am going to be demure, and you are going to be wildly in love with me. I want you to compliment me, fuss over me, and bring me lots of gifts. I'll pay you back for them."

"Compliment you? What do you want me to say?"

"Well, you are courting me, aren't you? Surely there is something not unappealing about me?"

He shrugged. "Of course. I wouldn't mind having you for a wife."

"There! See? Now just elaborate a bit."

"Well, uh . . . ." He scratched his head, as he'd been doing quite a bit lately, making Charlotte fear he had lice. "You're . . . I don't know . . . you have big breasts."

Charlotte dropped her face in her hands. "Please, Giles. Please think of something else. Anything else?"

"Sure uh . . . your face is all right. Not great, but all right."

"Something about my heart! My heart, Giles! My heart."

He scrunched up his nose. "What about it?"

Charlotte sighed audibly. "Giles. Can't you think of something nice to say that has nothing to do with my looks?"

"Sure." Again, he shrugged. "You're smart."

"I am? Thank you! Thank you, yes, that's exactly the sort of thing I'm looking for."

"I don't really like smart women," he went on, "but I suppose it's good. In a way. I don't know. I always thought you were sort of drab for doing so well in school, but . . . I guess it's all right."

"All right," she said, tossing up her hands, "that's it. I'm going to give you a list of compliments and I want you to memorize them. Then every time Shaun . . . or, every time anyone is in the room, I want you to say one of them to me. Can you do that?"

"What's in it for me?"

Charlotte sighed. "Well, you did say you wanted me for a wife, didn't you?"

"Yes."

"Well," she winced back the pain of it, "if you do this for me, then . . . well then, I'll consider it."

"All right. You have a deal." He held out his hand and they shook. Charlotte liked that gesture, and for one moment, hoped that some day, somehow, they might have more moments like this. Moments in which he seemed like a friend or a partner. Moments in which she didn't feel she had set her sights lower than any woman ought ever to be forced to do.

EIGHTEEN

December 1832

As Shaun traveled the slippery road to Peacham, watching the rounded hills rise majestically in the distance, he felt as though he were coming home. He'd been to Vermont only once before, but it was the sort of place that became home very quickly. Alive with pine, quiet like snow, it felt like anyone's home, or the home that should have been. Peter had been mercifully silent for most of the ride, perhaps because they'd not shared even a moment of friendship during the school year. Shaun had come to the realization he didn't like him. And though Peter seemed to hold a bizarre admiration for the boy who had nearly been his chum, Shaun had been rather in a hurry during every encounter. Now, one of the few things Peter said on their long, awkward sleigh ride was, "Are we almost there?" It was a question neither Shaun nor the driver bothered to answer.

Shaun felt very uncomfortable as the sleigh moved past houses and stores that were familiar to him. They were nearing Peacham, and it was going to be a very awkward Christmas, indeed. He felt bad about it—returning when he was no longer friendly with either the son or the daughter. But he'd had no choice. He couldn't spend the holiday with Miss Shepherd. The badgering from both families, the pressure from the young lady

herself, the expectation of marriage hidden in every exchanged gift—he just couldn't. And he had to admit, as
selfish as it was, he was glad to return to the lovely, natural land of Vermont and enjoy Mrs. Bass's johnnycakes,
no matter how awkward his arrival. Already, he thought,
catching a glimpse of the white, pitch-roofed schoolhouse where he'd taken Charlotte to the dance, this
place felt like the home he'd never had. He felt like
someone who had a right to return, as though the town
itself had invited him.

He was surprised and delighted by the warm welcome
he received at the Bass house. Margaret Bass raced from
the porch, hiking up her apron, a big, happy grin on her
face. Shaun was thrilled to see her. Her flour-streaked
face and stringy, graying hair was a familiar sight to him.
He kissed her cheek as though she were his own mother,
and this gesture meant more than she would ever understand. As Margaret moved to welcome her "other
son," Shaun was put to the task of introducing himself to
George Bass, the master of the house. Shaun extended
his hand politely, though in truth, the presence of a
grown man was a disappointment to him, which seemed
to diminish the gay atmosphere. "Hello, sir."

Mr. Bass broke into a friendly smile, displaying a
mouth full of giant, crooked teeth. His long chin and
unremarkable brown eyes made him modest. And he
gave Shaun a handshake that was as sincere as Shaun
could have hoped. It was clear that Mr. Bass was not an
intimidating presence in the household, father figure
though he was. The Christmas would still be joyous, after
all. "You must be the gentleman I've heard so much
about," he said brightly.

Shaun nodded gracefully. "I certainly hope not."

They shared a chuckle, and it was then that Shaun
glanced around and noticed that Charlotte had not
come to greet him. It didn't surprise him, of course. He

knew what she must be feeling. But at the same time her absence left him with a mild sense of dread. He'd hoped to get their greeting over and done with. It was going to be hard on them both. If only she knew—it would be hard on them *both*.

Shaun's worry grew worse when Charlotte did not arrive at the supper table. Settled into his chair beside the crackling winter fire, he had changed his clothes and was looking forward to the scrumptious-smelling stew Mrs. Bass had laid out before the family. He noticed there was a new picture on the wall, a portrait of George Washington. And though it was a fine work of art, he quietly wished it away, for any change to this cozy, familiar house was unwelcome in his eyes. "Where is Charlotte?" He was glad it was Mr. Bass who asked the question, and not himself. He didn't wish to pry, at least not openly.

"Heavens if I know," said Margaret in a tone that implied wherever Charlotte was, she would be in serious trouble when she returned. "Please go ahead and eat. Don't mind her."

The three men seemed rather anxious to follow her instructions, and dove eagerly into their fare while Mrs. Bass continued to wait on them. "So," Mr. Bass began in a tone that Shaun recognized as the standard paternal voice. Still, it didn't have the threatening undertones that his own father's often did, so he was able to maintain a pleasant expression as the gentleman went on. "I understand that you come from a long line of Harvard men," he said, stuffing his napkin into his lap.

"Not so," said Shaun politely. "In fact, I am the first. My own father went to . . ." There was a pause. He looked first at Peter, then at George, and then at the expectant expression of Mrs. Bass, who was frozen in mid-pour. "Yale."

There were gasps. There was the dropping of forks.

Then the whole family started speaking at once. "You didn't tell me that," said Peter.

"Yes, I did."

"Is he sorry he went?" asked Mrs. Bass.

"No, I don't think so."

"He's not a conservative, is he?"

"Possibly."

"Oh, my."

Mr. Bass felt it was his obligation as head of the house to put their unfortunate guest at ease. "Well," he said in a most kingly sort of voice which silenced the rest of the family, "many young men exceed their own fathers. Really, that is the dream of procreation."

"Why, thank you." Shaun tried to hide a smile.

"I myself did not even attend a college," he went on comfortingly. "That's why I've worked so hard to send Peter. All parents want more for their children than they themselves had."

The conversation might have become even more amusing for Shaun, whose father was quite proud to be a Yale graduate and quite upset that his son had chosen Harvard, but unfortunately, supper was interrupted by a slam of the front door. It was Charlotte. She raced in, panting and grinning, uttering unconvincing apologies. "So sorry," she said, her eyes stubbornly fixed on her mother, straining not to look elsewhere in the room, "I didn't mean to be late. I was with my beau and we were just so caught up in watching the sunset, I completely lost track of time."

"Sit down!" said her mother crossly. "I am very angry. Just sit!"

"After I wash my hands," she said, racing to the kitchen. Her mother watched her go with a scowl. Had she not suspected the real reason for Charlotte's tardiness, she would truly have been furious. But as it was, she was pretending to be angrier than she really was. She could only imagine how hard this was.

Shaun was rather startled by the sight that had flown by. Charlotte looked beautiful. She looked much older than he'd remembered. Her face had more distinction, less baby fat. Her figure was a bit fuller in womanly places like the belly and hips, and more slender in the arms and around the neck. Her hair was tied up, just like a grown woman's. He supposed she really was a grown woman. Why it surprised him so, he wasn't sure. In his absence, he imagined Charlotte frozen in time, always the same as the last time he'd seen her. It was quite startling to see that not only had she blossomed, but that she had done so in such an appealing way. If he'd met her on the street, he'd have thought her a luscious beauty.

He was quick to rise upon her return. Realizing that he was displaying good manners, Mr. Bass joined in, though he normally would not have done so for family. Peter continued to eat. Charlotte thanked her father for standing, and then took her seat. Naturally, she said nothing to Shaun. Testing her, he stared hard at the side of her face, wondering whether any amount of staring would make her look. It did not. She was chatting nonsense with her father and struggling not to look Shaun's way. *Don't do this,* he thought. *You're trying to make it less awkward, but you're making it worse. Come, Charlotte, just be polite.* But his telepathy didn't reach her, and she continued actively to look the other way.

At last, Mr. Bass said, "Well, Charlotte, have you noticed our guest?"

"Oh, uh . . ." Unfortunately, she felt forced to spare him a very tight-faced smile. "Hi."

Shaun's nod was courteous but mercifully brief. He released her quickly from his gaze and tended to his meal. He had seen everything he needed to know. She was hurting.

"Shaun," said Mr. Bass, "tomorrow is Sunday. Would you join us for church in the morning?"

Shaun worried over his chewing a little, then answered, "Certainly."

"We're Congregationalists. I don't know which church you and your father attend."

Shaun used his swallow as an opportunity to mull over his answer. "We, uh . . . we haven't attended church very often since my mother died. But I'm happy to go."

"Oh, Father," Charlotte broke in, "they're Episcopalians, no doubt. Or Unitarians. Nearly all Bostonians are one or the other." That she was trying to impress Shaun with her knowledge of city folk, even she herself wasn't aware.

"Is that so?" asked her father.

Shaun nodded, bringing a napkin to his lips as he chewed. "Yes, Episcopal, but I look forward to visiting your church," he said when he'd swallowed. "I'm sure it will be lovely."

"Well, it will be different for you," said Mr. Bass. "I'm afraid we don't have quite the same flair. It'll be rather a simple service without much in the way of incense and costume. I understand the Episcopal churches in Boston are massive stone buildings with stained glass to the ceiling. I'm afraid we have nothing like that here."

"It'll be fine," he said.

And only Charlotte saw through him. In fact, she saw through him so well that she found the courage to look directly at him. As soon as she did, the bottom fell out of her stomach. Lord, but he was handsome, more so than she'd even remembered. "Dashing" didn't begin to describe it. He looked like a prince, his chiseled face so intelligent, his light brown hair perfectly waved. He was broad in the shoulders, yet so fashionably slender. It made her positively ill. It made her ill because she knew what he was. Not the charming gentleman her parents supposed him to be, but something much worse than even a cad. Her family surely mistook his genteel words as the open-minded sentiments of a very good guest. That's what they were meant to think. But Charlotte knew him too well. She could see the true meaning behind the intellectual glint of his silvery eyes and could hear it in the excruciating carefulness of his words. Their lovely guest, their ideal surrogate son, was nothing but a heathen and an atheist. That's why he didn't care what church he went to. How could her family be so blind? If only they knew him as she did!

"So Charlotte, it's good to see you again. Who is your new beau?"

He hadn't just spoken, had he? Shaun had not just asked her about her new beau. There was no way he would have had the nerve to bring up something like that under these tender circumstances. Why, surely he . . . he didn't care. She could see it in his pleasant smile and his nonchalant posture, the way he brought the fork to his mouth right after asking. He wasn't afraid of her as she was he. He didn't feel awkward. He had no feelings at all! "That's none of your concern," she replied haughtily.

"Charlotte!" Her mother cast her a scolding glance, then hurriedly explained. "I'm sorry, Shaun. She's been courted by a young man named Giles Williams. I apologize for her rudeness."

"Giles Williams?" His incredulous expression held a small taste of amusement.

It wounded her to see him gloating. "Yes," she said proudly, "that's quite right. Giles and I have been together for some time now."

"Oh, that makes sense," he said calmly. "I know you've always adored him."

Charlotte met his eyes hotly. How dare he laugh at her for what she'd been forced to accept. What he himself had forced her to settle for! She leaned into him quite conspicuously, but spoke so deeply and softly that she could not be overheard. "Who are you to criticize my choice?"

He shook his head apologetically, but she could tell he didn't mean it, he didn't feel it. "I didn't mean to criticize," he said, but she could tell he was still laughing inside. And it hurt.

"So Shaun," her father interrupted, "I was so sorry to hear that your mother passed away. How old were you when that happened?"

Charlotte looked at him incredulously. Was this her father's notion of lightening the topic? What was he thinking? Things were getting too tense, so it was time to bring up death?

Fortunately, Shaun was not offended by his host's social inexperience. His reply was admirably graceful, given the emotional import of the topic. "I was twelve. I'm afraid she passed away, a victim of consumption. I used to tell people 'consumption' meant that my father consumed her, but fortunately, I've matured."

This won him a few weak smiles, only because he said it so good-naturedly. Mr. Bass then asked, "It must have been hard to get over that, being so young."

"Oh, I haven't," he replied. "I've never gotten over it."

And there was something about the honesty of that which made even Charlotte pause reverently. This was all she needed. To feel sorry for her worst enemy.

"Charlotte," her mother said, "help me clear these dishes and bring out dessert."

On second thought, that *was* all she needed. To be forced to serve her worst enemy like some kind of a handmaiden. "Yes, Mother."

Shaun watched her move about the room with a heaviness in his heart. He believed his discomfort was awkwardness, the strain of being around her after all that had transpired. But poets knew what it really was. It was the ache of someone who had made a grave error. And was too proud to admit it.

NINETEEN

In truth, Charlotte slept little that night. She just couldn't concentrate on the act of falling unconscious when Shaun's breath was only rooms away. She didn't exactly long for him; he had hurt her too much for that. When she looked at his handsomeness, she felt only pain. When she thought of him lying in the guest room downstairs, she felt only tremendous humiliation. She couldn't believe she had once been so foolish as to bare her breasts to his heathen gaze. That their lips had touched, that his hands had wandered . . . it was all too awful to actively remember. She tucked the images deeply in the back of her mind where they could only spring forth when she closed her eyes and relinquished control to the force of sleep. That is what kept awakening her. She could not simultaneously relax and push the thoughts away.

In the morning, she was late to rise.

"Charlotte, come down here! We are late for church!" Shaun had been there for less than a day, and already Mrs. Bass was losing patience with Charlotte. It was not a good omen. "This is just awful," she told her husband, frantically tying her bonnet. "We can't wait for her. We're late as it is. It doesn't sound as though she's even dressed yet."

"Well, she can follow behind."

"And walk alone? It isn't right for a girl to walk alone

to church. Without the sleigh, she'll be a half hour behind us."

"I'll walk her."

The couple was surprised by Shaun's steadily spoken
offer.

"Oh, no," said Mrs. Bass, "no, we mustn't leave you behind. My husband is right. She can catch up to us."

"No," said Shaun, "I'm happy to do it. I'll enjoy the
walk."

They looked at one another as though each was hoping for permission. They didn't want to embarrass
themselves by being late, didn't want to have Charlotte
walk in alone, and this . . . this was the best solution. As
long as Shaun could assure them they weren't mistreat-
ing a guest. "Are you most certain?" asked Mr. Bass,
"because it is Charlotte's own fault. There's no reason
you should suffer for it."

"No trouble at all," he said with a light nod.

And so it was that Charlotte descended the stairs to a
most disturbing sight in the kitchen that morning.
Shaun was drinking cider—spiked, no doubt, with bour-
bon—and there were no other people, no buffers to
stand between them. "Where is my mother?" she asked
frantically.

"Gone to church."

"But . . . but . . ." Oh dear, she knew she was in terrible
trouble now. She knew she was late, but never dreamed
they would go without her. "But . . . have they all gone?"

"Afraid so."

"Then . . . oh well, then, I must run after them. Good-
bye!"

Shaun caught her by the elbow just as she raced for
her coat. "I'm walking you," he announced.

"Oh no, you really don't have to do that," she said,
shaking her arm to free herself.

"I want to. I want to talk to you."

For that, he got a stare that was calm and deadly. Charlotte suddenly lost interest in being skittishly rid of him, and found she had something she wanted very much to say. She said it in a tone that was deep and slow. "I do not wish to talk to you, Shaun."

"I know," he said casually, ignoring the burn of her blue eyes, "but I really must. Believe me, I didn't intend to have this out. I had no plans for it. But now that I'm here it's become clear to me. We have to speak if we're going to spend even two weeks together. We have to have this conversation."

"No, Shaun. I don't want to talk to you, I don't want to see you, and I will be very happy if you spend your holiday ignoring me, then slip quietly away. That is what I want."

Her determination only further convinced him that he had wounded her brutally and must do something to cause a truce. He said, "We can talk now or we can talk as we walk."

"Neither," she demanded.

But he reached for his coat, which hung on a peg by the back door. "Come," he said, jerking his head at the door, "we'll walk and talk. That way you won't have to look at me."

Charlotte supposed that she did have to go to church, and so she consented. But if he'd meant it as a joke that she wouldn't have to look at him, she was calling his bluff. Her eyes were hidden deep beyond the folds of her scarf and she did not once turn her head as they stepped into the biting wind. "So I suppose I should begin," said Shaun, his fists jammed in his overcoat pockets.

Charlotte did not reply.

"I, uh . . . I should explain why I didn't reply to your letters."

Again, she said nothing.

"You see, I . . . it isn't that I didn't wish any contact with you. It's just that I suspected your plea for friendship was truly a plea for marriage, and I didn't wish to lead you on by accepting. I may have misunderstood, but . . ."

"You used me."

Shaun was surprised to hear her voice, shaking with anger. "Uh . . . no. No, really, Charlotte. That was not my intent. I . . ."

"You used me."

He stopped walking and faced her. "Charlotte, no . . ." He tried to lift her mittened hand, but she yanked it from him.

"Don't touch me. Do you understand that? Don't you ever touch me again. If you didn't want to lead me on, you should never have kissed me or danced with me or left me seductive notes! What you did was unforgivable, so don't you take the moral high ground now."

"No, Charlotte, really. I didn't have any idea you were thinking about marriage until that day when . . ."

"Liar! Yes, you did. You're not so stupid."

He bowed his head, absorbing and accepting her scorn. "Charlotte, I'm sorry. You have to know I cared about you, but . . ."

"But you wished to marry a richer woman? Someone your father would like? You expect me to accept your spinelessness?"

"What are you talking about?" he asked incredulously, "Miss Shepherd? I'm not marrying her. Charlotte, have more faith in me than that." He was beginning to feel a little angry, and Charlotte was glad, for it made him less condescending.

"You're not marrying her? Then what was so bad about me? Why was I such a poor choice?"

"It isn't that."

"Then what?! Why don't you just admit it? You're not

man enough to stand up to your father and marry the woman you want."

"You're half right."

"What?" She was surprised it had been so easy to convince him he was a cad and ought to grovel at her feet. Arguments usually took longer to reach that point.

"You're half right," he said sharply. "Not about the marriage part. I'll marry whomever I want. But about my father, you're right. I feel beaten when I'm around him. He has a way of reminding me . . . that I'm not good enough."

Charlotte squinted at him as though trying to find a speck on his face. "Wait one moment," she said breathily, "wait now. Is that what this is about? You turned me away because I saw your father hit you?"

Shaun turned his head and stared into the wind.

"You're punishing me because *you* are ashamed?" She laughed cruelly at the revelation. "I cannot believe this," she declared. "All of this time, I thought it was marriage with me you didn't want. But in truth, from that day forth, you never wanted to see me again. Not as a lover, not as a friend, not as anything. You thought that if you sent me away, you could erase the memory of the afternoon. You didn't think you were any longer a man in my eyes."

"It isn't a punishment," was all he could say in his own defense. "I'm not punishing you. I . . . I'm just not the man for you, Charlotte. I'm not the one. I'm sorry if you thought I was but . . . trust me. You don't want me for your husband."

"No, Shaun. *You* don't want *me* for a wife. Because you don't want anyone who knows what you suffer."

"Th—that's not true."

"Yes, it is."

"It is not!" He raised his voice and leaned into his words, making Charlotte aware of his size.

"Are you going to hit me?" she asked, lifting her chin in the air.

His teeth were grinding, but he worked hard to shake his head. "No," he said after a strained swallow, "no, I don't hit people, you know that." He tossed both hands in the air. "I don't do that."

"I know," she said, surprising him with a lilt of compassion, "I know it, and I always loved it. Shaun, it wasn't I who thought less of you on that day, it was you. I never wanted a man who throws punches or utters curses. All I ever wanted was you." He looked at her quizzically, clearly moved. Noticing that, she shrugged. "It's a shame you had to ruin it. Too bad."

Shaun watched her move ahead of him down the road, and felt the shame he knew was proper for one in the wake of a woman's righteous scorn. He felt belittled, and was gentleman enough to accept his moment of defeat rather than resist it. Nonetheless, he found himself with very little to say for the rest of the walk, and frequently having to stop himself from thinking up good retorts. She had the right to be angry, he reminded himself; she had the right to lash out. To prolong the argument would be to deny her emotional release. It would be wrong. That's why he didn't prolong the argument, he told himself. That in fact he couldn't have won the argument because she was entirely right and he was entirely wrong was a thought so contrary to the masculine paradigm that even one as reflective as Shaun could not consider it.

Charlotte waited for him at the church steps. Peacham's was a friendly looking church, bright white all the way to its narrow, pointed steeple and weathervane. Tall, clear windows made it look open to the community instead of shut off in pious isolation. "Can't you walk faster?" Charlotte called cockily. "We're already late."

Shaun jogged to the steps and mocked, "Are you sure

you want to walk in with me? I'd guessed you were anxious not to be seen with a cad like me." He tugged at the door handle and gestured her inside.

"On the contrary," she whispered loudly, "church is a place to take pity on the wretched."

"Is it a place to patronize guests, too?"

"Yes, that, too."

"Charming," he said, taking her coat. The carpets inside were bright red, contrasting beautifully with the lily-white walls. Two spiral stairways wrapped to the left and right, both leading to the same place: the sermon upstairs, which they could already hear.

"I wish our pew were at the back," whispered Charlotte, "but the Basses always sit third from the front, on the left. When we get up there, we've got to move as stealthily as possible. We don't want the reverend to pause when he sees us."

Shaun nodded, waiting for her to finish unwrapping and hanging her scarves on pegs. When she was ready, he led her with a gentle hand on the small of her back. Following the wind of the stairs, they arrived. The chapel was beautiful, full of winter light, and warmed by a crackling fire. Nerves that may have betrayed Shaun at the thought of arriving late to a strange service were eased by the sight of cheerfully dressed Vermonters glancing his way with a smile and then politely turning back, pretending they didn't notice his entrance. They followed the red carpet, creeping against the bright white wall before settling in the seats left empty for them. "Sorry," whispered Charlotte, squeezing over in the wooden pew. But her mother turned her head away, pretending to be much too engaged in the reverend's sermon to pay her tardy daughter any heed. Shaun settled beside her and took an elegant pose, staring intently at the reverend as though he were actually listening.

Charlotte glanced over each shoulder and realized . . .

all the young women were looking. They still thought
Shaun was her beau. And they envied her for it. They
were stealing glances at him as though sinfully examining the treasure of another. They were blushing,
whispering, and patting dramatically at their hearts, only
freezing in mid-motion when they thought Charlotte
could see them. Of course, she had never told them of
his rejection. Why should she? They must have thought
Giles was only her "in between visits" beau. What a scandalous life they imagined her to have! It was wonderful.
If only it could all be true. If only Shaun truly were her
beau, and if only he were everything they and she had
once thought he was.

She spied him from the corner of his eye, concentrat-
ing hard on the sermon, his handsome jaw twitching
expressively in thought. Only Charlotte knew what was
really going on in that heathen mind of his. He wasn't
interested in the sermon. He was studying the reverend
like he was a sociological specimen. He was intrigued
by the service only to the extent that it was interesting to
observe religious country folk in their natural habitat.
She could see right through that respectful look on his
face. Why was she the only one who could see what a
wolf he was? How had he managed to charm the entire
town of Peacham, including her own family, without anyone save herself and a barmaid learning the truth of his
wretched nature? And why couldn't she stop caring?

When the sermon was over, Charlotte wished to make
a hasty exit. Many approached the reverend to tell him
how moving he had been, but she just preferred not to
draw attention to her tardy presence. She urged Shaun
out of the pew before it seemed a graceful time to stand.
This won her a mild look of annoyance, but he obliged,
following her to the stairs and down into the coatroom.
There was one good thing about all of the wrathful
words she had spoken, he mused. She was no longer

avoiding him, no longer making his visit any more awkward than it had to be. She seemed able to relax now
that she'd had her say and had maybe even got the better of him. This was good, he thought. He didn't want
her arriving late to supper in a fluster every night. He
didn't want her pining for him, hurt and angry, imagining that he had been her true love when, in fact, no such
thing was the case.

Giles approached them just as they stepped outside.
Shaun recognized him immediately but was startled by
the changes. Giles was his own height now, and rather
striking with his sleek black hair and shiny eyes. Somehow, it shook him to see Charlotte's beau looking so
handsome. Somehow it was easier to imagine her with
an oaf than with someone to whom she might actually be
attracted.

"Oh hello, Giles!" cried Charlotte, wrapping her arms
about his neck. "I'm so glad to see you!"

"Why?" he asked, trying to figure out how to return a
hug. Did he put his hands on her back or on her waist?
By the time he'd decided, it was too late and she had
withdrawn.

"Just because," she said, "just because. No reason. Oh,
you do remember Shaun Matheson, don't you?"

"Yes, he poured punch on me."

"Oh!" Charlotte covered her mouth and giggled delightedly, "oh, that was so silly. We were all so young
then."

"It was only last year."

Charlotte scowled. "Yes, well. It seems a long time.
After all, you and I weren't in love then, were we?"

"Uh . . . no, I guess not." He kept glancing nervously
at Shaun because he was receiving such a cool stare from
his direction. Instinctively, he knew it to be the glare of
a competitor, but he wasn't sure how he was supposed to
react.

"So . . ." said Charlotte, bulging her eyes at him, "Do you, uh . . . have anything special you wanted to . . . to . . . say or . . . give?"

"Huh? Oh! Oh, yes." Giles reached deep in his pocket and withdrew a paper sack full of sweets. "Here. These are for you, Charlotte."

"What? For me? Oh! You shouldn't have!"

Giles was actually rather pleased by her response. He'd never given a gift to anyone outside his family before, and even though he'd been ordered to give this one, he was nonetheless delighted to see the reaction it brought. If they were alone, this would have been the perfect time to kiss her; something she'd never let him do before. "Well, they only cost one penny," he assured her, hoping that would make her stop saying "you shouldn't have."

Charlotte positively glared. "Don't be so modest," she commanded, peering into the little sack. "It's clear you got all of the best candies here. I'm sure they cost nearly a nickel."

"No. They'd been on the shelf a long time and Mrs. Adams was anxious to get rid of them before they got chewy. She said I could have as much of the old stuff as I wanted for a penny. I got more but I ate the rest of it."

It was with much devastation that Charlotte observed Shaun's repressed smile. He was trying hard not to laugh, and even went so far as to gaze off in another direction to hide his amusement. She closed the bag of sweets with a bowed head. "Oh, and, uh . . . wait. There was something I wanted to tell you," said Giles, remembering his list of compliments, "Charlotte, your eyes are . . . your eyes are positively voluptuous today."

She closed them against his stupidity. "Why, thank you," she said stiffly.

"And your . . . your dress is . . . umm . . . very . . . big?"

"Charlotte!" A brightly dressed woman, red and

Christmassy against the white snow, rustled her way to the sullen-faced girl's side. "Charlotte, I hear you're participating in our crafts fair this year."

"Yes," said Charlotte, grateful for the distraction, "yes, I'm bringing some of my watercolors."

"How marvelous!" cried the narrow-faced woman with baby hairs curled tightly to make a fringe round her forehead. "I am anxious for everyone's participation. If it is a success, we shall begin holding Christmas crafts fairs every year. Please ask Sarah whether she might bring something as well."

"She's been doing some lovely quilting," said Charlotte, brimming with pride over her friend. "I'll be sure to ask."

"Wonderful!"

"My father's going to print an article about the crafts fair," said Giles.

"He is?" cried the woman, touching her breast. "That is marvelous!"

"Yes, and he's appointed yours truly to cover the exhibits. I'm going to write an impression of each one."

"Oh! That is just wonderful news," she said. "Surely, the more publicity it gets this year, the more people will attend in the next. Oh, do thank your father for me, Giles. I can't wait to spread the word." She departed quickly, as one set out on doing just that.

Charlotte turned anxiously to Giles. "You're going to be a reporter?" she asked excitedly.

Shaun turned anxiously to Charlotte. "You're going to display your paintings?" he asked excitedly.

"Yes, shush. Giles, is it true?"

"Why, yes," he said proudly, "and I can't wait to get started on the job. I'll be taking a slate and jotting down all my thoughts about the exhibits to be run in the very next edition of *The Green Star*."

"How thrilling!" she cried. "I can't wait to see what you'll write about mine!"

Shaun was still grinning at the thought of Charlotte displaying her art. "I'm very proud of you," he said.

Charlotte tossed her chin in his direction, as though his statement meant nothing to her. "What for?"

"For having the courage," he said. "You're really a beautiful artist. I'm proud of you for showing it off."

"Thank you, sir," she said stiffly, then returned her attention sharply to Giles. "So how long will your article be?"

"As long as I want to make it," he said. "My father says if I can do a good job, he'll trust me with more assignments for the paper."

"Will you also be displaying art?" asked Shaun.

"Oh, no," said Giles proudly, "my contribution will be the article."

"I see. Well, just remember then that your intention was to contribute. Arsonists are rarely welcome at a carpenter's fair."

"I don't know what you mean," he said confusedly. "I . . . I plan to be honest, that's all."

"Well, good. That's very good. Just remember the first rule of honesty—it's always selective. There's rarely enough time to tell the whole truth."

"Shaun!" Charlotte snapped angrily. "What are you ranting about? Giles is going to do a wonderful job, and you are only jealous that you aren't writing for the newspaper. Stop being so patronizing." She smiled flirtatiously at her beau. "Isn't that right, Giles?"

"Of course it is! I'm going to be fabulous!"

"Shall we go?" Mrs. Bass's voice startled the three of them. The stern set of her fixed jaw told them she had done all the socializing she felt required to do and was ready to return to work, which meant home.

"Yes," said Charlotte. "Uh . . . Giles, thank you again

for . . ." She looked down at her bag of sweets. "Well . . . just thank you anyway."

He puckered up for a kiss so wincingly, she gave him her cheek. "Yes, yes, I'll see you soon."

"Don't forget our agreement!" he called to her turned back.

Again, she winced and retorted, "Don't *you* forget our agreement!" letting him know that the stale candies had not quite upheld his half of the bargain.

The Bass family rode home in the sleigh, where Charlotte unfortunately found herself beside Peter. About two minutes into the ride, he punched her in the ribs. "Got you!" he laughed.

"Ouch! Aren't you getting old for that?"

He did it again. "Got you."

"Mama, do tell Peter to stop punching me."

"Try not to do that, dear."

He did it again, and this time, Charlotte hit him right back.

"Charlotte!" cried both parents. "What is the matter with you?!"

"I'm sorry."

The parents cast very worried glances at one another as though to ask what they were going to do with their unladylike daughter. And Shaun sighed wearily, his heart ready to break all over again. Could he spend one day around Charlotte without wishing to whisk her away and defend her? It didn't seem so. It seemed that as long as they both lived, he was going to be plagued by the feelings that had gotten him into trouble the first time. And it was on that ride home that he realized that his trouble wasn't in convincing Charlotte why he'd rejected her. His trouble was in explaining it to himself.

He stole a glance at the lovely young woman who always made him feel at home, even when she was trying not to. Such lovely blue eyes she had, such dark walnut hair. Her face was such a warm color of cream. He would have loved to take her in his arms, to keep her in his bed and let no one mistreat her again. But he believed he didn't love her. Really, he wasn't sure what was happening inside his twisted heart, but he did plan to give it more thought.

Until Giles came to call that evening . . .

TWENTY

The Bass home was cheerily decked for the holiday. All afternoon Charlotte strung berries on beads and shaped gingerbread into little men while her mother baked spice cake and warmed cider, and her father and Shaun hauled in a tree. "Don't let it brush the ceiling!" cried Margaret. "The needles are getting everywhere. Oh, Charlotte, can you help me with the sweeping?"

"After one more gingerbread man. Almost done."

"Where are the Christmas candles? Charlotte, did you find the candles to put on the tree?"

"In the attic, Mother."

"Oh, oh, oh." She tossed her head frantically about, wishing she weren't carrying a platter in each hand. "Peter!" she cried, "could you get the candles for the tree?"

"I'm on holiday!"

"Oh, all right. Charlotte, then. When you're finished. And hunt for my angel! The one with the porcelain face. I can't believe I've misplaced her again—she is priceless."

There was a knock at the door. "Oh, for heaven's sake!"

"I'll get it," said Mr. Bass, "you just stay on course."

"Thank you, dear." She kissed the air in his direction before hurrying off to the kitchen.

Charlotte was humming and shaping dough, thankful

she'd been allowed to conduct the task in the parlor rather than the dreary, smoky kitchen. She was feeling rather in the Christmas spirit, imagining that she might even join the carolers Christmas Eve and show off her strong singing voice. She was wondering what gifts she might get this year and hoping there'd be some surprises. But the murmuring at the front door interrupted her festive train of thought. She was quite sure she heard someone say, "I must speak to you, Mr. Bass," in rather a shaky, nervous voice.

She sprang to her feet, wiped both hands on her apron, and skipped to the door. There, dusted with snow that clung to his black hair and speckled his overcoat was Giles. "Giles?!" she cried, rather wishing she hadn't been so curious. "What are you doing here?"

"I uh . . . I came to talk to your father," he said.

"What about?" Her squint was something between curious and accusing.

"I uh . . . well, actually," he said, straightening up, "actually, I think you're supposed to be here, too."

"Of course I am, I live here. But what are you doing?"

"Well," said Mr. Bass, patting the young man on the back, wearing a sparkle in his eye, "let's just bring you into the parlor and find out, eh?" He winked at Charlotte, and did not notice her wide-eyed horror.

Mrs. Bass was no more delighted to see him than was Charlotte. Her reasons were different, however. He was another person to wait on, another concern before the big holiday in ten days' time. "May I get you some eggnog?" she asked brusquely.

"Yes, thank you!" he cried, giving the answer she did not want to hear. With stiff politeness she moved to the kitchen in compliance to her cheerless offer.

The men settled themselves on the couch. Even Peter joined in, as he was beginning to complain of boredom and desperately needed a distraction. The only man who remained standing was Shaun, who all but hid in the corner of the room, flexing his jaw. "So what may I do for you this evening?" asked Mr. Bass, grinning from ear to ear.

"Well, I'd like to ask you a question," said Giles, thanking Margaret for a hearty cup of nog.

"And that question is?"

Charlotte was shouting loudly inside her head. *No, no, no, no, no!*

"I'd like to know whether umm . . . well, whether I can marry Charlotte."

She clenched her teeth and tried to catch his eye, but he did not look at her. If she could have brought herself to it, she would have jumped up and down and hollered, "Not now! Not now! Later! Later! I never said I'd marry you now!" But instead, her eyes just bulged from frustration.

"Well, now!" cried her father delightedly, "good for you, son. I . . . I imagine that's a question you'll have to ask Charlotte, though."

Charlotte began mouthing, "Say no, say no, say no." But her father could not discern her lip movement, and soon, it was too late. Everyone in the room had turned to see her reply.

It was interesting to her to see the different expressions. Her father looked cheerful, as though in every way expecting this to be the most thrilling moment of her life. How little he knew of his own children! Her mother looked worried—apparently, she knew her children much better. Her brother seemed in awe, as though it were unfathomable that someone had proposed to Charlotte, as though he had just gained a new respect for her. Giles had a little snicker on his face, for he knew well that her offer to "think about" marrying him had not been made with such a sudden and public proposal in mind. And then there was Shaun. His expression was unreadable. Not blank exactly, but stoic. He was hiding his thoughts just as surely as he hid his body in the shadow of the room. He was so handsome, by God. But never had he looked so untouchable, so far out of her reach as he did while standing in that corner.

She couldn't have him. And it hurt. And maybe it was the hurt that made her do it, or maybe it was spite. But she lifted her chin high in the air as though she had never been so pleased by anything in her life. She looked directly at Shaun, but lent her hand to Giles and said, "Why, of course. I'd be delighted."

And suddenly, Shaun didn't look so stoic.

Soon after their disturbing guest had gone, Charlotte found herself face-to-face with a biting-eyed Shaun, who pierced her with his narrow, silvery gaze over a chessboard. "It was unkind of you to take my pawn," she declared haughtily. "For that, you shall have to pay with your bishop."

Shaun did not even look at the pieces. He was cutting her with the intensity of his stare. "You're not going to marry him," he said as though he'd found the answer in the back of her eyes.

"Yes, I am. Oh, drat. May I take back that move? I put my queen in danger."

He barely shrugged in reply. He wanted to say more, he wanted to interrogate her, to convince her of the conclusion he had reached, but Mrs. Bass walked in and offered to refill his glass. "Will you need more spirit in there?" she asked.

He tasted his cider and said, "Yes, thank you."

She hastily departed, for she had long forgiven Shaun for having such a taste for strong drink. The moment she was gone, he said, "You hate him. You've always hated him," then took her rook.

"I should warn you no one ever beats me at this game," she declared.

Shaun wasn't listening. He was still staring, leaning into his thigh, watching her like a criminal. "The moment I leave, you're going to cancel the betrothal."

"Oh, this is about you, is it? How self-confident. Check."

He made a swift motion to get out of check then asked, "How can you . . ." Mrs. Bass brought him a stronger drink for which he pleasantly thanked her. But the moment she was gone, he remembered where he was in mid-sentence. "How can you forgive him for the way he's treated you?"

"We were children," she said, for it was her practiced answer. "It would be silly to bear a grudge."

Shaun glanced at the board just long enough to move his queen and declare, "Checkmate. But why?" he asked. "Why would you have any interest in someone who's done so little to charm you?"

"It is not checkmate," she said, wiggling her ivory knight. "I can still move this."

He grunted, a little surprised that she was besting him, even as distracted as he was. "You didn't answer my question," he said.

"I don't have to answer your question."

He attacked her with a piercing gaze, but found her sparkling eyes to be just as fixed in their own stubborn way.

"How is it any concern of yours?" she went on. "You're not my brother or even . . . my friend," she added, nudging him to remember how he'd not returned even her overture at a simple platonic friendship.

"I'm a friend," he objected.

"Oh, really? When did that occur?"

"When I let you berate me," he said, lifting a corner of

his mouth. "When you take a scolding gracefully, particularly an unjust one, that makes you a friend."

"Well, my, we should have had a party. What have I done to deserve your gracing me with your holy friendship?"

"Don't be nasty," he warned, swiping another pawn. "I told you I want to make peace with you."

"Well, insulting my choice of fiancés is a good start. Besides," she said, letting down her hair, pretending that it needed to be fixed and reclasped, just so he could get a good look at it. "How do you know so much about Giles? You might be surprised just how romantic he can be."

"You wrote in your letter that you laughed when he tried to court you. That's how romantic you think he is."

"Oh, you actually read my letters, did you?"

"Of course. Check."

"Well, at least I cost you some money, then."

"That's a cheerful way to look at it," he said with a little smile.

"Can you think of a cheerful way to look at this?" she asked, trapping him in a checkmate.

He studied the move carefully, quite amazed that she could outmatch him. "Yes," he said at last, having made certain that the mate was legitimate. "Now that our game is over, you can show me your paintings. The ones you're showing at the fair."

Charlotte blushed naturally. "You really want to see them?"

It was a silly question. Of course, he nodded.

"All right then," she said, rising to her feet, "but I'll have to warn you. I drew some of them after having been painfully rejected by an unworthy cad. A few of them are morbid."

"Just so long as they're not of me hanging from a tree," he said, eagerly abandoning his chair.

"Oh, you know I'm much more subtle than that."

"I simply have a ring mark around my neck?"

"You'll see," she teased him, but she lost her smile when she added, "come." For now, she was inviting him to her sacred lair, where absolutely no jesting was permitted.

Shaun followed diligently behind to a place he had not been since the year before, the attic. Somehow, he expected it to look exactly as it had the last time he'd visited: dark and romantic, heavy with the scent of wood, soft with the spirit of a lovely woman, and quaint with the drifting snow framed by the frosty, multipaned windows. He was startled by the change. Charlotte's paintings were everywhere—leaning against walls, propped up on easels. They made the attic seem more alive, more cluttered with activity. A piece of him wished away the change, simply because it was a change. But a stronger side of him was simply enchanted by the paintings and welcomed their thoughtful presence.

"Color gives your work a whole new dimension," he said, kneeling by a loud red river.

"I have you to thank for that," she admitted softly.

"No. No, I gave you those paints because I wanted to see what you could do with them. It was entirely selfish." He studied the drawing with reverence, entranced by the complex color. It had looked red at first glance, but clearly, she had mixed some brown in there to achieve that dark, deeper-than-blood color. "Is it a river of blood?" he asked.

"I don't know," she said. "Is it?" She was wringing her hands awkwardly, once again uncomfortable about having someone examine her soul so carefully.

"Mmmm, maybe not," he said, squinting hard. "It's more likely about anger, I think." Another painting caught his eye. "My God," he said, standing up only to kneel down a moment later. "This is fabulous. When did you do this one?" His hand reached out to touch a drawing of a beautiful woman, or half of one. She was drawn largely, so that only a portion of her fit on the canvas. "What a beautiful statement. Too large to capture in a drawing. Too much to say and not enough time or space in one lifetime to say it. Charlotte, this is the best drawing you've ever done. And you know that says a great deal."

She was blushing, bowing her head, and trying not to grin. "Do you think I should show it at the fair?"

"Absolutely. How many are you allowed to bring?"

"Nobody said. But I think I shall bring only two this time. Perhaps if it goes well, I'll bring more the next."

"Well, I don't know how you're going to choose only two," he said. "This attic holds more treasures than the average art gallery."

"Stop it," she laughed nervously, crossing her arms round her middle. "You're going to make me vain."

"If I can do that, I'll really have achieved something. I've never known you to be vain, Charlotte."

"Stop it," she said again, this time more stoically. "Shaun, you mustn't be so kind to me."

"Why not?" But as soon as he asked, he immediately remembered the answer. She wanted him to be more than a friend. Too much kindness felt like flirtation to her. If only he could show her that just because they weren't lovers didn't mean he couldn't be kind. "Let me help you get ready for the fair," he suggested before she'd thought up a response to his question.

"Oh, I . . . no, no. You don't have to do that."

"Please," he said, "I love your work. Let me at least carry the paintings for you and stand with you so you'll have someone to talk to while people browse."

"Well," she hadn't wanted to ask this but . . . "there is one thing, actually. I was thinking that it would be a much nicer presentation if the paintings were framed.

But I don't have any idea how to build a frame, particularly not before next Saturday, and . . ."

"I'd love to."

Charlotte raised her eyebrows hopefully. "Really?"

"I'd love to."

Charlotte bit her lip and bounced up on her heels. This was going to be the grandest artistic debut ever! Everyone would be sorry for how they'd ridiculed her paintings in the past. Just wait until they saw her drawings now, all in full color and packed into frames. She had absolutely no doubt. She was going to have the last laugh after all! And over something much more dear to her heart than the mere acquisition of a city beau.

TWENTY-ONE

All week, Shaun whittled at wood, carving designs into pale birch and rosy cherry wood. He did it with such care, there could be no doubt that he held the task sacred. On the day of the art fair, when the frames were finally ready, Charlotte was moved beyond words by the sight of them. They had been carved not with Shaun's ego in mind, but with her own paintings in mind. It was apparent in the way they fit so snugly both in form and in color. Even the wavy lines drawn in the wood were understated, calling for the eye to ignore them as pleasant background and move immediately to the vibrant drawings they embraced.

"Those are lovely," said Mrs. Bass, knocking on the wood. "When do we get to see the paintings?"

"Not until the art show," said Charlotte saucily. "No one can look until it's time. No exceptions!" Wiping perspiration from her brow, she raced up the stairs, realizing she'd forgotten the scarf she planned to wear.

Shaun grinned at Mrs. Bass. "She's a tad nervous," he explained. "It's a big day for her."

"Well, I don't know what she's got to be nervous about. It's only a little community fair."

"It's important to Charlotte," he said. "It's been a long time since she's opened up and trusted people to look at her art."

"Sounds a bit vain to me," she murmured, squeezing

on her tiny gloves, "Charlotte! We've got to go! Why does that young woman have so much trouble being on time?" she asked Shaun, as he seemed to be the expert on Charlotte this afternoon.

"I don't know," he said. But in his mind, he mused, *Maybe she's sad. Maybe sadness inhibits motion. Maybe she's been sad for a long time.*

"Charlotte!"

"I'm coming, I'm coming." She ran down the stairs so quickly that she found herself perspiring again. "Oh, Mama, how do I look?"

"You look late!"

"Really, Mama, please. How do I really look?"

"Like a young woman who is taking a crafts fair just a bit too seriously. Now, come."

Shaun gave Charlotte's elbow a squeeze of reassurance. "You look beautiful," he whispered so near to her ear that it gave her goose bumps. He smelled nice, as though he were wearing some sort of spice.

"Thank you," she said, flushing a bit. "Do you like the white dress? I got it for my birthday and saved it for this. I thought it would go well next to the red painting if I should stand beside it."

"I agree," he whispered.

"Are you coming?!"

"Yes, Mama!" Charlotte searched Shaun's eyes for reassurance and nodded when she got it. She was ready to face the day, ready to come out of hiding. It would be the grandest day ever.

The church was packed. Nearly all the children in and around town had been forced by their parents to make and bring something to the fair, to show the rest of Peacham how very prodigious they were. There were an awful lot of child prodigies in that town, as there seem to be in most. Adults, both young and old, also brought crafts. The women, for the most part, brought needlework and quilts while many men brought woodworking. This reflected not so much a disparity in talents as the desire to incorporate the fair into something they had to do in their daily lives anyhow. Charlotte didn't know whether to be pleased by the large crowd, much of which had come from Barnet and even the metropolis of St. Johnsbury, or whether to wish her own work might not be at such risk of being ignored in the shuffle. It was difficult even to find a place to set up.

Fortunately, Shaun, having noted this problem the moment they'd walked in vanished quickly in search of an empty wall in a visible spot. So the moment it entered Charlotte's mind, he called out, "Charlotte!" with a wave of his arm.

Charlotte sighed her relief. "Thank you," she said, carrying her veiled painting with some effort.

"Here, let me get that for you."

"No, no, I can manage," she said, though too late, for he had already relieved her of the burden. She turned the other way as he unmasked the paintings and leaned them against the wall. She feigned disinterest. "I wonder where Sarah is. I would've thought she'd be here by now. Wonder where my mother went. Where's Peter?"

"There," he said, "they look perfect."

Charlotte had to steal a glance, and when she did, she saw her paintings, bright and passionate against the snowy white wall. A big grin crossed her face. They *did* look perfect! They were beautiful! And they were hers. Just then, the fair's director grabbed her by the hand and exclaimed, "Charlotte Bass! Thank you so much for coming!"

Charlotte was giddy. "Oh, Mrs. Fishman, I'm just delighted to be here."

"Well, you look lovely!" she cried, examining Charlotte from head to toe, "You look so lovely in white." It was true that there was little more striking on a blue-eyed brunette than a bright, crisp white. Charlotte looked and felt fabulous.

"Thank you," she said.

"And where are your paintings? Are they . . . oh . . . oh . . . hmmm." She spotted them and nodded rhythmically, straining to show appreciation. "I see. Well, thank you so much for your contribution! It is just wonderful to have you here."

"It seems the fair is a great success," said Charlotte, try-ing to hide the hurt of Mrs. Fishman's clear dislike of her work.

"Oh, yes!" she cried, "Yes, it is. Oh, I'm just so de-lighted. Well, I have a thousand people to greet, so please make yourself at home and enjoy the fair. There are brownies on the buffet if you'd like a treat."

"Thank you." But the minute she'd departed, Char-lotte turned to Shaun. "Let's go home. Cover the paintings, let's go. I can't stay here, I just can't. Quickly!"

"Charlotte," he said, calming her with a squeeze of her arm, "Charlotte, we're not going anywhere. You've pre-pared for this for months, and we're not going anywhere. Just sit. I'll get you a chair."

"Oh no, I'm too anxious to sit."

"Are you sure?"

"Yes. No sitting. I just couldn't. Oh, Shaun," she pleaded, "this is horrible. Did you see that woman's re-action?"

"Charlotte," he said soothingly, "listen to me. Are you listening?" He raised his eyebrows expectantly, but could tell she was still too scattered to really pay heed. "Char-lotte," he repeated, "are you really listening now?"

She forced herself to stop bouncing and fretting long enough to look him steadily in the eye. "Yes," she said.

"Good. Now hear what I say. All art is good in the eyes

of the right person. And all art is bad in the eyes of the wrong person."

She was already shaking her head in resistance. "If only I could believe you," she squealed. "You're so encouraging. If only I could believe half of what you say sometimes, I'm sure I would never be anxious again."

Just then, a pair of finely dressed women, strangers from out of town, came to gaze upon Charlotte's paintings. "Oh, my," said one softly to the other so Charlotte could not hear. "This is startling. How beautiful."

"Do you think?" whispered the other. "I have to say I don't care for it at all."

"How could that be? Just look at the raging river, flowing so rapidly that it is not tranquil enough for blue. The artist made it red. And just look at the vibrant sun behind it. It positively gives me chills."

"Mmm." The other tapped her chin disappointedly. "I really disagree. It's not very pretty, not very elegant. It makes me feel rather . . . hostile. I don't think I should like to have it hanging in my parlor."

"Oh, I would like it in mine. It would make the room come to life. Daily life can be so drab, it would serve as a reminder of passion."

"Mmm, not I. I just don't see the appeal, though I do like this other one. The partial portrait of the young woman. Yes, yes, I do."

"Oh, no, you couldn't," the other laughed. "Oh, no. The river is much more vibrant. Perhaps if the entire woman had been drawn, I would have liked it, but as it is, I cannot even see the full expression on her face for the way it's been cut off. Oh, no, I don't think it nearly equals the other."

"How wrong you are! Just look at the blush of the woman's cheek and the deep green of her one eye. It reminds me of my sister at a younger age. And she was always so much taller than I, so much more sophisticated and grown up, I often felt as though she loomed larger than life and I could not equal her."

"Mmm, no. I think that drawing is simply silly. The river, for me."

A gentleman in overalls casually strode by, overhearing just a fraction of their chatter. "I don't believe I care for either of them," he said, then moved along. The women rolled their eyes at him.

"Are you the artist?" asked one, noticing Charlotte for the first time.

Charlotte nodded, though she considered denying it.

"Lovely," she said, "absolutely lovely. And don't you just match the paintings standing there in your white dress! How darling."

"I agree," said the other.

Charlotte absolutely beamed. "Really? You really like them?"

"But of course! You are a very talented young woman."

Charlotte looked at Shaun as though to say, "I told you so," but then she remembered that it was he who had told *her* so. And that rather spoiled the moment. "Why, why, thank you," she said bashfully to the women.

The rest of the afternoon was very much the same. Her mother remained tight-lipped about both paintings while her father was really drawn to the red river. Sarah liked only the portrait of the woman, and Kevin liked them both. Charlotte began to understand something very important about being an artist—that she needn't fear the showing of her work, for they were not questions seeking an answer. There were no answers in art, only feelings. And that is when she decided beyond all doubt that she would be a painter for so long as she lived. "Oh, Shaun," she said, "if it hadn't been for you, I would never have done this."

"Really?"

"But of course! If you hadn't seen my charcoals and

loved them so, I would never have thought it possible for someone to like my work. I would never have shown a drawing again."

He nodded his thanks, for it meant the world to him.

"Do you realize," she said, "all of my worry turned out to be for naught? Not one single, solitary thing has gone wrong all day!"

The next morning, on the third page of *The Green Star* were four giant sketches of Giles. In one, he was thinking with a feather pen in hand, in another he was laughing, in another he was looking very puzzled, and in the fourth, he was posing stoically.

GILES WILLIAMS, MAN ABOUT TOWN
PEACHAM'S CRAFTS FAIR

Following is my report of the artistic endeavors of my neighbors as seen at Peacham's first crafts fair. (As it turns out, I am using the word "artistic" rather loosely.)

Shall I begin with the good news? There is so little of it that it seems prudent to get it out of the way.

Jacob Kalen makes a very reasonable chair. It is sturdy, and what it lacks in originality, it makes up for in strength. A little more work could have gone into the intricacies of detail, but I suspect, given his girth, he was too fatigued after the building to attend to subtleties. A little sweat reaps rich rewards, Mr. Kalen. Chop, chop!

Mrs. Pruitt weaves an excellent rug. However, even I was able to notice that blue does not blend well with orange. Perhaps at her ripe age of 85, she is losing her eyesight! Please do us all a favor, Mrs. Pruitt, and retire from your weaving before the colors blind us all.

Little Melissa Young did quite an admirable thing by

attending our little gathering. I wanted so very much to like her drawings that I went into the viewing with high expectations. Unfortunately, they were not fulfilled, and it seems this child is behind the schedule of even a normal eight-year-old. Perhaps her mother should tell her that the tops of trees are not perfectly circular.

Mrs. Shiloh was attempting to sell her silken bouquets, her husband having lost his job. Yes, you heard correctly. Sell them! I suggest that Mr. Shiloh find a new occupation as quickly as possible before his talentless wife drives the whole family into starvation. If you should see a poorly dressed woman carrying a mangy, scrawny bouquet of poorly cut silken flowers coming your way, I recommend you run!

Sarah Brown had an interesting display of needlework, if by "interesting" I mean horrid! There were so many errors in the stitching that I wonder whether she was awake while in the act of creation. The frightening thing is that she probably was.

There are so many others on whose work I'd like to comment. I apologize if I skipped any exhibits, but I shall reach you all next time, I promise! It was necessary, however, that I leave ample room for discussion of the many atrocities contained in the "artwork" of Charlotte Bass.

Where to begin? Oh, here is a good place. She drew a river in the wrong color! No, this is not a jest. And it only gets worse from there. Not only does this "artist" think that rivers run red, but apparently she doesn't believe in purchasing proper art supplies. During her painting of a young woman, which started off respectably, she ran out of space and could not finish! Not only was this partial painting an insult to the viewing public but a terrible waste of this reporter's time. I could have been busy looking at paintings of entire women! The errors do not end there, however. The violent appearance of the river produced a positively infuriating effect which I could not shake for hours afterward. Perhaps this amateur has never heard that paintings are meant to be beautiful. I certainly would never put such a thing in my parlor, nor would anyone else, I daresay. My recommendation, given the myriad errors in these works, is to burn them quickly before anyone else has to suffer what I did in the viewing.

Hope to see you all at the next crafts fair! I'll be there with my pen.

The quivering-lipped Charlotte had only one thing to say about this. "Giles!" she cried. *"You* are a dead man!!!"

TWENTY-TWO

A nasty winter storm was brewing. The sky was thick with swirls of misty white. No doubt there would be a blizzard and no one in her right mind would choose the present to flee from the warm fires of home. But Charlotte was not in her right mind. Her thoughts were murderous, and the threatening, strong winds seemed only appropriate to her mood. She did not fear them, but sympathized with their rage. It was a long walk into town, but it took less time at the speed of a sprinter. Charlotte was running so hard that she didn't notice when the snowflakes began to fall on her eyelashes. Yet, she did not lose her breath nor did she perspire. She was too focused to remember that running brings exhaustion.

When she reached the printer's she broke open the door without so much as knocking. "Oh, hello," grinned Giles. "Say, Charlotte, did you read my article? Did you think it was well written?"

"You pretentious, self-absorbed bastard!" she screamed, her eyes no more than slits within her purple face.

Giles glanced over each shoulder. "Who? Me?"

"Yes, you!" She rolled up the newspaper and began beating him with it.

"Hey, stop that! Stop that! Are you crazy? I thought you'd be happy!"

Charlotte stopped swatting and glared at him. "You thought I'd be *what?*"

"Happy," he said, straightening up and brushing off. "After people see how insightful I am, they're going to flock to my column. Then, when you're my bride, people will ask, 'Aren't you the wife of that wonderful art critic?'"

"What about my career!" she screamed.

"Well, Charlotte, I thought we could be a team. With your being such a terrible painter, you'll give me ample material for my column, and together, with your help, I'll be greatly successful."

"Giles, I have always known that you are mean. But this time, you have gone too far."

"Oh, come Charlotte. It isn't so bad as that. Look, give me that paper. Let me show you some places where I was clever."

"There were no places where you were clever, Giles! In all of the places, you were a weasel."

"Hey!" he shouted, "I worked very hard on that article and I don't appreciate your waltzing in here and belittling it."

"Oh, dear God, will you listen to yourself?"

"Charlotte, you don't understand my new career."

"New career?"

"Shush! Now you listen to me. What I'm doing here is a public service."

"A public service?"

"Yes! I help artists by informing them of their shortcomings, and I help the public, too. I have to make sure that they don't suffer as I did."

Charlotte was trying to determine something, and finally just asked it. "Are you stupid?"

"You're going to bring *that* up, are you?"

"Oh, my word. To think I was going to marry you."

"What? You're not?"

"Good-bye, Giles," she said, reaching for the door handle, even though the snow had began to pour down heavily.

"What? You're not leaving me. Charlotte, you can't be serious. How can you take this so personally? I find it most unprofessional."

"It's not personal, Giles. My leaving you is a public service."

"A public service?"

"Yes. I have to make sure you don't breed!"

She ripped open the door and fled into the blinding snow. Giles nearly chased after her before catching a sense of how cold it was out there. He crossed his arms and shivered. "You'll be back!" he called, "you'll be back. You'll never get anyone else to court you! You mark my words, Charlotte. No one else would ever have you." But she was still running. Frantically, he called, "Charlotte! If you don't get back here right this instant, I'm going to . . . well, I'll call off the engagement! That's right! I mean it. Very well, just keep running. Give it some more thought. You'll be back!"

But Charlotte would not be back. She would not be back to the printer's shop or even back home. For within minutes, she was quite lost in the blizzard, and within hours, she was on the brink of collapse.

TWENTY-THREE

Shaun was helping Mr. Bass in the barn when the blizzard struck. They knew it was coming and had tied a rope from the barn door to the house to help them find their way back, just in case. It turned out to be a fortunate thing they'd been so cautious, for the blizzard came like a blinding ball of white, cloaking the very air before their eyes. As their hands glided along their guide, leading them to the house, they found themselves laughing in snow, for the wind was so strong it was almost funny to someone rather nervous. By the time they reached the back door, their shoulders were heavy with the precipitation that had collected there. They brushed it off, but it replaced itself so quickly, they could not help splattering snow all over the kitchen floor. They apologized profusely to Mrs. Bass, both of them knowing well what a sin it was to dirty the kitchen. But rather than receiving a scolding, they received a most unexpected expression. Margaret looked blank, wide-eyed and pale. It was an expression completely uncharacteristic of her. Before they could ask why she looked like a frightened statue, she whispered in a voice exactly like a ghost's, "Charlotte's gone."

It took them both a moment to absorb the shock. It was Mr. Bass who was first able to reply. "When? I thought she was sleeping upstairs."

"No. Sarah came this morning and brought her the

paper. Look what it said." She handed it to her husband, who shook his head sadly as he read.

"May I see that?" asked Shaun. He tore it from Mr. Bass's hand a little rougher than he ought. He read it quickly, then threw it on the counter with a snap and a curse. "That son of a bitch."

Mrs. Bass gasped.

"I'm sorry," he said, "please forgive my language. Excuse me. I'm going to look for Charlotte."

"Son, no!" called Mr. Bass. And it was the fact that he used the word "son" that caused Shaun to turn. "You can't go out there," said Mr. Bass. "We'll look. We'll all look. But we have to wait at least till the worst of it's over."

"We don't know when that will be," said Shaun determinedly.

"Well," he sighed shakily, "if it doesn't let up soon, then I agree with you. We'll have to risk it. But the fact is that in this weather we won't be likely to find her, and we'll be very likely to lose ourselves. We should at least wait a tad, just to make sure it doesn't improve."

"And for all we know," added Mrs. Bass urgently, "she could have made it to her destination. She might be safe and snug somewhere."

Shaun looked falsely pensive for a moment, as though he were considering the wait. Then he announced, "Sorry. I can't risk it," and pushed past them both.

"Shaun!" Mrs. Bass cried frantically, "Shaun, no! You'll never find her!" But the gust of wind and the avalanche of snow that dropped from the door the moment he opened it blew her back, and she had to protect herself by retreating.

"Shaun!" Mr. Bass, too, was eager to retrieve him until he felt the powerful wind doubling him over and saw that Shaun was already lost to his eyes. "Shaun!!! Shaun, you come back here!!" But no matter how long he called, he got no reply. The silent treatment had always been Shaun's most aggravating weapon.

"Oh, God," Margaret wept into her husband's shoulder, now that no one else could see. "Oh, God, we're going to lose them both."

"No, we won't," he said emptily, for he had no reason to be sure, "The storm will let up soon."

"Oh, God, George. Not both of them, not both. My only daughter and . . ."

"I know," he said, "I like that boy, too. I know."

Shaun had a hard time telling which direction he was heading. He could see nothing but white. He tried to reach a tree so he could slice into it and mark his path home, and so he could hold on against the wind. But would Charlotte have headed into the woods? Not likely. Likely, she would have headed to town, to do what any sensible person would do—strangle Giles. But had she made it there? His plan was to check the path between home and the print shop, hoping that if she had gotten lost and strayed from it, she did not stray far. But where was the road? If he could just find a tree, he would know that he was on the edge of the forest, and he could follow the edge around to the road. But it had been only a few minutes, and he was already so cold that his gloves and boots had grown useless. It was as though he were standing barefoot in the snow, as though his hands were naked in the wind. Even when he reached a tree and aptly made his mark in it, it did not stop him from losing hope. He felt too cold to go on. He couldn't see six inches in front of himself, nor hear much over the howling wind. It was ridiculous. He was risking his life for nothing. He would never find her.

But when he tried to sit with that thought, he found he could not. Never find her. Never find her. He couldn't live with it. He couldn't go back without her. No! He shouted her name, pushing himself onward, blindly into the white cloud that had seemingly encompassed the world. He kept shouting her name even though snow filled his mouth, and he kept running even though he couldn't feel his feet and didn't know where he was going. "Charlotte! Charlotte! Charlotte!" He said it on every exhalation. But though his deep voice was loud and expressive with desperation, it could not have traveled far across the howling winds. He didn't care. He was going to find her. And he was going to keep running. Even if he died along the way, he would keep running through death. He would find her before the angels snatched him away. She would hear him and she would reply and he would find her. And there was no other option. It would be so. It was so already. He had made it so with the strength of his conviction, with the force of his mind. "Charlotte!!!"

He stopped running to catch his freezing breath and clutch the cramp in his side. "Charlotte!" he called, even in near collapse. "Damn you, Charlotte! Damn you, do you hear me?!" He was breathing so hard, it was hard to keep shouting, but he did. "Char—"

And then he heard it. It was a feminine voice. He lifted an eyebrow as he waited for it to sound again. Could all that nonsense he'd been thinking in his desperation about willing it with his mind actually be true? "Charlotte?!" he called again.

He wasn't sure that time. It was softer and might have merely been the wind. But he caught its direction and raced to it, marking trees along his way. "Charlotte!" he called.

There was no answer so he kept running.

"Charlotte!"

This time, he heard a weak whimper from very nearby, and raced around a tree to find a snowy mound of scarves huddled in a ball. "Oh, my God." He took her in his arms and squeezed. "Charlotte. Charlotte." He opened the snowy scarves to get a glimpse at her face, and was so relieved to see that it really was she, he felt compelled to weep. "Charlotte."

She was bright red and trembling badly. Icicles had formed on her lashes and brows. "I got caught in the blizzard," she whispered weakly.

"You don't say." He tried to smile, but it didn't work. He was nearly crying.

"I . . . I tried to make it to the Mastersons' old barn. But I got lost."

"Where is it?" he asked urgently.

"I . . . I don't know," she said, "it's north from the road, but I lost my sense of direction. I don't know which way it is now. I wound up just stopping because I couldn't keep walking in circles. I was so cold."

"I just came from the road," he said. "North is this way. Let's try to make it to that barn."

Charlotte was shaking so fiercely it seemed she could move little more than it took to cross her arms and chatter her teeth. He realized he'd have to carry her and apologized for doing it. "I'm going to have to take you over my shoulder," he said. "Is that all right?"

She nodded as best she could, then gasped when he followed through. It always surprised her how strong he was. And hanging upside down was rather unpleasant. But she closed her eyes and tried to be grateful that she'd been found and that he seemed to know where he was going. It seemed almost a miracle, but a hazy, dreamy one, for she was getting awfully sleepy.

Shaun found the barn. The moment he saw the color red, his pace miraculously hastened. He suddenly had a goal, something to run toward. He put Charlotte down in the snow and slid the giant barn door sideways, revealing a giant room with a domed ceiling and soft beds of hay. It was as though he'd thrown open the door to paradise. "Get in," he said, lifting her by the elbow, "get in." As Charlotte stumbled forth, he closed the door behind them, sealing it as tightly as he could. There were still some spaces around the edge, so he went busily to work filling them with hay.

Charlotte was surprised how much warmer it felt inside, even though there was no fire. It seemed that the wind had carried the worst of the cold, and that stillness itself brought some degree of warmth. Instinctively, she snuggled under some hay and pulled more on top of her like a prickly blanket. "Shouldn't there be some animals in here?" he asked, brushing snow from his coat.

"It used to be a chicken coop," she explained drowsily, "but they haven't used it in years. They simply store hay and grain in here now. Sarah and I used to come here and play when we were young, pretending we'd be in great trouble if we were caught. It made it more exciting to think so."

Shaun saw a dreaminess in her eyes, as though she were a very old woman wistfully recalling days long gone by. He saw it as a bad sign, actually. It was the reminiscence of someone who was done for. It was the way his mother had looked in her final days—always chattering about her youth with cheeriness and resignation. Lord, but he wished there had been animals in the barn. It would have helped them a great deal if he could cut one open for warmth. Charlotte would not have liked it, and he would agree with her that it was gory, but the fact was that there was a limit to how long they could survive in the barn. Yes, they were out of the wind, out of the snow, and that would help tremendously. But they had no fire. Charlotte was not strong enough to walk home in this storm—that is, if he could find the way. And he was no longer strong enough or warm enough to carry her that distance. If this were a fleeting blizzard, then they were truly safe, for they could shelter in this snug barn for a good while. But if the blizzard went on for days . . . they were done for. He wondered whether Charlotte knew it.

"How far is the Mastersons' house from here?" he asked.

"A half mile."

Shaun sighed. "Looks like we're stranded for a bit then, eh?" He limped to a bed of hay, tastefully distant from Charlotte's. But something was heavy in his heart, something he wanted very much to tell her. He unlaced his boots, deeply immersed in his thoughts. He rubbed his feet, worried about returning feeling to them, worried that he could lose some toes. But really, he was so relieved that Charlotte was alive and breathing only a few feet away from him, where he could watch her and see for himself that she really was safe, he hardly cared about his feet. When at last a stinging pain shot through his ankles, he knew it was a good sign, but again, his heart and his hopes were lying in a bundle on the far side of the barn. "Shaun," she said, shifting in her cozy bed of hay.

He gazed upon her attentively, his courteous response implied.

"Shaun, you didn't come out in the blizzard just to look for me, did you?"

He didn't answer. Not with words, anyway. But there was no mistaking the truth in his heavily lined eyes, scarred with worry.

"Oh, Shaun," she said, "it seemed like such a dream when I saw you coming. Somehow, I imagined our paths crossed by chance before you heard my cry. But that isn't so, is it?"

He looked away.

She noticed that his hands were purple, and that he hid them in the hay, perhaps to warm them, but perhaps to hide his suffering from its cause. "Oh, God," she said, "what have I done?"

To this, he replied sternly, "You did nothing. It isn't as though you got lost on purpose. I'm only glad I found you."

His kindness only made her feel more guilty. It had been more her fault that he imagined. "Shaun, I knew there was a storm coming. I've lived in Vermont all my life, I know the signs." She glanced up tearfully in confession, "I was a fool. Would you believe me if I said I ran out in the thick of it just because I couldn't stand to spend another moment with Giles?"

Shaun cracked a smile. "I would think it's a difficult decision between Giles's company and death."

Charlotte laughed naughtily, cupping a hand to her face in a show of shame. "Shaun, stop it."

Thinking laughter was an awfully good sign that the warmth was waking her up, Shaun encouraged it by adding, "Well, at least you didn't kill him. That took some self-restraint. You know, I wouldn't be surprised to learn of Vermonters all across the state trapped in this storm because they were after Giles. You were probably one of the lucky ones."

Charlotte laughed until her lips would smile no more, and she was forced to say in earnest, "Oh, God, Shaun, you're so kind. Here, I got you trapped in this barn, made you risk your life, and now you're trying to cheer me up. I feel like an oaf." She dropped her head in both hands and said quietly, "What if I've led us both to our deaths?"

"No, we'll be all right," he said so confidently that she nearly believed it. "The storm'll let up soon." He saw the doubt in her eyes, and looked away before she could see it in his own. "Umm, are you warm enough for the time being?"

She just stared at him, and for the first time, tried to

come to grips with what had really happened out there. She was lost. And nobody had dared search for her—not her father, not her mother, not her brother, not even her fiancé. It was Shaun who had come. Why? "Why don't you sit closer that we might talk," she said.

"Uhh . . . all right." He limped across the barn with less strain this time and flopped down beside her. For a moment, he was stiff as though this were all he planned to do. But he spared her a glance and caved in, wrapping his arm about her shoulders in as friendly and unsuggestive a manner as possible. "Is, uh . . . is that better?" he asked. He gave her a squeeze and a peck on the top of the head.

Her answer was a liquid stare and a chilling question. "Why did you come for me?"

Shaun met her honest gaze for only a moment, then lowered his gaze. Something behind his eyes was quivering. The answer was so heavy within his breast, he had to work to push it to his lips.

"Shaun?" she asked, daring to touch his cheek, a gesture he all but shrugged away, "Shaun, did you hear my question?"

He nodded, but did not look at her. His eyes were filling with powerful tears.

"Oh, my God," she whispered, "Shaun, I'm telling you right now. If you tell me five minutes before our death that you love me, I shall never forgive you the irony."

He tried to laugh, but it seemed that he would cry if he did, so he swallowed it down. "Charlotte," he said, allowing her to glimpse his face well enough to see the tears, "When I thought you were lost, I . . ." He took a piece of her hair and fondled it like a precious symbol of her life. "I thought I would die."

A big smile spread over her face. "That is the nicest thing anyone has ever said to me."

He nodded his understanding. "Sadly," he said, "that's

probably true. And it kills me the way some people treat you."

"They can't help it," she said, "they just hate me. It's been a school tradition to hate me ever since I developed, you know . . ." She glanced at her bosom.

"No," he said, "no one has ever hated you. You take them much too seriously. Believe me, I live with a man who knows nothing but hate. People just get caught up in the workings of their own minds. It has little to do with what's outside them. If they want to hate, they'll find something to hate. You're nothing but a prop for their personal dramas, a character in their own plays. They don't notice you even when they're spitting on you."

"But you do?" she asked hopefully. "You see me?"

He released her from his embrace and cupped her ivory chin. "Yes, I see you."

His fingers moved across her jaw so lightly that she felt as though he were treasuring her face. She felt pretty all of a sudden, as though she were made of perfect porcelain and he had every reason to admire her. When his finger brushed her lip she felt a chill, and instinctively opened her mouth. She wanted him to see every inch of her, to look at the beauty he'd summoned with his tender words. She knew she was beautiful. She may never have been before, but at that moment, with her tangled hair dripping with melted ice, her messy bundle of clothes primly concealing her, and her chapped, flushed face, she was breathtaking. And she knew it. "Why don't you look at the rest of me," she said, her voice wet and soulful.

"Charlotte, I . . ."

She interrupted. She could not let him go this time. Not without doing the one thing she'd always secretly wished she'd done the last time she had his heart: bask in it. "Don't talk to me about the future," she said, her voice trembling with impatience, "don't tell me what I can't have. Just answer me this. Can I have you now? Once?"

Shaun's hands trembled with anticipation as he brushed the hair from her face. "Charlotte, we're not going to die here. I know you're scared but . . . but this really isn't the end. We don't have to do anything foolish. This isn't our last chance. We're going to live."

Charlotte sucked in some salty tears. "Oh, it isn't that," she said. "Don't you understand? I am sad." She met his eyes with burning frankness, making sure he understood the depth of meaning behind a word so simple as "sad." "I have been sad for a very long time. I don't even remember joy except—" There was no need to say it, was there? "Listen to me. I don't care what happens tomorrow. I just want you. I just want you now."

She had a way of melting him, of making him want to shield her and absorb her warmth. He kissed her, and she felt consumed by his lips. She moved her tongue along his mustache line that was growing manly and rough at the close of the day. She wanted every inch of him. She wanted every one of his muscles flexing around her, and all of his warm, bare skin encompassing her, eating her alive. She wanted him to teach her what it is he'd been doing for years and she had only imagined. "Do everything to me," she whispered in his ear. "Show me what men do."

He responded with ferocity and with love. She smelled sweet as the hay under her hair. He pinned her wrists so he could look at her, and see the beautiful virgin that was his for the ravishing. God, but she looked like a virgin, her face so creamy white and her hair so dark in the shadows, spread across the hay like a beautiful Medusa's. He wanted her desperately. He wanted to see her shy away from a touch and a pinch in a place she thought no man could caress. He wanted to open her wide and enter, to ruin her, to be the one and the only one who would ever break open her thighs. But he wanted to love her, too. Because every time he stopped kissing long enough to look down at her pretty face, a voice in the back of his mind said, "This is home."

Charlotte gave in completely to the moment, breathing in the darkness of an early nightfall, loving the feel of Shaun's strong hands wrapped so firmly about her wrists. He released her so he could tear off his coat and shirt, apparently oblivious to the cold. His arms were rippled with fine, slender muscle and his skin was a warm color all the way from his handsome, taut stomach to his elegantly carved face. The next thing she knew, his hand was under her skirt and her pantalets were yanked down. He wore a sly grin as he fondled her inner thighs, watching her carefully for a sign of shyness or resistance. She smiled right back up at him until she felt a tickle on her most private place. For that, her eyes flung wide. He was touching her in the raw, teasing her with dancing fingers. "I'm going to eat you alive," he said, the huskiness in his voice giving her chills. And from the way his handsome jaw was grinding, she knew that he meant it.

Daringly, she opened her coat and tore down her dress, tugging her breasts from captivity, letting them bounce freely before his greedy eyes. Thinking it was a fine place to start, he gave one breast a good twist, just enough to make her bite her lip. She looked so sexy with her lip caught in her teeth. He loved the sheer weight of her breasts so much that he jiggled them a bit in his hands, enjoying her embarrassed, excited reaction. Then he dove in to suckle one, rubbing the other with an open palm. Charlotte grinned helplessly as he wet her and kissed her in a place no man should dare. Then she looked down at herself and saw that she looked beautiful. Her torso was milky white, the tip of her free breast rather dark, and she was being devoured by the most handsome man she had ever seen. She looked around her, past her spread arms, and basked in the moment of sin. When he came up for air, she wiggled both breasts a bit, enticing him to adore her some more.

But Shaun had greater plans. "I'm not done kissing you yet," he said with a smile that was both friendly and sly, "but this time I need you to open your legs wide."

"Not there," she laughed. "You can't possibly mean to kiss me there."

"Open," he repeated, giving her thigh a friendly swat.

She put a finger in her mouth and sucked it in a sexy gesture of security as she parted her legs. Shaun put her coat over her breasts for warmth, then knelt between her thighs and crept under her skirt where he began to kiss her. Charlotte wanted to laugh at first, she was so nervous. But it was hard to laugh when he closed his mouth around her bud, and began fluttering his tongue. Her eyes rolled upward like she was thanking heaven, and she gave in to the feeling that something was inflating inside her. His mouth was on her and he was wetting her! She could feel his breath. It was so unthinkable it made the blood leave her mind and fill her thighs. But before she broke into shudders, he stopped, and left her in the mood to try more.

"I want to kiss you," she said, when he sat upright, his beautiful physique glistening with sweat in the cold. He offered his lips, but she refused, saying, "No, that's not where I want to kiss you."

He raised an eyebrow most enticingly and said, "Be my guest."

And to this, she responded by urging him into the hay by her side. He allowed himself to be urged, and propped himself up on one elbow, watching casually but delightedly to see what she would do. With her tongue, she touched his bare chest, a gesture he rewarded by stroking her hair. She loved each muscle on his arm and chest. She loved with every squeeze of her hand and every delicious kiss upon his bare, hot skin. She loved him. There was nothing she could find on her journey across his flesh that she would not love, because it was all a part of him, and he was perfect. He was perfect not in the sense of flawless, but in the sense of being all that he was meant to be. When she kissed his muscled stomach, she looked up at him with a question in her eyes. He did not answer.

Again, wordlessly she asked. But she received only a stern gaze, an authoritarian stare. Then at last, the reply. "Go on if you're not frightened."

She wasn't frightened of him. Nor was she frightened even when she saw the size of him, and felt how slick and hard he was. "Careful," he said, teaching her to loosen her grip, "it's very sensitive."

"Sensitive?" she asked delightedly. "Men are sensitive? How ironic that the very thing which makes you a man should also make you sensitive."

"Ironic only if you listen to nonsense." They shared a smile. His was so warm and handsome, she thought she could die tonight and be glad of it if only he would gaze at her in just that way as she faded.

"I'm ready," she told him. And he kissed her for her honesty, gently as though they were the dearest of friends, just before turning her on her back like the most wanton of lovers.

He spread her thighs wide as she watched, keeping a tight eye on him to see what he would do. She wanted him, and she wanted to be his so desperately it gave her a thrill just to see him making ready. But when they touched, he warned her, "Some women bleed just a little," and that made her very unsure. He soothed her doubt with a fetching grin and a brush to her cheek. "Do you want to back out?"

"No," she said without a moment's hesitation, "never."
And the devotion he heard in her vow was such that he
had never heard before. He could not imagine what he
had done to deserve such love, but he let her love drip
over him, figuratively at first, and then literally, as he
thrust deep into her flesh, cushioned by her warmth and
trust. Charlotte bit her lip against the pain, and he
hugged her, cradling her even as he continued to thrust,
and would not let go until he could see the discomfort
had passed.

"You're all right?" he asked, when she seemed ready to
part from his embrace.

"Yes," she said, a smile dawning. "I like it."

He smiled right back, and held himself over her, moving gently, steadily, rhythmically, his beautiful muscles
flexing all around her. Charlotte knew somehow that he
could hurt her if he weren't careful. But she also knew
that he never would, and that helped her open her legs
wider and wider, making it ever easier for him to stroke
her insides. "Does this make me a whore?" she asked,
pinching her own breasts.

He cracked a grin. "Would it arouse you if I said yes?"

"No," she managed to laugh.

So he answered, "Then it doesn't," and kissed her. "I
think you look like a goddess," he said, fully in earnest,
for her face was illuminated in the dim light by nothing
but magic. And her dark hair blended into the shadows
of the falling night. Her body, plump and soft, was not
visible to him under the cloak he'd draped there, but he
could feel it, and he could smell the power of its sweet
scent. It was dark now, but Charlotte, too, could see his
face. It was as though each held a secret candle which
cast flattering light and shadows on the other's perfect
features even though the barn was pitch black. And their
features were perfect. They were both perfect on that
night.

As Charlotte was stroked deeper and deeper into joy, she lost her sense of time and circumstance. For her, their lovemaking was a little taste of death, for it was just as unspeakable and just as mysterious to her. And it was something she needed to meet if she were ever really going to live. For Shaun, it was a coming home. A place to plant his seeds and claim his stead. It was a rooting he thought he'd never have. And with every thrust he claimed her, declaring that he would have the home of his choosing, and that Charlotte was his choice. "Shaun, I . . ." She was moving over the edge, slickening and responding to his increasing speed. She didn't want him ever to leave her. She wanted him to keep moving, keep claiming her until it made her sore if he had to. And something was happening within her loins . . .

"I know," he said, moisture glistening on his forehead. "Me, too."

And miraculously, they burst open simultaneously, something Shaun knew was rare. She embraced him within her womb, holding him snug, refusing to let go, trembling around him in delight. He filled her open mouth with his warm tongue, caressing her with his sigh of release. She had never felt such extraordinary pleasure, and thanked the heavens that she had learned it in the arms of the one she loved. "I love you," he said, but there was no need. She knew it. She could feel it in the pulsing organ that still beat within her.

Gently, he withdrew with a kiss. She reached out to him, trying to stop him from going, growing frantic when she realized his departure would be complete. Even his strong arms were abandoning her. But she saw that he was only refastening his shirt and huddling into his coat. "Sorry," he said, tugging her onto his lap, "I'm beginning to feel the cold again."

Charlotte settled onto his thighs and snuggled into his welcoming chest. There was a time she would never have believed this to be, that she was sitting with him in the dark, sharing his love in the aftermath of sin. "I'm surprised you didn't feel it sooner," she said. "I would never have left off my shirt."

"Oh, I never feel cold when I . . ." He stopped himself nearly in time. There was an awkward pause.

Charlotte broke it by laughing, "It's all right, Shaun. I didn't imagine I had stolen your virginity."

He appreciated her humor with a squeeze and asked her tenderly, "Are you all right? Are you all right about what we did?"

She thought about it for a moment, then nodded. He could feel her face brush up and down across his shirt. "I really am, Shaun. I have no regret."

They sat in the hay for a long while, just snuggling and listening to the storm. The wind sounded wild and dangerous. And the darkness scared them both, for with it would come lower temperatures. And the barn would grow less snug with every passing hour. Already, the biting air was sneaking its way through cracks. It took a lot of willpower not to say to themselves *if only we had a fire*. But neither of them succumbed to the thought. They were grateful to be alive, grateful for the joy they'd shared, and there was no sense in frustration. Anyhow, there was still hope. Though it grew less and less as the darkness closed in and the winds only quickened.

"Charlotte," said Shaun after a very long while, maybe hours, "Charlotte, you're still awake, aren't you?" When he got no reply, he shook her harshly. "Charlotte!"

She stirred lazily and asked, "What is it?"

"Don't sleep," he said firmly. "If it gets any colder, we mustn't be asleep when it does. Come now, talk to me."

Charlotte could see her breath in the dark. She had begun to drift off, and somehow, it had made her colder to do so. She reached for her scarf and wrapped it tightly around her head and mouth, but it didn't seem to do much good. Even in Shaun's arms, she was shivering. Her ears and throat were starting to hurt. "I don't know what to talk about," she yawned.

"Something silly," he suggested, though there was nothing silly in the way he suggested it. "Tell me about . . . Sarah or something."

"Sarah? She's not silly. She's my dearest friend."

"Just tell me about her."

"Well . . ." Charlotte was interrupted by a fierce yawn, at the end of which, she slid from his lap and used him as a pillow rather than a chair. Her hands clasped cherubically under her head, she sighed beside the manhood she had enjoyed so well and allowed herself to be comforted by its nearness. Shaun played with her hair as she spoke. "Sarah and I have wanted to run away our whole lives. Ten years ago it would have been treacherous of me to tell you, but I think it's all right now. She hasn't suggested it since Kevin began courting her." Again, she yawned and settled deeper into his lap. But she was not entirely comfortable. The shivering just wouldn't stop.

"Where were you going to go?" he asked for no reason but to keep her talking. If she could have seen his eyes, she would have seen the emotionless determination of a soldier.

"Anywhere," she sighed. "You know, neither of us has ever left Vermont. Is that ridiculous to you?"

He wasn't listening very well so it took him a moment to realize a question had been asked. The pause tipped him off, making him backtrack and answer, "Hmm? No, I don't think it's ridiculous. Sounds lovely. I'd like never to leave Vermont."

"Well, that's because you weren't raised here," she said. "Believe me, it's a sad state of affairs when St. Johnsbury seems to be a metropolis. But that's the farthest I've ever been. And believe me, it was an adventure by my standard."

"So you were going to leave the state?"

"Oh, heaven knows. It was nothing but a fantasy to keep us occupied. The truth is, we weren't ever going to go anywhere. Women can't just pick up and travel the way men can. It's a terrible injustice."

"Where would you like to have gone?" His question was stiff because his mind was outside in the storm. It was only getting worse.

"Oh, I don't know," she said wistfully, "nowhere fancy. Maybe Paris or Persia." They both let out shivering laughs.

But Shaun couldn't carry on the conversation any further. He was too tired, too dreamy. He couldn't think of anything else to ask, nor remember to ask it. The only thing he could make himself do was hold her. She seemed the only thing that mattered in the world.

Time was so confused by their weary, blank thoughts that it may have been an hour later that Charlotte continued the conversation by saying weakly, "There's so much I would like to have done."

He snapped out of his stupor just long enough to reply, "You will."

"Shaun?" she said, "do you know? I don't believe I'm cold anymore."

Panic awoke him from his daze and he realized with horror that she was no longer shivering. He leaned over her, wishing his cold body had some warmth to offer. "Can you feel your hands?" he asked, rolling one frantically in his own.

"Yes," she said, adorned with a pleasant smile, though her eyes were nearly closed. "Yes, I'm very comfortable."

"Charlotte, don't drift off," he warned, a tear streaming from his eye. "Charlotte, I think the storm is lessening now." It was a lie. "I hear it. The wind is dying down. Stay awake with me."

Charlotte wore a big grin. She had never been quite so happy. "I just realized something," she said.

"What? What is it?"

"Do you know that the dead outnumber the living?"

"You're beautiful when you're morbid."

She widened her mouth as though in a laugh, but no sound emerged. "It's true," she declared, "more people know what it is to be dead than don't."

"Charlotte, you're not going to die. Stay with me. I love you. Your love was never unrequited, do you understand me? I want you to know that."

"I'm so happy," she said, but it was all she said. It was the very last thing she said.

Shaun wept openly as she drifted away, for he could no longer awaken her. He cried until his tear ducts were too cold to bleed. And then gently, carefully, he checked her undergarments to make sure they were all properly in place. He barely had the strength to move her, but he managed it. He settled her limp body in a stack of hay, and tore off his own coat so that she might use it as a blanket. He took off his vest and his shirt and laid them upon her as well. Then, beet-red with painful cold, he shuffled to the far side of the barn and found his rest. For when their bodies were found, he wanted no one ever to know that Charlotte had been ruined. And if she were dead, his bare chest should make certain that he would not bear the pain of being found alive.

TWENTY-FOUR

"Charlotte." The feathers were slick and the blankets were warm. Rolling back and forth was a delicious pleasure. "Charlotte, my love." The whisper was an intrusion upon a glorious slumber, so refreshing and light. "Charlotte, please come back to us."

"Oh, Shaun," she whispered, dragging her swollen eyes open. "I . . . Giles! What are you doing in my bedroom? Get out!"

"Charlotte! Mrs. Bass, it's a miracle!"

The daylight was too bright for her eyes. She recognized her room, but it looked different somehow, as though she had not visited for ages.

"Mrs. Bass, Mrs. Bass!" Giles kept calling.

"Mother! Get him out of my room!"

Margaret's footsteps were soon heard scurrying up the attic stairs at a frantic speed. "Charlotte?" she asked after every three steps, "Charlotte?" When she stormed into the room and saw her daughter's eyes open wide, she clasped her cheeks. "Oh my lord. You're awake!"

"What is Giles doing in my room?!"

"Oh, and you've got your spirit back, too!" She hugged her daughter as firmly as she dared, supposing she was fragile enough to break. "Giles," she demanded, "please light the fire. I think it's safe now. I think we can expose her to the direct heat." She rubbed her cold arms.

"Mother," Charlotte began, only now realizing that her throat was sore from the weather, "Where is . . ."

"Oh, I'm sorry about Giles," her mother interrupted, expecting another remark about that. "I left him alone here for only a moment, I assure you. I had to make a quick run downstairs. We've all been taking turns looking in on you. Oh, my dearest." She hugged her once more, but Charlotte's true question had not yet been answered.

"Mother, where is Shaun?" she asked into her mother's shoulder.

"In the guest room, darling. He's had a rough go of it."

"What?" She struggled free of the hug and asked, "He is going to be all right though, isn't he?"

Her mother's thoughtful hesitation said far too much. "I . . . I think he will be."

"You *think?* Mother, what happened?"

"Isn't it you who should tell me that?" she asked. "We found you in the Hendersons' barn a few nights ago. What on earth were you doing in that storm?"

"Trying to kill *him!*" she shouted, pointing at Giles. "Speaking of which, you'd better get out of my room before I've the strength to get up and strangle you."

"Charlotte!" her mother snapped, but then quickly relented with a sharp sigh. "Oh Giles, you'd best run along for now. We don't want to upset her." She cast her daughter a look of bitter disapproval. "This is no time to be holding grudges," she whispered. "You should see how helpful Giles has been during your illness. He even helped us shave your head."

"What?!" Charlotte touched her scalp to find that there was hardly an inch of her lovely dark hair still attached to it. "Not my hair!" she cried. "Why did you shear my hair?! Mama, it was my only beauty! How could you?!"

"You had fever," she said sharply, forcing her daughter to lie back. "The fever was caught in your hair. It had to be cut out."

"My hair!" she cried, "it's all gone! You let Giles do this to me? No!" She was sobbing at the feel of her humiliatingly bare head. "It will take forever to grow back! Mama!"

"Oh, stop being vain!" her mother shouted, incensed. "You're lucky to be alive!"

Charlotte sniffed, supposing this was true. But to have no hair was nearly as awful a fate as could befall a woman of her age. It meant she was unbeautiful for years to come, and that while others would be wearing their hair swept up and fancily styled for the first time in their lives, Charlotte would be bald. It was not a happy thing to wake up to. But she stopped her crying and sniffed, "But you're certain Shaun is all right?"

"Y-y-yes," she said uncomfortably, "and darling, your hair really will grow back."

"Yes, in five years' time," said Charlotte sourly, "but enough of that. Why do you speak so awkwardly? What is the matter with Shaun? What are you keeping from me?"

"Well, he has the same problem you have, darling. He was caught in the cold for too long. You yourself awakened only moments ago, and you at least had on covering. Shaun was bare to the waist. He had given you all of his clothes."

"He what?!" Charlotte tried to stand, but found that she did not have the strength. It was the worst feeling. Her muscles, on which she had relied all her life to do everything she told them to do, were suddenly not cooperating. She was forced to fall back on her feather pillows in defeat.

"Yes, it's true," said her mother calmly. "You must have

fallen asleep first. He is a true gentleman, that Shaun. I don't know how we can ever repay him for helping you."

For the first time, Charlotte had to agree with what had so often seemed a delusional sentiment. Shaun was a gentleman. He really was. "Is he all right then?"

Margaret didn't know whether Charlotte was ready to hear this or not. She thought perhaps it was best to lie. But truly, she was not a fibber by nature, and when she tried to tell even this most generous falsehood, she found that she could not. She had to tell her daughter the truth. "The doctor took his hand."

"Oh, my God."

"It's all right, Charlotte. He's lucky to be alive. You both are. Don't you see that?"

"Oh, my God."

"Listen to me, Charlotte. He's lost the use of it, but only part of the hand was . . . actually taken. He has a thumb and a finger left . . ."

"Oh, my God!"

"It's his right hand, Charlotte, and he uses his left. His father said so. Really, he's been very cheerful about it. He's a very strong young man."

"He's awake?"

"But he's weak," she said, preventing her daughter's frantic attempt to rise. "He's speaking very softly and he can't sit up without help."

"I must see him. This is all my fault. Oh, God, Mother, he came after me because I was such a fool. I made him lose his hand! It is all my fault. What can I do? What can I do? How can I undo it? Help me."

Her mother responded to her helplessness with forced determination. "No one blames you. I don't, your father doesn't, I know that Shaun doesn't . . ."

"You've spoken to him?" she asked tearfully. "He said that?"

"Yes, he said that. Charlotte, when we barely avoid

catastrophe, then we all point fingers and scold. That's how we prevent it. But when catastrophe occurs, then it's time to let go of blame and mourn. There's just no sense in blaming yourself. It's over."

"Oh, Mama," she wept, "how can I face him? How can I face him after what I've done?"

"Well, for the time being, you won't. You're too weak."

Charlotte sniffed. "How long have I been unconscious?"

"You've awakened many times, but I'm not surprised you don't remember. You were confused," she winced, as though the memory of it still scared her. "But it's been four days since we found you."

"Four days?!"

"Yes. Your father took the sleigh and went looking after night fell. He didn't think the storm was going to calm, and thought it was time to go after you both. As long as it had been, I was forced to agree with him. The first thing he checked was all the barns and huts. He knew if you hadn't made it at least to one of those that . . . well, that it was hopeless. The doctor says he must have found you shortly after you both fell away, only minutes after the worst of the blizzard passed. It was very late at night—past midnight, in fact."

"I don't remember waking up before now," she said, amazed that not only her muscles but her mind as well could be failing her. "The last thing I remember was the barn."

"Well, we've been filling you with warm tea in your waking moments," she assured her. "Shaun's frostbite was much worse. But you were far more delirious. You'd caught fever."

"Let me think. Four days, I—"

"I'm sorry," said her mother, "you missed Christmas."

For some reason, that really troubled Charlotte. She had been looking forward to it so. It was and always had been her favorite day in the year. And it was past. All because of her foolishness. All because she had the idiocy to care what Giles thought. Shaun's hand . . . "Mother, I must see him. You must take me to Shaun. Help me down the steps. I must see him."

"No, you mustn't. You're both so weak."

"Mama, I . . . you don't understand. I cannot lie here without seeing him. I won't be able to sleep, I won't be able to eat. I need to know that he doesn't blame me. I need to see what I did to him. I need to tell him I'm sorry." The last of it made her break down into racking sobs. She was so, so sorry. How could she ever show that to him?

Her mother took pity on her weeping, for she could see it was agonizing. She sighed heavily as one about to say something she may very soon regret. "All right," she said stiffly, "I'll have your father help you down. But only for a moment. Neither of you has the energy to visit."

"Yes, Mama," she said, "I'll only need a moment." She sniffed in salt as she was helped to her feet, reaching for the lace nightstand cloth on her way up. She wrapped it round her head, as she could not bear to face Shaun in her wretched baldness.

Her father came racing up the stairs at his wife's beckoning. "My little girl!" he cried delightedly. His friendly face was always a sight to see, for not even the near loss of a daughter could keep him from smiling at a miracle. "Should you be getting up so soon?"

"She needs to visit Shaun for a moment," Margaret informed him, carefully choosing the word "need" to ward off any argument.

"All right," he said, not daring to question his wife's twisted-lipped expression. "Then let me give you a hand here."

The two of them led her so carefully down the stairs, Charlotte thought she might as well be carried. She was so anxious to see him, so scared to speak with him, so eager to apologize, and . . . the most shameful thought also haunted her. What if it were gory? Yes, it pained her to look her own selfishness in the eye. But what if it were hard to look at the hand? She had never seen an amputated limb, not even a finger. Charlotte's anxieties surely weighed more than the rest of her, for soon, the threesome had arrived at Shaun's open door. His father was napping in a chair. Charlotte could see that even before she could peer around the corner to the bed. Gently, her mother let go of Charlotte and roused the gruff man. "We need a moment," she whispered when he was shaken to rouse.

"Hmm?" He glanced irritably into the hallway, but softened when he saw the young lady. "Ah," he said, "certainly. How are you, young lady?" he asked, whacking her on the back as though she were solid as a rock. "I see you're up and about."

Charlotte winced at the pain of being hit, but managed a smile and said, "I'm well, thank you." As soon as he was gone, she whispered, "How long has he been here?"

"Just a day," said her father. "Rode in expecting to enjoy Christmas yesterday. Found all of this instead."

"Oh, dear. Poor man."

Margaret checked on Shaun to make sure he was awake, for at first, he appeared unconscious. When she'd gotten him to open his eyes, she motioned for Charlotte to enter. And Charlotte did so on a heavy breath. She was almost too scared to look.

But all the anxiety faded away when she saw him. He was propped up in bed, looking handsome as ever with his hair roughed up and his bare muscles showing. She did not even notice the hand, she was so delighted to see his face. He smiled in the way of an old friend, happy to see her after a long parting. And she knew it was true.

He didn't blame her. "Oh, Shaun!" she cried, and some-how found the strength to break free of her father's hold and throw herself across the room, kneeling passionately by his bedside. "Shaun, you look so well."

Margaret, with a twinge of suspicion, nudged her husband and whispered, "Let's give them a moment alone." Not even to herself did she explain the necessity. The couple departed, though leaving the door wide open in their wake.

"I'm glad you're better," he said. She didn't even recognize his voice. It was nothing more than a gritty whisper. "It's good to see you."

"Oh, Shaun, are you truly all right? I heard that . . ." She forced herself to look, amazed that she had not even thought to before then. The hand was wrapped in wet bandages. She could see by the shape that all but a thumb and forefinger was gone, but she couldn't see the wound.

"Not very pretty to look at," he said with a soft smile. His gray eyes were so distant and gentle, it was clear he was not fully alert. "It's all right, though. I'm left-handed."

"Shaun, it's all my fault," she rasped, bowing down repentantly before him, burying her face in his blankets.

"Oh, no, no, none of that," he said weakly. "Don't do that. No, no. Nothing's your fault. Don't say that."

Charlotte could think of so little to say on the matter, she was at a loss. What more could she say than that she was sorry? Realizing she hadn't said even that yet, she did so. "I'm so sorry for causing all of this."

"You didn't," he said, trying to stroke her hair, but finding lace in the way. "Lots of things caused it. Your part was a small one."

She found that rather interesting somehow, and imagined that only Shaun could find just the thing to say that would intrigue her enough nearly to calm her sorrows.

He was squinting puzzledly at her lace, for it was a rather odd thing to wear. "Is this . . . a scarf?" he asked faintly.

She had only just realized that he would never again be able to fondle her hair. Not even his favorite strand. "Oh, Shaun," she said, wishing to weep, "they cut it. I had fever and they cut it all away. I've nothing but an inch of it left."

She couldn't bear to look up and see his disappointment. She couldn't lift her gaze until she heard him say, "Oh, well, that's not very important, is it?"

Compared to losing a hand? No, it wasn't. But somehow, she was relieved to hear him say so. "I'm sure it looks terrible," she murmured. "I think I shall wear a hood for a year to come."

"Ohhhh," he sighed sympathetically, "I'm sure it looks fine. Why don't you let me have a look?"

That really was out of the question. "No," she said, and truly meant it. "I would really rather you didn't see me without my hair."

"Let me see," he smiled faintly, fondling the edge of the lace. "Come."

"Please don't ask me to."

"You saw me without a hand, didn't you?" he said cheerily, eyes drooping already from the exhaustion of the visit.

That shamed Charlotte, who couldn't believe she was worried over her hair when she could only imagine how he must have felt awakening to the sight of his sliced limb, and the numbness. "All right," she whispered, her head bowed low.

And he was pleased. Because he wanted to tell her it looked fine. No matter how it really appeared, he wanted to tell her that she was still pretty. So he slid the lace from her head, noting sorrowfully that a tear fell down her cheek when he did so, and immediately he said, "It looks sweet, Charlotte. I like it." Was it a lie? Not quite. Had he said he liked it better than before, it would have been a falsehood. But he did like it, only because he liked everything about her, no matter how mildly unsightly.

"You don't mean that," she said, rubbing her head self-consciously. She dared to turn her face to the looking glass. "Oh, I look dreadful!" she cried, genuinely pained by the sight of it. "I look like a boy!"

"No," he said weakly, combing through the spiky locks, "no, you look nice. You look just fine." But he was fading quickly, and she could see that. It was a struggle even to keep his eyes open.

"Do you wish me to go now?" she asked, selfishly wishing him to say no.

"I'm a bit tired," he confessed. He was greatly understating the matter. Carrying on this conversation was killing him, he was so exhausted.

"Before I go, I must tell you we missed Christmas," she said.

He smiled dreamily. "Yes, I know. It's a shame."

"You and I should celebrate it late," she suggested. "I'd like to get you something. Is there anything you would like? And please don't say a painting. I'll be angry if you say something so selfless as one of my wretched paintings."

He nodded, though it was very slow and his eyes were hardly open anymore.

"There is something?" she asked, "Something besides a painting?"

He continued to nod. "Yes," he croaked, "there is something I would like very much."

"What is it?" she asked anxiously. "Anything."

He sniffed at his wrapped hand. "Could you get me a glove?"

"A glove?"

"Yes," he said, "A nice leather glove? I don't like the way my hand looks."

Charlotte nearly burst into tears, but stopped herself in time. "Yes," she whispered, close to his cheek. "Oh, Shaun, I will get you the finest glove you have ever laid eyes on."

He nodded thankfully, but could say no more. Charlotte knew she would have to go, but she hated to. She wanted never to leave his side again. It would be so lonely in the attic without him. But she signaled to her parents, who came quickly to her assistance. Together, they helped Charlotte hobble from the room, past Shaun's father who'd had a hearty snack and was ready to return. It wounded Charlotte to leave the two of them alone like that, knowing how Shaun was treated by him. But she assumed it was safe so long as Shaun was so ill, and tried to think of more pressing matters like how to climb the steps. She herself was feeling a bit weak and more than ready for a cup of hot cider. "We'll have Peter bring your supper to your room," said Margaret, and that put a twinkle in Charlotte's eye. Peter would have to wait on her hand and foot, eh? Perhaps some good would come of this after all.

The moment Shaun felt his father in the room, he forced himself slightly awake. "Father," he said as the door was slammed shut, "Father, when I get well, we're going to have to talk."

"About your not running out in storms like a damned fool?"

Shaun knew better than to answer that. "No. No, really, we're going to have to talk."

"About what?"

"My future."

"What? 'Cause of that . . . that thing that used to be a hand?"

Shaun was a little hurt by that, because he really did wish for his hand. He was still adjusting to the deformity. But he managed to overcome his hurt and say, "Well, it may be related."

"Money? Because you can't use an axe? I didn't send you to Harvard so you can be a farmer. You don't need that hand."

"Father, I can't talk about it now. I don't have the strength to fight."

"You never did," he laughed.

Shaun just let it slide, just let it roll off his back. "I'm warning you now," he said, "when the time comes, we're going to have to talk about Charlotte."

TWENTY-FIVE

"Oh, Peter! I'm getting thirsty again! Hee-hee." Charlotte was feeling much better, propped up in her tall feather bed, hands linked behind her head. All her life, she'd been called lazy, but she'd never quite agreed until now. It seemed that sleeping all day and doing little else suited her very well. And to be the one taken care of for a change . . . it was a fine development.

"Mama, I'm tired of hiking up the stairs," she heard Peter gripe.

"Your sister can't fend for herself now, Peter. Go."

Charlotte chuckled brightly, and waited for her brother with a taunting grin. "Why, thank you, Peter," she said when he burst in. "Oh dear. But I didn't want water. I wanted eggnog. Do be a dear and fix the mistake. I'll be waiting."

"You're not even sick anymore," Peter growled. "You're only pretending."

Charlotte feigned a cough. "Oh dear. I'm sorry, did you speak? I can hardly hear a thing anymore."

"Wait until I tell Mama."

"Yes, Peter, why don't you tell her that I was only pretending to be caught in a blizzard, and that falling unconscious was only a ploy to have eggnog brought to me in bed. I'm sure she'll be most interested."

"Well, you may be sick," he admitted, "but you're well enough to be up and doing chores."

"That's not what Mama says. And besides, so are you!"

"I'm a boy. I'm not supposed to do anything boring. I should be traveling the world, not waiting on you."

"Oh dear, look how dusty the floor's gotten. You'd better sweep or I might start sneezing. I know Mama wouldn't want that."

"I hate you, Charlotte."

"I love you, too."

"Oh, I know. On my way to get the broom, I'll go tell Giles you wish to see him."

"Peter!" she called to his turned back, "Peter, you get back here! Peter, I take it all back. I didn't mean what I said about sweeping. Peter, don't you dare! Oh, drat." She huffed her arms crossed and pouted. She supposed she had gotten just a bit too cocky there, and this would be a just punishment. On second thought, she mused as she heard Giles's steps growing near, nobody deserved the likes of this.

But Charlotte was pleasantly surprised. The footsteps did not belong to Giles after all. Peter had only been teasing her. It was her beloved friend, Sarah, who peered around the threshold, her bright eyes sagging from days of worry. "Charlotte?" she peeped, as though fearing her dearest friend dead.

"Sarah!" Charlotte leaped from the bed and embraced her tiny friend, proving herself robust and well on the mend.

"Oh, Charlotte," she gasped, "I've been so worried for you. I didn't want to come too soon, for I knew it was a family affair, and didn't want to intrude. But just as soon as I heard you were gaining strength . . ."

"Oh, Sarah! It is so good to see you!"

As their arms unclasped, Sarah wore a sorrowful frown, tilting her head pitifully. "Charlotte, your . . . your hair."

She had nearly forgotten. "Oh, yes," she said, touching her head, "yes, I had fever, you know."

"Oh dear." She looked as though she might cry.

In fact, her obvious pity was very unhelpful, as it made the loss seem more tragic than Charlotte had come to imagine. She had felt very much better about it since Shaun's remarks and was able to say truthfully, "I've gotten used to it, actually. You'd be surprised how much less fuss it is."

Sarah tried to laugh, though secretly thinking she would die if their plights were reversed.

"Oh, Sarah," said Charlotte, leaping on the bed, "tell me all that I have missed. Did you have a pleasant holiday?"

"Yes. Though I was so worried for you . . ."

"Don't let me think I've spoiled your Christmas. Tell me what gifts you received."

"I got some wonderful things!" she cried. "In fact, I . . . I had brought something for you, but . . ."

"Well, what is it? Let me see."

"I . . . I don't think so. I . . . I think I ought to trade it in."

"Why? What . . . oh, wait." Charlotte touched her head. "It must be something for my hair—is it?"

Mournfully, she nodded.

"Well, that's all right. It will grow back, you know, and I'll need all the combs I can get. Please, let me see it."

Bashfully, Sarah handed over the tiny box, wrapped in a ribbon of gold. Charlotte opened it, determined to gush over whatever she found inside. It was a pair of red ribbons, plush and velvet. They would have looked so lovely in her hair. She wondered miserably whether it would grow out in the same way. "Thank you," she said, setting the box aside, well out of sight and remembrance. "Thank you, Sarah." The two girls embraced,

and again, her friend seemed to have something touchy
to announce.

"Charlotte, there is one thing that has happened since
your illness."

"Yes?"

Flushing, she held out her hand, displaying what could
only have been a solitary sapphire wrapped in white gold.
Charlotte felt a tear in the pit of her belly. "Sarah. My God!
It is beautiful!" She lifted the hand and turned it this way
and that so she could observe the blue stone in all of its
translucent magnificence. "Does this mean—"

Sarah was already nodding.

"You mean, you're—"

She was still nodding, a smile creeping across her
mouth.

"You're getting married! Oh, Sarah!"

"Will you be my maid of honor?"

"But of course I will. Oh!" She covered her open
mouth and bounced, unable to fathom that this day had
really come. One of them was betrothed. Genuinely betrothed—Giles really didn't count. "Sarah," she laughed,
"what are you going to do with a bald maid of honor?"

"Buy you a hat!" she cried, and again, the two
bounced and hugged for joy. They laughed and specu-
lated about the wedding night for hours to come,
Charlotte pretending to be as innocent as she'd been
days ago. They named all of Sarah's future children,
starting with the seven boys they'd decided she must
have, and then the eight girls. Charlotte refused to have
one named after herself. It was an ugly name to her, and
she didn't wish it upon any of her godchildren. Sarah insisted, so after much debating, they named her first
daughter "Charlene," imagining it was close enough, but
much lovelier. They also picked out all the colors of the
home Kevin would surely build for Sarah, including the
fabrics of the furniture, the curtains, and the quilts. But

beneath all the playfulness and joy was a painful un-
mentionable. Sarah was getting married, and they both
knew that Charlotte truly was not. All of their lives,
they'd secretly known that Sarah would be the first to
win a husband. But they had both secretly prayed that
Charlotte would find one as well, someday. And on that
day, after all that Giles had done, it didn't seem likely
that anything promising was waiting on the horizon for
the second friend. Not unless there was something Sarah
didn't know about . . . Oh, how she hoped there was
something she didn't know!

In the meanwhile, Mr. and Mrs. Bass were doing their
best to endure the very uncomfortable company of Mr.
Matheson, without the buffer of his pleasant son to ease
the tension. "I really don't think Shaun is well enough to
travel," said Mrs. Bass, pouring her guest a cup of cool
water.

"Oh, he's well enough all right. Besides, I have work
to do and I won't pay for two carriages. I won't coddle
my son."

"I wouldn't consider it coddling," she said, "to allow
him another week's rest. I agree he seems better, but I'm
sure the amputation is still painful."

"He can travel. That boy is soft enough as it is. Always
has been. It was his mother, you know, who spoiled him."

The Basses exchanged glances of discomfort. "Oh?"

"Yes. She was sickly, you know, even before . . . well, before she was bedridden."

"I'm so sorry."

"Well, I imagine her illness is the reason she always had
a soft spot for the boy. He kept her in good company. No
doubt, her doting is what made him the way he is."

They hardly knew what to say. The way he is? What
ever did he mean by that? "We always greatly enjoy your
son," Mrs. Bass was quick to offer.

"Indeed," her husband chimed in, "we find him to be quite a gentleman."

"Bah. A pacifist and a coward. I curse the day 'gentleman' came to mean that."

The silence threatened to grow awkward before Margaret finally broke it. "So what sort of work is it you have in Boston?" she asked, another slice of cinnamon bread in hand. "I understand you run a number of art galleries."

"Hmmm? Oh, yes, yes. Some proprietors sit back and hire help to run their ventures, but I oversee every showing. I won't put my funds at the mercy of a stranger." He paused poetically. "No, the more I think about it, the more I'm sure. I have work to do and Shaun will come with me. We'll start the journey at dawn, whether he likes it or not."

The Basses shook their heads at one another, but knew they were powerless. All they could wonder was, how had Shaun managed to raise himself so well? Undoubtedly, it had taken more than brains—it had taken courage.

Charlotte. The whisper glided into her dreams, weaving through the folds of her mind like smoke. *Charlotte.* Growing louder, it caused her to stir, but she held to the sound like music, fluting the background of her sleepy imagination. *Charlotte, wake up.* Oh, it wasn't part of her dream at all. It was real. As painful as it was, she willed her eyes open. "Shaun!" she cried, "how did you climb the stairs?"

"Shhh, not so loud. I can't stay long." He glanced over his shoulder, then took her hand in his good one. He was beautiful in the dim morning light. Charlotte could see a dull orange sun, still a half circle on the horizon through her window. It made a streak of cornflower blue in the otherwise coal-black sky. It was beautiful, but not nearly so much as the fine bronze of Shaun's skin and the smart twinkle in his silvery eyes. And that smile. Oh, what a sight first thing on a cold morning! "Charlotte, my father's having me travel back to Boston."

"Now?" She tried to sit up.

"Yes," he whispered, "he's expecting me downstairs any moment, so I have to speak quickly."

"But you're not well," she objected.

"I'm much better," he said, "and I haven't got a choice."

"But you could tell him that . . ."

He stopped her with a finger to her lips. "Please, Charlotte. I only have a moment. You know I've got to choose my battles carefully. I can't argue with him about everything. But before I go, I wanted to tell you that I shall return by Christmas."

"Next Christmas? But that's so far away! I . . ."

"Shhh. Please. I only have a moment." He touched her face in that way that made her feel the most precious thing on earth. "Charlotte, I just wanted you to know that I love you and that I will return."

"Is that all?" she asked blankly.

"Yes."

Her eyes grew smaller in her disappointment. "I mean, Shaun, is that your only promise?"

His jaw flexed painfully, but he nodded. "Yes."

"All right," she said, bowing her head, "then I shall hold onto it with my life."

He kissed her full on the lips, for bald and pale as she was, she looked as beautiful to him as a rose in winter.

"Shaun, wait!" she called as he tried to flee. "Wait, I have a gift for you. Your Christmas gift, don't you remember?"

He paused at the door and smiled.

"I'm sorry it isn't wrapped. I got it from Papa—he's a

drummer, you know. Here." She sprang from her bed and opened her dresser. "Here it is. Merry Christmas to you."

Shaun agreed it was the finest black leather glove he had ever seen. It was soft and supple as a woman's breast. "Thank you," he said, pulling her toward him with his good arm for a kiss.

"Aren't you going to wear it?"

"Can't," he said, holding up his bandaging, "but as soon as the slicing heals, I swear I'll never take it off."

"Oh, Shaun," she said, forcing him into one last embrace, "I wish you never had to go."

"So do I," he said soulfully. "You've no idea."

But he left her once more, with tears in her breast and a lonely creaking on the stairway. Her stomach was heavy, and her face pained from trying not to cry. Every time she lost him, it hurt. Every time he left, she felt as though she'd nothing to do until he returned. She loved him. And their painful partings had joined the cycle of her life. A whole year, she thought, gazing out at the morning which looked so barren through all the mist. A year and no promise. She thought of Sarah and Kevin, and the joy they would share come June. Why was it? Why was it that she had been doomed to a life in which nothing came easily? What was wrong with her? Why did no one worth having seek her hand? Oh, well. If she had learned anything in that barn it was that moments of joy must be stolen, and that even "forever" can never mean forever. She would see him next holiday. And by then she would have hair. That was enough joy for now.

TWENTY-SIX

The journey, first by sleigh and then by boat, knocked Shaun backward several days on his road to recovery. When at last they arrived, he chose to recover in Cambridge, imagining that he could get a great deal more rest and relaxation surrounded by even his drunken and rambunctious friends than he could ever find in his father's formidable lair. He spent more than a week in bed, basking in his father's absence, relying on friends to bring his studies to him. Often, when his friends brought books to his bedside, they stared morosely at his deformed hand. At first, this troubled Shaun, as he was genuinely self-conscious about it. But soon, he learned that the best way to put everyone at ease including himself was to cheerfully invite questions. Often, he would begin himself by saying, "Wondering whether it hurts?" and offering the answer with a smile, "No, it really doesn't. I can't even feel below the wrist so the amputation feels like nothing. It unnerves me to unwrap it and look, though," he'd admit, just to prove his honesty. "I still tend to look the other way when I'm rebandaging it. Hey, didn't you get me ale? I said soup and ale." People learned to appreciate his candor about the hand, and their pity gradually bloomed into respect.

When his strength fully returned to him in early spring, the first thing he did was not return to class, but grab his multi-layered coat and trek to Boston. He did not utter a word of explanation to his classmates or his professors. In fact, he did not even hail a carriage. It was near enough to walk, so that is exactly what he did, practicing the words he had rehearsed for so long in his bed. All the way to Beacon Hill, he kept glancing at his hand. Because for once, it wasn't unsightly. The bandages were gone, and in their place was Charlotte's black glove. For the first time since the partial loss of limb, he enjoyed looking at himself. And it was a good thing, because he would need all the confidence he could get for the confrontation ahead.

He let himself into the town house, then did something he rarely did. He actually sought out his father in the study. His knock was not a question but an announcement. "Come in," called his father, coughing out some pipe smoke.

Shaun opened the door and stood there long enough to be acknowledged.

"What is it? Is it Sunday already? Why aren't you in class?"

"Father, I have an announcement."

"And you had no stationery?"

"I had to talk to you in person. Hear me out. I wish to marry."

"Hmm." His father tapped the ashes from his pipe and stood up. Sensing the powerful position he was in, and loving the feeling of authority, he wove around the desk, pacing before his son like a general. But Shaun did not flinch. "And I gather," said his father, "that it isn't Miss Shepherd that you wish to marry, else you'd not be so fearful to tell me."

"I'm not fearful." This appeared to be the truth, as his gaze was warm and steady.

His father's chuckle was cold. "I see. Well then, why don't you tell me who she is? Who is this dreadful bride who should drive my son from Harvard Yard in the middle of the week?"

"Charlotte Bass." He said her name in a strong whisper, for the sounds felt like a prayer to him.

"What?" His father seemed indeed shaken by the announcement. "Are you mad, boy?" His dense brows furled suspiciously. "Why would you wish such a thing? Have you ruined her? Is she carrying your . . ."

"No," said Shaun coldly, "no, nothing of the sort. My reason is the traditional one. She has a good heart, and I love her."

His father's eyes grew beady. He looked the way he always did right before an outburst. "So why are you telling me this?" he asked.

"Because I need to know what will happen to my circumstance. I need to support her, I need to have a home. And without my hand, earning a wage may be even more of a challenge, though I can still hold a quill."

"And what makes you think I would cut you off?" he asked, in an eerily pleasant tone. "What makes you think I would have my son hire himself out to strangers?"

Shaun dared not hope he was truly accepting his choice. But he answered truthfully, "I don't know. I never know what you'll do from one moment to the next. That's why I had to make certain, before I proposed, that I have a way to support the young lady."

"Ah, I see." There was that power again. "Then I understand the source of your dilemma. What you are wondering, no doubt, is which is worse to me—the prospect of a son who works outside the family business, or having a plain country bumpkin for a daughter-in-law?"

"You won't speak of her that way."

Shaun knew he had to make this clear from the start. He knew his father all too well, and was too wise to let Charlotte start her new life on such a footing. If he allowed him to call her a "plain country bumpkin" today, tomorrow it would be something worse, and never would she be treated as a legitimate bride.

Mr. Matheson was of a notion to be amused by his son's defiance, and was disrespectful enough to grin. "Willing to fight for her, are you? Oh no, that's right. You don't fight."

"Don't change the subject, Father."

"I wasn't! I thought my remark was quite on topic," he chuckled, patting his robust belly. "You march in here, expect me to heed to your wishes, expect to be treated as a man? But what reason have you given me to yield to you as a man? To believe that you are a man?"

"Violence doesn't make a—"

"Yes, it does!" he shouted.

The sheer volume forced Shaun's eyes closed. It took a great deal of willpower not to rub his eyes in his frustration, but Shaun managed not to. He simply replied, "I didn't come here to discuss war."

His father took a step closer, dangerously close. He was shorter than Shaun, but that hardly scared him. His son had come to him begging a favor, and this, he would exploit at all cost. He would clear that hard, smug look from the boy's face before he would give even an inch. Just once, he would get his son to stop looking at him as though he knew a secret of which his own father was ignorant. "What if I told you I think your Charlotte is nothing but a gold digger. What would you say to that?"

Shaun's stare was still cocky, still unfazed. "I'd say you were mistaken." He said it so calmly, it was clear he was not even shaken by the suggestion.

"Well, I say I'm not," his father challenged him. "I say that country bumpkin took one look at you and saw her chance at riches." He eyeballed Shaun for any sign of anger, but saw none. "What will it take to make you fight for something? How do you expect to marry if you can't even stand up for your bride?"

"You're tormenting me without cause, but I won't be baited. I came here for one purpose and one purpose only. To find out what will happen to my circumstance should I marry Charlotte Bass."

"And I'm telling you she's unfit. I'm telling you she's got her eyes on my fortune, and furthermore . . ." His beady eyes narrowed murderously as he went in for the kill. "I believe she's carrying your child. Those kind peasants found you alone in a barn with their daughter and were so gullible, they believed you'd been a gentleman. But they don't really know my son, do they, Shaun?"

His father so rarely called him by name, it was startling to hear it. Shaun was momentarily taken aback.

"I know you, son. A lover and not a fighter? Is that what they say?"

Shaun's heavy swallow gave away his uneasiness.

"Yes, I know what you did. Let me tell you, if they'd been friends of mine I'd not only have given away your secret, but I'd have helped them hang you from the nearest tree."

For some reason, Shaun couldn't argue, couldn't lie. He couldn't pretend he hadn't done it. He was too startled that his father knew him this well. He kept his silence.

"Do you know what I think?" asked his father, sensing he'd shaken his stoic son. "I think you've come here to tell me that you have no choice but to marry the girl. I think you received a letter from her, and that's what sent you fleeing Harvard Yard in search of me."

"You're wrong."

"No, I'm right. That's exactly why you're here. You can't keep your breeches up, and that Charlotte of yours can't keep her legs closed."

Shaun hit him. He hadn't hit anyone since he was a child, no more than twelve. But he hit his father square in the jaw, toppling him into the desk. And he didn't stop there. Though he had only one good hand, he managed to wrap it round his neck and slam his father's head against the hard wood, causing blood and a tooth to spill from the corner of his mouth. His father was rendered helpless, and for a moment, they both wondered whether Shaun might kill him. He had a cold, murderous look in his eye. But as he gazed down at the pathetic face spitting blood and the beady eyes wildly avoiding his own, he was reminded how useless it all was. He wasn't going to kill his father. The sad, old man wasn't worth it. It was sweeter revenge to walk away, to leave him with the knowledge that he'd been beaten at his favorite game. "You get out of my house," his father choked out the very moment Shaun retreated. "Go now, and don't you ever come back." He stood up and straightened his vest, imagining he was regaining some measure of dignity in the process. "And you'll never see another penny from me. Not ever."

Shaun rolled his eyes as he reached for his coat. He'd always known it would be thus. All those years, all that talk about being man enough to fight. He'd always known that if he ever so much as lifted a finger against his father, he'd be disowned. It was nothing but talk. His father was the weakling, his father was the coward. He never wanted Shaun to fight—he only wanted to belittle him for refusing. He turned and left without a word. "Did you hear me?!" cried his father, "I said you're disinherited! You're not my son! If Harvard would reimburse your tuition I'd have you on the streets today. You're never to come back here. Do you understand?"

Shaun was a long ways down the road already, but he did understand. He understood that he had no way to support Charlotte, and for that, he was dearly sorry. He understood that he could not propose, not until he'd finished school in three months and found some way to earn a living, one-handed and all. It was a tragedy. What if Charlotte did not wait for him? What if he couldn't earn enough ever to propose? All of this was horrific. But as for the loss of his father? It was hard to get teary-eyed over that. To hell with him, he thought. Good riddance.

TWENTY-SEVEN

As awful a turn as Shaun's life had taken, there was no one who thought himself more miserable in the spring of 1832 than Giles Williams. Not only had he been humiliatingly expelled from the Bass home at the mere whim of Charlotte, but it seemed that he was at odds with the entire community. Since the appearance of his article regarding the crafts fair, people whom he'd expected to thank him for his insight were instead treating him with disdain. He had always thought honesty a very appealing quality, but Charlotte had told him, "Honesty is only a virtue when you have a kind heart. People with hearts like yours should be as false as is required to hide it." Still, he would let no such ugly commentary infringe upon the integrity of his column, which he had every intention of expanding, so long as his father owned the paper.

Not even Charlotte's abandonment could dissuade him, though this was the consequence that hurt most of all. She would not invite him in when he called. She would turn her nose in the other direction whenever their paths crossed. It just didn't make any sense to him, that she would be willing to become something so pitiful as a spinster, just to express her anger. He was sure she'd no other prospects, and had thought it was only a matter of time before the pouting would cease. But it was already May, and still, she would not speak to him. It made no sense. He'd spent most of his life tormenting Charlotte. Wasn't she used to it by now? Didn't she understand that whether he wrote it in an article or flung it at her in a snowball, that "I hate you" also meant "I can't stop thinking about you"?

Apparently not, as Sarah Brown's wedding was approaching and Charlotte refused to go with him. He knew she'd be there, though, and he planned to attend, dressed in his finest and speaking in his most charming platitudes. It was well known that weddings made all women wish to marry. So he thought it an excellent plan to be right under Charlotte's nose when the white cake and flowery dresses sent her tumbling into the inevitable yearning for her own pretty party. He hoped desperately that it would work, for the truth of the matter was that not only did all of the other young women seem to be taken, but honestly . . . he had always been fond of Charlotte. He might not have known how to express it, but he'd always thought she seemed a pleasant person to be near. Whether he was calling her Peaches or pulling her hair, one thing had always been true. He'd spent his whole life trying to be near her. He'd spent a lifetime trying to get her attention. And he wasn't going to stop now.

Giles was not the only one distraught over the broken betrothal. Charlotte's parents, once hopeful that they would see their daughter merrily wed to a handsome local boy, had now resigned themselves to a different plan. They would have a spinster daughter, and make the best use of her they could. "I wouldn't mind it so much," said Mrs. Bass in a private moment with her husband, "if she were a bit more useful around the house. She does a fine job when she makes a go of it, but she moves so slowly and resents it so."

"Well, few work as pithily as you, Margaret. And she seems to be trying harder nowadays. I've seen her rise from bed twice without your beckoning in the past six weeks. Surely that's a record for her."

Margaret took housework too seriously to laugh. "Well, at least she'll be good company as I age," she remarked. "As long as she's willing to do chores, even at the pace she does them, I suppose it will be nice for me always to have a woman in the house."

George said nothing, as he was busily collecting items for his next business journey. Watching him prepare made Margaret all the more certain that keeping Charlotte at home would be a blessing in some ways. Without children in the house, her husband's long absences would leave her awfully lonely. Still, "It's not what I always wanted for her," somehow slipped from her lips.

"Well," he replied, "we hope for the best and then we settle for what comes. There are only a certain number of boys here in Peacham. There just didn't happen to be one for Charlotte."

"She set her sights too high," she said quietly. "I love Shaun Matheson. I shall always thank him for saving our daughter from the storm. But I do blame him for some of this. It was not his intention, I'm sure, but I believe he raised false hopes in Charlotte, just when she needed to become reasonable."

"Well," said George with resign, "that's how most spinsters come to be. Nearly all have a story of lost love."

"Oh, don't use that word, George. I don't want anyone ever to call Charlotte a spinster."

"Well, what would you like them to call her?"

"A devoted daughter who chose to stay home with her mother."

"Isn't that a bit long?"

She scolded him with a shake of her head. "I don't care how long a breath it requires, I won't have anyone speaking ill of her. The poor thing," she mourned. "No hair, no beau, and in three weeks' time, she'll have

Sarah's wedding to attend. I know it will be sad for her. George, you will be in town for it, won't you?"

"Just barely," he said, at last locating his favorite snuff-box and stuffing it in his satchel. "I'm making an important sale to a merchant with branches all over New England. I'll be speaking to the director in Boston and can't risk any delays costing me the agreement. I'll be leaving before dawn after the wedding, but I'll attend," he added reassuringly. "I won't miss the Brown girl's wedding."

And neither would Charlotte. She had never seen Sarah so contented as she was in the days leading up to her wedding. Sarah had always been the restless one, always so eager to be gone from Peacham, set out on some wild adventure. But no more. She wore the look of someone who had finally found her home, in a place that had always been right under her feet. Her small, round face had never before glowed with such life, her dark eyes had never been so peaceful. Vermont was a new place for her, now that she was getting married to Kevin. It was no longer a prison to which she was bound by family and lack of means. It belonged to her and Kevin now. It was a different world, one in which whispering pines would soothe her own children to sleep, and where the sparkling brooks would play music for her and Kevin whenever they made love in the forest. As husband and wife. Husband and wife. It was just so exciting! Even the words gave her a thrill. "I'm going to have a husband."

"Well, yes," said Charlotte, who had been sitting long and patiently through the fifth dress fitting. "That's what happens after a wedding."

"I know," she said, fidgeting with her mother's wedding gown, still too roomy in the bust, "but I just can't believe it. I'm going to introduce him to people as 'my husband.'"

"And you won't have to make love in secret."

"I know!" croaked Sarah, bending over deeply in her astonishment. "Isn't it the strangest thing? Our entire lives, being seen so much as kissing a boy has been a scandal. Now suddenly, after one short ceremony, there is nothing we can't do. Nothing!"

"Well, I think there are a few things. You'll have to check the law books."

"Oh, stop it, Charlotte. Honestly, who will know?"

They giggled through Sarah's excited fear of the unknown, crouched in a huddle as they had when they were girls. "Oh, Charlotte," said Sarah, glancing anxiously at the doorway to see whether her mother was returning yet with the pins she'd gone to fetch, "sometimes I feel guilty being the first to wed."

"Don't," said Charlotte. "I have told you I don't want your pity. But more importantly, I don't wish you to repress your joy in my honor. There is nothing that could honor me less."

"You are a true friend, Charlotte."

"And haven't you been? Through all the years, through all the teasing and heartache, have you ever once turned your back on me?"

"Oh, I couldn't, Charlotte. You're my dearest friend."

"And that's why I'm so happy for you." She squeezed the tiny woman into a warm embrace, her hands clutching layers of old, musty ivory lace.

"It'll still be the same," Sarah whispered in her ear. "We'll still be friends as we've always been."

"It shouldn't be the same," answered Charlotte in a low voice. "It's not meant to be the same. We'll always be dearest friends, but I've got to let you go a bit, too. I know that."

"Charlotte, I don't want to be let go."

"Oh, I'll always be here when you need me. But you can't expect things to be the same." She pulled back and squinted her way into a smile. "I don't know how it happened, Sarah, but I think we are . . . women."

"Then why am I still so short?"

This sent them both into a fit of laughter which did not cease until they were interrupted by Mrs. Brown's stern entrance. "What are you girls laughing about? Turn around, the shoulders are hanging oddly."

"Nothing," said Charlotte, holding her tongue. "We were just—" she cast Sarah a look of understanding, "just saying good-bye."

"Why? Are you going somewhere, Charlotte?"

"No," she said, "no, I'm not." And it was the saddest "no" she had ever uttered.

TWENTY-EIGHT

It was on the morning of Sarah's wedding that Charlotte finally heard news of Shaun. And it was only by accident that she learned. "It really is a pity," she heard her father say. He was so rarely mournful that his somber tone really caught her ear and made her freeze on the kitchen stairs.

"That man is a beast," said her mother, again causing Charlotte to raise both eyebrows. Her mother rarely spoke so plainly or so defiantly of anyone. She tended to think it improper.

"Well, I imagine the boy's been through it before. Hard to believe he's spent his whole life in that house and still emerged such a gentleman."

Shaun. They had to have been talking about Shaun. Charlotte's breath caught in her throat. Merely to have his name uttered in her house was enough to turn her knees to custard. There hadn't been a day gone by when she hadn't yearned for him.

"It's shameful," said her mother. "A fine young man like that, being tossed on the street, and with a shrunken hand."

Charlotte finished her descent in a sprint. "What?" she demanded before her parents had the chance to deny their conversation. "What happened?"

Mr. and Mrs. Bass exchanged worried looks, but knew she must have heard too much already. So Margaret said simply, "Shaun's been cut off. We heard it in a letter from Peter." Then she rose to tend to the sweet baked beans nestled deeply in the brick by the hearth.

"Why?" asked Charlotte.

Her father, slouching in a kitchen chair, said nothing, only twisted the end of a sideburn. But her mother seemed more willing to speak as she worked and answered, "Apparently, he finally lost his temper."

"He always loses his temper."

"No, not him. Shaun. Shaun lost his temper."

"What?" She looked questioningly at her father.

"It's true," he said reflectively. "Seems they got into something of a brawl. A very bad state of things."

"Wait, wait. We're talking about Shaun? Shaun hit someone? He hit his father?"

There were sullen nods.

"Oh, this is awful," she gasped.

"Yes, we know. We . . ."

"No, you don't know. You don't know how awful it truly is. Shaun despises violence. It really meant something to him, the fact that he'd never raised his fist since adolescence. You don't understand."

"Well, every man has a breaking point."

"Not Shaun. No. Not Shaun. This is terrible. Do you have any idea what triggered it?"

"None at all."

"And now he's . . . he's been cut off?"

"Apparently so."

"No. No, it's just wrong. He can't do this to Shaun!"

There she goes, thought her mother, *thinking Shaun is her beau again.* "Charlotte, he'll be just fine. I don't think he needs you to worry for him."

"Mother, you don't understand! You've never understood." The last of this she said on a quiet breath because it truly pained her. It pained her that Shaun, who was by far one of the most important people in her life, was always to be seen as above her and beyond her reach. That this was true was bad enough. That it should be thought so was unbearable.

Her mother moved curtly from the kitchen, a pair of freshly washed stockings in hand. A cool breeze from the pasture scented the room in her wake. Charlotte waited until Margaret's plain dress had grown small through the tiny kitchen window before turning to her father. "Papa," implored Charlotte, her hands clasped in prayer, "Papa, I have to speak to you."

"Oh, no," he said, tossing up his rough hands. "Don't ask me to interfere in any of this fiasco. There's little I can do about all this, Charlotte."

"I know," she said, tilting up her nose with pride, "there's probably nothing you can do. But that doesn't mean *I* can't. And I need your help to do it."

Sarah's wedding was held on the vast lawn behind the Congregationalist church. It was a beautiful affair, blessed with sweet sunshine and a constant trickle of breeze. Sarah looked ravishing in her mother's ivory lace, which after many adjustments, finally fit her tiny-waisted figure just perfectly. It was the prettiest she'd ever looked, according to Charlotte. Her round eyes sparkled in her even rounder face. Her sandy hair was plaited and worn in a bun, just like an adult's. An adult's. Charlotte couldn't believe it. When had her playmate become a grown woman? It was impossible to fathom that it had happened not in the turn of a year, but gradually over the course of all years, of all hours and minutes. That every breath had brought them both closer to adulthood. Sarah even had a bosom, Charlotte noticed with a giggle. It was not much of one, so it didn't show well through her everyday dresses. But in her wedding gown, so snug around the bodice, it was clear every time Sarah turned sideways. She really did have a figure.

Kevin was the only one who didn't seem surprised by Sarah's beauty. He had always seen it. To him, it was no more real on this day than on any other. He clasped her hands before the flowering arch, letting the reverend's words flow over him like music. He kept his eyes on Sarah, and never once had the tastelessness to lower his gaze to what the audience had never seen before today. He'd always known about her bosom. It was no surprise to him. He knew about it because he saw her. While others knew her by heart, or thought they did, Kevin had opened his eyes and really seen her. That's what made him wise enough to win her. And that's why he deserved her, while the other young men, watching so enviously all of a sudden, did not.

Charlotte herself looked ravishing, though she certainly didn't think so. Her hair was only at ear's length, but she'd managed to pin it all snugly to her scalp and attach a switch made from her hairbrush's sheddings. She was thankful her mother had made her collect "switch hair" over the years, though she never thought she'd need it like this. The switches were intended to further lengthen a very long mass of hair. Never had she imagined she'd be using them to compensate for having no hair at all. Still, her false tresses looked real enough beneath her red veiled hat. And red was a good color for her, as it brought out the brightness of her blue eyes and the shine in her chestnut waves, which were, after all, still her own in one way or another.

Giles inched up to her all the way through the service. He had started off in the rear, having arrived late. But as the sermon about love and trust and all that other dull talk had worn on, he had gradually woven through the crowd until his elbow bumped against hers. "Touching service, isn't it?" he whispered.

She shushed him.

He paused another minute before trying again. "Really brings tears to your eyes, seeing two people so happily wed, eh? I can see it's getting to you."

"No, Giles, that's not why I'm wincing."

"Ha-ha. I see. That was funny. You mean you're wincing because I'm standing here and you're still angry?"

"Shush, Giles. They're about to kiss."

He yawned as they did so. Charlotte joined the rest of the crowd in applause before turning to make her getaway. "Wait," he said, catching her by the arm. "Wait, I . . . I just wanted to talk."

"No, thank you." She tried uselessly to pry her arm free, but was not willing to make a scene by tugging hard.

"So, uh . . . so that's a lovely dress Sarah has on, isn't it?"

"If you'll excuse me, I'd like to get some cake."

"Oh, yes. Yes, we'll get some cake. Allow me." He was proud of himself for the "allow me" part, which was foreign to his usual speech. He had learned it by observing Shaun, and thought this had been an excellent opportunity to retrieve it from his repertoire.

"Thank you," Charlotte was forced to say, since he'd followed her to the outdoor buffet and sliced her a piece of white cake.

"You're welcome. Say, just look at this wedding. Doesn't it make you wish for one of your own?"

"Yes," she confessed, squinting at a bluejay chirping high in a maple, "yes, it does."

"That's what I thought. I mean . . . I mean, I agree. It makes me wish that, too."

"Well then, I hope you'll have one someday, Giles." She handed him the slice of wedding cake, one bite removed. "If you'll excuse me, I'd like to offer best wishes to the bride."

"Wait! Uh . . . uh, Charlotte . . ." He kicked awkwardly at a patch of moss.

"Giles, don't."

"Huh?"

"I said don't."

"Don't what?" he asked, grinning nervously.

"Don't poise yourself for rejection." She could not have said it more coldly, and would not have, if she'd been speaking to anyone but Giles. But Giles, she knew, had to be drenched to the skin in a bucket of cider before he could take anyone's meaning. And wounding his feelings would be no simple task.

"Rejection?" he asked. "But Charlotte, you already said you'd marry me. Remember? Charlotte," he said, glancing nervously over each shoulder, "just give me another chance."

"No," she said flatly.

"No?"

"You hear well."

"But . . . but why not?" he asked, for truly, this was puzzling him beyond reason.

"Because I'm not rejecting you for what you did, Giles. I'm rejecting you for what you are. And that will not change, no matter how many chances I give you."

His black eyes returned from their false good humor to their natural state—mean. "What are you talking about?" he demanded. "What I am? I'll tell you what I am. I'm the son of one of the wealthiest men in town, I'm a damned good columnist, and I'm going to be a huge success. That's what I am. And you are . . ." His hands grazed her from an inch away as he tried to summon the words to describe her, "You are . . . just a very unpopular girl with no real prospects for marriage—and no hair, I might add. It's true, your family is well-to-do by Peacham's standards, but that's all you have in your favor. You're too smart, and you're boring, and you haven't got more than one friend."

Charlotte's lips curled smartly at her opportunity to reply. Her head held high and her fists upon her hips, she told him in a voice like silk, "You have it quite wrong, Giles. On both counts. You see, I am none of those things you claim I am. I am a person you don't know . . . because you've known me too long to see me. And you . . . you are someone who needs to belittle me. Yes, needs. Why you do it, I don't know, but it really doesn't matter. It's something you've always done. And I know when I turn you away, you'll inflict your hunger on someone else. But I can't help that. I can only look after myself. You, Giles, are a parasite. You grow stronger only when others grow weaker. And I won't be your host."

She left him abruptly and did not turn back. Sarah was waiting for her, arms open wide.

"Oh, Charlotte!" she cried, "I am so excited! I can't believe this is real! I can't believe I'm Mrs. Gordon!"

"Are you nervous?" whispered Charlotte in her ear as they embraced.

"Not nervous," she whispered back, "I'm excited."

"Oh dear." There was so much Charlotte wanted to tell her about wedding nights. Things she ought not to know, but did. Charlotte had never told Sarah what happened between her and Shaun that night. She swore to herself she would never tell a single soul, for it felt holier somehow, more sacred when it was kept in secrecy. Still, she wished she could give her friend some helpful hints. That she would fail to do so only furthered the evidence that they had both grown, enough so even to keep secrets about young men. "Oh, Sarah," she said, clutching her lacy arms and looking deeply into her beautiful, moist eyes, "I wish the best for you."

"Well, remember, I'm not leaving!" she squeaked. "I'm less than a mile away."

"Yes, but I won't be able to speak with you again for several weeks."

That took Sarah aback. "You won't?"

"No," she said, "I'm leaving first thing in the morning. I'll be heading to Boston with my father. He has business there and so do I."

"What sort of business?" she asked, furrowing her tiny arched brows.

"There is someone I love, and something I must do."

"Oh, Charlotte," she gasped excitedly, "are you going to see Shaun?"

"No."

Sarah squinted quizzically. "No?"

"No. My intention is not to win him, but to win something for him. I would rather, should he live even a thousand miles away, that he should live happily."

"But Charlotte, what are you going to do?"

A wicked smile came over her face. "Somebody needs to stand up to that father of his once and for all."

"But what are you going to say?"

"Say?" Charlotte scratched her neck. "Hmmm. I hadn't thought of saying anything, but maybe you're right. I was just going to clobber him."

Sarah burst into a giggle that was immediately shared. "I think you had best think of a second plan," she said, clutching her trembling waist. "I think you may be a tad outmatched."

"Outmatched?" asked Charlotte, playfully thrusting her chin in the air. "I daresay not."

Sarah shook her head in wonder. "When it comes to fisticuffs, perhaps," she said, her eyes sparkling at her oldest and dearest friend, "but when it comes to nearly anything else, I know you can do it, Charlotte. There is no outmatching you."

This earned her another hug, and this one ended in near sobs. The sun was setting, and it was time to part. Sarah would be on her way to the marriage chamber. And Charlotte . . . Charlotte would just be on her way.

TWENTY-NINE

It was a misty dawn, like the one on which her lover had last departed. Once more, the orange sun, dim enough for the naked eye, rose through the smoky gray, leaving a streak of lavender in its path. The air was cool and the world was dark. Charlotte had slept little all night, but welcomed the morning with cheer. For once, a short night's sleep did not affect her, did not drag her down into yawning and a heavy heart. She strode across the pasture, the cold mist gathering at her ankles, and breathed in the sight of round, blue mountains in the distance. Shaun had gone to Boston on a morning like this. He'd gone to that imaginary land past the edge of the earth—a land called "not Vermont." She'd heard it was a big place. But his land would no longer be a mystery to her. It would no longer be somewhere he could run and hide, leaving her behind to wonder after him. She was going to Boston. She was going to intrude upon his world, and no longer be a stranger to the land that bred him.

"Charlotte, this is the worst idea you have ever had, and you have had quite a few horrendous ones. Here, don't forget your nice hat. You can't wear your everyday one in the city." Mrs. Bass thrust a decorative blue hat at her, but did so without hesitation. In truth, she would never have dreamed of depriving her daughter of her one grand adventure. True, she suspected this trip had something to do with seeing Shaun's stomping grounds. She suspected it was an outlet of this unhealthy obsession she had with the boy. And it was highly improper—and the list of motherly objections went on and on. But Charlotte would never have another opportunity like this, so far as Margaret could predict. After this journey, it would be a life of spinsterhood, of knitting by her aging mother's side. On sunny days, they could weave on the porch. On cold days, they'd be trapped in the smoky indoors. And that would be the cycle of Charlotte's life. She deserved this one outrageous journey.

"Come now," said her father impatiently, for he had never before had to wait on someone at the start of a business trip. "I've got to be in Boston before the week's out. Let's go."

Charlotte was so excited, she nearly forgot to kiss her mother good-bye. "I shall be very safe," she assured her on the way out the door.

"Keep your gown clear of the wagon wheels!" her mother called, frustrated that her husband and daughter seemed so very excited to leave her in their dust. She'd expected a tad more in the way of a tearful departure. But Charlotte was beaming at her from the carriage and George was frantic over the hour. Before she could get either of them to do more than wave politely, he had snapped the reins. "Well, if that doesn't beat all," she said, sighing as they clopped down the road. She turned to face the house. It was like an old friend, with its peeling white paint and loose, jangling windows. She'd slept in it every night since her marriage. Every single night. Of course, the same could not be said of her husband, but that was natural. Confinement to a house would be unthinkable for him. He was a man. He had work to do. And speaking of work . . . she moved into the woodsy-smelling house with an unintentional slam of the door. No one was home, but it still needed cleaning. It always needed cleaning. It always would.

"Oh, Papa," said Charlotte, sliding sensuously into a lazy recline along the hard wagon bench, "Tell me about our journey. How will it be?"

"Well," he said, quickening the horses, "we'll cross the Connecticut, then make most of our journey through New Hampshire."

"Oh, not that," she said, at last feeling the sleepiness of early morning and a shortened night's sleep. "I mean, for example, where will we stay?"

"Inns, mostly. New Hampshire has some nice family establishments I don't mind bringing you through. Boston has only the high-priced hotels, though. Once we get there, we'll get back out as quick as we can. There's no sense making a sale only to spend the profits on the journey."

"Papa, are the hotels fancy? Will they have carpets and wallpaper?"

He chuckled. "Surely they will. But as I said, don't get too accustomed. Boston is expensive. As soon as I make this sale, I want to get back on the road."

"Oh, don't worry," she sighed, snuggling into her thin, summer coat, "what I have to do won't take long."

The first two hours were a gentle thrill. The road was splattered with rocks, the wagon wheels stirred dust, and the constant jiggling tickled Charlotte's anxious heart. She was getting to see how her father spent his days, his weeks, sometimes his months. She was driving to the edge of the earth, which seemed periodically to swallow the men in her life, then spit them back out again. To Charlotte, the sun felt hot, beating down on the brim of her hat, though hot, to her, only meant something less than cold. She did not break a sweat. The mountains lined their journey from a distance, most of them a deep forest green. The pines smelled sweet and the berries grew wild in open fields.

For a while, she and her father were able to engage in a great deal of small talk about his business and his habits on the road. But by the tenth hour, there was little left to say. The scenery had failed to change. And the rocking of the wagon was getting a bit nauseating. "Should we stop for the night?" Charlotte's voice was scratchy from hours of neglect.

"Can't," said her father. "We have to get in as much driving as we can each day. If you're hungry, grab another of your mother's sandwiches."

"No, thank you." She crossed her arms with a sigh. Travel sounded so exciting, but it seemed there was nothing exciting about being in a wagon all day. The only thing that kept it interesting were the thoughts. The thoughts of what lay ahead, the thought that they could be attacked by bandits, the thought that they could go anywhere they pleased. How interesting, she mused. It wasn't the motion that made a traveler free. It was the mind.

When at last her father steered them into a small, unfamiliar town, Charlotte was so exhausted all she could think of was the tedium of climbing from the wagon bench, through an inn, all the way up a flight of stairs to a bed. It seemed impossible in her state. She wished the bed would just magically appear. But when the wagon pulled to a halt, the change of motion jolted her awake just a bit. The soft, yellow lantern at the front porch of a most hospitable inn helped tickle her eyes a tad as well. "Well, here we are," said her father. The only other sound was the crickets. They were singing voluminously through the chilly night. "Charlotte?"

"Mmm, yes." She could barely squint at him. She kept

imagining how feathers might feel under her back and wishing they were there already.

"I'll get us settled in," he said. "Why don't you stay here?" He knew he couldn't move her if he tried.

"Mmmm. Yes." She took a deep breath and gazed up at the stars, only vaguely aware of her father's gentle-footed departure. There must have been millions of stars up there, each of them huge and liquid white. The crickets were so noisy, it could have been deafening if it hadn't been so fascinating, the way they all chirped in unison. A nice cold breeze tickled her nose and eyebrows. It was a bit lonely all of a sudden. No one in the tiny town seemed to be awake, save whoever had kept the light on at the inn. Sleepiness seemed to long for familiarity. Had it been daylight, she might have been curious about the speck of a New Hampshire town; in the dream state, she wished only for her own. She wanted to be in her attic again and to smell her own familiar crackling fire.

But soon her father was at her side, whispering, "Come. Shall I carry you?"

"Mmmm, no," she yawned, "no, I can walk."

This turned out to be only a half truth, as what she did resembled stumbling more than anything else. But she did make her way onto a friendly, creaking porch, then into a snuggly parlor, heavily scented by burning cherry wood. The inn looked clean, the furniture well polished, and the floor rather free of splinters. "I'll put the young lady on a cot upstairs," said an elderly woman, hunched badly at the shoulder.

"As quickly as you can," chuckled Mr. Bass, alerting Charlotte that she must look exhausted, indeed.

"Yes, come with me," said the woman, leading them both up a narrow front stairwell into frightening darkness. "Will this do?" she asked, landing in an awkwardly small room with only a slice of a window.

It had a bed, so Charlotte said, "Yes indeed," and meant it.

Her father dropped her trunk on the floor. "I'll wake you at the crack of dawn," he warned. "It's going to be rough like this, the whole way. Perhaps you can learn to sleep better on the wagon."

Charlotte smiled politely. "I'm sure I'll adjust."

He wasn't so sure. His daughter didn't seem cut out for life on the road, but he said no more of it, and left her with a gentle hug and a wish for a good night's rest.

Charlotte, though she'd thought of nothing but deep sleep for the past half hour, found there was something about having readied herself for it and lying on her single cot, fully permitted to fall into slumber at any instant of her choosing, gave her a sudden burst of energy. Oh, bother. She hiked the knitted blanket to her chin and squinted at the narrow window for any sign of a view. There was nothing. Only a clock ticking downstairs which seemed suddenly loud, and prohibitive of any kind of slip into the dream world. What was really bothering her? she wondered. Was it being away from home? No, she had journeyed to St. Johnsbury before when Peter was attending the academy there. She and her father had seen him off at the start of each school year, and sleeping away from home had never bothered her then. Was it really the clock? She listened intently for a moment, and decided no. It really would not be that loud if her own mind were not resonating its sound. So there really was only one possibility left.

Shaun. He gave her such delightful jitters that even visiting his hometown made her anxious. But this trip would have nothing to do with her girlish infatuation, as her mother was always so callous to call it. This was a journey of love, a journey of justice. This was her one and only chance to do something for him, no matter how small and useless. And it was the responsibility that was keeping her awake. She had to confront Mr. Matheson and she had to win. She had to. Calm and dignified, that would be the secret. She would approach him with reason and the gentle persuasion of a lady. And she would succeed. She had to. Oh God. She just had to do this for Shaun.

THIRTY

After six days of jerking about on the rocky dirt road and growing weary of looking at a virtually unchanging landscape of forest and sky, Charlotte caught her first glimpse of the majestic Boston skyline. They had passed through many small towns before then, but none of them had been different enough from Peacham to startle her. They had all been brief interruptions of the seemingly endless forest, while this place, this city, seemed like the end of all nature and the start of a new kind of landscape. "Papa," she whispered, "where are the trees?"

"They've all been cut down," he chuckled brightly, "so they could put up those." He pointed to the buildings, some several stories high, in the distance.

"Look at all the people." Already, they were crowding her with their wagons and horses. "I didn't know there *were* so many people. I really didn't."

"Yes, we're a plentiful species, all right."

"Papa, look at the women's gowns! They're beautiful. Look at all the ruffles! Oh look—look at the colorful sashes they wear. I've never seen that before."

"Just a silly fashion. City folk bore easily."

"Do all of the women have beaux? Look at all the couples strolling about. I don't see any women on their own."

"Women aren't as free in the city, Charlotte. They have to worry for their safety."

"You mean, they don't even walk into town by themselves? Oh, wait! What am I saying? Where *is* town, by the way?"

"Everything is town here."

"Oh, Papa! Papa, look at the houses! They're so long!"

"No, no, Charlotte. That's not one person's house. It's a town house. Each door is a different family's front entrance."

"And they all live together in there?"

"No. Walls separate them on the inside."

Charlotte wrinkled her nose. "How awful. They don't even have their own homes? Don't they grow weary of listening to the other families' supper conversations through the walls?"

"They try not to listen. City folk ignore each other to be polite. To give each other a sense of privacy in such a crowded space."

"They ignore each other to be *polite*? That doesn't sound very polite!" Now that she was paying attention, it did seem that hardly anyone was tipping his hat to her or nodding in greeting. "Oh, Papa, look! There are some houses that are all by themselves. And see? They're huge!"

"Some very wealthy folks in them, I imagine."

"Not wealthy enough to have land, though?"

Her father chuckled. "I promise you, those houses are a great deal more expensive than our house and land put together. Some people will pay anything to live in the city. They think it has something they need."

"Oh, Papa, look! Look at that building! The brick one with the tall, half-moon windows. It looks like an Iroquois longhouse."

"That's Quincy Market. And I can't afford to buy you

anything there, so let's just enjoy it from the outside." He laughed.

The wagon was moving so slowly now, dodging pedestrians and stray dogs, Charlotte thought they might do better to walk. But their leisurely pace did give her an excellent opportunity to enjoy some long glances at very handsome men. Nearly all of them were dressed like Shaun. "Are all cities like this?" she asked on a swallow.

"Oh, no," said her father. "Boston is called the Athens of America. You won't find another city in our land where so many men are university educated. That's why all of the most scandalous reform movements begin here. Too many smart and well-informed folks—a sure recipe for dissent of all kinds."

Charlotte joined him in a smile. "Oh, look! A patch of nature is left," she jested. "What on earth is that doing here?"

"Those are the Boston Commons. Anyone with a cow is welcome to let her graze there."

"A cow? These people don't look like they have cows. Where would they keep one?"

"I know. It's something of a running joke. But it was the resolution to a dispute long ago. You'll find many odd laws around these parts."

"May we see the wharf, Papa? I brought my paints, and I'm determined to draw the boats coming in. I'll never have an opportunity to paint such a thing in Peacham."

"Surely, surely. But let's get settled into the hotel first. I myself could use a nap before supper."

"Oh, Papa! I wonder what supper at the hotel will be like. I have never tasted city food before!"

"And you won't this trip, either. I'm sorry for it, but we can't afford to dine out. Remember, everything we take for granted is a luxury here—privacy, space, safety, clean water, and even inexpensive food. I had Mrs. Nelstin from the last inn pack us a couple of meals. I'm afraid we'll have to eat those in our room."

Charlotte thrust her chin in the air. "I'm sure it will be the finest meal in Boston. Especially as I'll be enjoying it with my favorite supper companion."

He shot her a wink. "You're a good traveling companion, Charlotte. Few complaints and lots of cheer. That's what every journey needs."

They pulled up to an entry of white stone where a polite though facially unexpressive gentleman offered to tend their wagon. "I hate letting them do this," her father grumbled. "They'll charge as much for this as for the bed. But I've learned that we have no choice. Yes, thank you," he said loudly to the gentleman who tipped his hat.

Charlotte allowed her father to help her from the wagon, her eyes round as eggs as she followed him into a massive lobby. Its ceilings were as tall as her three-story house, and there was white marble under her feet. "Papa," she whispered, tugging at his cloak, "surely this is not the most reasonably priced establishment in town?"

He patted her gently on the back. "No, it's not. But I'm giving you only one night. And your heart was so set on wallpaper."

It was then that she noticed in awe that the golden flowers on the walls were not painted on as they were at home, but were indeed set on paper. "Yes, sir?" A lanky young man was running the desk. He looked a bit too smart for his job, which Mr. Bass knew was trouble.

"Yes," he replied, "I need a room for my daughter and me. Double-room suite if you have one. That'll be for Mr. George Bass."

"Your daughter, hmm?" He gazed boldly at Charlotte, and made no apology for allowing his eyes to land on her chest. "Certainly, sir," he said with a cocky, twisted smile. "Let me see whether we have a father-daughter special rate."

George cleared his throat. "Sir," he said softly, "she really is my daughter."

"Oh, of course. Of course." He examined her once more. "I have a daughter who looks a lot like that. We come here a lot." Again, he checked his appointment book with a smirk.

George glanced worriedly at Charlotte, praying she did not understand. "Just tell me whether you have the room," said George.

"Yes, I do," he announced, closing the appointment book. "Mr. O'Reilly! Will you kindly show these two to their room?" He dangled a lone key. "It has two beds, Mr. Bass, as I'm sure that's what you wish. But you'll note that they're both rather spacious."

Mr. Bass yanked the key from his knotted fingers. "Rotten kid." He led Charlotte by the arm as she was looking about her in such awe that he thought it unlikely she could walk in a straight line. "There's something else I needed to tell you about city folk," he said as they ascended the marble stairs. "They hold everyone suspect. Everyone."

Charlotte was barely listening. She was mesmerized by the grandiosity of it all. Every cut of wood on the banister was of the highest quality, and shimmering with fresh polish. There were enormous paintings on all of the walls—not intriguing ones, but impressive in size and detail. Many of them were of the ocean and the ships crawling into port. Charlotte grew giddy just looking at them, imagining what her own interpretation of the waters might be. Perhaps there was even a hint of egotism in her musings, for she quite imagined that her painting would be far more entrancing than the ones blocking out the wallpaper around her. It was the prerogative of an artist to fall prey to the occasional egotism, she supposed. It was a central part of the process of inspiration.

But when the bellhop opened the door to her room, Charlotte forgot all about paintings, boats, and even the ocean. She simply could not believe what she saw, nor that the room could truly be hers. It was small, adjoined by an archway to her father's. But what the square rooms lacked in size, they more than made up for with glorious clutter. The bedposts were as tall and shining as any she had seen. Bedside tables were clothed in delicate lace. The bureaus and wardrobes were nearly as tall as the ceiling, each piece intricately carved with designs like the ocean's waves. There was a breakfast table right by the window, set with the finest silver and white china. Sparkling crystal would serve as cups. There was a blue Asian rug under her feet, patterned with gold and black diamonds. But most exciting of all, there was a French door between the windows, and it opened to a slim iron balcony.

"Oh, Papa!" she cried, as her father grudgingly put a coin in the bellhop's palm. "Papa, look! We can watch the people from here!"

"And they can watch us, too," he warned, tugging her elbow. "Come back in here. Your mother would skin me alive for letting you make a spectacle."

"Oh, Papa, I've never been on a balcony before! Did you see? I was standing right on it and didn't fall."

"Yes, I saw, I saw. Come now, it's only a few hours to supper and I'm in dire need of a nap."

"Then I'll go paint at the wharf!" she cried.

"No, no. Didn't I tell you? It isn't safe for a woman alone in the city. I'll take you in the morning, I promise."

Charlotte tried to hide her disappointment. She didn't want to be sour, but between not being allowed on the balcony and not being allowed to paint, her excitement was dwindling a bit.

"Why don't you read a book in the lobby?" he suggested. "They've some lovely books down there."

"All right," she said. "That does sound pleasant."

If he saw the lack of enthusiasm in her eyes, he did not mention it. Instead, he just kissed her good afternoon and retired to the lesser chamber. Charlotte allowed the thrill of the day to consume her again, taking an indulgent spin about the room, landing before a looking glass encased in gold. She had never seen such a clear looking glass before. She had never seen her own face in such detail. Her fingers lingered on a cheekbone and then fell to her plush lips. Her face really was an oval. She turned to the left and turned to the right, observing her bright hair from both sides. The false switch really did blend perfectly with her own color. It was impossible to know that her hair was still short. She lifted her chin up high to see what she would look like if she were a city woman, a lady of expensive breeding and exaggerated confidence. It made her look rather silly. She flushed and giggled at her own vanity. Then she glanced down at her plain beige gown and country apron. She really didn't look like she belonged in a hotel. But never mind it, she would venture downstairs alone. She had to. When would she ever get to be a city woman again?

The lobby was rather empty, and she didn't care for the attention her footsteps brought from the manager. If that cocky lad at the desk really were the manager, which somehow she doubted. She returned his startled glance with a warm smile that made him leave her be. Then she settled in an ivory loveseat, a random book in hand. At least the sofa was facing the street, so she had a lovely view of the pedestrians, all of them so much more elegant than she. She flipped the leather bound book this way and that to see whether she could glimpse a title. But the cover was worn, and the writing cracked with time. She'd have to open it to see what she'd selected. Carefully, as though opening it were to commit to a lengthy story, she examined the first page. "In the beginning when God created the heavens and the earth, the earth was formless, void and darkness . . ." Oh, for heaven's sake. This wasn't exactly what she'd had in mind.

"I beg your pardon."

"Ahh!"

"I'm sorry," said a handsome gentleman, blond nearly to a fault. "Did I startle you?"

"Oh, no," said Charlotte, clutching her throat, "no, not at all." She forced a grin.

"I'm sorry to intrude," he said, a devil in his pale eye, "but I couldn't notice such a pretty woman without stopping to say hello."

Charlotte replied, "Well, any man armed with compliments is welcome to share my sofa," and was rather proud of it. It was, she thought, a very city-womanish answer.

He hopped over the arm of the loveseat in a gesture of youth and virility. When he landed he asked, "Are you here alone?"

"No, I'm with my papa," she replied, then wished she had used the word "father." She sounded just like a country bumpkin.

Strangely, that didn't bother him. He merely stuck out his hand and said, "Bob Barnett."

"Oh, there's a town near Peacham called Barnet," she said, then wished she could throttle herself. What an incredibly boring statement. What was he supposed to say to that? That he'd founded it?

"Oh well, they're always naming towns after me," he beamed.

She had to credit him for doing so well with her remark. "Is that so?" she asked. "Well then, you certainly have me bested, because I'm Charlotte Bass and I doubt you've ever heard of a town called that." All right, it wasn't brilliant. But it was in keeping with the tone of things.

"Anyone who knew how pretty you are would name a town after you in a heartbeat."

Charlotte flushed at her Bible. "One compliment is nice, Mr. Barnett, but I daresay that too many of them take on a ring of sarcasm."

"Sarcasm?" he scoffed. His arm had somehow stretched out across the loveseat, dangerously close to Charlotte's neck. "You don't have a high enough impression of yourself."

"You don't seem to have that folly." She had not intended to make a cutting remark, but it had slipped from her mind to her tongue to the air. And now it was his to rebuke.

"No, that isn't one of my weaknesses," he cheerfully agreed. "Mainly, my only weakness is for beautiful women." She did not reply and blushed at her book, so he gathered he was being too bold. He retreated from his inadvertent lean and changed the topic to something easier for a country girl to manage. "What's that you're reading?"

"The Holy Bible," she replied with a smirk.

"The what?"

She held it up so he could see the first page. "Would you like me to read it to you?"

"Whoa, no, I . . . I already know the gist of it." He studied her expression to see whether she was in earnest. He could not tell. "So are you . . . are you planning to stay in Boston very long?"

"How long would you like me to stay?" There was an underlying accusation in the question and in her eyes.

"A good long while, I hope."

Charlotte absorbed his seductive glare, and realized something. He seemed to think she was on the wrong end of a joke. She knew his expression well. It was the one worn by children engaged in a cruel taunt. It was as though trickery and courtship were similar games. She had never known before that there could be a cruelty in the art of seduction. There had never been any such thing in Shaun's romantic tactics. "Excellent," she answered dryly, "I'll tell my Papa you'd like me to stay. He'll be delighted, you know. He was beginning to think no one would ask my hand in marriage."

"What?"

Charlotte burst into laughter at the way he recoiled.

"Oh, you're joking," he observed, straightening his cuffs to regain his dignity. "I see. Yes, that was . . . that was funny." He forced a smile that was meant to put him on the sharing side of the joke. "I see, well, no, I really didn't have marriage in mind. Not so quickly, anyway. I had rather thought you might join me for a drink."

"And then what?" she asked in challenge. "What then?"

"Well, I don't know." He lowered his voice seductively. "Must we plan so far ahead?"

"Is an hour from now so far ahead?"

"Well, I . . ."

Her countenance remained pleasant. "Sir, if you are meaning that I should bid my papa farewell for the night and put myself at your mercy, I daresay you should tell me your plans."

"Well, I could show you around a bit," he said, stuffing a confident hand into his vest's pocket. "I attend the college in Cambridge, you know. I know Boston like the back of my hand."

"You attend the university all day and then spend your evenings in hotel lobbies?" Her smart grin took the sting out of the observation.

"No," he laughed, "I'm visiting another student. Maxwell over there."

Maxwell, apparently the young man who so saucily greeted the guests, offered a false salute.

"Ahh," said Charlotte, "so the two of you were meaning to enjoy the town after work, were you? I had no idea Harvard students had so much time to be idle."

"Oh, yes. We rarely study. Much too smart for it." He winked.

"Not my brother. His name is Peter Bass, and I assure you there's not a thing in this world for which he is too smart. Have you met him?"

"Can't say as I have. But with a reference like that, I'll be sure to go out of my way."

"What about Shaun Matheson?" she couldn't help asking, "He's a good friend of the family. Have you met him?"

Bob leaned awkwardly away from Charlotte, as though she might be contagious. "Why, yes," he said, "everyone knows Shaun. He's a good friend of mine. A friend of everyone's. Why . . ." His stare was quizzical, suspicious, concerned.

"Is he well?" she asked anxiously, "Have you seen him of late?"

He was too distracted to answer quickly, but at last absorbed her words and replied, "No, not lately. Not since he left school. Say, did you say your name was Charlotte?"

"Left school?!" she cried. "But he hasn't graduated yet!"

"Uhhh," he scratched his pale blond head. "No, not quite. I think he had only one course left to finish. You're not . . . you mentioned a town called Barnet. You aren't from Vermont, are you?"

"Yes. Now tell me what he's doing. You said he left school, but I thought his tuition was paid!"

"Uh yes, I think it was. But as I understand it, he was

in a hurry to make a living, had to save up because . . . well, just because."

"What work is he doing?"

"Penmanship, I think. Copying letters. He can still write fairly well with his left hand. Say . . . you know that I was only being friendly, just passing the time. I was only waiting for Maxwell's shift to end."

"No, you weren't." But Charlotte had better things to worry over. She threw up her hands and cried, "I cannot believe this! Where is he living now?" She had somehow gotten to her feet and was pacing.

"In a basement flat, I think."

"I'll kill him," she growled. "I'll kill that father of his. Shaun has lost not only his future funds but his education as well? And all because he finally gave that man one shot of his hand?"

Bob shrugged.

"I will tear him apart. I will throttle his neck. I will . . ."

"Well, whatever you do, you won't say anything about me to Shaun, will you? I really meant no harm."

"I'll make you a bargain," said Charlotte, glaring at his pallid countenance, "I won't tell Shaun I saw you tonight. And you don't tell anyone who murdered his father."

He hoped this was another joke, but he just wasn't sure. Charlotte suddenly had a very frightening look about her.

THIRTY-ONE

"You bastard!"

It was not what Mr. Matheson had expected to see when he'd come to the beckoning of his brass knocker. Initially, he barely recognized the girl, her face was so purple. But gradually it dawned on him that she was the country bumpkin who'd stolen his son's senses, and greeted her exactly as he saw fit. He tried to close the door.

Charlotte prevented it with her whole body.

"How dare you barge in here," he demanded, pushing the door against her weight, finding his strength inadequate against that of a determined woman. "How did you get my address?"

"It's on all of your letters, you fool."

At last, she succeeded in flinging herself into the foyer, glaring at him as she caught her breath. He made no attempt to calm her. He knew what she was, and he knew what she wanted. His wrinkled face held nothing but contempt. "Well, now that you've embarrassed yourself by barging in unwelcome, why don't you tell me why you're here. Hoping to marry my son?" An evil smile curled his lip. "I've excellent news for you—he's yours for the taking. Though he's a pauper now, and I suspect that makes him somewhat less appealing."

Charlotte had forgotten all about her resolve to remain calm and dignified. Shaun's losing his education had pushed her over the edge of reason and she found herself screaming, "Oh! You are evil! Pure evil!"

Something about that interrupted Mr. Matheson's cynical train of thought. He had expected one of any number of wretched things to spew from Charlotte's mouth. But "pure evil" hadn't been one of them. Despite himself, he asked guardedly, "Pure evil?"

"Yes!" she wailed at him, "you are like . . . like Goliath! And Shaun is like David, only you're so evil he can never win! No one can win against such hatred as yours! It's like battling Beelzebub!"

Mr. Matheson burst into laughter. It was her earnestness that made it so unbearably funny. He could see that she wasn't meaning to exaggerate or trying to amuse him. She was just so furious, she believed every word of it. He could see it in her wet, purple face and in the painful squint of her eyes. His laughter seemed to make her all the angrier. "Miss Bass, please . . ."

"No, *you* please!" What had looked like the sweat of anger was suddenly mingled with tears. "What is the matter with you?" she cried in earnest. "What is the matter with men like you? There is so much out there to fight. There's so much horror and sorrow and devastation, and . . . and what do you choose? You choose to fight Shaun. You fight Shaun! Shaun, of all people. And you fight me! And you fight anyone who's done you no harm but you think you might just beat. You're useless! Do you hear me? You're useless! What good is all that strength if you can't find a proper enemy?"

"Miss Bass . . ."

"Don't you interrupt me!" she screamed. "I came all the way to Boston just to give you a piece of my mind and you're going to listen!"

That seemed only fair. All the way to Boston just for this? Lord, but she must have hated him with a passion.

"You don't even know Shaun," she nearly sobbed on

her lover's behalf. "You thought he was weak. You thought you could beat him because he hadn't the strength to fight back. And now you're angry because you learned the truth! He isn't weaker than you—he's simply better than you. He beat you at your own wretched game and now you know what you always feared was true. He is stronger and better! What do you think of that?!"

"I think," he said soberly, for it had been so very long since he'd been thrashed by a woman's righteousness, "that you are not after my son's money."

She had no idea what a statement of defeat that was. She was merely annoyed that he sought to change the subject. "His money?! His income has no bearing on my life. We are not even marrying. He hasn't asked me! He has rejected me squarely and often. Can't you see this has nothing to do with me? I seek only justice for the man I love, and the man you ought to love as well. That's all!"

So his idiot son had not even told her of his intention to marry. Just like him. Of course, there was one thing that was not so idiotic about his child. From what he could see, he had excellent taste in women. She was exactly as stubborn and faithful as his own wife had been. "You make a compelling argument," he said, hoping to satiate her.

But she would not be calmed. "It is not my intention to argue!" she cried. "I wanted only to be heard. And now that I have been, I shall bid you farewell. My papa is waiting for me."

"Wait . . ." But he could not stop her from leaving any more than he had stopped her from barging in. Before he could so much as catch the door, she was gone.

He watched her go, storming down the busy brick sidewalk, completely unprotected from the advances of men, and completely oblivious to her vulnerability. He felt a sinking in the pit of his stomach. How could he have misjudged her so? Why hadn't he seen what she was? Not a plain country bumpkin, but a reflection of his own wife as she'd been when she was but a poor and modest creature with a heart of fire. Shaun must have missed his mother. It was the strangest thought, because never before had he tried to get inside the mind of his son. But looking at Charlotte in a new light, he suddenly understood what Shaun had seen in her. And he understood something about his son. He was still in pain over his mother's death. Mr. Matheson had been so consumed by his own sorrow, he had never once considered the matter of Shaun's lingering loss. And to see inside his heart even for one moment was to know him a little better. And to remember that they were joined by a familial thread that could not be broken.

He noticed something on the front step. What was this? Good heavens, it was lovely. How could . . . no. She didn't . . . no. No, it couldn't be. Could it?

"How was it?" her father asked stoically.

"Miserable," she said, loving the feel of the horses clomping before her, rocking the wagon toward home. "Oh, Papa, everything went wrong. I meant to be so strong and diplomatic. I meant to explain to him, to make him see that he should take Shaun back into his care. But I was just so angry from last night. When the boy told me Shaun had quit school. I just . . . oh, Papa, I lost my temper. And now I just know he didn't listen."

George frowned mightily, not so much at her words but at the pitiful way she spoke them. The poor thing had come so far, gone through so much trouble, all for a young man who didn't want her. "Well, you did your best, I know. I'm sure he'll come around someday." It was a lie, but he didn't see the harm in it.

"I don't think so," she said miserably, "but I just don't want to think about it anymore. I just want to get home. It is a beautiful city, Papa. Thank you so much for taking me. But I don't wish ever to see the city again. I just want to walk in the forest and see Mama, and start preparations for the next holiday. I was wrong to seek more from my life. There's nothing for me here. I just want to be home again."

"I was wondering when you'd realize how good we have it," he said, beaming with pride.

But Charlotte looked startled, as though she'd been pricked by a pin.

"What is it?" he asked worriedly.

"Oh, no, Papa."

"What?"

"Oh, no! Do you remember the painting I did at the wharf all morning? Papa, I left it on Mr. Matheson's doorstep when I knocked. I forgot all about it."

"Do you want to turn back?"

"No," she said, sinking in her seat, "no, I can't go back there. Not after the way I ran out. He might see me. No, it's no use. I give up. Just take me home. Just take me home and let me remember where I belong."

THIRTY-TWO

Shaun had spent his spring and summer tormenting himself over money. He spent almost nothing. His basement flat was like a stone cave with only a narrow slit of a window way up near the ceiling giving him a view of people's feet as they walked by. He ate like a pauper and drank nothing but water. Yet, his savings were growing at a snail's pace. Every time he thought his long hours of work would finally leave him with more than a penny in his pocket, an unexpected expense would arise—a tax, a trip to the doctor, or a raise in rent—and he'd wind up with nothing again. At this rate, he could never take a bride. He couldn't ask Charlotte or any other woman, for that matter, to share a dusty one-room flat. His only hope had been to save and to hope. But so far, if there was a way to get from copying letters to tremendous wealth, it didn't seem that anyone knew the secret.

Every day, he surrendered his most precious asset, time, to a task he did not like. He had never even had a knack for penmanship. His writing had always been sloppy and fast. But he'd slowed down and forced himself to excel because it was the job for which he was most qualified, since they'd refused to hire a one-handed man at the docks. He hated the task, but he would have relished it nonetheless if only it were truly bringing him closer to Charlotte. But as he lost hope of earning enough in time to marry her, he came to resent the long hours. Late at night when his time became his own again, he had to waste it on sleep. And this he found the greatest tragedy of being poor. Not the lack of money, but the waste of life in the form of bartered time.

On one occasion, he was given the day off. Though it meant a loss in pay, he delighted in it. It was beautiful in the autumn, and he so rarely got to see the daylight, stuffed in his office as he usually was. The crisp air, the way it chilled him just enough to wake him in full but not enough to cause discomfort, put him in a romantic frame of mind. He thought of spending the day making a collage of dry, red leaves in the shape of a heart and sending it to Charlotte. But he'd sworn he wouldn't give her false hope of marriage until he was sure he could provide for her. So he held off on the romantic gesture, and ended his thoughtful wanderings through the city on a much less pleasant note. He'd left some belongings at his father's house. As poor as he was, it was time to collect them. It wouldn't be much—some clothes and books. But he could hardly afford to repurchase them, so he decided to brave the lion and gather his things in one fell swoop.

He'd never relinquished his key, so he let himself in quite calmly. When he saw his father shuffling expectantly to the door, he put up a hand. "I'm just collecting some things I left behind," he said by way of a warning. "I won't be but a moment."

Shaun half-expected to be informed that his belongings had been sold or burned. But when his father opened his mouth, he said something entirely unpredictable. "Why don't you stay a while?"

"No, thanks," he answered with a quizzical glance. "I'd rather be fed to crocodiles."

"Son, wait."

Shaun cast a look of annoyance at the hand that restrained him from climbing the stairs. "What?" he demanded.

"I've been hoping you'd come," he said, without even a hint of goading. "Why don't you have a spot of brandy with me?"

"Why? Is it poisoned?"

He feigned a chuckle. "That's amusing. But I'm in no mood for taunts. There's something in my study I want you to see."

"What?"

"Just come."

Shaun sighed heavily but relented. Really, he didn't see any way around it. And his father was acting so strangely, he had to acknowledge a morbid curiosity about where this might lead. He followed his father to the scene of their last fatal confrontation and looked about for anything unusual. He spotted it immediately. "Do you recognize the painting?" asked his father.

Shaun approached it with reverence. It was a watercolor of only one wave in a harbor. Complex in color, it was composed of gold, forest green, a touch of pink, and, of course, the clearest blue. The wave was suspended in midair, conscious of its impending fall, where it would join the other waves and cease to exist by virtue of transformation, but not by destruction. "I recognize the artist," said Shaun, "though not the painting. How did you get this?"

"Suffice it to say I found it."

"So that's what you wanted me to see?" he asked shortly. "That you've discovered Charlotte's paintings? Well, good for you. Now, if you'll excuse me."

"Don't you walk out of here, boy!"

"That's exactly the kind of talk that makes me walk out."

Mr. Matheson fought to regain control of himself. He had not summoned his son for the sake of argument.

But the boy made it so hard! He had no respect—he was forever scolding his own father. Just this once, they were going to get through a complete conversation. "Shaun, I have something to tell you."

He raised an expectant eyebrow. There was some goading in his expression, but his father tried to ignore it.

He blurted out, "Shaun, I want you to take the East Gallery. It's rightfully yours. You've got your starring artist—I know you can keep it running."

Shaun's expression wasn't exactly the elated one for which Mr. Matheson was hoping. It was more a look of disgusted confusion. The only word which sprang from his lips was, "Why?" And he said it as though surely there must be some horrendous condition to the gift, one so awful that he could never think to agree.

"Because you're my son!" his father bellowed. "Isn't that reason enough?" He hadn't meant to shout it. But he had expected thanks, not skepticism. And if he'd known his own heart he would have described his disappointment as saddening. As it was, he believed himself angry.

"I thought I was disowned."

"Well, I am de-disowning you," mocked his father. "Do you need it in writing? Shall I spell out 'de-disowned' in some phonetically acceptable though grammatically unforgivable way? Will that help you?"

Shaun was still squinting. "What do you want from me?"

"How about a thank you!" he shouted, turning one of his customary shades of purple.

"Why the change of heart?"

"None of your concern!" Charlotte's gentle eyes, struggling so valiantly to look vicious, flashed in his mind, nearly prodding him into a smile. But smiling before his son was something he could never do, so he composed himself and said in his most diplomatic voice,

"You've always been interested in the arts." He paced back and forth so he would feel as though he had the upper hand. "I don't condone it, not for a man. Not for a man who doesn't also love war. But I see it. I see what you are, and I know that you would turn the gallery into a brimming success. I know that you have an eye for . . . well, for things of beauty." Lord, what a disappointment. With a deep breath, he went on calmly. "Though I have learned a great deal about art for the sake of my galleries, my passion is for business. You'll do a better job with the gallery. I'll start you with one, and if funds improve as I think they will, I'll give you the rest."

Shaun's stare was still mercilessly cool. "Why should I accept anything from you?"

"Don't be such a fool!" he bellowed. "I'm offering you the gallery! I'm offering your bride a future, a monied husband, and a place to display her talents! I'm giving you everything you asked, though the Lord knows you don't deserve a drop of it! Isn't that enough for you?"

"No," said Shaun stubbornly. "It's not enough."

"What the hell else do you want?!"

A smile sparked his silvery eye. "My mother's wedding ring."

"What?" Their eyes locked, at first in conflict, and then in understanding. An understanding of what the ring meant to two warring bachelors who had lost the same woman.

"You heard me," said Shaun. "I want her ring."

"Am I to take it I won't get it back?" asked his father, returning the thin trace of a smile.

"I don't know," said Shaun. "That would be up to Charlotte."

THIRTY-THREE

December 1833

"Have we ever had a normal Christmas?" Peter was home for the holiday, and nursing a pewter goblet of the thickest, sweetest white eggnog.

"This year will be normal," his mother promised him. "We'll keep Charlotte out of the snowstorms and we won't let a thing spoil our holiday. A gingerbread crisp?"

"Oh, Mama! You burned the edges."

"Well, don't pout. I can crumble those off for you. Here you are, good as new."

"It'll still have that burnt taste."

"Oh, dear. Charlotte! Charlotte, come in here! I need you to go into town for more brown sugar. Charlotte, where did you go?!" She patted Peter's sturdy shoulder. "Don't worry. I'll make some more just as soon as she comes back. It's so good to have you home." He squirmed within her embrace, cookie crumbs spraying in his lap. "I just miss you so when you're gone," she whispered to his hair, then yelled, "Charlotte! I am summoning you! Oh, she is always such a nuisance. I'll have to go fetch her. You stay put." She kissed him on the head, then grumbled as she hitched her skirts, "I can't believe I'll be spending the rest of my life this way." But she didn't mean it. Secretly, she looked forward to the years ahead. There was something comforting about having Charlotte around. She had such warmth.

"Oh, there you are!" she cried, her face frowning itself into wrinkles that no longer faded when she eased her mouth. "I've been calling you."

"I know, Mama. I've been coming. It takes a few moments to descend the stairs, you know."

"Well, hurry. It's not every day we have Peter home. I'm out of brown sugar," she said, dropping a coin in her hands, "and while you're out, if you could also get some of the lighter maple syrup. All we have is the dark and it's a tad bitter for your father."

"Yes, Mama."

"Oh wait, Charlotte!" she cried before the girl could turn her back. "Wait, I forgot to tell you. Mary Whittaker is betrothed so you must pick up a gift in town. Any small thing will do. I'll ask her and her mother to stop by after the holidays, and I'll want you home to congratulate them."

Charlotte bowed her head. Of course she would congratulate her old classmate. She imagined she'd have to congratulate them all before the next season. It seemed everyone was finding someone. Everyone except Charlotte. "Yes, Mama."

"You're not going to wear that face, are you?" Her brows furrowed in a scolding. "No one wants to be congratulated through resentment. Just because you didn't find a husband is no reason to hold Mary in contempt."

"Oh, it isn't that, Mother." How could she be so cruel? Sometimes she was so noble, standing over her frying pans, not worrying over the deep lines on her skin or the silver in her hair, both symptoms of her years of confinement in a dark, smoke-filled kitchen. She could be so admirable, storming about the house, keeping order in the home of the husband and son who held her prisoner and didn't even know they were doing it. And then, she could turn around and be so cruel. Charlotte wondered whether she even realized how wretched it was of her always to bring up her spinsterhood as though in punishment for her failure. "It isn't that I wish her unhappiness," she pleaded to her mother, "it is only that my own status will surely be brought up. And I . . ." It hurt to say it plainly. "Mama, I never told any of those girls what happened with Shaun. Some of them still think he is my long-distance beau."

"Why did you tell them such a thing?"

"I didn't. Believe me. They only assumed it, and I, well, I fear I let them go on assuming."

"And now you'll tell them that it was never so. There's nothing hard about that."

There were times Charlotte felt more like a distant relative than a daughter to Margaret Bass. "I know it shouldn't be hard," she said, "and yet, it is. I feel so foolish." She touched her reddening cheeks. "I really wanted them to go on believing."

"Charlotte, that is utterly ludicrous. For heaven's sake, you've never even had a beau, save Giles. How can you face yourself having let them believe such silliness?"

Silliness? Which part? Charlotte wondered. The part about Shaun? Or the part about Charlotte's having any beau better than Giles. She found the answer in her mother's pitying gaze. Charlotte could see the disappointment, the lack of pride. "I'll go fetch the sugar," was all she said. But the dark in her eyes let on that she was wounded, that there was still a truth she wasn't willing to abandon.

Margaret watched her go with a crinkle in her brow. She was pulling on her wraps as she moved to the foyer, to the porch, and beyond. And though she closed the door with a respectfully gentle hand, there was no mistaking the aggravation in her steps as her boots sank one after another into the snowy lawn. There was an element of flight in her departure. The way Margaret saw it, she was fleeing the truth, flying away from talk of a romance that never was. She was trying to hold onto the lie that had ruined her chance at marriage, the lie that Shaun Matheson had some romantic inclination toward her. And that flustered Margaret, because she was the sort of person who saw inherent virtue in honesty, even when its use served no one and its abandonment was harmless.

"Is something troubling you, my love?" Mr. Bass startled her with a hug.

"Oh, my!" she cried, clutching her throat before collapsing into a mournful sigh. "It's nothing," she said, resting her head on his shoulder. "It's just Charlotte."

"You must stop worrying," he said. "She's just fine."

"I know she is, but . . . she still hasn't gotten over the Matheson boy, and George, it's getting embarrassing."

"Embarrassing?"

"Yes. It seems she told all the young folks that he was her true love, and has never corrected it. Now she's going to have to face them all and tell the truth, and I feel shame for her."

"For her?" he asked, lifting her chin with a knuckle. "Or for you?"

"For both of us, George. To have the girl who was left out of the marriage bidding was bad enough. But to learn that she's been telling princess stories about city men longing to sweep her away? It's embarrassing, George."

Peter had been standing in the threshold for just long enough to catch the end of that. He could be bright when mischief was at stake, so he was able to deduce the truth. "Charlotte told everyone that Shaun was her beau?"

Margaret wouldn't have said it if she'd known he was listening, but since it was too late, she nodded. "I'm afraid it does seem your sister suffered a bit of an infatuation."

He laughed rudely, spraying cookie crumbs on his vest. "Did she think she was pretty enough for him?"

"I don't know what she thought, Peter."

"But I don't want you teasing her," said George. "Do you understand? Your sister has a hard road ahead, and the last thing she needs is your jesting."

"Oh, Papa! How could I resist? This is too good to waste on kindness. You mean to tell me she had the notion that someone as handsome as Shaun was going to take an interest in her, and because of that, she's spoiled her only chance at the one boy who really would have her? And now she's going to be a spinster with wrinkled, knotty hands whose house children dare one another to touch? This is fabulous!"

"Stop it," his mother snapped bitterly. "George, I don't know what I did wrong, why I didn't reach her, how I failed to show her what it was to count one's blessings and be realistic about one's assets."

"When she went with you to Boston," asked Peter excitedly, "did that have something to do with this? Was she hoping to see Shaun?"

He laughed through his father's nod.

"Oh, this is hilarious. How could she think she was good enough for him?"

"Or wealthy enough," added his father.

"I'm so ashamed," Margaret sniffed.

Just then, the door burst open. At first, no one was certain about who resided beneath the crust of snow that rapidly melted on their fine maple floor. But whoever it was, he was quick to shut out the stinging wind with a gentle closing of the door, and to politely hang his coat on a peg between heavy breaths. It was then that they saw who it was. They all blinked confusedly as Shaun Matheson breathlessly exclaimed, "Mr. Bass. May I have your daughter's hand in marriage?"

THIRTY-FOUR

George looked at Margaret, who looked at Peter, who looked at George. None of them could quite think of what to say. So the head of the household asked the question that seemed to be on everyone's mind. "You mean Charlotte?"

"Yes," Shaun said, struggling to catch his breath. It had been a long, arduous trek from Boston, even using his father's fastest team. "Mr. Bass I . . . I assure you I can take care of her. I've become proprietor of my father's East Gallery. It will bring me a reasonable income, and when Charlotte's artwork goes on display, we fully expect it to turn a substantial profit."

It was time for Mr. Bass to ask another rather obvious question. "Did you say 'Charlotte's paintings'?"

"Have you ever seen them?" asked Mrs. Bass.

"Yes, of course," he panted, "she's brilliant. And Mr. Bass, I swear I shall not keep her far from home. I shall never move her farther than Boston, and we shall return here at every Christmas season, should we be invited. I swear," he said to their blank faces, "that I will be a good husband to her. I would never mistreat her. I would see that she wants for nothing." He paused just a moment for a reply, and when none came, it sent him into a minor panic. He thought he'd better go on trying to convince them. "I cherish your daughter, Mr. Bass. I value her warmth and her intelligence. I see her worth, and I will never take it for granted. Please accept my word that I would never forget my fortune in having won a woman with such quality of heart." He looked around hopefully, but still could get no reply. "Mr. Bass?" he repeated at last. "May I have her hand in marriage?"

George was so mesmerized, he'd forgotten he was expected to say something. "Oh, umm . . ." He turned to his wife for help. "I don't know, uhhh . . . does that sound all right with you, dear?"

"Huh?" She had to shake herself into reality. "Oh! Oh, yes. Yes, of course. That is, if uh . . . uh . . . I don't see why not. . . uh . . ."

George nodded at them both as though this had been a most interesting and informative family discussion. "Well, then. Uh, are we uh . . . all decided?" They were all just staring at Shaun, so he announced, "I uh . . . guess it looks as though we are."

"Where's Charlotte?"

"Huh?"

"Charlotte."

"Oh! Oh, Charlotte. Charlotte is uh . . . where is she, dear?"

"At the store," said Margaret, "fetching syrup and sugar."

"Then I'll go after her," said Shaun, grabbing his coat. "Thank you! Thank you very much. I declare, you have made me the happiest man alive."

They all waved dazedly, too stunned to say good-bye.

In the silence of his departure, they all gazed out the window, watching him drive away as though he had been a dream. The first to speak was Margaret, touching a hand to her throat. "My daughter," she whispered, "my daughter is a brilliant artist?"

"My sister has a warm heart?" asked Peter with a sneer of confusion.

George broke into a broad grin. "Charlotte is marrying money?"

Shaun rode as though catching her in time would guarantee the answer he sought to his proposal. He sensed her even before he saw her. Her boots were kicking up white dust, her beauty was scarved to the hilt. She seemed to belong to a portrait of winter, to a scene of pine and unspoiled snow shimmering on a winding road. He pulled his horses to a halt, waiting for her to notice the silence, the hoofbeats which had ceased in her honor. It was with much trepidation that she turned. Her muffled joy held tightly behind a trembling smile told him how glad she was to see him, and how hard the waiting had been. "May I help you, sir?" she asked of the handsome intruder.

He could barely find his voice. It was a blessing that it was carried on the wind or it would have been too soft to hear. "I'm back," he said.

Her nod was rhythmic, her expression invisible behind the woolen barrier. "I see that you are," was her stoic reply.

Absently, he tied the reins. She looked so soft and warm, her eyes so crisp, such a transparent blue against a white world. He had to hold her, he longed to squeeze her without mercy. "But am I welcome?" he asked, hopping down.

"I don't know." She swallowed some tears. "Perhaps I've lost patience. I've waited an awfully long time for you."

He brushed off his snowy shoulders. He moved slowly to his intended bride, swaggering in his cool determination. The only defense he could offer was, "I'm here now."

"But for so long . . ."

"I was young, Charlotte."

Her eyes locked with his in a soft understanding, a gentle forgiveness. "That's true," she agreed, astounded by how the years had passed, touching him when he was within reach, squeezing his shoulders to make sure he was real. "Well . . . at least it was nothing incurable."

His smile was gradual and contagious. She stopped it when she urgently clasped his jaw and told him, "I would have waited forever." She wanted him to know.

He swept her in his arms and swung her around, basking in the scent of her flowery perfume and the natural, sweetly fragranced warmth of her alabaster skin. "I know you would have," he sighed into her shoulder, "you've always had more faith than I. Charlotte, you are my home."

"And you're my escape from home," she giggled gaily as she flew.

He set her down and knelt before her, ruining his trousers in the snow, "Charlotte, this ring belonged to my mother." Impatiently, he tore off her glove and cherished her fair, soft hand. "Would you do me the honor of wearing it?"

She tapped his chin so he might look at her rather than at the ground.

"Would you?" he pleaded to her eyes.

"Shaun, if it meant the seasons should never again part us, I would wear but a strand of grass round my finger." She kissed the white diamond, cold on a ring of gold. "And this is so beautiful and so close to your heart, I shall cherish it always. Yes, of course I'll wear your ring. Of course I'll be your wife."

Elated, he rose and kissed her hand. He relieved her of her shopping bundle and planted her grip in the crook of his bad arm. "Come on then, Charlotte Matheson. Let's go home."

Charlotte blushed furiously at the sound of her name mingled with his. She led the horses behind them as they walked through the quiet of winter, smiling in the chilly wind. When at last the old white house, grand though blemished by chipped paint, had fallen in sight, Shaun thought to speak through his joy. "Another woman might have asked," he said wryly, "but since you didn't, I imagine I ought to bring it up. I have good news for us. It seems that by marrying me, you won't become a pauper after all."

"Oh, that's good," she said. "I didn't think I'd make much of a chimney sweep."

His wink was kind. "I don't think either of us will be sweeping chimneys. Strange as it is, it seems my father has had a change of heart. That's why I didn't come sooner. I was able to finish school."

"Oh?" Peter had already told her.

"But that isn't the important part."

It was to her.

"What's important to us is that he gave me the East Gallery. It seems he's decided I'm a partially worthy son, after all." She had already celebrated in private, for Peter had told her that, too. "Though what changed his mind," he added wistfully, "I don't think I'll ever know."

"I quite agree."

"Hmm? You agree? With what?"

She flashed him a vibrant smile. "That you'll never know." She stopped his reply with a glorious kiss. It was a kiss of friendship and a kiss of yearning, but it was also a kiss brimming with gratitude that somehow, in some small way, she'd been able to help the man she'd loved for so long.

THIRTY-FIVE

Shaun was invited to stay the holiday, along with his father, who drove in as soon as he was able. As usual, the Basses felt that Shaun was the most honorable of Christmas guests. Not only was he impeccably polite, graceful, and charming at the dining table, but by God, he was taking their unmarriageable daughter as his bride. Now, that was a house guest. Of course, as was equally usual, Shaun was, in fact, the very worst of house guests, unbeknownst to his hosts. For on the night of Christmas Eve, after a day of charming the family while assisting in the hanging of mistletoe and holly berries, he decided it was time to pay a visit to the attic.

He waited until his hosts and his father were all in bed, knowing that Charlotte would stay up late with her paintings. He hated to interrupt her, and yet . . . well, there was no question in his mind that as a man, he was selfish by nature. It was an innate moral handicap for which he couldn't possibly be blamed. "Charlotte?" He knocked on the door with an open hand.

She rushed to answer it, unfortunately fully dressed, but beaming with expectation. "Shaun, my love, what are you doing here?"

"I came to give you my Christmas present," he said, casually moving past her.

"But you already have," she said, touching the enormous ring on her hand.

"No, that wasn't a Christmas present," he said with a wry grin, "that was a bribe."

"Well, shouldn't you put the other under the tree till morning?" she asked.

"I thought about that," he admitted, sliding something slyly from his pocket, "but I decided it would be more fun to do it tonight. Come here." He dragged her desk chair to the window and bade her to turn out the lanterns. Sitting down, he patted his knee, wanting her to make herself at home on his lap.

With a tremble in her stomach, she turned out the lanterns and obeyed. Awkwardly, she began her descent into his waiting lap, but he caught her in both arms and helped her the rest of the way down to ease her trepidation. "Isn't it beautiful?" he asked, nodding at the night sky beyond tiny, square windowpanes.

The snow was falling in tiny specks, much smaller than usual. Only those which fell before the half-moon were visible, for it was so terribly dark outside. They were sitting so near to the window, they could feel the cold of the glass. It was quiet, save the crackle of the bedroom fire. "I love Christmas," she whispered. "It's the only time that people forget to be practical, and work just as hard on celebration as they usually work on survival."

"I never looked forward to Christmas," he said, his voice masculine in the dark, "until I started coming here. Where I knew I would see my girl." He kissed her sweet hair, then realized—she was still wearing a false switch at the end. "Take it off," he begged of her, tugging at its wavy tail.

"Oh, no, I can't," she said shamefacedly. "Really, my hair is still very short. It's unseemly."

"It's grown for a year," he pointed out. "How short can it be?"

"It's to about here," she said, holding a hand just

above her shoulder. Somehow, telling him was not as painful as showing him.

"That sounds pretty," he said. "Come, let me see." He nuzzled her ear and fumbled with the knot, which presumably tied her real hair to the false piece.

"No," she begged. "Honestly, I'll feel unpretty."

He stopped what he was doing and looked her soulfully in the eye. "I'll never let you feel unpretty."

She paused a moment, soaking in that truth. Then she melted against him, tugging at the back of her hair, longing to be naked and natural in his embrace. She knew it was true. She knew that no matter what she looked like, whether or not she had hair or even a set of eyes, he would hold her on high for the heavens to praise. She would never be worthless again. When the switch had fallen carelessly to the floor, he combed his fingers through her soft, natural brown waves, not minding that they fell free at the end of a short run. He lifted her in the midst of a kiss and put her on the bed. She landed with a giggle from the fall, then swallowed hard as he seductively threatened her by removing his vest.

"Can't you wait for the wedding night?" she laughed nervously.

He pretended to think about it as he unbuttoned his silken shirt. "Mmmm, no," he replied, chucking himself on the bed.

Charlotte felt sparks ignite under his exploring hands. "Is this my Christmas gift?" she grinned.

"Oh, no," he said. "This is mine. You'll have to guess what yours is." He lifted her skirt without care of her shame and tugged down her pantalets and stockings.

"Shaun, stop," she protested, her face beet-red.

But instead of stopping, he touched something cold to her inner thigh and gradually moved it upward. "What are you doing?" she asked, every inch of her throbbing.

"Guess what it is," he teased. It felt like a chain. A tiny chain with which he tickled her plump lips, then wrapped it around her swollen bud. It felt as if he were holding her hostage, chaining up her most private self. "Can you guess?" he asked seductively.

Guess? She could hardly even speak. But somehow, she managed to say, "A . . . a bracelet?"

"Let me moisten it a bit," he suggested. "Maybe that will help you feel its shape." As threatened, he wrapped his mouth around the swelling he now held captive. As he licked her soft petal, he also licked the chain that encircled it. For a moment, he sucked. And then he kissed. And then he fluttered until he heard her gasp. "Can you guess yet?" he asked huskily.

"Whatever it is, I don't care," she rasped out. "Just keep doing whatever that was that you were just doing."

"Oh, no, no, no. I won't satisfy you until you've guessed correctly."

"Shaun, that's cruel."

"Sometimes a little cruelty can be fun," he suggested, "as long as it doesn't get out of hand, eh? Here, I'll give you a hint." He unwrapped the chain from her womanhood and glided something cool and prickly along her thigh. It was only then that she realized something was dangling from the end of the chain.

"Is it a pendant?" she asked anxiously.

"Not quite." He struggled to lower his trousers, and Charlotte absolutely shook in her eagerness to be violated.

"Yes," she urged him, spreading her thighs, "yes, please."

But what he thrust inside her was not himself but the cold end of the "pendant." It was small, but she felt every curve of its metal. "Can you feel its shape now?" he asked, thrilling to the way she welcomed it inside. She even tore down the top of her dress, squeezing at her own breasts in delicious anticipation. Her eyes were so wanton, he wasn't even sure she realized what she was doing.

"Do you want to suck on my finger?" he asked, letting go of his other task so he could offer her something to chew.

She took it greedily, nibbling and suckling, opening her thighs ever wider. Shaun had a problem, for he had no other hand to use, and needed to enter her immediately lest it be too late for them both. The sight of her loving his finger between her luscious lips was too much for him to bear. So he struggled to guide himself inside her without the use of a hand. And though it took several attempts, it was well worth it, for she throbbed around him, welcoming him home. She was slick and warm, and her body seemed to know just where to squeeze him and when to release. He wanted to bite into the generous breasts, but the moment his tongue touched a fiery brown tip, she lost control and began to shudder around him. Quickly, he pried his finger free and covered her entire mouth. It was a favor she would not understand until it was over. Her life would have been in ruins if her parents had heard her scream. Later, she wouldn't believe he'd had wits enough to remember such a thing. But then again, he was Shaun. In some ways, the most considerate fellow she'd ever known. In some ways, the most devilish.

He found his own release, digging deep inside her, pushing hard into her softness. His last thrusts were so brutal, he nearly frightened her. But immediately, he regained his senses and drew her into a warm hug, wrapped her in her own blankets, and shielded her in his strong arms. Charlotte snuggled into his neck. Somehow, he smelled like leather and pine trees. She wondered how he'd gotten that smell, whether it was from wearing leather in the forest, or from a scent he'd put on . . . just for her. She could hardly breathe, she was panting so hard in the aftermath of ecstasy. Somehow, she managed to rasp out, "Shaun, that was . . . that was very adequate."

He tickled her belly, making her laugh out loud, then said, "I'm glad you think so." He teased her breast with a little twist. "I'll try to do better next time so you won't have to feign all that emotion."

"Oh yes," she panted, "a little more creativity, if you would."

He kissed her shining hair and whispered, "So do you know what your Christmas gift is?"

"No, what?"

He held up the chain he'd quietly wrapped round his wrist. "It's a key," he announced, swinging it in midair. "I bought you an art studio in the North End. I think you'll like it. Very spacious, good light . . ."

"Oh, Shaun!" she cried, hugging his neck, "I can't believe it! My own work studio! How could you . . . oh, no!" Her expression changed instantly to one of misery at the turn of a thought.

"What is it?" he asked with great concern.

"I knitted you a stupid scarf. Oh, Shaun. I feel awful. You got me a studio and I knitted you a stupid, ugly scarf."

He chuckled with good humor in his pale eyes. "I'm sure it's lovely," he said.

"No, Shaun. It's really not. You've never seen my knitting—it's a really stupid scarf. I've never even mastered the art of weaving different yarns into one piece, so it's all the same color. A bright red berry that was supposed to be maroon."

He couldn't help chuckling, though he knew he shouldn't. "I'll treasure it," he assured her.

"You needn't treasure it. Just wear a straight face when

you open it in front of the family and that will be more than enough thanks. I'm so ashamed."

"Oh, don't be," he said, settling into relaxation. He wrapped his arm behind her neck and squeezed her to his side, urging her to settle on his bare chest for the night. She could still smell the pine. "It's a Christmas tradition," he told her, "always to be embarrassed by at least one gift you've given. It wouldn't be Christmas without that."

"Oh, and don't forget the traditional overgiving," she chimed in, finding comfort in the warmth of his skin and the feel of his arm holding her tight for the night, "There's always at least one person to whom I give much too grand a gift, and receive almost nothing in return. Usually, in my case, it's Peter. I always swear I mustn't regret the giving, even when I spend months on his gift and receive something as thoughtless as a left shoe without a right for my efforts. But it always secretly burns me."

"Then there's the person to whom we forget to give a gift because we didn't know there was a friendship until the package arrives."

"Oh, and have you ever given the same gift that you received, only in lesser value? Once I gave Sarah a hair ribbon from Richter's. And she gave me the one displayed right beside it on the shelf, which I had decided against on account of its price. She knew exactly where I'd gotten hers, I knew exactly where she'd gotten mine, and we both knew she'd paid more than I had."

"Or how about the wishful gift? Like when my father gets me a hunting rifle every year, in hopes I'll kill something just to say thank you."

"Or how about the distant relative nobody likes but everyone has to see on Christmas?"

"My father's volunteering for that role this year," he grinned.

Charlotte's mood mellowed quickly in memory of all

the Christmases which had come and gone in this creaky white house. It suddenly occurred to her—this attic would no longer be her own. Its slanted ceiling, its musty smell, its tiny paned windows would all be left behind, and she would be far away in the hustle and bustle of Boston. "Oh, Shaun, I hope you won't think me an ungrateful bride if I tell you I'm going to be homesick."

"Not at all," he assured her, stroking her shiny hair. "All brides are scared. But I promise I'll take good care of you. You've got nothing to be afraid of." He made her look in his eyes until she nodded in agreement. "And don't forget," he added, "how long you've wanted to leave this place."

"I know. But I look at Sarah, and I think of how long she's wanted to leave. Yet, she's so happy only a mile from where she always lived. And I think, maybe it wasn't the *place* she longed to leave behind. Maybe it was the *life*. And I realize the same may have been true for me all these years. Perhaps I blamed Vermont when all the while its beautiful mountains and brooks were the only things keeping me sane in a life that was entirely unacceptable in so many ways. Perhaps it's a mistake to leave."

"Your duties as my wife aside," he said, stroking her oval jaw with care, "you're an artist, Charlotte. Too good an artist to stay here. There are no art galleries in Peacham, and you're too gifted to be silent. I'll bring you home every Christmas. That, I promise. But you're not Sarah. You have a special calling, and you can't push it aside in the name of safety. You've got to get out there and let people see your work."

"Sometimes I believe that," she said, "and sometimes I don't."

"Then I'll be the one to believe. I'll do the bragging for you. I'll tie you up and drag you from Peacham," he grinned, "and you can blame it all on me."

She replied by taking his gloved hand in both of hers.

He resisted instinctively, trying to pull back. He was ashamed for her to feel the lifelessness, the limpness of the deformed hand. Sometimes when he got the courage to take the glove off and look, he had to admit it still made him want to sob. But Charlotte would not let go. She pulled the leather to her lips and kissed it—a kiss he could not feel except in his heart. And she whispered, "You don't have to drag me anywhere, Shaun Matheson. Anywhere you are is home."

He kissed her the way only a man in love can kiss. And not because she'd said it, but because she'd meant it. Like him, she was a person who could give—who could give everything and have no regret. If she asked him, he would show her his hand, or even cut it off. They belonged to each other. Just as surely as their destinies belonged to the Spirit of Christmas, who had taken them under her wing two years ago.

THIRTY-SIX

"It's going to be a normal Christmas!" Peter was so excited, he raced down the stairs at the first sign of sunrise.

Shaun groaned at being awakened. "Do you think your mother may have coddled him a bit as a child?" he grumbled in Charlotte's ear, rolling her into his chest to kiss her good morning.

"Oh, no," said Charlotte, "she's told him he's perfect ever since the day he was born, and forced both of us to wait on him hand and foot like a king, but I really don't think there've been any ill repercussions."

"Mama!" he shouted, "wake up! It's time to open gifts!"

"Ugh." Shaun rubbed the sleep from his eyes, "And you say he hasn't yet secured a wife? How astounding."

"She'll be a very lucky woman." Charlotte loved the feel of his bare arms all around her. His skin was so warm, his chest was all hers. She kissed it and drew in the manly scent of him, loving being free to do so. And then she became fully awake. "Shaun!" she screeched in a whisper. "Get back to your own bedroom! Quickly! Go muddle up the sheets or something. Go!"

He only laughed softly. "Why scruff the sheets? I'll only have to make them again before dressing."

"No, you won't have to! You're a man. A woman will fix it for you."

"I thought you hated that sort of thing."

"Well, I do, but . . . oh, just go. Go quickly before we're caught!"

"Charlotte," he said, taking a taste of her frantic lips, "we're nearly married, you know."

"Nearly? Nearly doesn't count for anything in the eyes of my parents! You know that. Get out of here! Quickly!"

"It's the difference of a couple days," he chuckled. "We'll be married in a countable number of hours."

"Oh, please let me have a normal Christmas," she begged. "Please stop arguing semantics and get out of my room. I'm begging you."

"You're sexy when you beg."

"Stop it!" she cried, making him burst into a squinty-eyed chuckle. "Please, go!"

"I'm going," he promised, planting one last kiss upon her forehead. "I'll tell you what. I'll head down first and when you hear us all conversing naturally, you can make your entrance."

"Just hurry!"

He fetched his shirt and started dressing, Charlotte shaking her leg in a panic as she watched. "You're not going to wear the same clothes, are you? They'll know if you don't at least put on a Christmas cravat. Something green?"

"Charlotte, you do credit people with a great deal more astuteness than they actually have. But don't fret," he said with a kiss, "I'll stop in my room and fetch something Christmassy. Stop worrying."

She did not stop worrying. Not when he left her with his shirt half unbuttoned, and not when she heard him descending the stairs, fearing she would hear an encounter along the way. She still worried when she heard the guest room door close behind him and even when she heard it open again, presumably heralding his descent to the parlor. She bit her nail and held her breath when he said, "Good morning, Merry Christmas."

It was not until she heard her mother's amicable, "Why, good morning, Shaun. Won't you have some mint pie for breakfast?" that she let out her breath. She was saved. Shaun had pulled it off seamlessly, and wasn't it just like him. With the heart of an angel and the mind of a devil, she began to believe there was nothing her husband-to-be could not do.

When Charlotte finally arrived to see Christmas morning for herself, she was treated to the sight of something that very much resembled a storybook drawing. The fragrant pine tree caressed the ceiling, dressed in candles and ropes of red berries and nuts. Gifts wrapped in cloth and tied with string were piled all the way to its lower branches, spilling out to the floor like the overflowing of a goblet. The tall parlor windows were bright white and frosty, the sky beyond bare of flakes but an electrifying color of winter. The fire burned at exciting and threatening heights, the loud flames stretching for the chimney, stray embers falling in the commotion, prevented from igniting the room only by a dainty iron fire guard of black vines. The room was alive and the house knew it was Christmas.

"Charlotte!" Her mother looked like a Christmas package herself, all dressed in green velvet to match her husband's cravat. It delighted Charlotte to see her dressed so gaily. "Won't you help me in the kitchen?"

In fact, she was delighted to agree, for she knew it would be one of the very last times she would toil away in the smoke of that kitchen. "Of course!" she cried, following joyfully behind. Shaun watched her go with a twinkle in his eye from the corner coffee table. She was wearing her berry-red dress, and with her heavy skirts whispering all around her, she looked as though she should have adorned the tree.

"What needs fixing?" she asked her mother just as soon as they'd stepped into the darkness. She saw some potato pancakes sizzling on a black stove. She could smell the plum puddings bubbling from deep within the brick oven and she saw that breads were all kneaded into tight balls, ready to follow. She saw the plucked goose turning round and round on the brick hearth's spit. She winced. The head was still on the counter, looking at her.

"Apple pie," said her mother, handing her a bag full of crabapples. "They've been drying in the cellar since fall. Make sure they're well peeled, please. And don't put too much sugar in the crust."

Charlotte took the bag with some trepidation. "Where shall I slice them?"

"On the cutting board, of course. Over . . ." With aggravation she picked up the goose head and chucked it away. "I'm sorry," she said curtly, "I always forget how sensitive you are."

Charlotte heard the hint of an insult in that seemingly sympathetic remark, but did not mind it. She knew that it was a matter of habit for her mother to keep her humble. Quietly and respectfully, she tended to the task of peeling apples. Her mother went to work as well, for even after having instructed Charlotte on the dangers of over-sugaring the pie crust, she couldn't quite bring herself to have trust, and couldn't keep her hands from the habit of working, and so instinctively set out to the task herself. A long silence ensued as the kitchen smoke curled their hair and seeped into their faces. At last, it was Mrs. Bass who spoke. "Are you looking forward to the wedding?" she asked, a hint of genuine thrill behind her stoicism. "I'm glad you're marrying at the church here at home. I wish you weren't doing it so quickly so I'd have more time to plan. But I know Shaun wants to get to work right after the holiday, so . . . I understand."

A smile curled Charlotte's mouth when she replied ever so quietly, "Mama?"

"Hmmm?"

"Mama, I want to hear you say it." She didn't look up from her slicing.

"Say what?" she asked impatiently.

Charlotte's face was turning red. "I want to hear you say," she answered in a near whisper, "that you're surprised Shaun loved me after all. That I have always been right about it and you have always been wrong."

"Oh, Charlotte," she snapped angrily, "that is very immature."

"I know," she giggled, "very immature. But please say it."

Her mother prepared to growl something cutting in reply. But she couldn't. Her daughter was flushing, burning with delight and victory. It was adorable. And it was only fair. Margaret put down her pie crust and wiped both hands on her apron. Stunning her daughter by taking her round the waist, she planted a kiss on her hair and said, "You were right and I was wrong." She swayed her back and forth on her feet. "And I am going to miss you."

Charlotte flung her arms round her neck and cried, "Oh, Mama, thank you. Thank you for saying it and thank you for missing me." She sniffed back some loving tears and added, "Now if you would admit your wrongness in front of at least ten people, I would consider it a wedding gift beyond all others."

"Charlotte," she growled warningly.

"Sorry, Mama. I got greedy. Oh, thank you. Thank you so much."

Once all had been fed breakfast, the next phase of the holiday was the much-anticipated gift exchange, beginning with the emptying of the stockings by the fire. Charlotte was delighted to find not only a penny in hers, but also a brand new pair of stockings. "Thank you,

Mama and Papa. I'll need these. I had to hang my old ones here on the fire."

There were so many gifts under the tree that the opening was disorganized. Everyone was tearing in at once and sometimes missed the unwrapping of one of their own gifts. It was a bustle of beautiful commotion.

"Ah, a hunting rifle," said Shaun, nodding rhythmically at his father. "Why, thank you. What a surprise."

"It's the finest quality, son. You won't find a better one anywhere. If that doesn't turn you on to hunting, I don't know what will."

"I don't know, either."

"For me?" cried Margaret. "Oh, Mr. Matheson, you didn't have to get me anything."

"But of course I did! We're the parents of the young couple now, aren't we?"

"Oh, my goodness. What could this be? Oh! It's uh . . . a rifle."

"Yes! In these parts, I imagine no woman should be without her own. Wolves, bears, unexpected visitors . . . you'll never know when that will come in handy."

"Why, thank you."

"I'm guessing I know what this is," said George, unwrapping a long package from Mr. Matheson.

"I'll bet you do!"

"Ah! Wonderful. I haven't seen a rifle as fine as this in all my trading. Thank you, sir."

"Mine is a pistol!" cried Charlotte excitedly.

"Charlotte, don't aim that at your brother."

"Sorry."

"Oh, boy! I can't wait for mine!" cried Peter, tearing open his package. "I've been using a slingshot to get the squirrels and chipmunks. I can't wait to have my very own . . . silken cravat?"

"Sorry," said Mr. Matheson with a shrug. "Somehow,

you and loaded firearms just didn't strike me as a good match."

"And here's one for you!" cried Margaret excitedly.

"Oh, my," said Mr. Matheson, shaking the tiny box. "Could it be? Yes, I'm guessing it's that tobacco pipe I've been dropping so many hints about."

Margaret and George exchanged miserable glances.

"Oh, no!" he cried diplomatically, lifting the watch chain by its clip. "I see it's a fine watch. Why, thank you. Thank you. I'll just . . . dispose here of the one I've got." He removed a ruby-studded, gold plated watch from his vest pocket, fully engraved with his and his wife's initials, and replaced it with the new plain silver one. "There, that's better. Thank you. Thank you very much."

"What a beautiful scarf," Shaun winked jovially at Charlotte. "I'd say it's maroon. Definitely maroon."

Charlotte could look neither at him nor the scarf. "Oh, stop it, Shaun. I promise I'll get you something better."

"Don't," he whispered, kissing her cheek with such tenderness that everyone watching missed a breath. "It's beautiful."

Charlotte bowed her head.

Ultimately, not one person received a gift that promised to be of any use at all, and thus, it was declared a successful holiday. It was time to feast in celebration, and there was not a soul, including Mrs. Bass herself, who did not anticipate tasting the source of the delicious aromas which had tempted the family all morning as they'd wafted around the tree. The goose wore a honey-sweet glaze. The bread was hot and soft. Russet potatoes were mashed and trickled with milk gravy. The cabbage-and-apple soufflé smelled tart. Beside each plate of the most fragile white china was a generous cup of plum pudding. And as the sun set early beyond the ice-cold windows, Mr. Bass bowed his head and said grace. Charlotte's heart filled with joyful tears as he spoke. She was leaving this place, leaving it for the adventure of a lifetime. And yet, she would be back, always to share in this holiday feast, perhaps someday with a baby in her arms. It was more than her once-hopeless heart could absorb. She touched Shaun's hand across the table, and he, in turn, gave hers a strong squeeze.

As soon as the eating began, Mrs. Bass glanced curiously at Mr. Matheson. There was something she'd been dying to ask, something that was strangely important to her, but it wasn't until the clamoring of silverware overpowered the room that she found the courage. "So, Mr. Matheson," she began casually, though her hands were trembling a bit on her fork, "will you tell me a bit about what Charlotte will be doing with the gallery?"

"Hmmm?" Gruffly, he tried to talk and shovel food into his mouth at the same time.

"The gallery? Is it true you've urged Shaun to show her paintings there?"

"Mmm, yes," he muttered, bringing a linen napkin to his lips, "though he didn't need much urging." He favored his son with a rare smile.

"How will that work?" Her eyes were strange and uncertain as she pondered this unfamiliar venture.

"Well, her paintings will be featured in the main showroom. Collectors will bid on them, and Shaun will manage the profits. It's as simple as that."

"And you . . . you say that Charlotte really is gifted?"

"Hmmm? Yes, of course."

"Can you explain that to me?"

Everyone looked. She wanted to know. She really wanted to know.

"Why, of course," said Mr. Matheson, a faint fog of tenderness in his eye. "You see, there's been a long trend of realism in art. The most popular paintings have been those judged favorably in terms of their likeness to the objects and scenery they represent. But new trends always start in the cities, and it's the collectors who like to capitalize before the new movements become well known. Lately, some artists have been experimenting with a type of painting based on emotionalism created by a caricature of an object or a surreal interpretation of a scene. It's going to take some decades for it to become a widespread movement. It's mainly in Germany at the moment, but it's clearly the trend for investors. Their wisest venture is always to invest in the future while they can still get their hands on it at a reasonable price."

"And Charlotte?" she interrupted, caring very little about the details of entrepreneurship, "Charlotte is one of these newfangled artists?" She didn't mean for that to sound as bad as it did. It's just that she couldn't for the life of her see what the Mathesons saw in her drawings. And she wanted to. She really wanted to.

"Charlotte is brilliant," he said, forcing the poor girl to blush into her napkin. "She's still young, will surely improve. But she has a good grip on using surrealism to make statements about reality that couldn't be made through the use of literal portrayal, and in the process, invoking raw emotion. The latter is a skill that can't be learned. Artists need to be born with it."

Margaret had no idea what he just said. "So she's really good?" she asked, starry-eyed.

"Yes," he said placatingly, "she's really good."

Margaret grinned with a motherly pride Charlotte had never known she had. She was proud of her! After a lifetime of seeming to disappoint the stern woman, the queen of competence, she had finally made her proud. Charlotte felt a warm bubbling in her chest. And Margaret felt as though she were sitting on a cloud. She had raised not one, but two successful children.

"Mama, Papa, I forgot to tell you. I'm dropping out of Harvard."

OK, only one successful child. But at least the balance had been maintained.

"You're what?!" his parents cried at once.

"I'm bored," Peter groaned, "I hate it there. I don't like the reading, I don't like the writing, I hate the discussions. Sometimes I feel as though I'm living your dreams, and not my own. It's you who have always wanted me to succeed. All I've ever wanted to do is relax."

"Now you listen to me," growled his father. "Have you any idea how much your tuition has cost me?"

"Half of your father's trips are to cover it!" chimed in Margaret. "You are going back and that is all the discussion we are going to have!"

"I can't. I've been expelled. Something about poor marks . . ."

There was a knock at the door. Everyone looked up, but it was a good while before Mrs. Bass could unclench her teeth enough to answer it. She straightened her apron and cleared her throat before reaching for the doorknob and forcing a grand smile. "Why, Sarah and Kevin! Welcome!"

Charlotte leaped from her chair. "Sarah!" She raced into the foyer, nearly running over her mother to do it. "Sarah!" she squealed, squeezing and hugging, and finding that there was a plumpness to her that hadn't been there before. "Sarah?"

"I'm with child," she whispered.

"Oh, my word!" Charlotte covered her mouth and gasped, then bounced up and down excitedly. "Oh my word! Is it going to be Charlene, do you think? Or Stephen?"

Sarah looked beautiful. Her round face was moist from life and good cheer. She touched her belly, which was draped so festively in a green-and-gold quilted dress and said, "Oh, Charlotte, please don't be angry, but if it's a boy, I've changed my idea for a name."

"What?" she pretended to scold, flanking her hips with fists. "You can't do that without consulting me first!"

Sarah giggled. "Well, Charlene is still for the girl! But if it's a boy . . . we've decided to name him Kevin after his father. I'm surprised we didn't think of that when you and I were choosing names." She tilted her head most curiously.

"I think we had forgotten all about Kevin," Charlotte admitted. "I guess he was more or less an afterthought in our plans for your children."

The girls laughed and huddled together to hide their shameful joke. "Oh, Charlotte," Sarah whispered as long as they were down there, "is it true what I've heard? Are you really moving to the city? Are you really going to be a famous painter?"

"Well, I don't know about the *famous* part," she hedged, "but I really am moving to the city right after the wedding next Saturday. And I will be a painter, famous or not. I suppose I always have been, really. But now I'm going to have my own studio!"

Sarah was speechless. To think she had felt sorry for her dearest friend only months ago. And now, here she was, on her way to a fantasy the two girls had dreamed about since childhood. But alone. "I wish I were going . . ."

"No, you don't," said Charlotte, looking boldly at Kevin. He was handsome in his dark gray suit that flattered his flaxen hair. He had grown more handsome every day and every week by virtue of confidence, the self-worth that had come from having a dear and devoted wife. They both had lots of color in their cheeks and an ease in their posture. "You're good for each other," she said. "This is what you've always wanted—you just didn't know it."

Sarah nodded her agreement, but still looked in awe at her dearest friend. "Still, your destiny seems much more thrilling."

Charlotte shivered as they locked arms. "I hope it's not," she said, "I hope it won't be as scary as it sounds right now. I hope I can make a narrow Beacon Hill town house feel like home."

"You won't be sharing it with your father-in-law, will you?"

"Heavens, no. He's scared of me. We'll have our own."

"Good. That's the way it should be."

Sarah and Kevin joined in the feasting. Fortunately, Mrs. Bass always cooked far too much on holidays, and had plenty to spare. Peter was awfully quiet, and well aware of his good fortune in that no one wished to bring up his expulsion while in the company of neighbors. Occasionally, he looked up and received a glare from his father. But all the chattering was about babies and weddings and hope. At last, when evening was in full bloom, there was another knock at the door. "I'll get it," said Mrs. Bass, wiping her hands.

No one paid a great deal of attention until they all heard, "Why, Giles Williams!"

Charlotte nearly spit out her pie.

Shaun squinted curiously, leaning back in his chair to catch a glimpse of the foyer.

Mrs. Bass hated to pull up a chair that didn't match the others, but was forced to as her midnight-haired guest made his cocky entrance. "Hello, all," he announced with a big, fat grin. Charlotte didn't even want to know why he had come. "Wondering why I came? I came to share my good news with you all." He waved a piece of parchment he'd been holding since he left his house. *"The Boston Daily Advertiser* has offered me a job, writing my column for them," he said, spreading the paper before Charlotte. "I'm going to be moving to the city! They say they find my remarks insightful and candid, and say I will add much-needed character to their publication."

"Giles," she drawled, without even looking at the parchment, "nobody finds your column insightful or candid. You are utterly obnoxious, thoroughly vindictive, and . . ."

"Look right there," he said, tapping his knuckles on the table.

Charlotte's eyes widened in her horror. "Dear God."

"See? Insightful and candid. Right there. And you said I'd be better off hiding my true self."

"No, Giles, not you. I said the rest of us would be better off if you did. I can't believe this. You're moving to Boston?"

"Believe it," he said. "I'm going to be rich. Well, not right away, of course. But once readers get a taste of my insightful and candid remarks, I'm sure to be a star."

"Will you stop saying insightful and candid?"

"Better get used to it. That's what they'll all be calling me." He slouched confidently into his chair, crossing an ankle over his leg.

Shaun squeezed Charlotte's shoulder. "May I get you a drink?"

"I think you'd better get the whole Boston art community a drink. They're about to need it."

"Will do."

"Giles," she ventured, "I'm just not sure that . . ."

But he interrupted her the moment Shaun had departed. "This wasn't the real reason I came over here," he announced.

"Oh?"

"No. I came over here to let you know," he said pointing, "that I am doing just fine without you."

"Oh. Well, Giles, I really am happy to hear that. But . . ."

"Now, I know," he interrupted, "that you were wounded when I jilted you."

She blinked curiously at the wall.

"But I'm not sorry that I did it, Charlotte. As you can see, I had a dream to follow. I couldn't be weighed down by a woman who would keep me tied to Peacham."

"Giles, I'm moving to Boston, too."

"I know. I know you had to take second-best with that Matheson fellow, and I'm sorry for it, Charlotte. I'm sorry you had to settle. But a man of my impending prestige has to be fussy. What would have happened to my career if people had learned I'd married such a lousy painter?"

Charlotte took a moment to carefully craft the seething reply she was about to deliver. But she was interrupted by her brother, who bounced into the room crying, "I've got a great idea!"

Charlotte and Giles turned. Mrs. Bass came in from the kitchen and Mr. Bass returned from the outhouse. "What is it?" asked Charlotte.

"Well, Giles, you say you're moving to Boston?"

"Yes."

"Will you have a flat there?"

"Surely."

"Well, that's perfect! I'll be needing a job soon, and the city is the only place to find a good one. I'll need a place to stay in the meantime, and I can't stay with newlyweds. I'll stay with you!"

Giles looked as though he'd swallowed something too large for his throat. "I uh . . . my flat will be small."

"That's all right! I'll sleep on the floor. It'll be fun, just us bachelors out on the town. And if you're an early riser, you can just step over me."

"Well, how long do you think it will take you to start paying half?"

"Just as soon as I find the right job!" he declared. "It

shouldn't take long. I just need to find one that pays very
well and doesn't require much work, and then, I'll be
out of your hair. Are you good at keeping house? Because I'm not good at picking up after myself."

"Oh, please take him," begged Mr. Bass. "Please don't
leave him here."

"George," his wife snapped.

"Well . . ." Giles hedged, "as long as it's only tem-
porary . . ."

"I'll be gone before you know it! I promise. I will find
the perfect job and, and when I do, I'll make so much
money you'll be visiting me at my mansion before long!"

"Are you sure?"

"Yes, but in the meantime, try to remember. I don't
like my scrambled eggs too dry. Just a little swishing in
the pan with just a touch of milk and pepper. Well . . .
Mama will show you how."

Shaun bent down and whispered in Charlotte's ear, "I
think they make a handsome couple."

Charlotte giggled fiercely into his shirt.

"Ah, yes," said George, wrapping an arm about his
wife's shoulders, "my hard-earned money was spent well
on that one."

"Curse that college for not taking girls."

As sleepiness grew thick in the air between the Basses
and their guests, the candles on the tree were lit and
everyone found refuge on the most comfortable sofas
and chairs they could find. It was time to sing carols.
Shaun took Charlotte to the windowsill, where they
could feel the Christmas air seeping in and still watch
the family. Holding her tightly by the waist, he was delighted to hear her sing for the first time, for she had a
lovely voice. He kissed her between verses and sometimes forgot about the song. The lights were low, and

everyone was mellow. Kevin and Sarah sat on the rug, holding hands. Mr. and Mrs. Bass shared a puffy chair, while she sang out in a high, perfect pitch from the arm of it. The three bachelors shared the sofa. And they all held leather bound songbooks, though they all knew the words to each carol.

Then the strangest thing happened. Mr. Matheson looked up from his verses, from where he'd been grumbling out a gruff tune, and he saw his son on the windowsill, holding Charlotte, that warm, feisty bride of his. And for just that moment, he saw Shaun the way she did. He looked like a gentleman. Elegant and graceful in posture, tender in his affections, and terribly handsome. And so bright. So very bright.

Giles and Peter, noticing their couch mate was no longer singing, followed his eyes and found where they lay. Both of them looked at Charlotte. She was beautiful. It wasn't just her blue eyes and her shapely figure in that flattering red dress. It was the way she kept looking up from her book to spare a friendly glance at Shaun. And the way he responded, so pleased to have her near. And she looked like a painter. She really did. She looked as soft and curious as a woman artist ought to look. She looked like a brand new Charlotte, though she hadn't changed a bit.

Mr. Bass also noticed how beautiful the couple looked, entwined in each other's arms, and whispered in his wife's ear, "Oh my, just look at them. Can you imagine? Can you imagine if we could all be seen through the eyes of that one person who loves us most?"

"How much more beautiful everyone would become."

He gazed at the fire and whispered, "God only knows how beautiful we may already be."

DO YOU HAVE THE
HOHL COLLECTION?

Thrilling Romance from Lisa Jackson

__Twice Kissed	0-8217-6038-6	$5.99US/$7.99CA
__Wishes	0-8217-6309-1	$5.99US/$7.99CA
__Whispers	0-8217-6377-6	$5.99US/$7.99CA
__Unspoken	0-8217-6402-0	$6.50US/$8.50CA
__If She Only Knew	0-8217-6708-9	$6.50US/$8.50CA
__Intimacies	0-8217-7054-3	$5.99US/$7.99CA
__Hot Blooded	0-8217-6841-7	$6.99US/$8.99CA

Call toll free **1-888-345-BOOK** to order by phone or use th
coupon to order by mail.

Name_____

Address_____

City_____ State _____ Zip _____

Please send me the books I have checked above.

I am enclosing	$_____
Plus postage and handling*	$_____
Sales tax (in New York and Tennessee)	$_____
Total amount enclosed	$_____

*Add $2.50 for the first book and $.50 for each additional book.
Send check or money order (no cash or CODs) to:
Kensington Publishing Corp., 850 Third Avenue, New York, NY 10022
Prices and Numbers subject to change without notice. All orders subject to availabi
Check out our website at **www.kensingtonbooks.com.**